The Pale Cast of Death

John Vance

BLACK ROSE writing™

ISBN: 978-1-61296-815-5
PUBLISHED BY BLACK ROSE WRITING
www.blackrosewriting.com

Printed in the United States of America
Suggested retail price $19.95

The Pale Cast of Death is printed in Gentium Book Basic

Special thanks go to Reagan Rothe and Dave King of Black Rose Writing; to my children Hope and Jimmy for their support and encouragement; to my wife Susan for her enthusiasm and keen editorial eye; and to Professor Richard Menke for his valuable suggestions.

The Pale Cast of Death

Chapter 1

January 1898

The Acropolis Theatre in London's West End

Waiting off stage for her next entrance as the "mad" Ophelia, Catherine Healy peered from the wings and saw her young friend, the seventeen-year-old Alice Pearcy enduring the annoying exuberance of her escort George Wooten, who was apparently acting out the moment in *Hamlet* along with the actors on stage. His hands were in constant motion, and Catherine saw him making a dagger sign as he leaned over to poor Alice as if to say, "He's going to kill him!"

Catherine silently laughed as Alice tried to hush her suitor, and it was clear the girl desired to be anywhere else but sitting where she was. There was no doubt Alice was overcome by a consuming wave of utter mortification. To Alice's left was her incorrigible younger brother—age fourteen and this evening's apparent chaperone—grinning with malicious glee at his sister's distress.

"Jamie, look at this." Stepping to her was James Millard, tonight's Claudius and Catherine's husband, although no one in the theatre knew they were married.

"What is it, Cate?" She pointed to Alice and George, just as the young man dug his fingers into Alice's arm and spoke loudly enough to be heard, "And . . . here . . . death . . . comes."

"This is not to be believed," whispered Jamie. "The lad is shaking her shoulder to a jelly."

Catherine wondered what those sitting directly behind Alice must have concluded watching the girl vibrate like one in the thralls of St. Vitus' dance. It would be nothing short of a blessing from God, she thought, if Alice's hair didn't come undone.

"From the stage tonight's Hamlet, the dynamic Edward Ludmore, spoke his line "Dead for a ducat, dead! The old man is done for!" In the audience, George Wooten raised his left hand in a gesture of finality while his right almost shoved Alice into the arms of her still-grinning brother.

As always, Ludmore's thrust through the arras brought an assortment of gasps, most coming from the uninitiated in the audience—those who had never seen or read the play. But on stage the action ceased. Ludmore, a handsome young thespian on the verge of becoming one of London's favorites, stood bewildered before the curtained area—the arras—through which he had thrust his rapier to kill the eavesdropping character Polonius. Catherine noticed that he glanced at Nedra Alexander, playing Hamlet's mother Gertrude. She seemed as confused as Ludmore. Charles Donovan as Polonius was supposed to have shouted behind the arras "O, I am slain"—the signature line of a Shakespearean character mortally wounded. But neither Catherine nor Jamie had heard the line delivered.

They knew Donovan was to hold up the padded effigy against the other side of the arras, the object into which Ludmore was to thrust his rapier—and that Donovan would immediately hand the effigy to the stage hand as he delivered his final line of the play and drop to the floor. Ludmore as Hamlet would lift the arras aside and discover that he had not stabbed Jamie's character Claudius, the new King and his mother's new husband, but rather the meddling old Polonius.

"Something's wrong." Catherine knew her words were superfluous, but they came nevertheless. The patrons waited for a resolution of the silence.

"Good." Jamie grabbed Catherine's hand as he heard Hamlet and Gertrude go on with their lines. As called for, Ludmore pulled up the arras and quickly let it fall. He dropped his rapier and turned to the audience.

"Please, a physician! Notify the authorities! It's not . . ." Whether Ludmore completed his thought was impossible to tell from the immediate explosion of sound from the 1,600 patrons watching the events unfold. Catherine rushed to the stage ahead of Jamie and gave a quick look to see if Alice was safe from being trampled. For once George Wooten played the role of proper and gallant companion, as he did his best to shield Alice and her brother Matthew from the others pushing forward either to see what had happened upstage or pushing past them to flee from the theatre.

Catherine stared at the body while Jamie tended to Nedra Alexander, who had fallen to the stage. "Oh, no. Dearest God, no." Catherine saw that it wasn't Charles Donovan but rather Morris Roberts-Smythe, the manager of The Acropolis Theatre. Jamie came and knelt by her side and checked the man for any signs of life. The other actors and members of the stage crew stood back and gave proper deference to Millard, the son of a noted London post-mortem physician, and to Catherine Healy, who just happened to be the daughter of Dublin, Ireland's chief criminal investigator.

"Look here, Jamie." Catherine Healy pointed to a wound on the torso from Ludmore's sword thrust. It was Roberts-Smythe's body that had pushed the arras forward, not an effigy, and the puncture had occurred in the upper right side of the chest—just below the collarbone—and therefore wasn't a fatal wound. Millard grabbed the coat fabric around the shoulders and Healy the pants material around Roberts-Smythe's knees, and in perfect synchronization they turned the body over. There it was. A dagger embedded deeply into the middle of the theatre manager's back, with only the ebony handle visible.

A physician ran across the stage toward them, but he saw in an instant that his presence was unnecessary. Members of the theatre staff and a few of the actors had moved down the stage to keep the curious patrons at bay.

"Cate?" Millard whispered.

"Yes, Jamie?"

"I don't see Charles anywhere."

"I know. And more than that, where is Patrick?"

Catherine Healy had been well taught by her father. That Charles Donovan—tonight's Polonius—was absent was fairly evident. But none of the others had given a thought to Patrick Copsey, the nineteen-year-old stage hand who was to take away the effigy as Polonius fell. During this mad moment on the stage of The Acropolis, both men were missing.

Chapter 2

Inspector Denham Phillpotts' reply to their offer was both immediate and unpleasant. "Yes, Miss Healy and Mr. Millard, I'm sure the both of you could *indeed* add much to the investigation. But at moments like this, it might be best for you to devote your time and energies to enhancing your theatrical skills and leave this business to those who know what they are doing."

Jamie looked at Catherine, who lifted her forehead and expanded her lovely eyes, suggesting to him the futility of volunteering their services to the chief inspector of the Yard. Phillpotts had little use for James Millard—that is, ever since the day almost a decade earlier when Millard's father, with his actor son in tow, offered a no-holds-barred critique of Phillpotts' investigation into the Whitechapel murders that had paralyzed so many in the city. Specializing in post-mortem medical investigation, Thomas Millard asked to examine the bodies of Emma Smith and Martha Tabram—the first of the "Ripper" victims, but Phillpotts refused him access.

As Catherine had learned, for almost four years afterward, Phillpotts endured the stares and mutterings of London's citizens and the reminders in the newspapers that the murderer had never been found. Phillpotts insisted they had in fact found their man—dead and half submerged along the shore of the Thames near the construction site of the now completed Tower Bridge. But neither the Millards nor the rest of London was convinced by Phillpotts' claim. Although he would never admit it, for the past decade the detective had been waiting for a crime at least approaching the sensational quality of the Whitechapel murders, and it was apparent to Catherine and Jamie that the detective believed that he might now have found it.

"If I may, Inspector Phillpotts, I think that—"

"If *I* may interrupt, Miss Healy. As it presently stands, I am satisfied the both of you were on the opposite end of the stage from where the body was found. But I will need to speak further with you about tonight's events. For instance, about those who are now absent from the theatre."

Millard politely raised his hand, holding it up until Phillpotts acknowledged him. "Inspector, I believe our assistant theatre manager Mr. Jaynes has everyone gathered near the apron of the stage—all that is except—"

"Except for Charles Donovan and the stage hand Copsey. I am already aware of who is missing, Mr. Millard."

Catherine took a step toward Phillpotts. "But, Inspector, we should also inform you that—"

"Miss Healy, I suggest that you and Mr. Millard return to your respective lodgings for the night. I have assigned one of my men to watch the residences of all the leading actors and the theatre owners. Good evening."

While on a case, Phillpotts preferred no interruptions, especially those that came in the form of questions or contradictions. Having dispatched the two meddling actors, he returned to his business at the back of the stage. The body of Morris Roberts-Smythe remained where it had been discovered during the third act of *Hamlet*.

Jamie touched Catherine's hand. "We had better do as he says. Besides, he doesn't yet know we turned the body to find the murder weapon. When he learns what we've done, he'll likely spontaneously combust from rage." Even at this dreadful moment, they enjoyed the image of Phillpotts literally exploding into flames, as Dickens had depicted his character the alcoholic Krook in one of their favorite novels, *Bleak House.* By the time they reached the lobby of the theatre, both could hear the inspector roar, no doubt turning his normally ruddy complexion to a throbbing beet red.

"Now he knows what we've done." Hailing a hansom cab, Jamie dropped his smile. "Cate, I wonder if Henry Jaynes will forget to tell him that two of the first-act performers left the theatre when they finished their parts for the evening."

Before they stepped inside the cabriolet, she brushed Millard's ungovernable forelock from his face. "Very probably he will forget, Jamie. It's likely just dawning on Henry that he must become temporary manager—at least for a few days." Catherine dropped her head. "I'm afraid Inspector Phillpotts will arrest him because he has the most to gain from Roberts-Smythe's murder."

"Did you see the way Phillpotts looked at him, Cate? I think he hates poor Jaynes as much as he does me."

"Jamie, you well know that Mr. Phillpotts dislikes me more than he does you."

"Not a chance."

"He does. Ten years ago, my father published in Dublin's *Evening Telegraph* his own indictment of Mr. Phillpotts's handling of the Ripper killings. The piece was reprinted here in London, and from what my father told me, Phillpotts was almost apoplectic with resentment over being taken to task by "some low-born Catholic Irish bastard constable.""

"Cate, I don't believe I have ever heard you say the word 'bastard.' I'm completely horrified."

"I'm merely providing you an accurate quotation. I haven't endorsed the use of the word, my love."

"Thank heavens for that. Other women who speak such words end up in one of London's many dark corners. Where I wish I had you right now. But this cab will do."

Catherine adored his ardent wit. "Well, we can't have any of that." Much to her relief, the driver paid no attention to them, only to his reins. "Very well, if you are quick about it, your Cate will permit one respectful kiss—but only on the cheek."

Catherine took pleasure in teasing him about his calling her "Cate"—a name that wasn't at all authentically Irish. He protested that he often found "Catherine" too formal, to which she replied that he only wanted an informal companion for his "Jamie," which his father had called him since boyhood, rather than his formal Christian name James. She had expressed mock indignation when he wrote his first note to her and spelled her new name with a "K." "We Irish don't carry a 'K' in our traditional alphabet," she lectured.

Millard stole his kiss. "Cate, I'm afraid we can't be with each other tonight. Remember that Phillpotts is assigning a policeman to guard each of our residences, and it wouldn't do for me to be away from home, at least for tonight."

Catherine pulled his neck forward and kissed him once more. "This isn't at all what I bargained for when I married you, James Millard."

~ # ~

Denham Phillpotts checked his pocket watch. It was 2:45 a.m., and his eyes stung with fatigue. Sleep would soon come, but not until he poured one last drink. Because he had failed to replenish his stock, he was forced to make the inferior brandy in his possession more palatable by cutting it with soda. Phillpotts smirked at the coincidence, for earlier he had learned that the missing Charles Donovan overcame his performance anxiety with short glasses of cheap brandy and soda, which he placed in several hiding places back stage at the Acropolis. Tonight, Phillpotts had only a cursory look at the nooks, crannies, and labyrinthine recesses of the theatre. He would of course return the following day and examine these areas more thoroughly, with the hope that something back there could tie the assistant manager Henry Jaynes, rather than the actor Charles Donovan, neatly to the crime. The very thought of implicating Jaynes gave Phillpotts the pleasure the inferior brandy failed to provide.

~ # ~

"Good morning, Alice." Catherine had come down the stairs on light feet.

"Heavens, Catherine, you startled me."

"But not enough to prevent you from sliding that volume under the cushion. What scandalous thing are you reading now?"

"I will never tell. I see you are up almost a full hour before you usually arise after a performance. Given last night's tragic event, I would have expected you to sleep the rest of the day."

"I slept very little—and only in annoying fits and starts. I believe it's the only restless night I've had since I've been living here. Thinking too much of the murder, I'm afraid."

"And how to solve it, no doubt."

"The idea did cross my mind."

Catherine smiled recalling the day Alice Pearcy asked when her house guest first became interested in crime detection. Catherine had answered, "Well, as a girl in Dublin my father had the habit of pacing the hallway outside my bedroom door when he was pondering a case such as this. When I was seven years of age I decided I would pace the halls with him, and he soon began sharing his thoughts with me. He would never have imagined it then, but he was teaching me the entire time he was muttering on about his assorted facts and speculations."

Catherine could see something impish modifying Alice's face. "And Catherine, I would guess that being apart from your husband last night didn't encourage a peaceful slumber either."

"Perceptive as always, Alice." Catherine dropped wearily into a chair and stared out to the street below. It had snowed during the night. The view was serene and inviting, but this morning she found it difficult to appreciate winter's nocturnal gift.

"I must admit I have become delightfully accustomed to your living here with us, Catherine, but I know eventually you will be with Jamie openly as his wife." Catherine said nothing and continued gazing at the new-fallen snow. Alice walked to Catherine's chair. "Catherine, you have the most breathtakingly beautiful hair. When it is down I wish I could run into it and have it swallow me up."

Catherine took a moment before she replied. Genuinely modest, she nevertheless wished to absorb the compliment. "You are exaggerating again, Alice. It's thick and healthy, but it's also reddish brown—in fact, more reddish than brown." She smiled impishly. "And only women who are depraved or demonic should have red hair. And only those who are mad or about to be murdered should ever have it down in a public setting. Those are the unalterable rules of the theatre, as well you know."

"Catherine, may I ask how soon it will be before you can make public your marriage?"

"I fear it will be more of a confession than an announcement." She found it difficult not to laugh at Alice's bright-eyed expression.

Catherine was used to Alice's interrogations about her relationship with Jamie. Two afternoons ago, they had both taken a delightful walk in the crisp January air and Catherine spoke more specifically about the occasion of her marriage.

"I married him on November the fourth, which was most appropriate, seeing that it was Mischief Night." Alice laughed at hearing the date. She knew Mischief Night was the evening before Guy Fawkes Day, when children from eight to eighteen behaved naughtily just for the exhilarating sake of being wicked.

"Jamie thought the day was apt, seeing we were in effect eloping without parental consent—or parental knowledge." Catherine explained that she and Jamie were returning to London after an engagement playing Sheridan at the Theatre Royal, Edinburgh. They stopped to visit mutual friends in North Yorkshire—in Whitby—and in the evening as they were looking out at the North Sea, Jamie pronounced that they ought to do something outlandish on Mischief Night. "I thought he meant simply stealing a pie from a window. I had no idea he would instead steal a clergyman from his bed and convince him—how, I do not know—to marry us in the middle of the night. Our friends and several of their friends served as our witnesses and wedding guests."

This morning, however, Catherine's thoughts were on more dreadful events, although she still was curious about the book Alice had put under the sofa cushion. Further prodding and teasing convinced Alice to hand it to Catherine. "Here. It's only a volume of Mr. Browning's poetry. I am reading this one here. The 'Soliloquy of the Spanish Cloister.' Don't be horrified, Catherine. It's not really an indecent poem, not at all unfit for a woman to read. Surely you know it. It's a monologue by a friar who secretly despises one of his fellow servants of God who lives with him in the cloister—and wishes all misfortune to befall him."

Catherine knew the poem. She remembered that under the humor of the piece lay the troubling fact that hatred and dreams of revenge have no limits. Catherine recollected as well the line Jamie was to have spoken last night as King Claudius: "Revenge should have no bounds."

Catherine's thoughts shifted from the cloister to the theatre and the sight of Morris Roberts-Smythe's body, with the ebony handle of the large dagger protruding from his back. As her father had taught her, she went back to the moment she arrived at The Acropolis and reconstructed all she had seen and heard, second by second. Staring at the snow aided her concentration as well as relaxed her spirits.

~ # ~

"So, James, tell me. How deeply was the blade embedded?"

"To the hilt."

"Directly into the spine or slightly on either side?"

"From what I could see, it might have been slightly off the middle of the spine."

"To the right or left?"

"Slightly . . . to the right."

"Directly thrust in, or was the blade leaning a bit?"

"Leaning slightly."

"In which direction?"

"With the handle leaning a bit to the right. Like this." Jamie demonstrated the angle with the palm of his hand.

"Well, my boy, you likely have a right-handed killer to find. Or should I say for the police to find. Leave it to them. Don't be seduced into getting involved by that Irish detective's incredibly charming though highly dangerous daughter."

"Dangerous?" Millard sighed amusingly at his father's latest attempt to suggest the wrongheadedness of his son's affections. Jamie could only imagine Thomas Millard's reaction once he learned Catherine Healy was in fact his daughter-in-law.

"All right, father, tell me how you know the killer was right-handed."

"Look and learn." Thomas Millard put down the severed hand he had been examining and positioned himself with his back turned toward his son. "Now grab the top of my coat, pull me toward you, and thrust your fist into my back exactly where you found the dagger." Jamie did as instructed. "Now do you see what I mean?"

"I do." By pulling his father toward him and swinging his arm to the middle of the spine, the younger Millard realized the blade would have entered on a slight angle and likely to the right of the spine.

"Good."

Jamie smiled. "So we can narrow the possible murders down to only those who are right handed."

"Don't mock me, boy. In any event, you might be able to use what I've just taught you the next time you act Macbeth or Hamlet."

"Neither character performs a stabbing in that particular fashion. Besides I'm out of the Hamlet game now."

"Ah, too old for the part then, I take it."

"No, not really. I may be thirty-four, but the great Henry Irving has played him throughout his forties. The truth is we have a new Hamlet at The Acropolis—the dashing Ned Ludmore. Twenty-five years of age, insufferably conceited, and highly aware of the name he is making for himself with the public. If there weren't a murder involved, I might have taken considerable delight in the fact that we left last night's Hamlet undone."

"Ludmore. Ludmore. Never heard of him."

"You will—if he has anything to say about it. But tell me why you think I wish to be involved in investigating the death of Morris Roberts-Smythe?"

The elder Millard lifted one of his thick gray eyebrows as if to say, "And you are *really* asking me that question?"

"I see. You think it's only because Cate will want to follow it up, is that it?"

"Never let it be said that I raised an idiot. Of course that's it. You are spoon-eyed in love with that girl. What is she, the eighth or ninth actress you have fallen madly for since you became a thessalonian?"

"A thespian."

"Makes no matter. Damn it, boy. You are, as you say, thirty-four. You are too old for the girl. What is she, seventeen?"

"Twenty-four."

"She looks seventeen."

"You were a full eleven years my mother's senior—or have you forgotten?"

"It was a different time then. Besides, she looked my age—if not older."

"She did not."

"And your mother didn't have enticing blue eyes. They were dismally muddy brown."

"Indeed."

"Have you given any thought to what your mother would think if she were alive now?"

"I truly believe she would have been deliriously happy to know I have found such an incredible woman to love."

"Bah." The senior Millard resumed his study of the severed hand. "Jamie, I've been thinking about the reattachment of hands and feet. If I have another ten years in this ancient carcass of mine, I may come up with a way to do it. Or if I don't have ten years left—which being sixty-four I likely don't—it would be a comfort in my declining weeks and days to know that my son would be carrying on my work. Just to know that the name Millard would be forever associated with hand and foot reattachment would be . . . well . . ."

"You find Cate a darling, don't deny it."

"Fine. I will confess it. I do find her a darling. An exquisitely beautiful creature. But she is also a child next to you. And more, she is Irish. And even more than that, a Catholic. And finally, not the kind of woman you should marry—although God knows I long ago gave up any hope you would find a spouse and give me grandchildren."

"You are sending me contradictory messages, father."

"Get you gone now. Get you to your stage studies. Tend to your blank verse. Leave me to my body parts."

"You know I've learned so much from you about medicine and the human body—and that I've had frequent use for what you have taught me."

Thomas Millard took the severed hand, and with it waved a silent goodbye to his son.

Chapter 3

Denham Phillpotts returned to The Acropolis at 10:30 a.m. and found a crumpled and haggard Henry Jaynes sitting behind Roberts-Smythe's desk. No other man filled Phillpotts with such disdain.

"I had little sleep last night, Inspector, as you might imagine. I was unable to erase the image of Mr. Roberts-Smythe lying dead on the upstage floor."

"And now you have new responsibilities to ponder, at least temporarily, isn't that right, Jaynes?"

"I suppose it is, Inspector."

Phillpotts examined several books on Roberts-Smythe's shelves. "And you're certain neither Donovan nor the stage hand Copsey returned later last evening or early this morning?"

"I assure you no one has seen them, Inspector." Jaynes knew Roberts-Smythe kept a bottle of spirits in his desk. He pulled one of the drawers open to retrieve the bottle—more as a peace offering to Phillpotts than as a calming agent for himself. He found no spirits; instead, he discovered an ornate case, decorated with engravings suggestive of the Ottoman Turks.

As soon as Jaynes pulled the case from the drawer, Phillpotts seized it. "Here now. And what might this be?" Noticing that the small latch was undone, Phillpotts lifted the top piece and opened the case. It was empty—the felt bottom revealing a depressed outline that could hold only one thing: a dagger of some kind. "Jaynes, have you ever seen this case before?"

Jaynes opened his mouth but failed to formulate a response. His complexion lost every hint of color.

"I asked if you have ever seen this case in Mr. Roberts-Smythe's possession, Jaynes." Phillpotts leaned over the front of the desk and lowered his torso until his eyes were even with the now acting-manager's. "Well?"

"I . . . I gave that box to him last October. I received it as a gift myself, but I felt he would appreciate it more than I. Jaynes closed his reddened eyes. His head weaved side to side. Phillpotts believed he was about to swoon.

"Was there anything inside the box when you gave it to him?"

"Yes, Inspector."

"And what the devil was in it?"

"There was a dagger inside the box."

"A dagger?"

"Yes, Inspector. With an ebony handle. The very dagger we found thrust in his back."

~ # ~

"And that's all I can possibly tell you, Inspector Phillpotts. I have scoured my mind for anything that might shed further light on this matter, but I can come up with nothing more. Please, must we speak here in Mr. Roberts-Smythe's office? Can't we at least go to mine?"

Jaynes confessed that Roberts-Smythe had little respect for him during their time working together, but that he fully respected the theatre manager's dedication to The Acropolis. Phillpotts kept his eyes drilled into Jaynes's lamb-like countenance. "You claim you gave him the ceremonial dagger that resided in this case. Yet you didn't know why you decided to award him something originally given to you? A gift then for a man who, as you have just admitted, had abused you in front of the actors and stage hands."

"But not physically. It was all verbal humiliation . . . . in the manner of what I judged as superfluous criticism."

"Might it be you had imagined using that dagger if the verbal humiliation failed to cease? That you were in effect sending him a warning to stop the 'superfluous criticism,' as you phrased it?"

Jaynes slumped in Roberts-Smythe's chair and lowered his face in the palm of his hand. "Inspector, I cannot deny that he threatened to relieve me of my position on at least one occasion. But I assured him there would be no need to take such a drastic course. I vowed to dedicate all of my time to becoming better at my duties. Yes, Inspector, I disliked him for holding the dismissal over my head like some sword of Damocles, but I assure you I could never have killed him. Inspector, look at me! I'm not capable of it. You have to believe me."

"I suggest that you solicit counsel, Jaynes."

Jaynes knew his plea was futile. Denham Phillpotts wasn't the type of man who would ever forgive past injuries—even those thirty years past.

~ # ~

"No, Jamie, it's colder this morning than it's been all winter." They had walked twenty or thirty yards from the house belonging to attorney Oliver Pearcy. Catherine squeezed Jamie's arm and nestled her body as close to his as possible while he hailed a hansom cab. How he had missed feeling her touch last night as he slept apart from her at his residence.

On the way to the Pearcy house this morning, Jamie indulged his fancy by recalling the circumstances under which he and Catherine had met and fallen in love. Seven months earlier, he had arrived at the theatre for an important meeting of all members of the company, who gathered on the middle of the empty stage. There Henry Jaynes introduced the new manager of The Acropolis, Morris Roberts-Smythe, who had been hired by the owners to bring needed competence if not luster to the company. He vowed to make the theatre rival the eminence of The Lyceum before the century was out.

Brutally efficient in both word and deed, Roberts-Smythe asked the company to look about. Millard was confused by the request until he realized that fully a dozen of the familiar faces were nowhere to be seen. Roberts-Smythe ceremoniously cleared his throat, at which everyone returned their attention back to him.

"You will notice that some of your old friends are no longer with us. The reasons for their dismissals should be apparent to each of you. Most lacked an acceptable level of commitment and some had failed to prevent the erosion of their skills and commitment to this theatre. We will no longer tolerate any member of the company who is guilty of either. Now, look about once again."

Millard understood that, for The Acropolis to survive, such a purge was probably necessary, but he also knew it would take time to forgive the new the manager for the callousness he demonstrated in making these necessary changes. Still, Jamie did as he was told and once more contemplated the others in the room. Now he saw seven unrecognizable faces—all new actors, he assumed. One face, however, struck him more than the others. It belonged to a young man with flowing light hair, a more than respectable physique, and an unmistakable attitude of privilege. The man was Edward Ludmore, Robert-Smythe's protégé and heir to all the parts requiring a romantic male lead.

While Millard nodded to some of the new members, a current member of the company made his tardy entrance on stage. It was Charles Donovan, looking rather sheepish with both hands massaging the rim of his weather-beaten bowler derby. Jamie winced, believing Donovan was about to learn he was no longer employed by The Acropolis. His skills had clearly deteriorated in the several years Millard had been with the company. Donovan's commitment to his craft was always questionable, and his reliability highly suspect, especially as he became more devoted to his backstage brandy and soda.

"I have brought her, Mr. Roberts-Smythe, just as you have asked. She is waiting in the wings."

"Good, Donovan. Bring her on stage and then go and stand with the others."

Millard felt relieved. It seemed that the old rapscallion Donovan had escaped the executioner—at least for the present.

In a moment Donovan ushered in the most fascinating young woman Jamie had ever gazed upon.

Roberts-Smythe again cleared his throat. "I wish to introduce all of you to Miss Catherine Healy. I had the good fortune of seeing her in Dublin acting Rosalind in *As You Like It.* The most impressive performance of the role I have yet witnessed. Miss Healy was intrigued by the challenge of winning over a London audience, and, after a spirited negotiation, she agreed to help me elevate The Acropolis to unprecedented heights. She, along with Mr. Ludmore, will make the 1897/98 season one of the most memorable ever in our good city. Right before Christmas we shall debut a new production of *Hamlet* with Mr. Ludmore as the Danish prince and of course Miss Healy as Ophelia. Mr. Millard, I trust you will agree you are now ready to concede the part to Mr. Ludmore and assume the role of Claudius. I have every confidence that you will make yourself worthy of that important role."

"I hope to indeed, sir." Jamie's eyes locked on Catherine's. She smiled at him warmly.

Yes, that warm smile. Later she would tell him she was highly impressed and most delighted by the manner in which he responded to Roberts-Smythe's patronizing remarks. She also confessed to feeling embarrassed by being so highly praised before she had had the opportunity to prove herself.

But prove herself she did, and for all his insufferable manner, Roberts-Smythe knew what he was about. The company was invigorated by the excellence of each production. Jamie's only complaint at first was that he would likely never be Catherine Healy's love interest on stage. He began the autumn season by playing the madcap and ill-fated Mercutio in Shakespeare's *Romeo and Juliet*, with Ned Ludmore and Catherine Healy in the title roles. In the next ten weeks, Jamie was also cast as Healy's elder brother, her unrequited suitor, and her cruel uncle in contemporary plays. At least he was able to play her husband when they went to Edinburgh in November. True, he depicted a curmudgeonly and old husband to Catherine Healy's rebellious and much younger wife in Sheridan's *School for Scandal,* but at least they were married on stage.

By then deeply in love and feeling confident she shared the emotion, he announced to Catherine that the experience on stage in Sheridan's play just had to be paralleled off it, and so they married while in Whitby.

As they rode in the hansom cab, Catherine noticed her husband was smiling for no obvious reason. "Where is your mind, Jamie?"

"Hmm? Oh, it's off thinking about our history, my lovely Cate. So tell me where your mind is."

"Mine's thinking of where Donovan and Copsey might have gone off to last night. I fear for them both."

"That either or both might have killed Roberts-Smythe?"

"No."

"That one of them killed the other *after* killing Roberts-Smythe?"

"No, my dearest. I'm rather thinking that neither of them killed Roberts-Smythe or each other—yet I'm fearing that one or the both of them are now dead."

Jamie instructed the driver to let them out before crossing Russell Street. Helping Catherine alight from the cab, he whispered to his wife— merely to get his face close to hers. "Cate, let's walk in this direction. I think we can discover if Patrick Copsey made it to his home last night."

~ # ~

"Oh, Mr. Millard, please don't keep asking me. I can only inform you that Patrick did come home briefly last evening, but he made me promise not to tell a soul where he went off to. Mr. Roberts-Smythe murdered? And you believe my son knows who might have done it? You can't believe he was responsible, do you?"

Jamie gently patted the right forearm of stage hand Patrick Copsey's mother. "And what time did he come home, Sarah?"

She gazed at Millard, as though he was the only man who could save her son. "Half past ten last night. He seemed utterly terrified."

Catherine placed her hand on Sarah Copsey's left forearm. "Did he say whether he had left the theatre earlier than usual?"

"No. But what he said was confusing to me. He had gone back to the theatre but then had to come here and collect some clothing—and that I would hear from him in a day or two. I didn't know what to make of it. Oh, dear."

Jamie softened his voice. "Sarah, I know he made you promise, but please—for his sake—tell us where he went."

Brushing the tears from her cheek, the woman looked at Catherine, who nodded her head. "Trust Jamie, Sarah. Please tell us."

Copsey's mother emitted a strained sigh of resignation. "All right, I'll tell you. And God forgive me for breaking my word to my son."

~ # ~

Patrick Copsey opened the door only after he identified Catherine and Jamie's voices on the other side. "So, how did you find me? Never mind, I know. My mother. Of course she'd tell you. I should have known better than to confide in her." Catherine was struck by the normally placid Copsey's agitation. He almost invariably maintained a sunny disposition at The Acropolis, and there were few who didn't enjoy his company backstage. But it was clear he didn't wholly believe she and Jamie were there for his benefit.

"Patrick, Miss Healy and I are not here to harm or betray you. We know you had nothing to do with Robert-Smythe's murder last night."

Catherine wondered if her husband really believed so. She was of the opinion that Copsey had some involvement in the events of the previous evening. After all, it wasn't like him to disappear the way he had.

Copsey looked over their shoulders before closing the door. "I am afraid to trust you, that's all."

Millard placed his hand on the young man's shoulder. "Just tell us why you weren't at your post last night during the third act. We both saw you backstage in the second act. All seemed well. You joked with us as you always do, Patrick."

"Is there is no one outside waiting to arrest me?"

"No, Patrick, there is not." The three of them sat in a small lodging on the south side of the Thames, right off Westminster Bridge Road, not far from the Bethlehem Lunatic Hospital. The police were frequently called upon to apprehend those who sought an escape from "Bedlam," as it had often been called, and return them to their caretakers. In fact, Copsey had a friend who worked at the hospital, who provided him sanctuary at his lodgings.

Copsey was startled when Catherine touched his hand. "Patrick, you can indeed trust us. Just tell us what happened."

Copsey emitted a deep breath as he raked his fingers through his thick hair. "At the beginning of the third act, when Mr. Millard and Mr. Donovan left the stage for Mr. Ludmore's 'To be, or not to be' speech, I arrived at my small desk upstage left to be in position to grab the stuffed effigy as soon as Mr. Donovan made his way around the stage to the spot. I then saw a note lying open on my desk."

"In whose hand?"

"That's the thing, Miss Healy, I really can't be sure. I didn't recognize it."

"Then it wasn't signed?"

"No. I first assumed it was Mr. Jaynes's handwriting, but I soon became curious about it, seeing that Mr. Jaynes had written me several notes before, and this one didn't look like any of the others."

"What did the note say?" Jamie kept his hand on Copsey's shoulder as if to steady him.

"It said I was to leave the theatre and go to The Lyceum to meet a Mr. Pratt, who had a package that was to be delivered immediately to Mr. Roberts-Smythe's office. The note also informed me that someone else would hold the effigy for Mr. Donovan's scene. But when I arrived at The Lyceum and began asking for this Mr. Pratt, not a soul knew anything about any such man or any such package. When I returned to The Acropolis, I discovered many patrons were outside talking about the murder of Mr. Roberts-Smythe and at what point in the play it had occurred. The police had arrived and had begun asking questions of some of the theatre patrons. I comprehended that they would discover I was not in the theatre as I should have been. I then dismissed the idea that Mr. Jaynes was the author of the note. Surely someone sent me away so that everyone would discover my absence from my place backstage at the time Mr. Roberts-Smythe was killed, and I would be taken into custody as the possible murderer. I knew they would come to my small lodgings near the theatre, so I went to my family's residence, took some clothing, and came here. I am at a loss as to what I should do now. Please tell me what I should do."

Catherine squeezed his hand. "Stay here for now. Let us have the note. You have it don't you?"

"Yes, it's in the pocket of my coat." Copsey retrieved and handed it to Catherine.

Jamie steadied Copsey further by grabbing both his shoulders. "Patrick, we'll examine this and try to find out who wrote it."

"But if something happens," Catherine added, "and you are apprehended, tell them to contact us and we'll do what we can to get you released as soon as possible. My good friend the attorney Oliver Pearcy will get you free."

After stepping into the hansom cab, Catherine and Jamie studied the letter carefully. Neither could recognize the handwriting. "I'll tell you this much, dear husband. There are at least three different styles in the handwriting on this note."

"Three different hands you mean?"

"No, only one hand, but it is evident the author was doing all he could to disguise his own."

Chapter 4

Lord Oxley finished examining the papers and handed them to his secretary. "David, give these to the Prime Minister. Tell him I see no reason why we cannot bring this matter to Her Majesty."

"Yes, Lord Oxley." Young David Isaacs excused himself and took the papers to the office of Robert Arthur Talbot Gascoyne-Cecil, the 3rd Marquess of Salisbury.

Oxley had been bitterly disappointed upon Lord Salisbury's most recent election to head the Queen's government, because he thought the new Prime Minister would appoint him Foreign Secretary. But Salisbury declared he would maintain the post for himself, while Oxley would serve as First Lord of the Treasury, the position traditionally held by the Prime Minister. Even so, Oxley realized that at age forty-eight his prospects of succeeding the nearly sixty-eight-year-old Salisbury seemed likely, provided the Conservatives remained in power.

Oxley had to admit that remaining more often in England did have its benefits. And the one Oxley was concentrating on at present was the frequent opportunity to attend theatrical productions in London's West End. Before the previous autumn he had summarily dismissed the pleas of his wife and daughter to escort them to the theatres, but in mid-November—upon a request to accompany two German ministers—Oxley found himself sitting in a box at The Acropolis gazing down at the achingly lovely Catherine Healy performing Shakespeare's heroine Portia in *The Merchant of Venice*—the one play, the German ministers teased, that ought especially to intrigue the First Lord of the Treasury.

Oxley returned to The Acropolis as often as possible, more often alone as the weeks went by, to admire a young woman he had become completely enraptured by. Oddly, he hadn't yet been introduced to her, even though his appearance behind the scenes following the final curtain would have been proper form and a special treat for the actors and management. Yet he felt the time hadn't been quite right to take Catherine Healy's hand and kiss it as a gesture of appreciation for her performance. From there he would of course send a few notes and gifts before asking to meet with her alone.

"Anything else, Lord Oxley?" Isaacs had returned from his errand.

"Yes, David. Take this note to The Acropolis Theatre and give it to no one except to the addressee—Miss Catherine Healy."

"Yes, my Lord."

~ # ~

Upon arriving at The Acropolis, Catherine and Jamie spotted Ned Ludmore and Henry Jaynes standing near one of the downstage audience boxes. Ludmore was shouting at Jaynes, who in his apparently fragile condition was ill-equipped to deal with the intensity of Ludmore's verbal assault.

"Damn it, Jaynes. And you are going to allow them to shut this theatre down? And for how long?"

"I don't know, Ned. I have spoken this morning to one of the owners, who informs me that we can expect to keep our doors closed for at least the next three nights."

"At *least* the next three nights? Didn't you point out that we're committed to these productions regardless of the loss of an actor or stage hand? Didn't one of your actors have a heart attack off stage in the middle of a performance—and the production continued and no further ones were canceled?

"But it was a heart attack, Ned, not a murder."

"You refused even to make the argument for our carrying on, isn't that so, Jaynes?"

Millard interrupted. "I'm sure if you had the heart attack, Ned, you would have been highly insulted if the performance continued without you."

Because Ludmore had not sensed Millard coming up behind him, he was jolted by the remark, but quickly recovered.

"Keep out of this, Millard. And you can take your elementary wit and thrust it up your . . . ." Ludmore caught sight of Catherine and immediately suspended his insult. He excused himself only to her and made his way from the theatre.

Catherine was sympathetic to Jaynes's mental state. "Henry, you look as though you haven't slept."

"I haven't. And I know I'll likely be arrested at any moment. Inspector Phillpotts believes I killed Roberts-Smythe. I haven't a doubt he believes it. He has advised me to seek legal counsel."

The mention of legal counsel again brought Oliver Pearcy to Catherine's mind. "We know an attorney we can ask to speak with you."

"I have a member of my family in the profession. I've already sent him a note."

Healy and Millard shared a look, each wishing to see the note Jaynes sent in order to compare the handwriting to that on the message Patrick Copsey received at his backstage desk. Whereas Jamie's face registered regret that they couldn't do so, Catherine's countenance took on the expression of one about to jump a precipice.

"Henry, might I ask you to look at this? Do you recognize the hand?"

Jaynes's face tightened as he took the Copsey note. As was his habit when he perused cast lists, documents, or invoices, Jaynes wet his lips with his tongue and swallowed once, with his prominent adam's apple lifting and falling, before dropping his eyes to the paper. He examined the writing only briefly. "No. I don't recognize the hand. But it is rather peculiar. I'm sorry, dear Catherine. Now if you will excuse me, I have to meet with a representative of the city to discuss the length of time the Acropolis must remain closed to the public."

Looking toward the back of the house, Catherine observed two newspaper writers from the *The Daily Telegraph* and the *Pall Mall Gazette* heading toward Jaynes for yet another series of questions. These and other newspaper men had been peppering the poor man since eleven o'clock last night—and had probably followed him as soon as he left his lodgings this morning. Jaynes walked as quickly as his slight legs could take him. But he needn't have hurried. The men from the newspapers actually had James Millard and Catherine Healy in their sights.

~ # ~

"But father, you must assure me you will help Catherine and her husband if for any reason they get caught up in the horrible events of last night."

Oliver Pearcy took his daughter's hand. "I can see no reason why they'd be in any legal jeopardy. Then again, given this city's and this government's peculiar sense of justice, anything could happen, I imagine."

Pearcy was the only one in London, other than his daughter, who knew of Millard and Healy's marriage. Since he had years earlier ceased his weekly excursions into an Anglican church, his conscience wasn't much disturbed by the unconventional arrangement between the two actors. After all, he wasn't harboring two lovers, one of whom was married to someone else. He simply made it possible for a husband and wife to perform the legally sanctioned role of lovers. Pearcy understood that the occupations of each and their difference of age, nationality, and religion would pose difficulties for their fathers, whom they loved dearly and wished slowly to reconcile to the idea of their marriage before announcing it as a *fait accompli*.

To the ever-jaundiced eye of the public, Pearcy served as a surrogate parent to Catherine Healy—giving the actress a room and the companionship of his daughter Alice. He never protested when she wished her husband to remain the night with them, during which time Jamie would eventually make his way to Catherine's room. That Pearcy's son Matthew was but fourteen and for the most part myopic and oblivious—and a profoundly deep sleeper—permitted the deceptions to occur under the boy's nose without questions being asked or deductions being made. Even with all that, Pearcy hoped one day to have some of the charity women with whom he was often forced to conduct business find out that Catherine and Jamie were spending the night in each other's company. How he would relish telling these women that yes, it was all true. And worst of all, Miss Catherine Healy and Mr. James Millard were—of all horrors—actually married. Besides, his secretly aiding and abetting a married couple in this manner was nothing compared to another more dangerous activity of his, of which not even his daughter, Millard, or Catherine Healy were aware.

~ # ~

After Catherine and Jamie dispatched the reporters, they considered their good fortune in being employees of the recently renovated Acropolis

Theatre, which was in many ways reflective of the other London houses with which it competed, such as the grand Lyceum. It was horseshoe shaped and included the new stall seating, separate boxes, dress circle, upper circle, and gallery areas. Here one could admire the vibrant splashes of color in the wallpaper, seats, and gilded trim, as well as in the patron's clothing. Catherine Healy told her father that what first appealed to her about The Acropolis was its color, especially its amber satin and dark red color scheme.

Before the opening curtain, one could glance about and see many important persons now more comfortably and properly placed. The amenities—as well as the seating, entrances, and exits—had been greatly improved with the arrival of the theatre's new administration. Morris Roberts-Smythe was excellent at coming up with novel ways to make his important patrons satisfied with their own significance. For example, The Acropolis included four segregated bars as yet another way in which the classes were kept separate.

But unlike many of his competitors, Roberts-Smythe did something about the poor sanitation conditions, which at times made attending a performance a most unpleasant hygienic experience. On certain nights in other theatres, members of the audience were forced to watch the proceedings with a perfumed handkerchief pressed firmly to their noses. In addition, the electric lighting, which had not become common backstage until the previous decade, was improved and became less of a fire hazard. The dressing rooms, usually insufficient at other theatres, were enlarged for the comfort of the actors. As much as the company disliked Roberts-Smythe's generally abrasive personality and frequent demands on their energy and time, all were grateful he didn't follow the lead of other commercial managers who were especially conscious of cutting expenses. Jamie believed Roberts-Smythe's commitment to improvement was motivated by his desire to be viewed as London's finest theatre manager—and indeed he had been the subject of two praiseworthy newspaper articles, which prompted ridicule from several of the envious actor-managers at London's other houses.

Most intriguing perhaps were the architectural adjustments Roberts-Smythe ordered for the backstage area of The Acropolis. Several large recessed spaces held painted scenic pieces of flat and three-dimensional kinds. In fact, Roberts-Smythe added so many new recesses, alcoves, niches, and nooks of varying dimensions that the company called the backstage area "The Honeycombs" owing to its appearance. Because he had drawn up a master chart to show where everything should be stored, Roberts-Smythe could blow a tempest when a stage hand, carpenter, scenic painter, costumer, or actor placed an item in the incorrect storage area. Soon the actors began to speak of the theatre manager's ultimate punishment as having an offending member of the company stuffed in one of those recesses and left to rot. "So much for the improvements in sanitation," Jamie had once quipped.

It was with these thoughts in mind that he and Catherine made their way behind the stage area to search for clues that might assist their unsanctioned investigation of Roberts-Smythe's murder. As they greeted and moved past one of Inspector Phillpott's photographers, who was taking pictures of the crime scene from several angles, Jamie whispered to his wife, "You know that Phillpotts will soon want both of us to pose for a photograph, so he can put us on his wall along with the other vandals, thieves, and cut-throats he has proudly on display."

"That's where your father already has me, isn't it, my dear?"

"We have nearly won him over, Cate. I can feel it."

"What makes you conclude that?"

"Because he waved goodbye to me this morning with a severed hand, that's why." Jamie felt the expression on his wife's face was indeed worthy of a photograph.

As they walked into the "The Honeycombs," Jamie desired a kiss before Catherine traded pleasantry for seriousness. But she was first her father's daughter. "All right. Let's start our examination with this crevice—where the stage cups, dishes, and glasses are kept."

Chapter 5

Sitting in his cluttered office, Dublin Metropolitan Police Inspector Michael Healy had a few moments to read the correspondence from his daughter and another letter he had received from London. He opened first the one from his dearest Catherine. After reading the accounts of her more recent theatrical endeavors, he came to the meat of the matter.

My adored Father, as for your suggestion that I at least find an Irish actor with whom to "act out my social inclinations until I find someone better suited for me," I can only say that of the four Irishmen we have in our theatre company, two are married with children, and the third is unlikely ever to be wed, given his only periodic regard for his own cleanliness. As for the fourth, the unhappy Mr. Donovan, he enjoys his brandy and soda a little too much to make a satisfactory social companion. I can hear you now muttering that the fault lies in the soda, not in the brandy. But let me say in all seriousness that I will socialize only with a man who possesses my heart, regardless of his other qualifications, and I hope that counts for something in your estimation. Please understand I do not beg your approval of whatever man to whom I may chose to award my heart, for you long ago insisted that I always maintain my dignity and never beg for anything. But when that time comes, having your blessing would mean everything to me.

But even without it, I remain
Your loving and dutiful daughter,
Catherine

Re-reading the last part of her letter, Healy understood that for his daughter the time had already come. Evidently, she had awarded her heart to someone her father might find objectionable on one or more grounds.

Healy had raised Catherine without a wife since she was four years of age, and he taught her to be fearless and spirited. And yet she had never lost her charming ways and loving nature. He wondered how that could have happened, seeing he had said nothing to her about cultivating either of those qualities. That he loved her she always knew. The charm must have come from her deceased mother, for he found that attribute wholly incompatible with his life's calling.

Still, if she married an actor at The Acropolis or at one of the other London theatres, she would remain until her old age a mere object of public amusement and curiosity. Healy was uncomfortable with the fact that others evaluated her efforts and physical appearance as they sat smugly safe from the arena in which she exercised her talents. Healy knew what it was like to be criticized for an assortment of failures. Dublin had too many crimes unsolved and too many criminals roaming its streets for him and the Metropolitan force to escape criticism. But he never felt himself on display as was his daughter whenever she mounted a theatre stage. Catherine's marriage to an actor would do nothing to remove her from periodic embarrassment and emotional distress. The papers were replete with tales of disastrous unions between stage players. Even though all indications pointed to her being one of the darlings of the London theatre scene, Healy still feared for her future, especially given the capricious nature of the public.

"Excuse me, sir."

"What is it, Maguire?"

"Word has just reached us that there was a murder last night at London's Acropolis Theatre. The message just came in by telegraph."

Healy jumped to his feet. "My God, man. The Acropolis?"

"Yes, but the victim was a male, so your daughter must be all right."

"A male? Who? A patron? An actor?"

"It only says the man was connected to the Acropolis Theatre."

"Thank you, Maguire. I'll need to send a message to London."

"I'll prepare that for you now, sir."

Healy dropped back into his desk chair and attempted to regain his equilibrium. His daughter was almost certainly unharmed, but had she witnessed the slaying? Had the murderer been apprehended, or was he still a danger to anyone who worked at the theatre? Healy trusted his daughter to know well enough to keep out of harm's way, but he worried that her instincts, which he helped to shape, would make her curious enough to investigate what had happened. Healy slammed his already clenched fist down upon his desk.

Under his hand he felt the second piece of London correspondence. He had momentarily forgotten about it. The letter was short—less than a page. Following the correspondent's introduction of himself, there was a straightforward request to meet when the sender arrived in Dublin later in the week. The correspondent wished to speak about serving as patron to Healy's daughter Catherine. The letter concluded,

Be assured that I will better explain my motives and intentions when we meet.

Healy didn't bother to read the letter again. He simply ran his finger back and forth over the signature of Oxley, England's First Lord of the Treasury.

~ # ~

"Jamie, here—look at this." Catherine stood in front of one of the backstage recesses holding two coat buttons in the palm of her hand.

"Buttons. From Roberts-Smythe's coat?"

"No, my love. Look. These are silver. Last evening, Roberts-Smythe was attired all in black."

Roberts-Smythe deplored ostentation in his own dress, and neither Jamie nor Catherine could recall his ever wearing silver or gold buttons."

"But, look again, Jamie. These are costume buttons. From an Elizabethan coat."

"From *Hamlet*, then?" She nodded, still absorbed in thought. "Cate, they could have been dropped here at any time."

"No, not dropped. Look at the thread still attached to each of them. These buttons were pulled or ripped off in some manner." She turned from him and placed the extended fingers of her right hand to the side of her face.

Millard understood the gesture, having seen it before. She was evidently close to recalling something important.

"These came from Charles's Polonius costume, Jamie."

"Torn off while he was backstage last night, I suppose. Perhaps in a struggle with Roberts-Smythe?"

Catherine shook her head forcefully. "But Charles couldn't have murdered Mr. Roberts-Smythe. I refuse to believe it."

"Cate, he had reason, and he was becoming more reliant on alcohol to get through an evening's performance."

"Yes, he did have cause, seeing that Roberts-Smythe was soon likely to sack him. But how many at this theatre also had reason to do it—for a host of justifications?"

"All right, Cate. So, did Roberts-Smythe grab at his coat? Or if Patrick Copsey is lying to us, did he jerk the buttons free? Or . . . something else?"

While Jamie debated the possibilities, Catherine began pulling out the rolled up theatrical banners and tapestries Roberts-Smythe insisted be stored in one of the wide recess areas some twenty paces from where his body was later found. "Please help me, Jamie. I'm having difficulty pulling out this large tapestry."

Millard gently moved her aside and grabbed the tapestry at both ends. "I've done this before." The tapestry slid out more easily because the floor inside the nook was slightly raked—higher in the back and lower in the front. Jamie let the tapestry down on the floor, while Catherine peered into the recess.

"Dearest God, Jamie. It's Charles."

He thrust in his head and saw the splayed body, seemingly frozen in an attitude of terror. Jamie crawled into the recess, as Catherine cast her eyes further down "The Honeycomb." She soon found what she was looking for. The rest of the rolled banners and tapestries rested on the floor, underneath three other nooks. Whereas a visitor might think these were placed there for quick use on stage, Catherine knew none of them were employed in the current production. Someone had taken them out to prepare the tapestry recess for the depositing of Charles Donovan's body.

"Cate, you might not want to see this." Jamie pushed himself back out of the nook, dragging the stiffened body with him.

"My darling, I have seen more than my share of dead bodies following my father around Dublin."

"But did you actually know any of them, Cate?"

"No." For the first time she would see the corpse of someone she knew, liked, and often consoled. Still the lessons of her father were paramount in her mind— "A good detective must put all personal feelings aside. Serve the process, dear daughter. Serve the process."

Millard had regained his footing on the floor. Donovan's body lay on the very edge of the recess, some four feet off the ground. For his part, Jamie was also conscious of the experience he had gained from his father, who would periodically assist the Coroner's Court by retrieving a body and bringing it to one of the post-mortem rooms for examination.

Jamie sounded much like his father now. "The skin is waxy. The hands blue. The head and neck showing slight evidence of blue-green color. His eyes are beginning to retreat into his skull."

Catherine opened her nostrils and was much relieved that the state of decomposition had not yet advanced to the point of nauseating putrification. Yet she easily detected the odor of death. "He's in full stiffness, Jamie."

"Yes, and will be for another day or so. Then he'll become limp once again. No, don't lean forward, Cate. There are already flies around him, laying their . . . I'm sorry. That detail was completely unnecessary." For Catherine, part of her husband's charm was his always being the gentleman and protecting her without making her feel inferior.

Catherine pointed. "Can you see that? There on his neck."

Her husband saw the impression easily enough. "Clearly he was strangled."

"Probably right near where we are standing. And then lifted up and rolled into the recess—pushed far enough back to make room for this tapestry to block the body from anyone passing by. That was probably why the body was somewhat on its side. Look down there at those banners and tapestries on the floor. It's evident the murderer took pains to prepare this recess for Charles's body."

"Since I was on stage with him not long before Roberts-Smythe's body was discovered, Charles must have been strangled as soon as he returned back here for his final scene. He couldn't have been strangled *after* Roberts-Smythe was killed, for the murderer would have made his escape before the arras was pulled aside by Ludmore."

"Yes my love, but how long before Mr. Roberts-Smythe was stabbed? And why was Roberts-Smythe backstage at that moment?"

~ # ~

"Good God man, you must return to The Acropolis and state where you were last night at the time of the murder. Here, down this pint and then

37

go there or to the police and account for yourself." The proprietor of The Red Swan public house—north of the West End theatres, right off Charing Cross Road—had spread before him a copy of the halfpenny *Daily Mail,* which had just begin publishing less than two years earlier. "Quite a story here. I see it mentions a Donovan and a Copsey being unaccounted for after the killing of the theatre manager, but it says nothing about you being missing, Bernhard."

Bernhard Schneider nodded weakly and returned to his pint of stout. He said nothing about the fact that there were three of them the newspaper failed to mention as absent from the theatre. Schneider, Alfred Nichols, and John Metcalfe had all left the Acropolis at the conclusion of the first act of *Hamlet,* for their work was done for the night. They had portrayed the characters Marcellus, Bernardo, and Francisco respectively—the three men on the platform of Elsinore Castle when the ghost of Hamlet's father appears. Metcalfe was done first, for his role merely consisted of nine lines, followed by Nichols, with a slightly larger part, and eventually by Schneider, whose Marcellus was a more substantial character, remaining on stage the longest and uttering one of the many famous lines of the play, "Something is rotten in the state of Denmark."

Schneider found the line apt—especially when he considered the foul state of affairs at the Acropolis Theatre. Whereas the public was captivated by the theatre's luminaries—Catherine Healy, Edward Ludmore, James Millard, and Morris Roberts-Smythe—no one cared much for the lesser members of the company, who acted with scant recognition and minimal financial reward. Even though it was rare for someone in the ranks of the bit players to rise and command a leading role, almost all of them—at least those under the age of thirty-five—held out hopes of doing so. They soon came to resent the Hamlets and even to distrust the Marcelluses among their number. That is, instead of a familial environment, with all hands happily committed to providing the public excellent and memorable performances, it was too often a contentious atmosphere, with every small part analyzed for the number of lines that accompanied it and the number of scenes in which one appeared.

These members of the supporting cast came to see the jealousies not as petty but rather as necessary. Most of them found solace and stimulation in plotting against fellow small-role actors. Schneider moreover felt an antagonism towards him owing to his strong German accent, which a seventeen-year residence in London had failed to efface. As Schneider and the others were aware, in Shakespeare's day and later, actors who played such parts as Marcellus, Bernardo, and Francisco would often take on another role or even two later in the play. Schneider had played multiple parts before. It was a small consolation for being relegated to minor roles. But desiring to work into the company newer and younger performers, Roberts-Smythe avoided giving an actor a second role in the same play. It was therefore perfectly fine with him if Schneider, Nichols, and Metcalfe left the theatre during or after the first act.

Finishing his pint, Schneider walked out of the Red Swan and headed south on Charing Cross Road. He wondered if Nichols and Metcalfe had already spoken with the police regarding their whereabouts the previous evening. Schneider recalled that he hadn't actually seen Nichols and Metcalfe leave The Acropolis. Had one or both of them remained, therefore being accounted for during the initial investigation the previous night? If so, Schneider feared he might well be the prime suspect.

Chapter 6

"No, Mr. Millard, it would have been the 'better course' had you contacted me *before* you decided to go about exploring as you did. You may well have disturbed the area to the point that good evidence might now be irretrievably lost."

"I strongly doubt it, Inspector."

Phillpotts pressed his teeth together in a manner that gave his face a comically macabre expression. It was obvious he wasn't used to contradiction and was only restraining himself with Jamie because of Catherine Healy's presence. "Fingerprint evidence, Mr. Millard. That's what you might well have destroyed by your actions." Catherine mildly grunted. "Something the matter, Miss Healy?"

"Not at all, Inspector Phillpotts. I'm just thinking."

She was indeed thinking of a conversation with her father when he had come to London in the autumn. Michael Healy had been going on about his London rival, whom he without affection called "Inspector Pisspots." Healy scoffed at Phillpotts's conservatism when it came to investigative procedure, noting that the Inspector had dismissed the growing interest and application of fingerprint evidence. Whereas Healy and many others found Sir Francis Galton's book *Fingerprints* a fascinating and significant analysis, Phillpotts would have none of it when the book first appeared six years earlier. Apparently, Catherine thought, he must either have changed his mind or simply decided to grab Galton's book to swat Jamie with.

"Inspector, I don't believe either Miss Healy or I rubbed the frame around the nook. The imprints, if there are any, might still be there. Have your man examine the frame and the wall three feet on either side."

Phillpotts looked incredulous. "I think I know my business, Mr. Millard. And, as I have already said, I would most appreciate it if you and Miss Healy kept to yours."

Ignoring his suggestion, Catherine stepped toward Phillpotts, "When you investigated last night, did you or your men know the depth of these recesses, Inspector?"

Phillpotts maintained enough composure to avoid rudely dismissing what he deemed an impertinent query. As for his presence at the West End theatres, he had only attended when the audience included those he was about to apprehend. An arrest at the Haymarket Theatre three years earlier led to his being lampooned in the papers and ridiculed by none other than Oscar Wilde. Because Phillpotts hadn't waited until intermission to make the arrest but rather interrupted the first act of Wilde's *An Ideal Husband*, the newspapers gave him such titles as "Inspector Bit Part" and "Constable Clap Not." Wilde was widely quoted as saying of the event, "Interruption is the tribute mediocrity pays to genius." Few therefore were as gleeful as Phillpotts when a few months afterwards the court found the playwright guilty of gross indecency and sentenced him to two years hard labor.

Phillpotts answered Catherine in a measured tone, "Mr. Jaynes should have told me about the recesses, but he didn't. I have sent for him at his lodgings. I will expect him to account for this omission."

Jamie turned to Catherine. "At his lodgings? I wondered why he wasn't here."

"Yes, Mr. Millard, at his lodgings. I ordered him there earlier today."

"But why, Inspector?"

"I have my reasons. Besides, why either of you expect that I must account to you for every decision I make, I cannot make out."

At that moment the three of them reacted to an explosion of flash powder. Phillpotts chose to unleash his pent up frustrations on the hapless police photographer attempting to record the scene backstage in "The Honeycomb." The young man had already taken several pictures of Donovan's body before it was removed from the recess. Apparently, only the photographer believed a picture of Inspector Phillpotts investigating the crime scene would be worthy of the permanent record.

The young man was highly embarrassed, but that didn't suppress his delight in being this close to Catherine Healy. He smiled gawkily, and she responded with a pleasant nod. Only he knew the last photograph had the actress in center frame. He trusted that Phillpotts would reject it. The young man planned all along to keep the photograph of Catherine Healy for himself.

When the smoke from the magnesium powder and potassium chlorate finally dissipated, they found Henry Jaynes standing before them.

"You called for me, Inspector?"

"Jaynes, did you know that a little while ago we found Donovan's body lying in this nook?"

Catherine and Jamie both thought, "*We* found?"

"I was . . . was just told so when . . . when I arrived, sir." Jaynes could barely get the words out.

Catherine did her best to help. She had always felt badly about Jaynes's social awkwardness, unhandsome face, and general appearance of vulnerability. "Inspector, Mr. Jaynes is distraught, as you can see. May we not postpone this questioning for a time?"

Phillpotts ignored her request. "Well, Jaynes? Why didn't you inform me this area included spots where a body might be concealed?"

"I wasn't . . . thinking of that, seeing that his . . . Mr. Roberts-Smythe's body was at the rear of the stage, and I wasn't considering the possibility of course that Charles might be dead, but . . ." Catherine took his hand. Her touch and Jamie's look of encouragement steadied him. He took a deep breath and finally spoke without halting. "When we talked last night, I wasn't thinking of anyone else being found murdered here at The Acropolis. I merely assumed that Mr. Donovan and the boy Copsey had fled out of fear for what they had seen. I was naturally concerned for their safety, but if Charles was to turn up dead, I would have expected it to be somewhere else, and not here."

"Is that so?"

"Yes, Inspector. Why would I think Charles would also have been murdered? Instead, if anything, I was thinking that he . . ." Jaynes dropped his eyes.

"Go on, Jaynes."

"No, no. That was horribly unfair of me. The man is dead."

"You were thinking that Donovan had killed Roberts-Smythe. Is that what you were going to say?"

"I only thought it a possibility, Inspector."

"And Copsey?"

"No. I don't know why exactly, but I don't think young Patrick could

42

have done it. But, Inspector, are you suggesting now that he killed both Mr. Roberts-Smythe and Mr. Donovan?"

Jamie and Catherine read each other's thoughts. They would say nothing at present about their visit to Copsey or about the note, which was still in their possession. But would Jaynes mention the note to Phillpotts?

Phillpotts stepped closer to Jaynes, who instinctively backed away. "Please let go of his hand, Miss Healy. You are not his mother."

"Very well, Inspector."

"Jaynes, do you know where Patrick Copsey is at this moment?"

"No, I . . ."

"Do you know if he is alive at this moment?"

"I cannot . . . say with certainty."

"Do you know, if he is dead, how he might have met his demise?"

"Inspector, I don't know. Now please stop badgering me." Jaynes's legs began to give out on him. He fell back against the edge of the recess where Donovan's body had been found.

Jamie grabbed Jaynes and pulled him away. "Fingerprint evidence, Inspector. We can't risk wiping it away."

Phillpotts offered a half smile, satisfied he had learned something new or had corroborated something he had suspected. "Escort your acting manager back to his lodgings. Have a pleasant evening, Miss Healy. And you as well, Mr. Millard."

~ # ~

"You must both relax and forget about what happened last night at The Acropolis—at least for the rest of this evening. Father will be down as soon as he changes out of his heavy clothes. It's so toasty warm down here, isn't it?"

Alice Pearcy was delighted to have both Catherine and Jamie home for a light supper and some sherry—and the fine claret her father recently received from France. Jamie seemed surprised by the quality of the wine. "I must say, this is especially fine, Alice. And I'll be sure to tell your father so as soon as he comes down. And by the way, where is your brother Matthew?"

"In his room inventing some mischief to plague me with for the next week."

Jamie laughed and raised his glass and took another sip of the claret. Catherine flashed a "Medusa look," as her husband termed it—the one to discourage him from either talking or in this case drinking too rapidly, which often led to his speaking inappropriately—but Jamie saw nothing but the claret inside the glass as he brought it up to his lips. Still, Catherine appreciated that the events of the past twenty-four hours had taken their toll on the both of them and that an evening's escape into modest hedonism was sorely needed. The Acropolis was dark tonight and would be for the next few days at least—normally the perfect opportunity for extended relaxation—yet she understood her mind would be constantly wrestling with the murders of Morris Roberts-Smythe and Charles Donovan.

Catherine failed to notice Alice's pouring Jamie a second glass of the claret or hear his witticism that had Alice chortling uncontrollably, because another thought commanded her attention. Other than Patrick Copsey, two others of the company were missing from the accounting of the previous night. It was true Inspector Phillpotts refused to allow Jamie to inform him of that fact, but did Henry Jaynes mention the missing actors to the detective? But then Jaynes was so completely flustered and intimidated that it was probable he had forgotten.

Oliver Pearcy appeared on the stairs. "Finally, your delinquent host has arrived. Thank you, Alice, for performing my duties while I changed clothing." Now sporting a bright green vest, Pearcy resembled a character out of Dickens, as if he and Fezziwig were about to host a Christmas party. "How do you like that claret, Jamie? I first had it when I visited Mr. Wilde in Paris. It was his payment for my legal efforts on his behalf, even though they were ultimately unsuccessful."

"Is Oscar Wilde really a bad man, father?"

"Not if you can overlook his behavior, my dear Alice. As Wilde once told me, he has 'the spotless soul of a true church-goer but the lurid habits of an Anglican bishop.'"

Catherine gestured to Pearcy that she was now ready for a small glass of sherry. She added, "Would that Mr. Wilde could end his exile in France and return to the theatre. His loss as a playwright is severely felt, it seems to me. I would most like to be in one of his plays, but who knows how long it will be before they stage them again, given the scandal and sensational trial of three years ago."

Alice's green eyes lit up, matching the color of her father's vest. "Tell me more about that scandal, Catherine. Mr. Wilde is Irish, is he not? Did you know of the trial in Dublin?"

Pearcy interrupted, "Forgive my intrusion, Catherine, but Alice shouldn't hear anything about that, especially at her age. He shifted the conversation to the slightly less enthralling topic of the weather.

~ # ~

Trusting that Phillpotts's men would assume Jamie was spending the night with his father—as Jamie's housekeeper Mrs. Leavis was always led to believe—Catherine saw no need to place him in a hansom cab and send him home for the sake of appearances. Oliver Pearcy insisted Jamie remain in any event, and within moments of lying down in one of the guest rooms, Millard was asleep, assisted in the endeavor by his general fatigue and the several glasses of claret he had consumed throughout the evening.

It was a little past eleven. Catherine lay in her bed unable to sleep. Yes, she thought, Roberts-Smythe was the kind of man who made enemies. He cared little for gentlemanly decorum when it came to his business, and many resented his manner if not his methods. Yet, why was he backstage at the time of his death? His body couldn't have been dragged or carried there, for all the blood traces were in the immediate vicinity of where his body lay. Had he come to confront Donovan? He surely knew the actor had become more and more unreliable and more dependent on his brandy and soda. Or had Roberts-Smythe received a message, such as the one Patrick Copsey found, telling him to come backstage to that spot?

And what of Charles Donovan? Had he reacted to Roberts-Smythe's presence or something the theatre manager told him? Did he stab Roberts-Smythe and then attempt to flee, only to be detained and then be strangled by someone else? If so, then who? Catherine decided that she and Jamie would revisit Copsey in the morning.

Smiling with relief at her resolution, she sensed the heaviness of her eyes. Now she could sleep. She hoped for comforting dreams, but expected worse.

Chapter 7

"Show him in."

Although it was only half past eight in the morning, Phillpotts lit one of his favorite Indian cigars. He was agitated over his failure to learn until late last night that an actor had exited The Acropolis before the murder of Roberts-Smythe. Phillpotts had assumed only stagehand Patrick Copsey was unaccounted for.

Phillpotts had a team of men interviewing patrons and the employees who worked at the entrance of the theatre in order to determine if any audience members left their seats before the climactic moment in *Hamlet*. But Phillpotts knew a murderer wouldn't simply walk down the staircase and out one of the front doors. Nor would he leave his seat and find his way into one of the interior side entrances that would have taken him to the spot where Roberts-Smythe was stabbed.

That damned theatre. As his men reminded him, there were exits at both sides of the backstage area the perpetrator could have used to make his initial entrance and then escape. The backstage was a labyrinth, with its quick turns, corners, doors, and recesses. Jaynes had shown him that much, but Phillpotts knew he hadn't seen everything. He would return to The Acropolis in the afternoon to do an even more thorough examination of the edifice.

"Come in, man." Phillpotts saw the visitor standing nervously in the doorway. "You may sit down. Tell me your name."

"The name is John Metcalfe, sir. I'm the actor at The Acropolis you wanted to see."

"I've been told you left the theatre before Mr. Roberts-Smythe was found dead."

"Yes, that's true. You see, Inspector, I only have a very small role in the play, and my part is over after the first minute of the first act. Since we've been running *Hamlet*, I've been leaving right after I come off stage."

46

"Why haven't you been waiting until the play was over? Was there nothing you could do to help out during the other scenes?"

"No, sir, not really. Mr. Roberts-Smythe insisted we stay out of the way of the other actors and the stage hands. I didn't want to cross Mr. Roberts-Smythe, so I obeyed that law right down to the letter, sir. Indeed I did."

"Then he knew you left when you did."

"Oh, yes, sir."

"And what about Mr. Jaynes? Did he know as well?"

"Him? Not sure he knew that, sir. If I won't be quoted as saying it, I can tell you that Mr. Jaynes didn't always know what was going on half the time, sir."

"He was the assistant to Mr. Roberts-Smythe and he didn't always know what was going on?" Phillpotts offered Metcalfe a cigar. Metcalfe shook his head no.

"Half the time he didn't, Inspector."

"Yes, so you said. Half the time. Now you returned to The Acropolis after the murder, is that correct?"

"Yes, sir. As I told your man, I was heading for my favorite pub across the street after arranging with a lady to . . . well, perhaps I shouldn't be admitting to anything like that."

"At present, I'm not interested in how you waste your money, Metcalfe. Go on."

"Well, before I got to the pub I saw the commotion going on at The Acropolis. People running out, making all that noise. I went back inside the theatre and saw what had happened. The other actors saw me there. You can ask them. Then I left and went home."

"So you didn't go to the pub and meet up with that woman?"

"No, Inspector. After seeing Mr. Roberts-Smythe dead, my stomach didn't think much of drinking or anything else pleasurable, so I went home to bed."

"All right. But Mr. Roberts-Smythe knew of your early disappearance—you are sure of that?"

"As I say, he insisted we three leave as soon as we came off stage for the last time."

"We three?"

"Yes, sir, Mr. Schneider, Mr. Nichols, and myself."

~ # ~

Catherine sat at the vanity dressing her hair. She glanced at her husband staring into the mirror.

"I hope you realize I was lonely sleeping in that other room, Cate." Millard bent over and kissed her ardently on the neck.

"And whose fault is that?"

"You shouldn't have let me drink so much claret."

She rapped his hand with a brush. "*I* let *you* drink?" Smiling, she stood and placed her head in his chest. "You must know how much I do love you."

"I should like to stand here for the next hour so you can convince me of your sincerity."

"I should like that too, dearest Jamie, but for two reasons we cannot spare the time. First, we must go to where Patrick Copsey is hiding and talk to him again."

"And the second reason would be?"

When he gave her a puzzled look, she pointed to his mouth, took his lips, and squeezed them together. "The second reason would be this unpleasant residue from all the claret you consumed last night."

~ # ~

The temperature had crept above freezing by the time they crossed the Thames. Precipitation had been predicted for the afternoon and evening, not the most cheery portent for Catherine, who was forced to battle a touch of winter melancholia whenever the late afternoon and evening mixed cold rain with the darkness. Yet she adored snowfalls of any amount, and the rains from late April through September never affected her, but weather such as they expected for today always left her with feelings of anxiety and occasional dread.

Still, her stage performances on the bleak days were invariably her most memorable. To Catherine Healy, acting was an escape, a fleeing from the reality of one's existence, and the farther and faster one wished to run from anxiety and fear the more intense and committed the performance. That was the reason she preferred to play tragedy during the late autumn and winter months, and why she was looking forward to late February, when she would be doing the tragic Nora in Mr. Ibsen's *A Doll's House*. How fervently she had pleaded with Morris Roberts-Smythe to let Jamie play Nora's husband—the ten-year age difference between them would have thus worked beautifully for their characters. But Roberts-Smythe refused, reminding her that the younger Edward Ludmore was now the leading male actor of the company.

"Here we are." Jamie asked the driver to wait and assisted Catherine in alighting from the cab. They walked to the door and knocked lightly. After a few moments it opened. A young woman stood before them with just her head and shoulders visible. Jamie judged her as no more than fifteen or sixteen.

"Yes?"

Catherine stepped in front of her husband. "We'd like to see Mr. Copsey. He knows us. We are actors at The Acropolis."

"Oh yes, I know you both. You are Miss Healy, and he is Mr. Millard." The young woman lowered her head almost out of deference.

"You have been to the theatre, then?" Jamie offered a comforting smile.

"Oh yes, sir. I have seen you from the top gallery. But never up this close." Once again she lowered her eyes.

"Are you Mr. Copsey's younger sister, by any chance?"

"Oh no, Miss Healy, I am not. I am rather . . . not his sister."

"Here let us go in. You'll be chilled if we stand here much longer." Millard pushed open the door to the lodging they had visited the previous day, but there was no one else in the room. Catherine could plainly see the girl was at least eight months with child. It wasn't difficult to guess the child was Copsey's.

"What is your Christian name?"

"Clare, Miss Healy."

"It's so nice to meet you, Clare. Can you tell us where Mr. Copsey is at present?"

The young woman handed Catherine a folded note. After a quick survey, Catherine passed it to Jamie. It was in the same unusual script on the note left for Copsey backstage at The Acropolis. It told Copsey to come immediately to an address on High Holborn."

Millard refolded the note. "I know where this is. It's near Gray's Inn Field."

~ # ~

"Dr. Millard?"

"Yes, boy, what is it?"

"I'm sorry to interrupt your examination, but there is someone here who wishes to speak with you about a death."

"I already know. Besides I can't do anything about it. Where the death occurred is not in my jurisdiction. Remind me again. What is your name, my lad?"

"Wooten, sir. George Wooten."

"And who is it that recommended you to me?"

"Oliver Pearcy, sir."

"The attorney?"

"Yes, sir."

"With the pretty daughter named Abigail?"

"Alice, sir."

"Are you smitten by her, Mr. Wooten?"

"Oh yes, sir."

"The more important question. Does she have any interest in you?"

"I think so, sir. I took her to the theatre the other night."

"To The Acropolis?"

"Yes, sir."

"On the night of the theatre manager's murder?"

"Yes, sir."

"You have the gift of timing, my boy. You must have all the girls fainting at your feet." Thomas Millard made a surgical incision the entire length of the dead man's torso. "Here. I'll show you something that can make all the pretty young ladies swoon."

"But, sir, there is someone here to see you."

"About the death of Mr. Dodgson, you mean?"

50

"I don't know that, sir."

"Show this person in—that is, if he has the stomach for it."

As Millard continued with his examination, Denham Phillpotts entered the examining room. Millard didn't look up from his work. "Whoever you are, I already know about Mr. Dodgson's death. Do not ask me to go down to Guildford. It's some thirty miles and it's not in my jurisdiction. Besides, from what his sister told me, he had pneumonia. He was in his mid-sixties—not at all a surprise and not at all anything I need to look at. In addition, he was a friend. And a damned good writer of stuff, although I couldn't understand the half of it. 'The Jibberwicky' or whatever it was he penned. Yes, Charles Dodgson, better know to the world as Lewis Carroll, is now dead. What else can be said? Sorry you have come for nothing, sir."

"I haven't come here about the death of Lewis Carroll, Dr. Millard." Millard recognized the voice. The same uncompromising baritone he had heard ten years earlier, at the time of the White Chapel killings. Millard continued with his examination.

"What can I do for you, Inspector?"

"You might first pay me the courtesy of looking at me while I speak to you."

"I owe more courtesy to this man here, Inspector. Before he was murdered on the street, he might have actually done something worthwhile during his wretched life."

"Amusing, especially coming from a man now relegated to examining corpses."

"I often get them after you are done with them, Inspector." Millard paused and lowered his head to more closely examine the body. "Now this is interesting. Evidence of a second bullet seemingly fired through the same hole made by the bullet I initially took out. But it seems I extracted not the first bullet, but rather the second."

Unable to resist, Phillpotts stepped down to the table. Millard continued, "Can you see this residue around the wound, Inspector? The gun was clearly pressed up against the man's stomach and fired twice, making what looked to be a single entrance hole. This man was either held up or restrained in some way so that his body couldn't move after being struck by the first bullet."

Previously, Phillpotts refused to believe what he had been told about the elder Millard. That this eccentric medical crank, long ago having ceased treating living patients successfully, had become touched by brilliance whenever he came in contact with the deceased.

"Ah, and see this?" Millard pulled some fabric from inside the wound. A piece of lavender colored cloth—I would guess from a man's handkerchief—was blown into the wound. The murderer likely had the weapon pressed into the cloth in an attempt to muffle the sound and drove some of it into the wound. If I were you, Inspector, I would be looking for some kind of dandy who prefers lavender or lavender trimmed suits. There you may find your murderer."

Phillpotts knew he was right to come to Thomas Millard, despite the toll it took on his pride. "Very impressive, Millard. Now, to the purpose of my visit. I want you to look at the body of Charles Donovan and tell me what similar clues you might be able to find there."

"Why don't you take him to your barely competent man at the Yard? You let him examine Morris-Smythe, didn't you? But then I suppose you had to do that, since that booby is the nephew of Her Majesty's personal physician."

"Yes." Phillpotts wasn't at all satisfied with his man's handling of the theatre manager's post mortem. Others at the Yard strongly advised him to seek the opinion of Thomas Millard as it related to the body of Charles Donovan.

"Donovan was killed how again, Inspector?"

"Apparently strangled. But you might detect something about the wound on the neck or on the rest of his body that might assist in our investigation."

Phillpotts noticed a broad smile shaping on the old physician's face. Millard was amused by the fact that he had already talked to his son about examining Donovan's body.

~ # ~

"Well, Jaynes, have you given any further thought to when we might reopen The Acropolis? Edward Ludmore had taken a seat in Jaynes's parlor. He hadn't been invited. Without any hint of politeness, he refused tea.

"Mr. Ludmore, I say again. The choice is not mine to make."

Ludmore noticed Jaynes's hand shaking as he poured himself tea. "From what I understand you are not without influence, Jaynes."

Jaynes offered an anemic laugh. "Influence? Would I be in this miserable state with Scotland Yard if I had influence, Mr. Ludmore?"

"What do you mean?"

"Inspector Phillpotts suspects me as the murderer, of *both* Mr. Roberts-Smythe and Mr. Donovan, I am afraid."

Ludmore laughed robustly. "Donovan weighed at least fifty pounds more than you, Jaynes. What do you weigh—ten stone if you've had a full meal?"

"Nevertheless, I am suspected."

Ludmore reached for the small cake. "Well, you did have a motive, Jaynes."

"Many at The Acropolis had motive, Mr. Ludmore."

"Not I, Mr. Jaynes. Roberts-Smythe was shepherding my career. I couldn't have asked for anyone more supportive of my work."

"And now you fear that the wool has been pulled off your career, is that it?"

"My, how very witty. I wouldn't have expected metaphors from you. But to return to my reason for coming, I . . ." Ludmore began to cough from ingesting the particularly dry small cake. Jaynes smiled wearily and poured the actor some tea. "Thank you. So, Jaynes, as I was about to . . ." Again Ludmore coughed.

Ludmore was one of those young men who loathed being in any situation that made him appear less than the most assured, handsome, and talented leading men of the London stage. He had no sympathy for actors who lost their concentration or forgot their lines, therefore forcing him to improvise—a skill at which he was not at all proficient. He once attempted to chastise Catherine Healy backstage when she had stumbled into him during a stage cross, knocking a cup from his hand. Unfortunately for Ludmore, she expressed to him in no uncertain terms that he was supposed to move upstage instead of downstage of her and that the collision was entirely his fault.

"Jaynes, I fear that The Acropolis will suffer the same fate as that theatre in Washington after Lincoln was shot. It hasn't been used for over thirty years and from what I've been told will likely never will be again."

"Mr. Ludmore, you are engaging in exaggeration. But then again, the assassin Booth played both Romeo and Hamlet, now two of your signature roles, Ned."

Not expecting such a retort from Jaynes, Ludmore rose angrily, knocking the small cake to the floor as he banged against the table. "Just make sure that The Acropolis reopens by the beginning next week—or else." Ludmore stormed out of the house, as Jaynes held the teapot, which he had prevented from falling when Ludmore rose to leave.

~ # ~

Catherine and Jamie arrived at the address on High Holborn, a very short distance from Gray's Inn—one of London's four Inns of Court. The house looked uninhabited as well as in considerable disrepair.

"Cate, did you know Dickens served as a junior clerk at Gray's Inn when he was the age of Matthew Pearcy?"

"I do hope he didn't have lodgings at this place. It looks horribly dismal, although it probably was once rather fine." She felt the first drop of cold rain spatter on her cheek.

Jamie knocked on the door. Immediately they heard footsteps scurrying inside and then running across the floor boards. He knocked again more forcefully. They heard nothing further.

"Cate, go down to the cab and wait for me."

"What are you going to do?"

"I'm going in."

"No, Jamie. Not yet. Not yet."

"Please, Cate. Go down to the cab." He turned the knob. As Catherine took several steps toward the street, Jamie pushed open the door, but before he could take a step inside, she called to him, "Lower your head and torso as you go in." Her father had once spoken of making himself a smaller target whenever he entered a dangerous situation. Jamie did as she requested and stepped into the front room.

After several moments of hearing nothing, Catherine headed back toward the house, no longer concerned for her own safety, only that of her husband's. She peered inside the open door and saw him standing still, looking at the darkened staircase to her left. Lying face up on the first four steps was a man's body.

"Recognize him, Cate?"

She stepped closer. "It's Alfred Nichols." He had played Bernardo the night of the murder. "He was supposed to leave the theatre after the first scene."

The lighting being insufficient on the staircase, they bent over the body to see what had killed the man. The small and neat entrance wound was located in the forehead above his left eye. Millard pushed his wife back when he saw the pool of blood from the exit wound trickling down the wooden stairs.

"We didn't hear the shot, Jamie."

"The murderer must have waited around for some reason, only leaving when he heard our approach."

"Perhaps, but . . ."

"Cate, I suppose I should go the rear of the building and look for him."

"By now he's nowhere near this place, Jamie."

"Not 'he,' Cate—but rather Patrick Copsey. What the devil made him shoot Alfred? We must alert the police and inform Phillpotts of everything."

As they returned to the cab, the chilling rain began to fall more steadily. They noticed the driver looking straight ahead from his stand-up place behind the carriage. He hadn't moved a hair's width since they had arrived.

Chapter 8

"I am delighted you've chosen to join me, Inspector Healy. And especially here at the Shelbourne. This hotel is without question your island's finest. I have lodged here on several occasions. In fact, I'll sleep nowhere else when I come to Dublin. The structure is most impressive and the view of St. Stephen's Green is one of my favorites in all of Europe."

Sitting at the dining table, Michael Healy found Lord Oxley's praise of the hotel overly complimentary only in the grandiose way the First Lord of the Treasury delivered it, because Healy agreed completely with Oxley's assessment of the Shelbourne. But Healy was also put off by Oxley's appropriation of the surroundings, as if this fine hotel were an example of English and not Irish taste and cultivation. If he could have his way, Healy would bar anyone residing in London, save his daughter, from entering the hotel, let alone spending a night in it.

"I have always found the food exceptional here, Inspector Healy. If I were forced to live in Dublin I would take all of my meals at the Shelbourne."

"Excuse my getting to the point, Lord Oxley, but you mentioned in your letter a desire to talk about my daughter and what you could do for her as a patron. Is that not correct?" Healy pulled Oxley's letter from his coat pocket and placed it on the table.

"That is correct, Inspector Healy."

"And you say in this letter that you would 'better explain' your 'motives and intentions' when we met."

In ordinary circumstances, Oxley would have expressed indignation at the tone and implication in Healy's voice. Indeed, he wouldn't have ever invited the Irishman to sit at the same table. "I've come to Dublin on government business, Inspector, and I thought I would take the occasion to speak with you about your daughter and how I might be able to assist her."

"I am aware of that from your letter, sir. What can you say that I don't already know?"

Oxley squeezed his right hand into a fist. He saw by using the mere "sir," Healy was in another way showing disrespect. Still, Oxley's desire to form an intimate relationship with Catherine Healy forced him to ignore the insult.

"Inspector Healy, I think you would agree your daughter would greatly benefit from my patronage."

"I'm not sure that I do. In what way might she benefit?"

"As you may know, many who engage in theatrical activity—however loudly applauded any one of them may be—bear always the heavy weight of their profession. What I mean is that many in London judge the occupation of actor and actress as illegitimate—as something perhaps entertaining but not socially acceptable. I don't agree with such a view, but in truth many more hold to it than attend theatrical performances. Many, many more. As a result, the reputations of actors suffer unfairly, especially those of the women who step on the stage. Many in the city believe a woman who appears in public portraying another woman who has lost her virtue or her soul or who expresses herself in unacceptable ways—well, they believe that the actress is little better, if any better, than some of the women she depicts." Oxley could see the frown deepening on Healy's face. "Again, I'm not suggesting there is any truth in such an opinion—particularly where your daughter is concerned—but it is a widely-held opinion nevertheless."

Healy couldn't help accepting the veracity of Oxley's assessment, for he had the same argument ready for his daughter ten years earlier when she began appearing on the public stage. But he didn't present that argument, appreciating her unalterable decision to make theatre her life's calling. He only hoped the yearning would disappear after a year or so. But it never did—not even for a moment.

Oxley continued, "Therefore, Inspector Healy, no one would dare impugn your daughter's character or motives if I were to become her patron. I simply wouldn't permit it. Finally, it's a sad reality of the profession that the public becomes weary of actresses just as quickly as the public becomes enamored of them. I hope your daughter's career will be a long and successful one and that she will have the love of the public for many, many years to come. But if not, having my patronage would protect her from the scandalous gossip and exaggerated accusations one often reads in the daily papers."

Healy recalled his daughter's concern for the reputation of one of her company, a Miss Nedra Alexander, around whom rumor of unacceptable personal conduct had swirled. Even so, Healy found it hard to imagine that a man as educated as Oxley would honestly believe that Catherine's having his patronage would prevent a single person from casting such aspersions. Healy thought instead that having Oxley as a patron would only increase the likelihood of "scandalous gossip and exaggerated accusations."

"So, Lord Oxley, you are here to ask my permission to be my daughter's patron? Or is it my blessing? And, if I may ask, have you informed her of your wishes?"

"No, she doesn't yet know. I'm here of course to receive your approval. I would hope you would then encourage her to accept my offer before I make it. I wouldn't wish my motives to be in any way misconstrued."

Healy's eyes bore into Oxley's. It would be enough if the First Lord of the Treasury were merely asking to serve as Catherine's surrogate father, although Healy could never abide another man assuming that role. But Healy knew Oxley's true motivation was to seduce his daughter and make her a kept mistress. Healy recalled tales of the actress Lillie Langtry's love affair with the Prince of Wales a number of years earlier. Although, as Catherine pointed out, Langtry began her acting career *after* the affair with Prince was over, the image of his actress daughter becoming the plaything of a powerful man still remained uppermost in Healy's mind.

Healy knew what he wanted to say to Oxley but thought better of so expressing himself while sitting at a table inside the Shelbourne Hotel.

"May I have your reply, Inspector Healy?"

"Lord Oxley, you may. And here it is. When you return to London, visit my daughter and repeat to her all you have said to me. And then articulate your desire to be her patron. If she says yes, then return here to the Shelbourne. I will again meet you and will then tell you whether or not you have my approval."

Oxley was stunned, unable to speak for several seconds. Finally, his indignation overcame him. "Healy, I wish to be left alone to dine. Your company is no longer welcome at this table. Let me add that it may benefit you to recall just whose government rules here in Dublin and whose faith has been deemed since the time of Elizabeth to be the only acceptable religion of *all* subjects of the realm. Oh yes, you might also take some time to regret the sins of your youth and remind yourself that home rule for the Irish has been and always will be rejected."

Healy understood Oxley's allusion. It had long been rumored, correctly, that some thirty years earlier a young Michael Healy was a member of the Fenians, those who began an ill-fated insurrection to end British rule in Ireland. Fifteen years later, a branch of the Fenians—the Irish National Invincibles—boldly assassinated in Dublin the Chief Secretary for Ireland and the Permanent Undersecretary. Rumors also linked Healy to the Invincibles, but in truth he was then part of the police investigation which brought the guilty parties to prison and then to the gallows.

Healy rose at Oxley's parting words, and left the hotel. Oxley turned to his meal and took his first bite of food. The dish was more than satisfactory, the flavors being made all the more pleasant by the accompanying thought of Catherine Healy in his bed.

~ # ~

"Now *three* are dead?"

Henry Jaynes dropped into the seat behind Roberts-Smythe's desk. He looked helplessly at the drawers on either side, as if he wanted something in them but hadn't the strength to pull them open.

"You'd like something to drink, Henry?"

"Yes, Catherine, thank you. I most certainly would."

Having on occasion witnessed Roberts-Smythe's returning a bottle of spirits to the bottom left-hand drawer, she walked around the desk and retrieved the bottle. Jamie pulled a glass from one of the side tables and placed it before Jaynes.

"Here. Allow me, Miss Healy." Denham Phillpotts stepped forward and poured the blended Scotch whisky into the glass. "Drink it down, Jaynes. Then I want you to answer some questions."

"Must we go through this again, Inspector?"

"Not 'again,' Jaynes. These are new questions." After Jaynes swallowed the Scotch whisky, Phillpotts proceeded. "Thanks to Miss

Healy's and Mr. Millard's continued meddling earlier this evening, we must now speak about what you know of Mr. Nichols, our latest victim, and more of what you know of Mr. Copsey, who most probably killed him. Take your time, Jaynes. Have another swallow and then sit up straight and steel yourself, man."

Catherine and Jamie noted the pleasure Phillpotts took in instructing Jaynes. What might Jaynes have done to the Inspector to elicit such aggressive and derisive remarks?

Jaynes refused another swallow, even after Phillpotts had picked up the glass and held it in front of the acting manager's face. "No, I don't want anymore. Let me just answer your questions."

"That would be helpful, Jaynes. However, may I ask that you also answer them *fully* this time?"

"Of course, Inspector. All right, then. Alfred Nichols was brought to The Acropolis by Mr. Roberts-Smythe. I had nothing to do with engaging him."

Catherine was desirous of helping Jaynes through the uncomfortable interrogation. "That is quite true, Inspector Phillpotts. Mr. Nichols came when I did."

"Thank you, Miss Healy. But please allow Mr. Jaynes to speak for himself. Should I require your recollections or corroboration of Mr. Jaynes's answers, I will specifically request such information of you or of Mr. Millard. Now continue, Jaynes."

"Nichols was a dedicated member of the company, even though he was always assigned the smaller parts. I cannot recall his ever missing a performance or showing up late for one."

Phillpotts pulled a cigar from his coat pocket. "Go on."

"He was a talented actor, who might have done a credible job in more substantial roles had he been given the opportunity."

Recalling his recent discussion with the actor John Metcalfe, Phillpotts walked directly behind Jaynes's chair and placed the unlit cigar in his mouth. "I understand that Roberts-Smythe sacked a number of other bit players in favor of actors like Nichols and Metcalfe."

"Yes, that is true, Inspector."

Catherine and Jamie knew where Phillpotts was leading Jaynes.

"Of those replaced by the likes of Nichols and Metcalfe, how many of them had you hired, Jaynes?"

"I was never manager of this theatre, Inspector. I was always the assistant. I wasn't responsible for engaging new members of the company."

This time Catherine's shoulders sagged, as she folded her arms, each hand grabbing the opposite wrist. Phillpotts removed the unlit cigar from his mouth and returned it to his pocket.

"Finch, ask the lady to step inside." The policeman nodded and went out the door. Jaynes looked more perplexed than frightened, Jamie thought. In a moment Finch escorted Nedra Alexander into the office.

"Thank you for coming, Miss Alexander."

She could barely push out the words. "It's 'Mrs.', Inspector." Catherine turned toward the far wall and softly sighed.

"My apologies, *Mrs.* Alexander. Now you were on stage when the murder of Mr. Roberts-Smythe occurred, is that correct?"

"Yes, Inspector. I was playing Gertrude. She is Hamlet's mother."

"So the two characters, Gertrude and Hamlet, were the only ones on stage at the time?"

"Yes. You see, James—I mean Mr. Millard here—was playing my husband, King Claudius, but he wasn't in that scene."

"Good. Thank you. May I ask how long you have been with the company, Mrs. Alexander?"

"Over a year, sir."

"So were you engaged by Mr. Roberts-Smythe?"

Jamie wished to curse Phillpotts for the manner in which he was about to refute Jaynes's previous assertion.

"No, sir. I came here before he did."

"Oh, excuse me. I remember now. Mr. Roberts-Smythe had only arrived at the end of last season. So, then, who did engage you for the company?"

"Why Mr. Jaynes, sir." Throughout the questioning, Nedra's eyes remained riveted to the floor.

"Mr. Jaynes? You mean the gentleman presently sitting in Mr. Roberts-Smythe's former chair?"

She nodded hesitantly. Catherine sensed Nedra's fear that she might have said the wrong thing.

Phillpotts came from around the desk. "You may go now, Mrs. Alexander. Thank you for coming this evening."

When she closed the door behind her, Phillpotts once more removed the Indian cigar from his pocket. He took his time lighting it. "So you say you never once engaged anyone as the managerial assistant, Mr. Jaynes?"

Jaynes continued to sit impassively, the half drunk glass of Scotch directly before him.

Phillpotts blew a perfect smoke ring toward the ceiling. "Your theatre keeps impressive records, and from what I understand, you are in large part responsible for the meticulous accounting of receipts, performances, and information regarding members of your company. Oh, Finch."

"Yes, Inspector?"

"Bring me the book with the blue spine."

"I thought you would like to see what you wrote about Mrs. Alexander in the accounts book, Jaynes. Finch brought in the large folio volume. Phillpotts opened to the page he had already marked. "Here it is. The entry dated December 4, 1896. 'Nedra Alexander. Formerly of the Meridian Theatre'—and here it lists seven or eight roles she apparently played there, including Lady Macbeth and Gertrude from *Hamlet*. 'Age thirty-one.' So that would make her thirty-two now. And I see this interesting annotation. 'Mature face. Mother/Queen roles.' And let's see what else we have here. Yes, a pair of initials after the entry. 'H.J.' Take a look at this page, Jaynes and tell me if you recognize the handwriting."

Jaynes's voice was lifeless. "Inspector, I wrote the entry, and I engaged her."

"I see. So is it possible you might have engaged other actors?"

"I did. But only supporting players."

"Any of them victims . . .? Jaynes snapped his head toward Phillpotts, who continued. ". . . victims of Roberts-Smythe's purge of last summer?"

"Yes, Inspector."

"And so I must ask—why didn't you admit that to me?"

"Because I know you are only interested in pursuing me as your suspect. I failed to tell you the truth because . . . because I was afraid to give you any further . . ." Jaynes didn't finish. His head bent forward until he cupped it in the palms of both hands.

Jamie's face registered his frustration. "Inspector, with all due respect, perhaps you might—"

"Save your plea, Millard. I'm finished here for now. Tomorrow I'll return for a fuller investigation of the backstage area. I have the original and the renovated building plans. I request you and Miss Healy join me at eleven in the morning. I shall see you then." Phillpotts took his hat and heavy coat and made his way through the office door.

Jaynes's head remained in his hands—his entire body in an attitude of exhaustion and despair. But as she attempted to sooth him, Catherine stared at the entry in the opened folio volume on the desk. Jaynes's handwriting was, as it always was, most neat and legible. "Poor Nedra," she thought. "That she continues to claim that she's a 'Mrs.'"

Phillpotts stepped back in. "Oh, Jaynes. One more thing. Did you engage any of the stage hands in the past year or so?"

Jaynes raised his head from his hands. He answered Phillpotts with his eyes shut. "Yes, Inspector, it was I who engaged Patrick Copsey."

Chapter 9

Accepting that he couldn't return to The Acropolis or go anywhere near Scotland Yard, Bernhard Schneider boarded the train for Hatfield, in Hertfordshire, just north of London. For once he was grateful he was only a secondary actor in the company, since he wouldn't be recognized at the congested railway station. Schneider was on his way north to Manchester, where he would decide his ultimate destination. He could travel further north, all the way to Scotland, where lived a relation and several friends. But he could stay there only temporarily, for they would surely find him in Glasgow. There was Ireland, but again he couldn't remain long there either, although sailing to America would then be possible. Or he could return to Saxony or some other place in Germany, where he could feel safe. As Schneider settled uncomfortably on the train's wooden bench, he pulled his comforter higher on his neck to help ward off the chill from the cold and steady rain.

He reached into his coat pocket to feel the folded five pound notes he had received anonymously. And he was told in another kind of note that he would receive the rest of the promised payment if he simply appeared at an address off High Holborn near Gray's Inn Fields, which he had done. But now it would be impossible for him to receive any more five-pound notes. Schneider pulled out the short letter and read it again, a task made more difficult by the murky lighting on the train. When he finished, he refolded the note and returned it to his pocket. He was still struck by the odd handwriting on the paper.

~ # ~

Following a light supper with the Pearcy children, Catherine excused herself and headed upstairs to her room. Apparently, Oliver Pearcy was still tied up at the Sessions House in Westminster regarding a legal matter—January being one of the designated months to hear appeals. Jamie was presently with his father, who by special request of Scotland Yard was examining the body of Alfred Nichols. Alice had just begun practicing her Schubert, while her brother, reluctantly obeying his father's instructions, had trudged off to his studies.

Catherine decided to finish the correspondence she had begun the previous night.

And so my dearest friend, I can only add to my apologies for having taken so long to read your book, which I have found in so many ways simply exhilarating. The character of Mina will forever be one of my favorite literary heroines. There is much I see in her that I see in myself. My heart went out to poor Lucy, as I am sure you meant it to. I shouldn't confess this, but Lucy intrigues me in ways I cannot express. As to your vampire, I will keep my feelings for him strictly confidential. (Please note that I smile as I write this.) I do hope you can convince Mr. Irving to portray your vampire on stage at The Lyceum, for I have no doubt that Mr. Irving inspired your portrayal.

Allow me to say in closing that I so deeply appreciate your remark, recently quoted in the papers, that you found me to be "one of the brightest stars in the theatrical firmament." These words spoken by the business manager of The Lyceum and the assistant to the great Sir Henry Irving would have been more than enough to thrill, but knowing they also come from a fellow countryman, someone whose father was the close friend of my grandfather, makes your generosity to me more than anything I could ever repay.

With deepest friendship and affection,

Catherine

Smiling as she sealed the letter, Catherine looked forward to the day when she could tell Bram Stoker that she and Jamie Millard were married. Then she would playfully chide the author for choosing Whitby as the location for the vampire Dracula's arrival into England—in the very town where she and Millard had decided to wed. Had she read the book before December, she would never have set foot in Whitby—or so she would have teased Stoker.

Arriving at the window to see if the weather had cleared, Catherine pressed her beautiful face against the cold pane and observed that the chilling rain had not abated. Affected by the slow waves of melancholy she couldn't control, she kept her face against the window until the biting cold pushed the tears back in her eyes.

Yet soon enough she smiled again, recalling her husband's offer to stay with her if she was feeling too low. Her beloved Jamie, her loyal Sir Knight. So admirably brave and so charmingly chivalrous. She shook her head at the conflicting influences in her life. How could a woman so moved by tales and images of romance and rescue be so analytical about crimes of passion and violence? Depicting such characters of misguided passion as Juliet and Ophelia challenged and delighted her considerably, but there were few roles that could compete with the satisfaction of solving a real-life mystery—one involving even the vilest of human behaviors. Up to this point in her life, she had only assisted her father from time to time in his investigations. Yet, she always had occasion to talk and think about other crimes, even though she never took a practical hand in solving them. Therefore, becoming this active in investigating the murders of Morris Roberts-Smythe, Charles Donovan, and Alfred Nichols failed to intimidate her in the least.

~ # ~

"Collect your things. We need to leave immediately." Copsey rushed into the small room where he and the pregnant Clare Paget had slept the previous night.

"But why, Patrick? Did anything happen where you went to?" Clare searched for any indication that he knew she had revealed to Catherine Healy and James Millard where he had gone.

"Just get what you brought with you, Clare. Now hurry!"

"Are we going back to our home?"

"Home? We had no home. Just a place to stay. And now we must find another."

"But where? Here in London still? I wish you would tell me. You frighten me when you leave me so uncertain like this."

Copsey had seen some of his acquaintances—even his own father—strike women when they argued or hesitated as Clare was doing now. He felt these women were either very stupid or very brave to prolong their stubbornness, since they risked further physical harm by doing so. As a boy, he couldn't understand why his mother remained with his abusive father, but he soon came to realize she had no other place to go.

But now he was agitated, both by the fact that he couldn't take the time to comfort Clare and by her seeming even more reluctant to accelerate her pace. He was certain others, besides Catherine Healy and Jamie Millard, knew where he was hiding and would soon find him. He looked at Clare, who hadn't moved, still waiting for him to explain why they must flee. He dropped his head. He couldn't escape the fact that her physical condition would severely hinder their flight.

The events hours earlier raced through his mind as he kept staring into Clare's anxious eyes. He had arrived at the house on High Holborn near Gray's Inn Fields, as he was instructed to do in the note. All would be explained to his satisfaction, he assumed. He would then understand the true reason he was told to leave The Acropolis a short time before the murder of Roberts-Smythe. When he walked to the door of the abandoned dwelling, he had no idea how the next minute would so change everything.

"I believe I'm ready, Patrick. But I won't be able to run." She touched her stomach to make him understand.

Copsey frowned. "No. Not quite ready yet. You don't have enough clothing on you for the rain and cold. "Here." Copsey removed the frayed black comforter from around his shoulders. "Now stand still." Copsey stepped behind her and placed the comforter around her throat. In a moment her eyes expanded. Her mouth opened, emitting a cry of pain. She sagged to the floor.

~ # ~

"Well, father, I assume then that the shot likely came from at least ten feet away."

"Not a bad assumption, Jamie my boy. But I'd put it at fifteen. Here." Thomas Millard picked up Alfred Nichols's head by the hair and turned it enough so Jamie could see the wound at the rear of the skull. "The bullet made its way through the forehead bone above the left eye, traveled through the brain, and then barely made its exit the rear of the skull. Given that you found this man lying on the stairway suggests to me that the spent bullet is likely resting somewhere on the stairs above the body."

Jamie glanced at young George Wooten, who was in the process of determining whether he was fit for work as gruesome as this. Staring at the head wound, Wooten's face blanched. He turned abruptly and staggered away from the examining table. Jamie laughed. "It looks as though George will have to find himself a different kind of apprenticeship."

"Not necessarily, my boy. If he comes back in a few minutes, he'll be fine. If I don't see him for the rest of the night, he'll be begging Oliver Pearcy for a legal clerkship in the morning." The elder Millard's smile matched his son's, but it quickly disappeared. "One thing bothers me about where you said you found the body."

Jamie repeated the facts. "Lying on the bottom five steps of the staircase—with his head on the fifth step, his right foot hanging off the bottom of the last step, between it and the floor, and the left foot curled somewhat so that it rested on the first step. What troubles you about that, father?"

The elder Millard again pulled up Nichols's head and pointed to the exit wound. "See where this exit hole is, my boy? Now look again at the positioning and the shape of the entrance above the left eye."

Jamie examined the two wounds. "I see. The exit wound should be located higher than the entrance hole because Nichols was likely standing on the first step when he was shot—and it is—but yet . . . ."

"But yet . . .?" The old man's face registered a twinkle of pride at his son's thinking.

"But this exit hole is up toward the top rear of the skull. If he were standing on the first step the exit would be lower."

"You have it, my boy."

Jamie was afraid his father was going to break out in a jig. "Yes, I see. Unless the shooter was a very small child, the wound should have been lower on the rear part of the head if Nichols was standing on the first step. So he must have been standing farther up on the staircase. But wait. The one who shot him might have been squatting or sitting when he fired the shot."

The elder Millard threw up his hands. "For the love of God, Jamie. Squatting or sitting? And I was so proud of you there for a moment."

"All right, that seems very unlikely, I'll admit. But I was simply trying to consider all possibilities. You taught me that, remember?"

"So I did. All right, I'll let it pass—this time."

"Thank you. So Nichols was standing higher up the stairs when he was shot. Could he have slid down to the position in which I found him?"

"Unlikely, for as you said earlier the wood on the stairs was jagged and split. Not smooth enough for a body to have been hurled back by the shot and then to have been able to slide down what looks like another four or five steps."

"All right father, then how do you think he ended up where he did?"

"My guess is he was dragged down the stairs to the position you found him in. Did the stairs go up into darkness?"

"Yes. Past the first five or six steps it was impossible to see anything."

"I believe the one who shot him—or perhaps another who was there—pulled the body down by the legs so it could be examined in whatever light was available."

"Examined? Then Nichols may have had something the shooter wanted?"

"Yes."

"What about a simple robbery following the killing?"

"Here." Thomas Millard walked to a table and came back with several five-pound notes. "These were in his coat pocket when they brought him here. Whoever killed him was probably looking for something else of value. What that could have been I don't know."

"I see. Was there anything else you found on the body?"

"No, Jamie. Nothing out of the ordinary."

"And was there anything on the body that might have belonged to the one who shot him?"

"Again—nothing. What is needed is a careful investigation of the house and especially of that staircase."

"I'm sure Phillpotts is taking care of that."

"Still, I should like for us to go there tomorrow, especially if the weather clears and there is good sunlight. I am most anxious to determine if there's any blood from the head wound on the higher steps and then to retrieve the spent bullet. And there may be more than blood to discover."

"I'll make the time. And I'll ask Cate to join us."

"Somehow I assumed you would."

"As I say, you need only give her a chance. She'll win your heart."

"That's the easy part, Jamie. Its winning my head that will pose her the bigger challenge."

~ # ~

Ned Ludmore hadn't yet climbed into bed. It was only a few minutes from midnight—the end of a day marked by most depressing weather. Ludmore stared out the bedroom window and saw the wind making a good effort at chasing the rain clouds away. Tomorrow would likely be clear and very cold. Perhaps there would be flurries of snow before dawn, but only those living miserable existences would be awake to see them. Ludmore usually slept until eleven, although tomorrow he had a furtive meeting scheduled for nine.

Two sips of expensive Spanish brandy had thoroughly warmed him. As he twirled the remaining brandy in his glass, Ludmore picked up one of the photographs he purchased anonymously a few days before Christmas. He had looked at it often since, almost always late at night. It depicted an unknown young woman from the waist up. She was wearing nothing but a black ribbon around her throat. Her breasts were modest but alluring. Her head was arched away from the viewer, her eyes and face expressing indifference. Her lovely thick hair cascaded down her neck, some of it disappearing behind her back. The black ribbon looked as though it held her there against her will, and yet she showed no signs of fear or helplessness. She was just beautifully aloof.

Ludmore imagined how shocked his adoring public would be to know how often he contemplated this and similar photographs during the past several months. Didn't they realize how simple it was to secure such erotic images—either as pictures or as literature? The city was teeming with prostitutes, well over one thousand Ludmore was told, not to mention with sin and perversions of all kinds imaginable—and not all of them relegated to the filthy East End. And yet the vague thing most called "society" in the reign of Victoria, personified for almost a century by the watchful eye of the old theatre character "Mrs. Grundy," insisted that

70

proper expressions were necessary to soften images and protect delicate sensibilities.

He finished the brandy still transfixed by the woman in the photograph. Part of him would have given anything to know who she was. He could then imagine meeting her and paying court to her loveliness— even if he could never possess her. Returning the photograph to a small plain wooden box where he kept similar images, Ludmore reached for another that had only recently come into his possession. It too was alluring in the same manner, although the woman in this photograph was older and less beautiful, although still desirable. He knew that this woman, unlike the other, could easily be possessed. She was what he liked to call "a most useful woman." And Ludmore knew that indeed she would be.

Chapter 10

"Yes, Mr. Ludmore, the offer still stands. I won't take advantage of the terrible misfortune that has befallen The Acropolis by altering the terms I initially proposed."

"I appreciate that, Mr. Northcot." Ned Ludmore understood he wouldn't have been able to enter this negotiation if Roberts-Smythe were still alive. The contract Ludmore signed at the end of the previous July seemed more than generous, including the freedom to move to another theatre within six months if he wasn't happy at The Acropolis. As he understood the terms of the agreement, if he hadn't expressed a desire to terminate the agreement by the end of the day on February 1, 1898, he would then be exclusively in the employ of The Acropolis for three years from that date.

But when Ludmore visited Morris Roberts-Smythe's office on the second of January, the manager informed him he would now be exclusive property of The Acropolis through January 2, 1901, and he offered a brandy to "celebrate" the sealing of their relationship for the next three years.

His shock quickly turning to indignation, the young actor refused the drink and mocked Roberts-Smythe's knowledge of basic mathematics. "Mr. Roberts-Smythe, six months from August 1st is the first day of February, not January."

"May I ask you to take a close look at this?" Roberts-Smythe calmly pulled out the contract signed by Ludmore the previous summer. The two-page document included the terms on the first page and the place for the signatures on the second.

Ludmore re-read the agreement. "What the devil is this?" The document noted that the stipulated time frame ended on January 1st, rather than on February 1st, as Ludmore knew it had stated when he signed the contract the previous summer. "Are you serious, man? You can't bind me to The Acropolis with such a transparent and amateur trick as this."

Roberts-Smythe affected complete surprise at Ludmore's response. "I am most disappointed by your reaction, Ned. I took you for a gentleman and a professional. My guess is you have sold your integrity for another offer—most likely from the Americans. However, I cannot let you violate the terms of the contract. I'm afraid you'll then force me to begin legal proceeding against you for a breach." Roberts-Smythe put the contract in his desk. "I must say, your disloyalty deeply pains me. You forget it was I who brought you to The Acropolis and I who have nurtured your career. And there is much I have done you don't know about. I've been able to prepare the way for your positive reviews in several of the publications, *The Athenaeum* and *The Stage*, most notably.

"Are you are telling me you bribed the reviewers on my behalf?"

"Of course not. Your talents are genuine. You lack only a little seasoning to put you in the first rank. But if I paid for an extra superlative or two in the reviews, it was all to your benefit and to that of The Acropolis."

"And to your management and reputation?"

Roberts-Smythe ignored the insult. "In any event, by the time this contract expires in three years, you will be in the first rank, especially on the assumption that Mr. Irving will retire before that time."

"You complete bastard, Morris." Ludmore knew Roberts-Smythe had simply replaced the original first page of the contract with another reflecting the five-, and not the six-month period, leaving intact the second page which only contained their signatures and that of Henry Jaynes as witness.

But now Morris Roberts-Smythe was dead, and Ludmore was entertaining the renewed offer by William Northcot, the London representative of New York's recently established Manhattan Island Theater, located in Madison Square. It was Northcot's job to encourage tours of New York by the established London troupes and, more importantly, to convince many of the young London talents to cast their lot with the new American enterprise. The owners of the Manhattan Island Theater were wealthy men, determined to elevate the company rapidly to the top of the New York theatre world. Yet, they knew the shortest path to esteem would be employing actors who could enhance a young theatre's reputation by their English pedigree.

Northcot continued, "Mr. Ludmore, as I explained in our first meeting right before Christmas, you will make half again more than what you are paid here. In your first year, you will have the choice of what roles you'll perform and at least some influence in deciding those with whom you will share the stage—that is, in the major parts. Your contract will be for a single year at first. If you wish to remain with the company, you can sign on for another year or more if mutually agreeable. You will also be allowed a forty-five day absence between September and May so you may return here for whatever engagement you can work out. I think you'll agree the offer is most attractive, and it requires only a calendar year commitment on your part. If you wish to come to New York, let us say, at the beginning of February, the company will mount a production of your choice no later than at the beginning of March."

Ludmore listened carefully for any deviation from what Northcot told him two weeks earlier. Every term of the offer was the same.

"I have one request, Mr. Northcot."

"Of course, Mr. Ludmore."

"If I accept your offer, I should like to sign two copies of the contract—one of which I will keep."

"Certainly."

"And I must insist that the language of the contract and the signatures—every single word—be on one page—with not a syllable on another page."

Northcot raised his eyebrows at the stipulation but quickly agreed. "Then may I draw up the contract so we can have you become the *leading* member of The Manhattan Island Theatre Company?"

By his recent and rude protests to Henry Jaynes about the reopening of The Acropolis, Ludmore had cleverly prepared Jaynes for his leaving the theatre with the words "Just make sure that The Acropolis reopens by the beginning next week—or else."

Ludmore extended his hand. "Mr. Northcot, I beg one further indulgence. Give me two days and you'll have my answer."

Northcot wasn't at all pleased by the request, but he agreed nonetheless. After all, taking the new offer today might be akin to a widow's socializing before the proper period of mourning has expired. Surely, the young actor didn't wish to leave the impression that he had killed Morris Roberts-Smythe in order to get out of his contract and sign a new one with, of all things, an American theatre.

~ # ~

The elder Millard was waiting for them when Catherine and Jamie arrived at the vacant house on High Holborn.

"Well? Have you gone in yet, father?"

"No, I haven't gone in, my boy. I decided to wait out here in the cold until you arrived, assuming you'd be here punctually. But, as usual, my assumptions proved incorrect." Much to Catherine's surprise, the old doctor winked at her.

When they entered the frigid and vacant dwelling, Jamie's father headed directly toward the staircase. He moved up six steps before the shadows obscured his vision. His son lit the oil lantern his father brought with him and joined the old man, while Catherine examined other areas of the room.

"And here we are." The elder Millard easily found the blood stains on the ascending steps and a larger pool on the ninth step. There also lay the spent bullet, which apparently worked itself out of the skull when Alfred Nichols fell back against the steps.

Jamie patted his father on the shoulder. "You were right. Nichols was standing higher up and was pulled down."

"In order to be examined for something he had on him, my boy. But whether he actually possessed anything of interest to the murderer, we can't yet say." The men stepped back down to the floor level.

"So, father, did you find anything on Charles Donovan's body when you examined it?"

"I found no evidence belonging to the murderer on Donovan's body, or in his hair, or in or on his clothing. Donovan was strangled as you know, and the markings on his neck were shallow and broad. And I can say the murderer was right handed, taller than Donovan, and fairly strong."

"Why do you say that?"

"The damage done to the bones inside the throat. The assailant was either very strong or motivated by intense hatred of Donovan."

The younger Millard looked about and failed to find Catherine. "Catherine?"

"I am out here."

Her voice came from the rear of the abandoned house. When the men made their way to her, she was holding something in her hand. "I found this a few steps from the rear of the building. She handed her father-in-law a black velvet woman's belt. The fabric was folded in half.

The elder Millard ran his fingers the full length of the belt. "Interesting. The size of this article, as so folded, matches the width of the wound around Donovan's neck."

Catherine extended her hand. "May I see it again?" She turned the belt over and stared at something attached to the velvet.

~ # ~

"It's blood, Inspector."

"Yes, I can see that, Finch." Phillpotts and his men stood inside the lodging south of the Thames—the one to which Patrick Copsey had fled after leaving The Acropolis on the night of Roberts-Smythe's murder. Phillpotts learned the address from Copsey's mother, who furthermore informed him that James Millard and Catherine Healy also knew the address of the lodging near Bethlehem Hospital.

"Foul play, Inspector?"

"A possibility worth pursuing, Finch." Phillpotts pointed to the blood trail leading to a small room. "We best have a look in there."

While they were in the room, a young man knocked on the door frame. "Excuse me, Inspector sir?"

"And who might you be?"

"My name is Moffat—Dick Moffat. I work at Bethlehem Hospital. I live here, Inspector." As the young man stared at the blood pooled on the floor, every trace of color left his face. "Dear God. I was so afraid this would happen."

~ # ~

Nedra Alexander folded, unfolded, and refolded the garments lying on her bed. They had been sent out to be washed and flat ironed, as they had been every month since the actress began working at The Acropolis. Living with an elderly and often bed-ridden uncle, Nedra was sole mistress of the house. She had never wed, but wished not to convey that fact to those outside the theatre. Her uncle employed a nurse and several servants, only one of whom lived on the premises. Nedra closely guarded her privacy. It was necessary to do so, for there was too much to risk if she didn't.

Her impulse to complete a task and then undo it—only to do it again—was a more recent eccentricity of character. Other members of The Acropolis's company found more amusing than unsettling her donning her costume, only to remove it entirely, before donning it again in time to make her first entrance. Catherine Healy believed Nedra had her heart stolen and then broken when she was young and had never fully recovered. Jamie Millard thought the odd behavior stemmed from unresolved guilt for some serious mistake. Catherine and Jamie would roll their eyes and laugh, confessing to each other that they had been swept up in the recent mania for psychological explanation, especially on the continent.

Nedra Alexander never acknowledged she was so often the topic of others' speculations. As a girl, she had cursed God for making her features too plain, but as she grew older she cursed him for making them too desirable. Perhaps what she had endured in her life was punishment for her reckless and sacrilegious impertinence.

"Miss Alexander?"

"Yes, Betty?"

"Ma'am, a man is at the door to see you."

"This early in the day?" Nedra immediately regretted uttering the remark in front of the servant.

"I don't know that, ma'am, but he insists on seeing you."

"He has come here to see me?"

Betty observed that her mistress was distressed. "Yes, ma'am, to see you."

"All right. Show him in. Tell him I'll be down in a moment."

"Yes, ma'am."

"No, wait. Help me first."

Nedra opened the wardrobe and pulled out another dress. But she became agitated when she couldn't locate something else she was looking for.

"Now where is . . .? Betty have you seen it?"

"Ma'am?"

"It was here . . . and now I can't seem to . . ." Nedra stopped her search and dropped her shoulders in an attitude of capitulation.

"Then perhaps I should go down and show in Mr. Ludmore—yes, that's his name. I had forgotten it for some reason."

"Mr. Ludmore? It's Mr. Ludmore who is here?"

"Yes, ma'am, Mr. Ludmore. He's your fellow actor at The Acropolis, isn't he?"

Nedra smiled broadly and walked quickly out of the room and down the stairs to greet her theatrical colleague.

Chapter 11

"May I ask what you're doing rummaging through Mr. Roberts-Smythe's desk, Jaynes?"

Jaynes couldn't believe it. Phillpotts had come yet again to harass him.

"I'm not stealing anything, Inspector, if that's what you think. There are files here I wish to move to my desk. They pertain to theatre business. Business I must tend to until a new manager is found."

"Or until you are named Roberts-Smythe's permanent replacement?"

"As I say, I simply wish to move some of these files to my office."

"Why not leave them where they are and move yourself into this office?"

"Because I don't think it proper to inhabit this office at this time."

"'At this time.' Yes, at this time. In any event, you seem disturbed about something you've found—or perhaps *didn't* find in Roberts-Smythe's desk." Phillpotts moved behind Jaynes, leaned over his shoulder, and picked up a stack of the documents on the top of the desk. "What are these?"

Feeling Phillpotts's chest pressing against the back of his shoulder, Jaynes reached for one of Roberts-Smythe's cigarettes lying in an ornate box. His trembling hand made difficult securing the cigarette in his fingers. Expecting Phillpotts to make another cutting remark at his expense, Jaynes volunteered his own. "Perhaps, for just this once, you'll overlook my taking what isn't rightfully mine, Inspector."

"What?" Phillpotts hadn't noticed Jaynes's taking the cigarette. He was going through the stack of contracts Jaynes had pulled out of the drawer. "Is your contract in here as well, Jaynes?"

"I imagine it is, Inspector."

"Ah, here we are." Phillpotts stood erect as he examined the contract, allowing Jaynes to return his torso to a normal sitting position.

Phillpotts walked around the desk as he finished reading. The disappointment on his face informed Jaynes that the detective found nothing in the document of any evidentiary value. "So—the entire company's contracts are in this stack?"

"Yes, Inspector. And I was merely transferring them to my office. Take the time to examine them and you will see that several of the actors are coming up for renewal at the end of the spring. I should like to talk with them now to express the theatre's interest in keeping them for one or more seasons to come. Mr. Millard, for example."

"And that is troubling to you?"

"Troubling to me, Inspector? What do you mean? Why do you say that?"

"You seem particularly concerned about something other than renewals, and I should like to know what it is."

Jaynes dismissed Phillpotts's assumption, disguising his anxiety over not being able to find the one contract he was looking for—that of Edward Ludmore.

~ # ~

Lord Oxley's train passed through Birmingham on the return trip from Dublin. The special accommodations of the railway carriage brought no protest from His Lordship. The food was splendid and the champagne acceptable. Even though it was only a little past noon, Oxley and his traveling companions had already consumed three bottles of Perrier-Jouët Brut 1878. After asking the other men to leave, Oxley's secretary David Isaacs returned with both the fourth bottle and a young woman whom Oxley had spotted as he boarded the train after the crossing from Ireland. The young lady was persuaded to separate herself from her party for the privilege of meeting the First Lord of the Treasury.

After the young woman had taken her first sip of champagne, Oxley ascertained she was both inexperienced in such imbibing and doggedly determined to disguise that fact. He gauged exactly how many glasses he'd allow her to consume before attempting to seduce her. But as he peered into her angelic though somewhat insipid face, his imagination fixed on another—on the more intriguing beauty, Catherine Healy. Oxley knew it would take more than several glasses of Perrier-Jouët Brut to have the actress in his bed.

Perhaps Miss Healy might be moved to return his passion when reminded of Oxley's influence, which had a very long reach and could make difficult Michael Healy's retaining his position as the lead inspector of the Dublin force. Oxley would take pains to remind the actress that rumors of her father's earlier associations with the Irish nationalists and their violent history would be believed—especially if they were coupled by a public accusation made by the First Lord of the Treasury. It didn't matter to Oxley whether Catherine Healy was initially willing or not, just as long as he was able to have her fully. And he would do more than keep her. He would assist her career, just as he had promised her father.

Oxley smiled genially at his young female guest, who much too rapidly finished her first glass of champagne in a clumsy attempt to prove her sophistication. Yes, he wanted the body of Catherine Healy moving passionately under his own, but in the meantime he would amuse himself with someone more easily taken.

~ # ~

"No, thank you. I wouldn't care for tea right now, Inspector."

"If you change your mind, Finch will be happy to make it for you, Miss Healy."

Sitting with Jamie in Roberts-Smythe's office at The Acropolis, Catherine was surprised by Phillpott's politeness to her, although he showed nothing of the sort to her husband.

"All right, go on, Millard. You say you met your father at an abandoned house off High Holborn today and chanced upon something I might find of interest. I am ripe with anticipation. What did you find?"

They went over the details of their discovery with Phillpotts, except for Catherine's encountering the black velvet belt. She wished to pursue the matter of ownership before she gave it to Phillpotts. The item was a necessary accessory for most women, of course, but what was sewn on the inside of the black velvet led Catherine to believe she might know to whom it belonged.

Phillpotts refused to indicate the slightest appreciation for what they had found on High Holborn. "I'm surprised you have revealed all of this so quickly after your discovery, Mr. Millard, considering that you neglected to inform me that you and Miss Healy had gone to the lodging where Patrick Copsey was hiding. Oh, yes. I know all about that from a recent conversation with his mother."

Catherine was tempted to ask Finch for tea after all. "Inspector, we decided then not to come to you—out of fear that Patrick might flee London if we didn't search for him immediately."

Jamie repeated to Phillpotts the contents of the note telling Copsey to go to the abandoned house on High Holborn. Once again, the Inspector accepted the information with affected detachment. "Well, then. It seems I'll have business to attend to on High Holborn as soon as we are finished here."

"And there's one more thing, Inspector."

"Somehow that doesn't surprise me at all, Miss Healy."

"There was a young woman staying there with Patrick."

"Is that so?" Phillpotts petulantly decided to keep from them what he and his men discovered at the lodging. "Let me advise you to forget about Mr. Copsey for the time being and show me the backstage area of The Acropolis before another murder leads us astray." In spite of his anger at the interference of Healy and Millard, Phillpotts refused to take immediate action against the two meddling actors. They could help him, and he damn well knew it.

~ # ~

When they arrived at the spot where Roberts-Smythe's body was discovered, Phillpotts posed his first question. "I have spoken with those who originally constructed this theatre and have examined the architectural plans. But I'm convinced there is more back here than I was shown in the drawings. Tell me truthfully. Are there any hidden rooms, alcoves, or passageways—other than the area where Donovan's body was placed—that might have been constructed *after* the initial round of renovations? For instance, what is behind that door at the far end there—just past the offices of Jaynes and Roberts-Smythe?"

Catherine answered, "Behind that door reposes a few seldom used costumes, furniture, and other stage properties. Those more frequently needed are in the larger room there. She turned and pointed to the much wider door at the other end of the backstage area. "The new storage space was part of the renovation done soon after I arrived last summer, isn't that correct Jamie?"

"Yes, it is. Mr. Roberts-Smythe found much time wasted having to sort through so much of what was rarely used. Therefore, he made the division of costumes and properties, which has worked rather well, I must say."

Phillpotts gestured to Finch, who jotted down the information. "Let's take a look at the area where the lesser-used pieces reside."

When they made their way to the door, Millard stopped Phillpotts from reaching for the knob. "We'll have to find the key in Roberts-Smythe's office. He always kept it locked unless we needed a specific old costume or stage piece. He made reference to actors pilfering from his previous theatre."

"Come, then. We had best look for the key in Roberts-Smythe's desk."

"That won't be necessary, Inspector Phillpotts."

"No? Why not, Finch?"

"The door's unlocked, sir."

"Good fortune smiles, it seems. Light the lantern, Finch, and let's have a look about."

The room was half as large as the new costume and property repository at the other end of the backstage area. As he stepped through the door, Phillpotts detected a mustiness from the seldom-used costumes hanging on one side of the room, many in need of a good seamstress should they be chosen for a future production. On the other side were miscellaneous and tarnished weapons, several incomplete sets of armor, and a large cluster of broken and scarred furniture—tables, chairs, and benches. At the far end of the room hung a faded green tapestry, torn on all four corners.

Phillpotts walked to the tapestry and stood before it, his thumb and index finger stroking his bearded chin. "Finch, give me that lantern and pull back the left bottom corner of the tapestry."

Finch did as instructed, assisted by Millard. The men pulled enough of the tapestry away from the wall for Phillpotts to notice another door. This one was of more recent vintage than the one they had come through.

"Know anything of this, Miss Healy?"

Catherine was just as surprised as the others. "No, Inspector. I had no idea this was here. But then I've looked into this room only twice since I joined the company."

"Was this tapestry hanging here both times?"

"Yes, I believe so."

Millard and Finch had pulled the tapestry further away from the door and kept it in place by laying some of the heavier furniture against it.

"Millard, did you know about this door?"

"No. I've been in here a dozen times or so—under Roberts-Smythe's supervision of course—and I never thought anything was behind the tapestry but a wall."

Phillpotts opened the door and pushed the lantern through it. There was another area the size of a large closet space. A table and a chair were against one of the side walls. Both furniture pieces looked as though they came from the cluster in the storage room. But on the other side wall was a narrow door, again more recently constructed. Phillpotts pulled it open and once more extended his lantern through. He saw a narrow spiral stairway that surely led to the ground level. He couldn't see beyond the staircase but he didn't have to. He knew it went down to yet another door or opening that led to the alley at the back of The Acropolis. "Yes, yes," he muttered. "The very route someone likely took the night of Roberts-Smythe's and Donovan's murders."

Phillpotts went down the staircase, and when he returned he was a bit dustier and almost completely out of breath.

"Find anything on the spiral staircase or between it and here, Inspector?" Jamie had gone out one of the side doors and made his way around to the narrow lane at the back of The Acropolis.

"Very clever, whoever added this entrance. Look. Because it's hidden by the short brick wall that angles away from the rear of the structure, you can't even see the door unless you're a foot away. The question is why Roberts-Smythe would ask for this and the two other portals on the backstage level to be included last year. Now how is it, Millard, that none of your company witnessed any of these renovations being made?"

"Much of the work was done after the midnight hour or in the early morning—that is, at the only time they could be made—after the company left following a performance and before the actors arrived for late morning rehearsals. Mr. Roberts-Smythe instructed us to stay far away from the workmen, for fear of injury and interference. It seems Roberts-Smythe wanted an anonymous escape route from the theatre.

But as you say, Inspector, why?"

"Or perhaps he required a discreet way to accept deliveries of a special kind."

"If you mean opium, Inspector, I've seen no evidence he was addicted to the drug." Millard heard from several American friends that London was popularly perceived as a city teeming with opium dens and stupefied citizens, but he knew London's reputation on that score was highly exaggerated, owing to the fictional employment of opium smoking in the works of master craftsmen like Dickens, Wilde, and Arthur Conan Doyle. Besides, why would Roberts-Smythe purchase or smoke opium at The Acropolis, when he could have done so even more discreetly elsewhere?

"So, Inspector, did you find anything?"

"No, nothing. We will need to come back with more light to make an adequate survey of the area. Yet we can at least conclude the murderer likely knew of the hidden doorway in the old costume and properties room and the spiral staircase taking him to this exit. And you're certain neither you nor Miss Healy knew of it?"

"Inspector, I assure you neither of us was aware of its existence. Nor had anyone else at The Acropolis ever said anything to me about it. The only thing I can come up with—and it's an innocent explanation considering what happened—is that Roberts-Smythe had this route constructed so he could leave his office at the rear of the theatre and make his way around to the front, only to slip into the house and watch us in rehearsal while we all thought he was still in his office."

Phillpotts reached for a cigar. "You're not telling me you actually believe that, are you?"

~ # ~

Catherine Healy had remained backstage to examine the hidden room at the rear of the old costume and properties storage area. The cramped chamber had nothing in it, other than a well-worn chair and table, to counter the eeriness of the surroundings. With both doors closed and the faded green thick tapestry covering the door to the storage room, a person would feel uncomfortably isolated more than comfortably protected. Even though the tapestry was pulled back and the door to the storage area now wide open, Catherine wasn't immune to feelings of stifling claustrophobia. But she steadied herself and manipulated the lantern so that she could look up and down the side of each wall, as her father had taught her when she would occasionally assist him in similar searches for evidence. There were no holes where something might have fired a pistol and no depressions or gouges on the walls or furniture to suggest a struggle.

Seeing nothing else out of the ordinary, Catherine dropped to her knees and examined the floor. Under the table she spotted a key. She stood and moved immediately through the storage room until she reached its outer door, the one leading to the confined backstage area. Inserting the key, she heard the voices of the Inspector and her husband as they ascended back to the top of the spiral staircase. She remained at the door until Millard and Phillpotts made their way to her. "Look what I found on the floor of the inner room." She closed the door and demonstrated that the key locked and opened it easily. The murderer might have either dropped or tossed the key in the secluded room when he made his way toward the spiral staircase."

Phillpotts led them back to the inner chamber. Millard took the lantern and dropped to his knees to continue the search of the floor. He was only at it for a moment when he found something. He handed Catherine a pair of women's cream-colored and scalloped dress gloves. "They were resting one on top of the other between the front chair legs."

Phillpotts took them from Catherine. "Are these costume gloves, Miss Healy?"

Catherine shook her head. "They might have been used in one of the productions, but they seem to be dress gloves any woman would wear if she intended to impress her companion or anyone else who might see her."

"And what might this be?" Jamie reached against the bottom edge of the far wall and lifted from the floor a dark colored handkerchief, properly folded.

Phillpotts took the item from Millard. "A dark blue male's handkerchief."

"May I see it?"

"Of course, Miss Healy."

Catherine held the lantern close to the fabric. "There is a stain on the handkerchief."

Phillpotts hardly needed to be told what it was.

Jamie crawled another two feet to his left. "Cate, take your lantern and look at the bottom of the wall here. Looks like specks of blood to me."

Chapter 12

Sitting in a house a mere hundred yards from Dick Moffat's lodging, Patrick Copsey gazed at the older woman as if she had come down from above. He was completely spent—his arms dangling at his sides and his legs thrust straight out from his chair. The woman softly brushed the hair from his eyes. She offered a warm smile and took his hand.

"Patrick, she's going to be all right. She had heavier bleeding than most, but she has eaten and is now asleep."

"And the baby?"

"The same. I am most grateful I was returning at the same moment you were running toward the house."

Caroline Reed, the married sister of Copsey's friend Dick Moffat, had assisted with another delivery earlier in the morning. It was the service she had provided for many in the area. And a good number of the births took place at her home, where she kept all in readiness. But Clare Paget's delivery was too sudden to have afforded Caroline the familiarity of her own lodging. She had to deliver Copsey's baby girl at her brother's lodging, in the small room where Copsey and Clare had been staying. When she was assured of Clare's post-delivery condition, she had both mother and child carried to her home for a more comfortable stay.

"May heaven reserve a special place for you, Caroline." Copsey dropped his head in utter exhaustion and relief.

Once more, she stroked the young man's hair. "Patrick, I think you should follow the example of Clare and your new daughter by eating something and then sleeping."

"But the police?"

"I have spoken with them. They will return late this afternoon or this evening and take you to see Inspector Phillpotts."

~ # ~

Another employee of The Acropolis, actor Bernhard Schneider, stepped off the train in Manchester, having made the decision to sail to America. He pondered the advantages and disadvantages of living in New York and speculated on the degree of cooperation between the police forces of both that city and London. Could he be arrested by the local authorities acting as agents of Scotland Yard, even if he was situated across the Atlantic?

What would he do to support himself? Could he still make ends meet as an actor? It was possible that in a city such as Cincinnati or Milwaukee his Teutonic accent would serve him well. Surely no one in London would look for him if he was further west than Manhattan, Boston, or Philadelphia. As he remained on the platform pondering his options, two men approached in tweed winter coats and bowlers.

"Bernhard Schneider?" asked the shorter of the two men.

Schneider was stunned. He didn't recognize either man. How could they know who he was? His voice quivered, "No, I am not, and I know no such person."

"My name is Farmingham, and this is Stephens. We are detectives from the Greater Manchester Police. If you are someone other than Bernhard Schneider would you present some identification that proves who you are?"

Schneider stood mute in the blustery and frigid conditions. The burly Stephens pulled at his arm. "Come with us, sir. And without protest, if you don't mind."

"Wait a moment. How could you possibly know who I was?"

The men from Manchester shared a knowing look. Farmingham responded, "Your hat, sir."

Schneider's shoulder's dropped. Of course. He had given himself away by wearing his trademark short top hat with a yellow band and a prominent green feather—the hat being his one glaring concession to vanity. Apparently Scotland Yard had sent a description of the hat to the police in Manchester and likely to other cities in England.

~ # ~

Henry Jaynes stood before the headquarters of the London County Council at Spring Gardens, near Trafalgar Square. He had been here two weeks earlier, sent by Roberts-Smythe to deliver documents to Sidney Hawkins, one of the many officials responsible for the regulation and licensing of the city's theatres and other entertainments. Each time he approached the building, Jaynes could think of little but the bloated bureaucratic sluggishness characteristic of the Council.

How long would it take the city to permit the re-opening of The Acropolis? As Jaynes mounted the impressive staircase leading to the principal floor, he feared that disagreements among the conflicting governmental bodies would force The Acropolis to remain dormant long enough to destroy everything the theatre had gained in the past year.

"Sit down, Jaynes. Would you care for tea? "

"No thank you."

"Then how about a scone? You look like a man who needs a daily scone or two in his diet. These are still almost warm. My daughter brought them in only a few minutes ago."

"I'm fine, thank you." Jaynes fidgeted in his chair, unable to settle comfortably. He found Hawkins of a type—a man in his early fifties, without ambition or any desire to alter his daily routine. "Mr. Hawkins, as you must know, I am here to discuss the re-opening of The Acropolis."

"Yes, it's quite unfortunate. Had the murders taken place outside the theatre—or perhaps even inside the lobby area—that would be one thing. But to have occurred right on the stage itself—yes, such misfortune. You have my every sympathy, Jaynes."

"That is very much appreciated, but I would also like to have your assurance that the closing won't be a long one. I and all the company hope we may reopen by the beginning of next week—at the very latest."

"Ah, simply splendid." Hawkins's face radiated satisfaction at the scone. Such a treat. Clotted cream and jam. Are you sure you won't have one?"

"No thank you." Jaynes continued lurching about in his chair. "As I was saying, if your office can see fit to allow the reopening by—"

"Well, you must understand, Jaynes." Hawkins spoke with the clotted cream and jam drooping from both sides of his mouths like an unruly moustache. "The decision isn't mine to make. In fact, it's not entirely the decision of this office. Scotland Yard has a say in this, and I've been told that they won't consider any reopening until the murderer has been apprehended."

"But that's preposterous." Jaynes stood with both palms pressed flat on Hawkins's desk.

"I'm afraid it isn't, sir. It's what I've heard."

"And what if the murderer eludes detection? Are we to remain closed forever?"

"Don't be so theatrical." A smile exploded on Hawkins's face. "What? Did I say 'theatrical'?" Hawkins guffawed at his unintentional witticism, spraying half-chewed pieces of the scone unto Jaynes's hands and coat sleeves. "Now man, from what I've also heard, the Yard has a good suspect or two, so the arrest shouldn't be too long in coming."

Jaynes felt his hands and lower arms giving way. He pulled them up quickly. Had that bastard Phillpotts announced him as a suspect?

"Jaynes, if I were you I would take this up with someone much higher in government. Don't you or your theatre have any friends at Court or on Downing Street?"

Leaving the building at Spring Gardens, Jaynes thought of the one recent patron of The Acropolis with enough influence to help in the matter—the First Lord of the Treasury. But Jaynes knew Oxley wouldn't speak to him about the matter. Someone else would have to do it. Someone perhaps more pleasing to Oxley's sensibilities.

~ # ~

Catherine stepped away from the Pearcy front door with a letter just delivered by an employee of The Acropolis, who had received it from "someone looking official, as if he had been sent by the Queen." Glancing at the envelope, Catherine understood why the messenger thought it had come from the Queen. Could it have something to do with the re-opening of The Acropolis? But such good news would have been sent to Henry Jaynes, not to her.

Before she could open the letter, Alice was at her side. "Who is the letter from, Catherine?"

"Alice, I am going to my room. When Jamie returns, tell him where I am." Catherine hurried up the stairs, pulling open the envelope as she went.

~ # ~

91

Thomas Millard took a healthy swallow and expressed complete satisfaction at the high percentage of rum in the concoction. "No one makes these better than tavern master Bill Shackey here." The elder Millard raised his drink in salute to the proprietor of The Pelican's Foot, who saluted him back with his bar towel.

"Well father, is this the first or second one of the evening?" Jamie always enjoyed the ritual of inquiring.

"I had all intentions of stopping after one, my boy, but since I knew you'd be meeting me here, I ordered a second so you wouldn't have to drink alone."

"Nothing more heartwarming than a father's devotion to his son."

"You can say that again, lad. Here's to Her Majesty." As Thomas raised his rum-dominated beverage, he lowered his voice. "Almost seventy-nine and not for the longest time been kissed. Nor will she ever be again."

Jamie followed his father's lead. "To the Queen." He paused for only a moment. "All right, then, so much for the requisite pleasantries. You say you have some information regarding the death of Roberts-Smythe."

"Indeed. It seems my old enemy Inspector Phillpotts and I have become quite good friends over the past two days."

"I always knew you were both destined for reconciliation."

"As you were always destined to be cut from my legacy." The elder Millard quickly dropped his smile. "Phillpotts asked me to check Roberts-Smythe and his clothing one final time before they handed the body over to the family."

"And what did you find?"

"Death caused by knife penetration, as we all know. No other marks suggesting trauma to any other part of the body. The evidence of previous tears to the flesh were very small and of considerable vintage."

Jamie so enjoyed the sound of his father's voice as he spoke of what he loved and did best. "Anything in the hair?"

"Nothing out of the ordinary for a man who likely washed it once a week and kept it daily pomaded with oil."

"Anything on or in the clothing then?"

The old doctor peered over his shoulder before leaning forward across the small table. He reached into his pocket. "Of consequence? Only this." Thomas pushed a photograph face down across the table.

Jamie saw that the photograph had a crease running across the middle. As his fingers reached to flip over the photograph, he felt his father's strong grip encircle his wrists.

"I found it folded in a special pocket on the *inside* of his waistcoat. Turn it over discreetly, my boy."

Jamie did as instructed and understood why his father seemed so secretive about the photograph. It depicted a man and a young woman engaged in a sexual act of the most socially unsanctioned kind. The French inscription read "*Amusement un après-midi.*" Jamie muttered, "An afternoon amusement indeed." But there was something else written in ink across the bottom. The words were "Is this proof satisfactory?"

"Do you recognize the hand, Jamie? Someone at your theatre, perhaps?"

"No. I don't." It was nothing like the script Millard saw on the notes to Patrick Copsey. "But I couldn't really identify anyone's handwriting at The Acropolis, except for Cate's and Robert-Smythe's. And it isn't his, although it's clearly the penmanship of a man."

"Let me have it back, my boy."

Jamie placed the photograph face down on the table and slid it back to his father, who deftly slipped it into his pocket while once more looking over his shoulder.

"And does Phillpotts know about the photograph, father?" Jamie saw the twinkle in his father's eye. "He doesn't, does he?"

"Not yet. I thought you might like to see it first. Perhaps you or your Conan Doyle Holmes of a lady friend might want to ponder it a bit before I hand it to the police."

"First of all, the author's name is Arthur Conan Doyle and his character is Sherlock Holmes. In any event, I'm not sure that I should take possession of that photograph, even if you insist, father. I wouldn't look forward to explaining to Cate how I came in possession of it." Jamie wondered if his speech or manner had informed his father he had already had pleasurable intimacy with Catherine Healy.

"As you wish, my boy. I'll give it over to Phillpotts and see if he blushes the same way you seem to be doing now."

Chapter 13

"Finch, bring the lad some tea."

"Yes, Inspector."

"Now Copsey, the sooner you can satisfy me as to the reason you were at the abandoned house off High Holborn, the sooner you can return to your wife and child."

Copsey wasn't about to correct Phillpotts's characterization of his relationship with Clare. "I understand, Inspector, but as I have told you three times, I went in response to a note I received instructing me to go there."

"The note being in the same hand that wrote the one sending you on a fool's errand to The Lyceum the night of Roberts-Smythe's murder?"

"Yes, Inspector, in the same odd hand."

"And in spite of that fact, you still went off to High Holborn?" Phillpotts wished at this moment for nothing more than a good meal, a strong drink, and flavorful smoke. It was past seven o'clock on a bitingly cold January evening, and he was clearly feeling the effects of the long hours spent on The Acropolis murders. "And you have no idea who wrote these notes?"

"As I said, I first supposed the one at The Acropolis was from Mr. Roberts-Smythe, but the second one couldn't have been from him since he was dead."

"Tell me truthfully. Could the notes have been written by Mr. Jaynes?"

"Yes, sir."

"Yes?" Phillpotts was for the moment reinvigorated. "And what makes you believe he was the author, Copsey?"

"But I don't, Inspector."

"What? Damn you, man. You are contradicting yourself."

"I mean Mr. Jaynes *could* have written them—just as anyone else could have written them. I didn't recognize the hand. So it naturally could have been anyone, including Mr. Jaynes. But I wasn't trying to imply that I thought Mr. Jaynes had written them."

Phillpotts grunted and turned the page in his notebook. "Again, why in God's name did you obey the summons on the second note seeing the first one might have had some connection to the slaying of Mr. Roberts-Smythe?"

"Because I feared the second one *might* also have had something to do with his death, Inspector."

"Blast it, boy. You are severely trying my patience."

"Forgive me, sir. You see with Clare about to give birth, I feared that if I didn't go as summoned, someone would come to where I was and harm her and the child she was carrying. I'm sorry, but I felt I had no choice but to go to the lodging off High Holborn." Copsey's hand trembled as he reached for the tea Finch set before him.

Phillpotts absorbed the young man's reasoning. "All right, lad. Then tell me what you saw when you arrived at the abandoned house."

Copsey finished the tea in two swallows and began. He said he had approached the darkened lodging with considerable uneasiness, expecting that someone was waiting to assault him. He didn't walk to the front door, but rather moved slowly around the house to the rear, looking in several windows, but seeing nothing.

"I reached the rear door, Inspector, and once more looked in. I saw only the darkened outline of the few pieces of furniture. I didn't illuminate my lantern for fear of being discovered myself. I tested the doorknob to see if it would open. It did, and I stepped inside—but only barely. I had by now made up my mind to call out and see if anyone was there waiting for me. If a voice sounded threatening I would run back out the way I had come in. If I heard nothing I would light the lantern and make one quick inspection of the surroundings and then leave. And that's what I did, Inspector Phillpotts, after no one replied to my calling out. Then I saw the man lying there, on his back on the bottom stairs. I walked to him and lowered the light toward his face. There was the wound on his forehead and the blood. I was sickened by the sight, and I immediately left the house. That was all I saw, Inspector."

Phillpotts stood and walked slightly behind Copsey, placing his hand on the young man's shoulder. "You saw the blood and wound on the man's forehead?"

"Yes, Inspector. It was quite horrible."

"And yet you've not even hinted the victim was someone you knew fairly well." Phillpotts hand clawed into Copsey's shoulder.

"Someone I knew well? No, no. I don't understand, Inspector."

"You are one of the stage hands at The Acropolis and you didn't recognize the actor Alfred Nichols?"

"Mr. Nichols? The man was Mr., Nichols? I swear I didn't recognize him, Inspector. I immediately saw the wound and didn't examine the rest of his face. I swear I didn't." Copsey tried to rise, but Phillpotts kept him pressed down.

"Keep seated, boy. I am not through with you yet."

~ # ~

Catherine gazed into the upstairs bedroom window, studying her own reflection in the panes. The opened letter from Lord Oxley was in her hand. She hadn't let go of it since she read it ten minutes earlier. When she opened the envelope, she looked immediately for the signature. As she began, she hoped Oxley's would express regret about the murders at The Acropolis and assure her he would use his influence to reopen the theatre as soon as possible. But the letter said nothing about the misfortunes at The Acropolis, giving not the slightest hint Oxley even knew of Roberts-Smythe's murder. The letter had no date. Had it been written before that night's performance of *Hamlet?*

Disappointed in herself for being unable to resist the impulse to read it a second time, she returned to the table and placed the letter under the lamp.

Miss Healy,

Please excuse my intrusion on your valuable time, but I could no longer deny myself the pleasure of writing you. As you may know, I have been to The Acropolis on several occasions. I will admit with some embarrassment that I had not been a devotee of stage productions and went initially only for political reasons. But my perspective on theatre changed immediately and dramatically after seeing you perform the role of Portia in Mr. Shakespeare's play about the Merchant of Venice.

I found your loveliness, exuberance, communicative skill, and intelligence far exceeding any exalted praise I could possibly express in this letter. I hope I am within the bounds of proper decorum when I shamelessly admit to you that I returned to the theatre expressly to observe you again on stage. I have since seen some of London's acknowledged finest young actresses, such as Miss Winifred Emery and Mrs. Patrick Campbell. But none of them seem to equal your combination of artistic gifts.

Please know I am grateful to you for opening for me such a new and beautiful world. I feel I have been enriched by my exposure to the pleasures of the theatre— especially to the pleasure of your performances.

I should stop now before my praise overstays any welcome you might have so far given it. But do know I am most interested in seeing your career and the success of The Acropolis flourish in the years ahead—and I am ready to assist in whatever way I can.

To that end, would it be at all possible for us to meet and discuss what I might do for you and your theatre? Afternoon tea, perhaps? Or if your schedule permits, a dinner at the Charing Cross Hotel?

I end this correspondence with the deepest apology if I have offended you with either my flatteries or my invitation to tea or dinner. I am simply offering my sincere estimation of your extraordinary theatrical talents and of my desire to assist you and The Acropolis in the months and years to come.

I will send someone to solicit your answer to my invitation that we meet.

All of this from the pen of Lord Oxley, the First Lord of the Treasury. Catherine folded the letter and placed it in her correspondence box. She wanted to show it to her husband as soon as he returned, but she dared not. Jamie would see past the flattery and offer of assistance and judge the letter as something more ignoble. She recalled that in the late autumn, after they had been informed Oxley had attended one of their performances, Jamie noted with disdain that the man had a kept mistress and a history of seducing younger women.

Although everyone remarked on her generally modest character and demeanor, Catherine Healy was always exhilarated by the public's praise and the generous compliments of the accomplished, such as the brilliant thespian Henry Irving and her dear friend Bram Stoker. Lord Oxley's epistolary attention, then, was impossible to dismiss with indifference, even though Jamie's assessment of Oxley's reputation offered wise counsel. She of course couldn't put herself in the position of having to ward off an attempted seduction. She had seen but never met Oxley and judged him as handsome, but not in a way that stimulated her sensibilities. "Dear God," she whispered upon the reminder that her marriage to Jamie couldn't be revealed quite yet. But would knowledge of her marriage deter Oxley, if his true motives were unacceptable to her? Sadly, she realized, the First Lord of the Treasury wouldn't be deterred at all by that fact.

But the man offered his assistance to The Acropolis as well as to her. Perhaps she could meet him for tea or an evening meal in order to encourage a quick reopening of the theatre. Would he be charmed enough to assist in the matter, even if she made it plain she would never agree to any offers or expectations of intimacy between them? But again, what would her husband say to all of this? Would Jamie even approve of her seeing Oxley in order to encourage an intercession on behalf of The Acropolis? She was almost certain Jamie would say it was up to Henry Jaynes, not Catherine Healy, to solicit the government to hasten the theatre's reopening. Catherine was also confident Jaynes would do all he could on that score, but given his often tepid personality, he might not be able to make the case as well as she could.

Catherine's now accelerated pacing was halted by a knock on her door. "Yes?"

"Catherine, it's Alice."

Considering her agitated state, Catherine was most grateful for the intrusion. "Has Jamie come home?"

"No, not yet. But there is someone downstairs waiting for your reply to this." Alice handed her a folded note.

Catherine opened it and saw that it was in Oxley's hand. It included only a succinct request.

"*Will you do me the honor of dining with me tomorrow night at the Charing Cross Hotel?*"

"What does it say, Catherine? Does it have anything to do with the letter you received earlier?"

"Alice, please give me privacy. Just wait outside for a moment."

Catherine closed the door and sat down to reply to the invitation. She reached for the pen, but her fingers wouldn't spread wide enough for her to pick it up.

~ # ~

Denham Phillpotts examined several statements provided by the latest victims of fraudulent financial schemes. It was all he could do to assign his men to investigate these deceptions, seeing he had little patience or sympathy for anyone foolishly entrusting his money to another who promised large returns and financial security. But since the latest targets of fraud included gentlemen of high standing and political influence, Phillpotts felt he had no choice but follow-up on the complaints. Besides, it was just possible Morris Roberts-Smythe was involved in financial chicanery of some kind, therefore leading to his death.

"He's here, Inspector."

"Thank you, Finch. Bring him in."

It was past 11:00 p.m. when a weary Bernhard Schneider stepped into Phillpott's office at Scotland Yard.

"Can't this wait until the morning, Inspector? I've been on the train for the entire day. I'm afraid I'm too exhausted to be of much use to you tonight. Surely, you too would prefer to be in bed at this hour."

Having had his sleep interrupted by news of Schneider's impending arrival, Phillpotts suppressed the urge to second the man's assumption. "Tell me, Mr. Schneider, why you were travelling so far north of London. Planning on leaving the country, perhaps?"

"The Acropolis was shut up, Inspector. No performances. That offered me the opportunity to leave the city for a time. Surely you understand. Haven't you ever wished to put all this behind you for a few days?"

Phillpotts slid a small glass of Scotch whisky to Schneider. "Here. Take it."

Schneider downed the contents. It was the most comfortable moment he had experienced the entire day.

"So, you were about to tell me why you took the train to Manchester. You have family up there, I suppose?"

"No, Inspector. No family. The reason I went to Manchester is simple. I hadn't been for several years, and I thought I would investigate any theatrical opportunities available to me at the new Palace Theatre there. With The Acropolis being closed . . ."

"And you expect it never to reopen?"

"No, I imagine it will, but . . ." Schneider fell silent.

"I see. You were having problems at The Acropolis, then?"

"Nothing beyond what others of my kind were experiencing."

"There are other Germans in the company?"

"No, Inspector. I wasn't speaking of my nationality. I meant the problems I and my fellow bit-part actors were having with the kinds of roles assigned to us."

"I see. Have you been at The Acropolis long enough for a promotion to larger parts?"

"It rarely works that way, Inspector. The reality is once a small-role performer, always a small-role performer, I'm afraid."

"So it didn't upset you when Mr. Roberts-Smythe brought in newer actors last summer—Mr. Ludmore in particular—who took parts you might have coveted?"

Schneider's agitation was impossible to disguise. "I just said it doesn't work that way, Inspector." Schneider pointed to his empty glass. Phillpotts poured him another drink. "The one most resentful would have been . . . never mind."

"Go on, Schneider. Would have been who?"

"James Millard."

"Millard?"

Schneider began to relax, his expression suggesting the arrival of a helpful thought. "You see, Inspector, Roberts-Smythe made clear to him that he'd no longer be playing the romantic leads."

"Have you heard Mr. Millard express any frustration with Roberts-Smythe's decision on that score?"

Schneider folded his hands on Phillpotts's desk, like an attentive schoolboy. "He didn't speak to me about it, but I was told he frequently voiced his displeasure to others about being denied the roles he had been accustomed to playing. Especially since his leading lady would have been Miss Healy."

"But it's very evident to me that he's not had to do without Miss Healy's company."

Schneider again reached for the Scotch whisky. Phillpotts could see his eyes dancing over the glass. "Yes. Well, . . . it's just that . . . that his feelings for Miss Healy are of the kind that even thinking about her playing the love interest of another man—even in a stage production—has given him considerable unease."

"And you were told that as well?"

"I have also seen that, Inspector."

"Very good. I appreciate your candor, Mr. Schneider." Phillpotts leaned back in his chair.

Schneider rose to go. "I'm glad I could be of service, Inspector. I trust that will be all for tonight?" Phillpotts didn't reply. "Might I ask if I have your permission to return to Manchester—again for the purpose of evaluating theatre opportunities there?"

Phillpotts stood and poured more whisky into Schneider's glass. "I'm afraid we have a little more to talk about tonight, Mr. Schneider. Please sit back down." Schneider began a protest but knew the effort would be futile. He reluctantly dropped into the chair. All the equanimity he had regained in the past several minutes had evaporated in an instant.

Phillpotts walked behind Schneider and placed his hands on the actor's shoulders, as he had done earlier to Patrick Copsey. "So tell me, Mr. Schneider. Have you been to an abandoned house on High Holborn, not far from Trafalgar Square?" Phillpotts could feel Schneider's shoulders jerk upwards. "Just relax, Schneider. So, have you been to the residence I just described?"

~ # ~

"He did find something the police missed, but it's unclear how much relevance it might have." Sitting in the drawing room at the Pearcy's, Jamie didn't wish to be specific about his father's having located an erotic photograph folded in an inside pocket of Roberts-Smythe's waistcoat. Since falling in love with Catherine Healy, Millard had become even more careful of offending feminine sensibilities with any allusion to something socially untoward.

"Jamie, you're not identifying the item found on Mr. Roberts-Smythe's person. From your manner, you're telling me it was something no lady would wish to hold in her hands." She smiled, as her husband looked down. "But many men might?"

"You know me too well, my darling."

"I could never know you well enough. Now, tell me what your father found." With some hesitancy and embarrassment, he explained what the photograph depicted. Catherine showed no signs of discomfort at the description. "I see. And you say it was folded?"

"Yes. The murderer likely folded it and put it in his pocket."

"Might Mr. Roberts-Smythe have folded it himself before putting it into his pocket?"

"But why would he do that, Cate? The photograph would have easily fit into his pocket unfolded. Surely, the murderer placed it in there right after stabbing him in the back."

"My husband—and how I so enjoy saying that, by the way—we should ponder both possibilities. Just why would anyone wish to place that photograph on his person?"

"To embarrass him, I would suppose."

"Even after he was discovered dead? Is it probable the murderer would think Roberts-Smythe's reputation would be forever damaged by public knowledge of such a possession? You must also remember the pocket was cut on the *inside* of the waistcoat. Clearly, Mr. Roberts-Smythe was used to concealing what he didn't wish others to see."

Jamie sighed. "You have me again, dearest Cate."

She kissed him in appreciation of his congenial admission. "So, have you spoken to your father about what we found in the hidden chamber at the back of the old storage area?"

"Yes, a pair of gloves and a handkerchief with an apparent blood stain. He asked if the amount of blood on the handkerchief and at the bottom of the wall was all the blood evidence found. When I said there was no indication of any more—either in the room or immediately outside of it—my father suggested the handkerchief might have been used to staunch a cut of some kind."

Catherine yawned. It was almost midnight. "I only wish we could determine whose blood it was."

"My father reminded me that the blood might have been the handkerchief's owner, or . . ."

"Someone who was with him in that chamber—yes. The glove points of course to a woman. But how would she have been cut? There weren't any nails protruding from the walls or any broken glass." She yawned again.

"We need to get you up to bed, Cate."

"In a moment. If the blood came from a woman, it might well have been inflicted by the man to whom the handkerchief belonged. It seems to me that the small room hardly gave enough space for the kind of intimacy requiring the removal of a woman's clothing."

Jamie laughed. "As I said, it's time to get you to bed. You are violating the code of acceptable feminine speech."

Catherine touched his hand. "I only hope I'm not lessened in your eyes when I speak more like a Dublin crime investigator than a lady. Quite simply, I am my father's daughter. I have no other defense for my forwardness."

Millard desired nothing more than to postpone any attempt on her part to be too much of a lady.

"Jamie, remind me to send a note to Nedra Alexander in the morning."

"A note to Nedra?"

Catherine was thinking of the gloves and the black velvet belt at the abandoned house on High Holborn. "I must talk with her tomorrow morning or afternoon. I do so hope she won't be gone down to Sussex for the day. She often does that when she hasn't a performance. She never gets back before evening."

"If so, then why not meet her in the evening after she returns, Cate? We haven't any performance either, you know."

Catherine's face burned with concern and at least a modicum of shame. She knew that she couldn't meet Nedra in the early evening. At least not tomorrow evening, for she had agreed to dine at that time with Lord Oxley at the Charing Cross Hotel.

Chapter 14

Checking to see if everyone was asleep, Oliver Pearcy stepped into the morning room and noted the time—12:50 a.m. In recent months, Pearcy had come to relish the silence and serenity of this time of night. He poured a drink and nestled into his favorite chair. Over the past several days especially, he had worked hard and accomplished much. Still some of what he had done had to be kept from everyone in the house, although he fancifully imagined bragging to Catherine Healy about his furtive activity. Yes, Catherine. How he appreciated her filling several empty spaces in his domestic life, which had been so fractured by the death of his wife several years earlier.

Pearcy smiled recalling how insistent Alice had been that he accept Catherine's invitation to tour The Acropolis last October. He found the structure intriguing, especially the byzantine backstage area. Three weeks after the initial visit he would go again, only this time remaining backstage with Alice during an entire performance. Alice was utterly fascinated by all the theatrical comings and goings, while he found the backstage area largely reminiscent of the legal profession. The constant bustle of activity, followed by periods of inaction. Labyrinthine weaving and disappearances. Jarring collisions and secretive communications.

Pearcy recalled as well Jamie Millard's assessments of his fellow actors and backstage crew. If he couldn't be enthusiastic, Millard was at least charitable to them all, with the exception of Ned Ludmore, whom Millard praised for his talent but ridiculed for his vanity. Ludmore never wore a hat to cover his luxuriantly long hair, Jamie noted, adding that the young actor lived only to be pointed at—on stage and off. In the several times he had seen Ludmore since, Pearcy believed the actor was annoyed by Catherine Healy's never being familiar with him. Pearcy assumed Ludmore blamed her aloofness on the influence of Jamie Millard. Ludmore once claimed in front of Catherine that Millard resented him for taking the parts Jamie used to play with considerable success. Although he was an attorney and not a theatre person, Pearcy couldn't understand why Roberts-Smythe brought Ludmore in to replace Jamie in those leading roles. As Alice informed him, the patrons of The Acropolis didn't revolt only because Millard was still featured in important parts, such as Claudius in *Hamlet*. Still, Ludmore seemed to be the resentful and suspicious one.

But Pearcy knew only too well that there was another resentful and suspicious member of the company. Of that person too he could say nothing.

~ # ~

The following morning, Nedra Alexander arose still grappling with the doubt and anxiety Edward Ludmore had instilled in her when he had come to visit. Nedra examined her face in the mirror. She had never understood why men like Morris Roberts-Smythe deemed her appearance "older than her years." She believed her eyes and nose were her best features—the latter so aristocratically Greek in its straightness, the former hauntingly bluish gray, with a hint of mystery and promise of reward for anyone who could command their attention.

But these qualities were best appreciated at an intimate distance—not at all possible on a stage far removed from so many of the theatre patrons, especially those who sat toward the rear of the house. Other actresses, Catherine Healy most notably, seemed to transcend such distance with their beauty and manner, but Nedra's could only be adequately judged from a close proximity.

"Miss Alexander, the cab is here."

"Thank you, Sanders." She smiled at the servant and moved toward the door. "Isn't it a most beautiful morning?"

"Yes, ma'am. Very cold. Bracing cold."

"It stimulates the blood in one's face, Sanders. I've long believed we never look more youthful than we do on a cold winter's morning."

Sanders delivered his reply without changing expression, a talent possessed by so many in his profession. "Perhaps that's true of women such as you, Miss Alexander, but I believe such harsh conditions only age one such as I beyond my years. And I'm afraid I've almost completely exhausted the parameters of how much further age my face can accept."

"Oh, Sanders, you delight me so. Whenever I need to be invigorated by a good laugh, you are always there to encourage it. And I've needed your assistance much more often these past several months, haven't I?" Nedra managed to keep her smile in repair. "Well, I must go. I am to meet Miss Healy for a late breakfast." She held the note Catherine had sent earlier in the morning.

After informing the cabman of her destination, Nedra began squeezing her hands together. She was anxious over what Catherine Healy wished to see her about.

~ # ~

"Are you getting in, sir?" The driver was anxious to get moving.

"In a moment." Ned Ludmore took another look at The Acropolis, at which he had arrived twenty minutes earlier. He had easily gained entrance when the policeman guarding the door recognized him as the leading male actor of the company.

"My missus and I have seen you on several occasions, Mr. Ludmore. She's quite keen to sing your praises, sir. She has one of them theatrical postcards with you decked out as Romeo on it. She shows it off to everyone who comes by."

"That's especially gratifying. Please send my regards to your wife."

"I will, sir. And we are looking forward to seeing your next performance, whenever that might be."

Ludmore thanked the man and walked into the theatre. Twenty minutes later he came out, pleased he hadn't found Henry Jaynes in his office or anything incriminating in the vacant office of Morris Roberts-Smythe or in the secret chamber at the rear of the old costume and properties area.

~ # ~

"And how, may I ask, were you able to afford breakfast at this hotel—on the mere wages of a stage actor?"

"You shouldn't ask me such personal questions, Catherine. Some things should remain unspoken, even with one's dearest friends."

Catherine wondered at Nedra Alexander's comment, regardless of its facetious nature, for she and Nedra were hardly 'dearest friends.'

"But, the Savoy is such a beautiful hotel, isn't it, Catherine?"

"Indeed it is. The interior is quite—"

Nedra interrupted. "I know its history well."

Catherine was struck by Nedra's refusal to look at her while she proceeded to go on about the hotel. Nedra's eyes moved back and forth over Catherine's head, as she examined the room. "Perhaps you are unaware that the Savoy Theatre was the first public building to be illuminated entirely by electricity. Then it became a hotel, financed of course by the proceeds of the Gilbert and Sullivan operas."

"Yes, I would assume they had a large hand in the financing." Catherine heard the slight sarcasm in her own voice. Why was Nedra force feeding her the history of the hotel and the Savoy Theatre? Was she refusing to hear what was on Catherine's mind?

"It was the first hotel with electric elevators."

Catherine couldn't help smiling. Nedra's loquacious nervousness was becoming comic. "Well, Nedra, I must admit I wasn't aware of that particular fact."

"Perhaps we can ride them after breakfast. Would you like that, dearest Catherine?"

Catherine could manage only a nod before Nedra plowed on. "Oh, I so regret that you came to London a year too late."

"Oh, and why is that?"

"Had we been here last year, I could have introduced you to Mr. Ritz."

"Mr. Ritz?"

"Yes, dear César." At least Nedra now looked at Catherine. "He was the manager here. And such a charming man. Do you know he made the Savoy the place to be for many women of elevated society who formerly never allowed themselves to be seen dining in public? Sadly, he was dismissed by the owners for some ridiculous claim that he made several thousand pounds worth of wine and spirits disappear. In any event, Mr. Ritz will be opening his own hotel in Paris in the next several months. When it opens we must go. I will introduce you. You will adore him."

Suddenly, Nedra's face sagged from weariness. She had exhausted her knowledge of the Savoy and knew not what else to say.

"You seem tired, Nedra."

"Oh, forgive me. It's only that I've not yet had my breakfast."

"May I ask again how it is that you have been here previously in the past year or more—or long enough to remember Mr. Ritz?"

Catherine heard enough of Nedra's own history to find the matter intriguing. According to common belief, Nedra had escaped from a life of want in London's East End when she was sixteen, living for a year in France before returning to London, where she began acting at one of the now-defunct West End theatres. After a dozen years performing there, so the story went, she moved to The Acropolis. Nedra never spoke of her childhood experiences as far as Catherine was aware, nor had she ever admitted to her depressing place of origin. All anyone seemed to know was that Nedra's life had begun in France at age sixteen.

Catherine learned about Nedra's humble origins from Charles Donovan, during the theatre's recent Christmas party. As usual, Donovan had consumed too much of his favorite brandy and was sharing all forms of gossip and revelations to Catherine, his most polite though reluctant listener. She now regretted terminating the conversation when Donovan offered to reveal "more naughty secrets about our dear *Miss* Alexander."

"Well Catherine, if truth be told, I have always had my admirers. Not everyone falls at the feet of the lovely Miss Healy, you know."

Catherine simply looked away following the two-edged compliment. Nedra immediately grabbed her hand. "Oh, dearest Catherine, I didn't mean that the way it sounded. Forgive me. I've just not been myself these past few days. I'm still horrified by what happened several nights ago and still deeply depressed at the possibility that we may never again act at The Acropolis."

Forgiving the insult, Catherine squeezed Nedra's hand. "We will perform there again, and I believe it won't be much longer before we do. In point of fact, this evening I . . ." She caught herself a bit too late. It wouldn't do to let Nedra or anyone know that she would be meeting the First Lord of the Treasury for dinner. "This evening I'll be writing several letters to express all the good reasons why the theatre should reopen immediately."

"I wish you well in that endeavor, my dear. If anyone can convince the government to raise the curtain, it would be the lovely Miss Healy."

Nedra was oblivious to the fact that this attempt at a compliment was punctuated by the same phrase she had used as a mild insult moments earlier.

When breakfast arrived, Nedra attacked the eggs and bacon with the clumsy exuberance of a man, striking her fork too loudly against the plate. Wishing to change the subject, she halted her attack and put down her fork. "Catherine, what do you think of the 'New Woman' of our age?"

"I am utterly fascinated by her."

"Really? Then have you become one? Are you indulging in any of the political talk about voting rights for women?"

Catherine was grateful for Nedra's sudden teasing and wide-eyed, girlish manner.

"You forget that I'm Irish, and such matters as suffrage are serious issues for us. My father instilled in me the importance of being properly represented and having the right to be properly heard."

"Have you discussed your views of suffrage with Mr. Millard?"

Catherine knew Nedra was angling for some kind of admission as to the nature of the relationship. "Mr. Millard and I are fellow actors. We never speak of politics." Catherine enjoyed the expression of disappointment on Nedra's face. "But I'm certain Jamie shares my views of this matter."

"Do you really?" Nedra erupted into laughter.

Because Nedra's earlier pedantic manner had evaporated, Catherine decided now was the time. She opened her bag and pulled out the black felt belt discovered at the abandoned house on High Holborn. Upon seeing the item, Nedra's laughter was cut off as suddenly as if she were strangled.

"So is this yours?" Catherine placed the belt in Nedra's hands, with the inscription facing up so Nedra couldn't miss it.

Nedra closed her eyes after a brief glance. "Yes, it's mine."

Catherine allowed her a few moments to formulate her thoughts. Realizing she wasn't about to offer an explanation, Catherine continued. "What does the inscription say? The language seems to be Bulgarian or Romanian or of some place near there."

"That is correct. It is Bulgarian."

"Who gave this to you?"

Nedra attempted a smile. "Oh, just an admirer who saw me on the stage. Surely you have received your share of similar gifts. His name is unimportant."

Catherine had learned from her father the strategy and patience necessary for successful questioning of a hesitant witness. "Then can you at least tell me what the inscription says?" Catherine accepted the possibility that Nedra, by not inquiring where the belt had been found, knew exactly where it was discovered. Had she been at the house on High Holborn when Alfred Nichols was killed?

"I don't read Bulgarian, Catherine. I have no idea what it says."

"I see. But you know the language is Bulgarian. Please, let me see the inscription again."

"Here. You may keep this belt, as have no further use for it. It holds for me no sentimental value." Nedra placed the velvet belt back into Catherine's hands. "Perhaps you can find someone to translate the inscription for you."

Catherine regretted her ignorance of the tongue as she attempted to decipher the phrase sewn inside the belt on a separate piece of silver cloth. "*Кой обича роза ще издържат своите тръни.*"

~ # ~

Jamie stopped at his residence to change his overcoat for the hundred mile journey to Bristol. He agreed to his father's request to accompany him on the train in order to assist in an examination of a husband and wife shot to death the previous afternoon. The local coroners were unable to tell whether the bullet wounds were inflicted by a third party or by either the husband or the wife, and so the coroners invited the elder Millard to advise them on the matter. And since his father was petrified of train travel, Jamie had little choice but to accept the invitation.

Jamie also gave thought to Cate's odd reaction when he apologetically announced he would be with his father in Bristol for the entire day and most of the night. She actually seemed relieved by the news. Usually, she offered at least a playful protest whenever he needed to be away for several hours, and always expressed concern whenever he had to travel outside of London—or even to its East End. Perhaps she had now reached a point, as his wife, where she felt more comfortable and confident in their relationship. Yes, his darling Cate was legally his wife. Yet without the public admission of the marriage, it seemed almost a fantasy.

"Father, are you going to release your grip at any point between here and Bristol?"

"When the train arrives and comes to a complete stop, I shall do so."

Jamie shook his head at the sight of his father's right hand latched on to his left wrist.

"Have you always had this fear? I don't believe we've ever talked about it before."

"No, my boy. You might be surprised to learn that from the time I was a lad and all the way through my twenties I adored rail travel. And then in 1865 I happened to go to one of Mr. Dickens's public readings. He informed his audience that he had recently been on a train that came off the tracks on a bridge being repaired in Staplehurst, Kent. His was the only one of the seven first-class carriages that didn't plunge into the stream, but it was left dangling over the bridge like a wilted sock over a dresser's edge. Dickens showed his heroism in saving others in his carriage, but some fifty persons were unfortunately killed. His tale sent chills through every one of my internal organs, and from that time, I have avoided train travel whenever I could. You rascal, why are you laughing?"

Jamie waved his hand in front of his face. "It's not the account I find amusing—and I believe it happened the way you describe it. I'm simply diverted by the way you have related it. A 'wilted sock hanging over a dresser's edge'?"

"Well I suppose I could have come up with a better descriptive image than that one." Thomas couldn't help joining in the mirthful moment, which temporarily eased the anxiety he felt with every dire clatter of the train's wheels across the track.

Jamie thought it best to keep his father thinking of other matters. "To be completely serious for a moment, have you come up with any other thoughts on the killings at The Acropolis and the abandoned house on High Holborn?"

The elder Millard nodded affirmatively. "Yes, my boy, I have. Especially on the shooting of that Nichols fellow on the stairway of the empty house."

"But I think you got it perfectly right. He was up several of the stairs and was shot by someone standing on the floor below, therefore accounting for the upward angle of the shot."

"Yes, yes, I know all that. What I mean is that I've been thinking about *why* Nichols was standing there."

"Trying to escape the one who shot him, more than likely."

"Then we might expect the bullet to have entered at the rear of his head. But it was a frontal shot, and he was found on his back."

"Perhaps he turned around. The one with the gun might have called out for him to stop and turn around. Nichols did so and was shot."

"Still, why not shoot him in the back?"

"I don't know. Some kind of perverse code of honor on the part of the murderer?"

His father paused for a moment to consider that possibility. "I would think the murderer would have ordered Nichols down to the floor level and shot him there—that is, if 'honor' was in any way involved. No, I rather imagine Nichols had been upstairs and came walking down, not expecting anyone would be waiting for him. Or . . ."

"Or?"

"Or that he was there with the murderer but had no inkling that his life was in danger."

"I see. Perhaps we need to go back to the house on High Holborn and go up the stairs to the rooms above."

"Yes." Jamie saw his father's grip again tighten on his wrist. "If we can manage to survive the rest of the damned way to Bristol and then all the way back again."

Chapter 15

"And where is he now, Finch?"

"At the theatre, Inspector."

"In his office, I assume?"

"Forgive me. Mr. Jaynes is not at The Acropolis, but at The Royal Victoria Hall—or the Old Vic, as they like to call it."

"The theatre still managed by that woman Mrs. Pons?"

"It's Mrs. Cons, Inspector. My son and his wife go often. They informed me she is still in charge there."

"All right Finch. Thank you. And what of the German actor Schneider?"

"He has spent his time at two places. Lodging with friends—a husband and wife—on Craven Street and drinking with the husband at a pub off the Strand."

"Keep watch of him."

"And Mr. Jaynes as well?"

Exasperated, Phillpotts took a moment to respond. "Yes, Finch, Mr. Jaynes as well."

Phillpotts had allowed Schneider to go about his business, provided he remained in London for further questioning. Schneider's discomfort at the conditions imposed upon him informed Phillpotts that he knew more than he was revealing, but Phillpotts's instincts told him that the German wasn't the murderer of three men connected to The Acropolis. Yet was it really his instinct or simply his strong wish that someone else, and not Schneider, was responsible for the series of murders?

Phillpotts grabbed his hat and heavy winter's coat for the hansom cab ride to The Old Vic. He would confront Jaynes there and pose him with difficult questions while the acting manager was talking with the Cons woman. The recent events at The Acropolis had finally given the inspector the opportunity for revenge he had long hoped for. True, he was violating his office by seeking retribution, but Phillpotts also accepted the basic truth that in certain cases personal grievance took precedent over oaths and the codes of his occupation. Phillpotts had been told as much when he was a young detective, for his mentor at the Yard taught him that all a man had to do was find a way to exact his revenge in the line of duty.

As he buttoned his coat, Phillpotts looked at the items he, James Millard, and Catherine Healy discovered in the secret chamber at the end of the old costume and properties area at The Acropolis. Yes, the two actors. What else did they know about the murders and about any possible suspects? How much were they keeping from him? Given the identity of each of the actor's fathers, it wouldn't be simple charging them with unwarranted interference of a homicide investigation. Were his old mentor at the Yard still alive, he would suggest that his protégé find a more clever way to suppress Millard and Healy's curiosity.

~ # ~

It was late morning when Catherine exited the cab on Great Russell Street and made her way toward the intimidating British Museum. A clowder of stray cats magically appeared at her feet. The "feline plague," as Jamie's father called them, such homeless cats were, as one writer put it, "as common as blackberries in September," especially in the London slums. This gathering of toms and queens seemed out of place in front of the august British Museum, which stood slightly north of High Holborn and to the west of the abandoned house where the body of Alfred Nichols was discovered. Catherine had come to speak with Aydin Kormaz, a middle-age Turkish scholar working with the Egypt Exploration Fund, which the British Museum established in the early 1880s.

"No, I am afraid he cannot be disturbed at all today. He is too busy cataloguing. Please come again next week."

Catherine was face-to-face with the intrepid keeper of the gate, an Italian named Moretti, whom Catherine and Jamie had met in November when Kormaz invited them to examine some of the Egyptian treasures in the Museum's holdings. On that occasion, Moretti was reluctant to allow them passage inside, but gave way when Kormaz insisted. Catherine doubted the Italian ever remembered a face that didn't belong to the staff at the British Museum, for visitors were all the same to him—all nameless intruders.

"Dearest Miss Healy." The brightness in Kormaz's voice made Moretti wince. "And what do I owe the pleasure of your visit? Please don't tell me you are leaving London in the wake of the horrors of the other night."

"No, not at all, dearest Aydin." She found his first name so wonderfully apt, as he had told her it meant "enlightened" in Turkish. "We are all waiting for governmental permission to reopen the theatre and then we will resume entertaining wonderful patrons such as you."

"And to think I was there just one night before the killings. Oh, did you receive the little gift I sent as a condolence?"

"I'm sure it's waiting for me at the theatre. With all the confusion and police investigation, you know . . ."

"Well, it's only a trifle."

"I'm sure it's much more than that."

"You are too kind. It is Egyptian, I will say that much."

Kormaz was yet another of Catherine Healy's devoted male admirers, but whereas so many others lacked grace and acceptance of the proper distance required in such a relationship, Kormaz's infatuation never interfered with his charm or respect for her privacy.

"And what are you cataloging, Aydin?" Catherine smiled at Morelli, who remained impatient for her to leave. The man was as before stoically unsocial, the only Italian male she ever knew to whom romance would have been an imposition.

"I am cataloging part of the bequest left by our most distinguished antiquarian Augustus Franks, who unfortunately died last year. Over three thousand finger rings, porcelain of all kinds, jewelry and plate, and over thirty thousand bookplates. An immense gift. Simply immense."

"Yes." The pale sound of her reply told Kormaz she had another reason for visiting, other than discussing his current activities and the Museum's future plans."

"Dear Catherine, you seem preoccupied. Is there something I can assist you with?"

"Yes, Aydin, there is. Can you translate this inscription for me? She showed him the inside of Nedra's Alexander's belt.

"Ah, well it's not in my native language—but I suppose you knew that I am well versed in six other languages."

"Yes, I am aware."

"Where did you get this?"

"It was found at . . . outside an abandoned house."

"Near High Holborn?"

She dropped her eyes. "Yes."

"And may I assume that it might have something to do with the killing of your fellow actor there?"

It had not dawned on Catherine that Kormaz was aware of the shooting. "It might."

"All right, "*Кой обича роза ще издържат своите тръни.*" It is Bulgarian and literally says, "Who loves a rose will endure its thorns.""

Catherine's brow furrowed as she attempted to make a connection between the words and Nichols's death. She repeated the words "endure its thorns."

"But, wait. The meaning in English is something like 'If you care for or love something, you must embrace or at least accept its undesirable aspects.' Or to put it even more plainly, 'Everything good has its consequences.'"

Catherine removed a pencil and a folded piece of paper from her handbag and wrote down the translations. "Thank you, Aydin. Thank you so very much."

"Whatever I can do for you, dearest Catherine." Kormaz waited until she had turned and taken several steps before adding, "Tell me. Have you shown this belt to the police?"

~ # ~

"I'm so sorry you've had to wait, Henry. I hope you'll forgive me. Unscheduled theatre business, I'm afraid."

"It's quite all right, Emma. While waiting, I've learned quite a bit from your less-discreet employees about your plans for next season." Jaynes couldn't resist teasing her about the competition between The Acropolis and the Old Vic.

"And have they also informed you we'll be making a concerted effort at the end of this season to steal Miss Healy from your company?"

Jaynes looked into the inscrutable face of the formidable Emma Cons. She just might be serious about making an offer to his beautiful Irish actress. "Well, Emma, we'll just have to see about that."

Still vigorous nearing the age of sixty, Cons believed she had sized up the situation. "Henry, I would like to think you've come to tell me The Acropolis will soon be up and running again, but I fear such is not the case."

Jaynes offered a strained smile at her accurate assessment. There was no one in the business he respected more than Emma Cons.

She smiled knowingly. "Henry, have you come to ask for a reference?"

"What do you mean, Emma?"

"You of course should be appointed the new manager of The Acropolis. There is no one more qualified for the position."

"Actually, I've come to ask a favor not for myself, but for my theatre. I realize what I'm requesting will make no sense to you since we are competitors, but if you could see your way to make a case to the government to allow The Acropolis to reopen its doors immediately, I'd be eternally grateful. I'm just afraid that if too much time passes with the theatre remaining dark, then . . . well."

"Say no more, Henry. I will be more than happy to assist."

"Thank you, Emma. You are the most exceptional woman I have ever known."

Indeed, ten years earlier, she had become the first of her sex ever to serve as an alderman on the London County Council, which infuriated many of the men on the Council and many others who served in other areas of city governance. Jaynes had little doubt she would have a much better chance of effecting action than he ever could. "May I add that I would be most appreciative if you could as well endorse me as the next theatre manager of The Acropolis?"

"I'll tell you what, Henry. I'll do that on the condition that you release Miss Healy from her contract so that she may begin performing at the Old Vic before this season is over." Again her face gave him no hint as to how serious she was.

~ # ~

Phillpotts was bristling with agitation by the time he crossed the Thames on his way to Lambeth and the Old Vic. He had the great misfortune of drawing the most tentative cab driver in London to take him across the Thames to Waterloo Road. Instead of steering the light hansom around snarled traffic, the driver waited patiently for the blockage to clear. Phillpotts vainly exhausted his supply of profane encouragements for the man to take the cab around the impediment, but the old driver was likely as deaf as he was cautious.

But he made it to the Old Vic just in time, for coming down to the road ready to hale a cab was Henry Jaynes. Phillpotts signaled his driver to wait, and he walked briskly to where Jaynes was now standing.

"Going back across the Thames, Jaynes?"

Jaynes seemed both surprised and intimidated by Phillpotts's appearance. "Yes, as a matter of fact I am."

"Did you and Mrs. Cons have a pleasant chat?"

"It's Miss Cons, Inspector. She has never married." Jaynes didn't need to ask how Phillpotts had found him. He was certain the inspector was having him watched and followed.

"May I offer you a ride in my cab, Jaynes? I'm returning north of the Thames myself."

"Thank you no, Inspector. I'd much prefer to take my own—or perhaps I'll walk."

"Now I'm sure that walking all that way on a winter's day wouldn't be good for your health. It's a dangerous time of the year for a man of your years and of your relatively delicate constitution. Come. Let's ride back across the Thames together. We'll take you to wherever you were planning to go. And where exactly would that be?"

"I'll at least accept your advice and avoid walking in this weather, Inspector." Jaynes began to signal another hansom cab when he felt Phillpotts pull at his arm.

"Come, come, Jaynes. I insist you ride with me. Besides, whatever money you save now might be quite useful in the days ahead—especially if The Acropolis remains closed for any length of time."

Jaynes knew the man relished tormenting him in this fashion, but he also understood Phillpotts wouldn't allow him to travel on his own.

"Very well, Inspector. I'll ride with you."

"Good, good. Watch your step as you get in."

The men didn't speak for the first hundred yards of the return trip, although Phillpotts had turned toward Jaynes the entire time. Finally,

Jaynes broke the silence.

"Is there something about my person you find fascinating, Inspector?"

"I'm afraid I don't follow you, Jaynes."

"You are staring at me."

"Am I? Well, forgive me if I've unhinged you."

"I'm not unhinged. I've only been made uncomfortable by your staring."

"Tell me. Have you made a formal request to be named manager of The Acropolis?"

"No, Inspector. I have not."

"Then you aren't interested in the post?"

"I didn't say that. You asked if I had made a formal request—and I answered that I had not. I said nothing about my desire to be the new theatre manager."

"You want the position, then?"

"Yes, I would like to have it. Is that so illogical?"

"Not at all. So the tragic death of Morris Roberts-Smythe has worked in your favor, wouldn't you agree?"

"I see what you are about, Inspector. So let me again answer your most thinly-veiled real question. No, I did not murder Mr. Roberts-Smythe. Nor did I murder Mr. Donovan. Have you invited me to ride with you on the assumption that I would confess to crimes I did not commit?"

"On the contrary. I know you are far too clever of a man ever to do that."

Jaynes sighed. He could avoid the matter no longer. "Would it do any good for me to apologize for past transgressions—that is, as far as you personally are concerned? Would doing so satisfy you enough to leave me in peace?"

Phillpotts didn't answer until the cab began to cross the Waterloo Bridge. "Do you know that some fifty years ago, some poet called this "The Bridge of Sighs"?

Jaynes curled his fingers on the underside of the seat. "What are you getting at, Inspector?"

"Seems that the poet was immortalizing a female suicide at this spot.

And since that time, the Waterloo Bridge has been known as the place where women have come to end their miserable lives. Yes, right here where we are now. Here is where they ended their miserable lives. I have often thought—what made them want to do that? Have you ever asked yourself that same question, Jaynes?"

Chapter 16

"It's a pleasure to meet you. My name is Alice Pearcy."

Alice scrutinized the man who had just stepped inside the Pearcy home. Even though he wore a heavy coat, she easily detected his muscular form. His hands and fingers appeared powerful and scarred. Yet his ruggedly handsome features were softened by traces of sensitivity in his eyes.

"Is Catherine here?"

"I'm sorry, Mr. Healy, but she is out. Please do remove your coat. Can I get you tea?" She smiled conspiratorially. "Or something stronger?"

Healy smiled and shook his head. "No thank you. Is your father present?"

"Father is speaking with a gentleman in the next room, but they should be finished shortly. Please sit. Are you thirsty or hungry? Mary can bring you something, if you like."

"No. I'm fine." Healy looked about the attractive furnishings and seemed satisfied that his daughter was boarding with a respectable family. "I cannot stay, Miss Pearcy, but might you know where my daughter is at present?"

Alice had no idea. Catherine had been uncharacteristically secretive about where she was going, especially so late in the day. She only told Alice she had to meet someone about the immediate fate of The Acropolis. Alice didn't need to ask if this "someone" had any power to influence a quick reopening of the theatre, for a coach had been sent to collect Catherine, not a mere a hansom cab. Six persons could have fit into the vehicle, but from what Alice could see, her friend had the coach all to herself.

"She has gone to speak with someone about reopening The Acropolis, Mr. Healy. You did hear about the murders there, didn't you?"

He nodded. "Can you tell me the name of the person she has gone off to see?"

"I don't really know who it is, but I'm willing to wager that the person is very important in the government. I'm not sure when she'll return exactly, but you are welcome to stay here until she returns and . . ."

Alice saw the futility of finishing her invitation. Healy had already exited the front door. She looked out the window and saw him moving quickly toward the street.

~ # ~

"Welcome to the Charing Cross Hotel, Miss Healy." She took the man's hand and alighted from the coach. "I hope the journey through the streets was relatively uneventful."

"Oh, yes. There were even moments when it bordered on delightful. And you are?"

"David Isaacs. I am Lord Oxley's secretary. He has asked me to escort you inside. Have you been to the hotel previously?"

"I must say that I have not."

"Then it should be even more of a treat for you. We are in the very heart of the city here."

"Indeed." Catherine's expression suggested to Isaacs that she was immediately taken by the hotel's impressive façade.

"It's of the French Renaissance style."

"How old is the hotel?" Catherine wished to compare the Charing Cross with the Savoy."

"I believe it has passed forty years now, although it had been extended twenty years ago—in 1878. I know the year well, for my father was involved in designing the addition."

"How fascinating." Catherine shook her head, refusing to believe her morning and evening meals would be taken at two of the city's—if not the world's finest hotels.

"Let us go in, Miss Healy. Lord Oxley is waiting for you at table."

A few moments later, after a very rapid examination of the hotel's striking interior, Catherine and Isaacs approached the First Lord of the Treasury, who was standing by the table, speaking with the maître d'hôtel. After the introductions were concluded and Catherine was seated, Oxley took the chair to her left, rather than the one directly across from her.

"My dear Miss Healy, how incredibly charming you look this evening."

"Thank you, Lord Oxley." She didn't wish for the conversation to begin with any discussion of her. "May I say that I deeply appreciate your willingness to help The Acropolis at a time when—"

"Now, now, Miss Healy. Let us first enjoy a few pleasantries and our meal before we commence our business."

"Certainly, Lord Oxley." Catherine had no choice but to accede to his wishes.

The conversation began innocently enough, with mutual concern for the Queen's health.

"You weren't in country for last year's Diamond Jubilee, were you, Miss Healy?"

"No, Lord Oxley. I believe that took place in June and I arrived the following month. But it must have been something incredible to see."

"Oh, it was. So many mass displays of affection for Her Majesty. Sixty oak trees planted in the shape of the Victoria Cross—one for each year of her reign, which has now surpassed that of Edward III as the longest in our history. Would that you could have been here and have seen the glory of England on such spectacular display."

Catherine knew her father would have evaluated Oxley's concluding remark as a criticism of the Irish. She wished to believe such was not the case.

"Lord Oxley, I understand that Her Majesty remained in her carriage during the ceremonies."

Oxley frowned. "That is true."

"Lord Oxley, is something the matter?" Oxley's face had completely lost its handsomeness. He was obviously mulling over something unpleasant.

"You do know that there was an assassination attempt on the day of her Jubilee, don't you?"

"I had heard that there was, yes." Now, it was Catherine's turn to frown. She knew what Oxley would say next.

"By Irish nationalists, I regret to say." But there was no regret in Oxley's voice—merely contempt.

"If my presence here is discomforting to you, Lord Oxley, perhaps it would be best if I returned home."

123

Oxley's somber face registered surprise. "My dear Miss Healy, I . . ." His hand reached for hers, but he stopped before he touched it. Instead, he dropped both hands in his lap and slightly lowered his head like an offending schoolboy. "I must apologize to you for allowing my concern for politics to intrude on our evening together. Forgive my allusion to the Irish nationalists. In truth, during her reign Her Majesty has endured at least four other attempts on her life, as well as an assault on her person. In any event, it is not a subject we should be talking about this evening. Will you accept my solemn promise that I will henceforth keep all political matters far away from our table?"

Catherine responded favorably to his apologetic manner. She understood that any chance of Oxley's assisting the quick reopening of The Acropolis depended on pleasant communication between them.

"I will accept your assurances and the promise they imply, Lord Oxley. Thank you. As you know, tonight I would so like to discuss with you matters of considerable significance to me." Recalling from Oxley's letter that he wished to assist her career, she was immediately concerned that he would take the conversation in that direction. "What I mean is the matter of getting The Acropolis reopened very, very soon. We are all concerned that the recent and horrid events there will lead to such a long enough of a delay in the reopening that all of our livelihoods will be greatly jeopardized."

The waiter and *maître d'* interrupted, and Oxley attempted to impress her with his suave manner of ordering everything for the both of them. After the two men left, Oxley moved his right hand a mere two inches from where Catherine had hers resting on the table. "You know, Miss Healy . . . Wait. I believe we have known each other long enough, even surviving our first difficult moment together, for me to call you Catherine. Might I have that distinct privilege?"

Catherine quickly considered the several good reasons why she should demur and at least postpone granting his request, but her mission on behalf of The Acropolis wouldn't allow it. "If you wish."

"Good. Now, let me again tell you how your appearances on stage have won my appreciation and my admiration. And, if I may be so bold, how they have expanded my imagination. Hearing you deliver the speeches of the women you portray has inspired me to understand these women, to feel for them, even to cheer them on. I had never known that such a personal involvement with the words an actor speaks would ever have been possible. Thank you for opening my eyes, my mind, and yes even my heart with your incredible talents."

Her shoulders sagged. She wanted to discuss no other subject other than the situation at The Acropolis. "Lord Oxley, I cannot tell you how flattering your words are to me, but I have come to . . ." She stopped when she saw him looking over her right shoulder to the other side of the room. Did he see someone? Had he made a subtle nod of the head? She couldn't be sure.

"Dearest Catherine, forgive my interrupting, but it seems as though Mr. Isaacs is requiring my attention." Oxley waved him forward, rose, and took several steps to meet him some ten feet from the table. In a moment, the *maître d'* joined them in whispered conversation. Catherine saw Oxley frustrated by whatever it was Isaacs told him. Finally, the First Lord of the Treasury returned to the table, his face reflecting considerable disappointment.

"Dear Catherine, I had assured you that politics would be forbidden for the rest of this evening, but the Prime Minister has little concern for any promise I might make to such a lovely creature as you. Something has come up, and I must go. I am dreadfully sorry that we cannot take our meal together and especially that we cannot talk about the reopening of The Acropolis, but I swear to you we will meet two nights from now in order than we may discuss *only* that matter. I will send you a note regarding the place and time." Oxley managed a smile and a clipped laugh. "Perhaps we should meet in some place where they cannot find me. Dearest Catherine, I have dedicated my life to serving my Queen, but every so often I would like to defer that service so that I may do the bidding of the patient, intelligent, and beautiful empress of the London stage. Mr. Isaacs will see you to the coach. I am so truly sorry. Adieu." With that, Oxley hurried off toward the rear of the hotel, escorted by the *maître d'*.

As Isaacs helped her into the coach, Catherine recalled every word Oxley uttered right before he parted from her. His compliments were so effectively phrased that she distrusted them even more. She well understood the danger even in Oxley's jocular suggestion that they meet in some secretive place. But what mattered most was his claim to be anxious to do her "bidding," which could only mean that he was willing to use his position and his enormous political influence to reopen The Acropolis at once. Everything else he had uttered was secondary to the implied promise of those words. Catherine wished to smile with at least some satisfaction at the result of her abbreviated evening at the Charing Cross Hotel. She wanted to, but couldn't. Unfortunately, she would have to keep her husband unaware of whom she was with this evening and then, somehow, find a way to break free of Jamie's company two night's hence.

~ # ~

Oxley went upstairs and finished his meal alone in the room he had reserved for the evening. He toasted himself in the mirror with the champagne brought to him by the *maître d'*. One of the two bottles remained unopened.

The meeting with Miss Healy had gone perfectly. He had phrased his flattery cleverly enough to both please and to disarm her. And how well her face revealed her acceptance of all that nonsense about having his heart touched by her acting. He was particularly delighted by the way he had dangled the hope of reopening The Acropolis through his efforts.

Isaacs did his part perfectly, as did the *maître d'*. Oxley laughed thinking that the three of them were good enough to perform at The Acropolis or at The Lyceum. Even though tonight was too early to attempt a seduction of Catherine Healy, tonight was the vital first step in that seduction. Perhaps two evenings from now? If not, how long could he postpone his attempt? Yet there were ways to release the intense frustration of being denied her physical charms.

A soft knock came at the door. "Come in." Stepping inside the room was the young woman Oxley had seduced on the train while returning from Dublin. This girl would do for now.

Chapter 17

"It is a pleasure to know you both. Mr. Millard, I have attended many performances at The Acropolis and I recognized you immediately."

Nearing the end of their return journey by rail to London, an affable gentleman had made his way to James and Thomas Millard and begun a casual conversation. The elder Millard quickly offered a comparison of theatre "in his day" to the sadder state of dramatic affairs at present. Jamie was surprised to hear his father speak almost rhapsodically about the male stage performers during that time. When the gentleman questioned why he mentioned no actresses, Thomas ridiculed the very notion that women ought to be acting in public theatres at all.

"It was better during Shakespeare's time, when no woman was permitted to stand upon a public stage. These days, there is too much emphasis on the female actors. At least in my day, we barely tolerated the women players."

The gentleman disagreed, "Dear, sir, you cannot be serious. The annals of theatre history have paid much deserved respect to the great women players of earlier times. Have you never heard of the famous Sarah Siddons?"

"Before my time" was all the elder Millard offered in reply.

The gentleman politely continued his rebuttal. "And I must also take issue with your estimation that theatre was better at mid-century than it is now. It has *never* been more accomplished and exhilarating—in both the productions offered and in the performances of *both* the men and women actors, sir."

Thomas raised his eyebrow. "And how old are you, if I may inquire?"

"I am twenty-nine."

"Then you were born at the time when the theatre made its turn for the worst. That fact alone wins me the point."

Completely delighted by his father's curmudgeonly exchange with the poor man, Jamie still decided it had gone far enough. "Please excuse my father, sir. He's not an advocate of train travel, and as a way of diverting his mind from thoughts of railway disaster he chooses to indulge his contrarian nature." Jamie also knew that the comment about actresses was nothing more than a jab at his involvement with Cate. The sly smile on his father's face told him as much.

The gentleman seemed well satisfied by the explanation and took no insult from his skirmish with the elder Millard. "Well, we are now pulling in, so let me again tell you how much I have enjoyed your performances Mr. Millard."

"Thank you very much."

"And those of Miss Healy."

The elder Millard groaned.

"I do hope the theatre reopens shortly, for I have enjoyed productions at The Acropolis more than at any other venue. Still, the loss of your manager and Mr. Donovan will be felt."

"Indeed it shall."

"But I will personally feel the loss of Mr. Nichols more."

Jamie and his father exchanged looks. "Did you know Nichols, sir?"

"Yes. Very well, actually. What I have been able to gather from the newspapers, he was shot to death in an empty house. Is that what you have understood to be the case?"

Jamie stood and put his hand on his father's shoulder. "Yes, that is what happened."

The gentleman sighed wearily. "I could tell you something about Mr. Nichols beyond what the public knows, but what would it matter? In a fortnight, all will be forgotten. So please forgive me. Let me just say that it has been a pleasure meeting you both. I wish you a delightful evening." The man turned to exit the train. Jamie stepped toward him.

"Wait. Can you tell me what you were about to say about Alfred?"

"It would take a little time, and I'm afraid I haven't got it now. My wife is waiting impatiently for me on the platform. I have been away from her for almost a full week."

"I understand. But can I meet you somewhere in the next day or two?"

"Well, I'm not . . . What I mean is that I find it painful to speak of Mr. Nichols's death, but . . . . Now why is it you want to speak to me about him?"

Jamie saw that the man was both suspicious of his motives and very anxious to leave the train. "He was a friend and fellow actor, sir." Jamie didn't want to let the man know that he, Cate, and his father were doing their own unauthorized investigation of Nichols's murder.

The gentleman stared into Millard's eyes. "Forgive me, Mr. Millard. Of course. You were theatre colleagues. I suppose if I speak with anyone, it should be someone who cared for dear Alfred. Here. I can be at this location tomorrow evening from eight to nine." The man smiled. "My wife's mother is visiting at that time, and I'd rather be elsewhere than at home, if you get my meaning." The man gave Millard his card and quickly joined the flow of passengers leaving the train.

"What does the card say, my boy?"

"No name, father. Simply an address. On High Holborn."

~ # ~

Michael Healy entered the Charing Cross Hotel at 7:30 p.m. Being the chief inspector of the Dublin force had its advantages, even in London. Two visits were all it took to inform him that Lord Oxley had earlier gone to the hotel "for a meeting." Healy was almost certain that the First Lord of the Treasury planned to join Catherine there for dinner, at which time Oxley would begin a seduction in the guise of wishing to speak about his daughter's career and the fate of The Acropolis. Healy continued to chastise himself for not immediately informing Catherine by telegraph message—or even by the damned unreliable telephone contraption—of his discussion with Oxley in Dublin. But he had chosen to say nothing, owing to Catherine's insistence that she be allowed to take care of herself without his intrusion into her affairs, regardless of his motives. Yet what purpose would it serve to honor her request for independence if doing so put her in a precarious situation?

Having stayed at the Charing Cross the previous September, Healy knew his way around. He walked to the dining area in the hope of finding his daughter with Oxley. Seeing neither of them, he sought one of the hotel's staff. There would be no point speaking with the *maître d'*. Oxley would have already secured his services and his silence.

A young man passed him on the way to removing a dining party's salad forks and first-course wine glasses. When he returned, the Irish detective followed him toward the kitchen area.

"Excuse me, young man."

"Yes, sir?"

"As you can perhaps tell from my speech, I've come from Dublin for the purpose of delivering a letter to someone at this hotel. Perhaps you know her. She is the actress Catherine Healy."

The young man's face turned pink. "Oh, yes, I know her, sir. She's simply the most divine woman acting upon the stage."

Healy managed to keep his fatherly instincts in check. "Yes, yes. She's the one."

"Imagine my reaction tonight when I beheld her sitting there dining with Lord Oxley." The young man pointed to the empty table, which had been far enough separated from the others to insure at least a modicum of privacy.

"But she's not here any longer?"

"Well, I didn't see her leave, sir. I was in the kitchen when she did, for when I come out again, she wasn't here any longer."

"Well, I suppose that Lord Oxley left with her. If so, would you happen to know where they might have gone?"

"I have no idea where the lovely Miss Healy went off to. But Lord Oxley hasn't gone, sir. He's still here. That is, he's in one of the rooms in the hotel."

"Is that right? So he and Miss Healy parted company down here and he went up to his room—is that what you mean?"

"I suppose so, sir. Wait. Wait a second, sir." Not surprisingly, in his exuberance the young man had totally forgotten every lesson he had been taught regarding employee discretion. "I overheard from a conversation in the kitchen that Lord Oxley had two bottles of the highest quality champagne sent up to his room. It seems that he was going to entertain someone up there."

Healy was barely able to remain in his character. "So Lord Oxley is up in the hotel's finest room, then?"

"No, sir. That one's occupied by some important visitor from India or Ceylon—one of those places. His Lordship is in the room at the other end of the hall. I also heard that he wasn't happy about getting the second-best room."

"Thank you for your assistance. Here you go." Healy handed the boy a one-pound note.

"Oh, thank you, sir. Say, do you think his Lordship is entertaining Miss Healy up there? I do hope it's someone other than her."

"So do I, my boy. So do I."

Healy knew exactly where Oxley's room was located. He made his way to the floor as rapidly as possible without calling attention to himself, his anxiety increasing with every step. How had Oxley managed to lure Catherine to his room? Surely she wouldn't have gone willingly. England's First Lord of the Treasury had somehow incapacitated Catherine and had her brought up to the room. It could be nothing else. When he was ten paces from the door, Healy heard it opening. He froze in his tracks, spread his fingers, and then closed them into fists.

Out into the hallway stepped a young fair-haired woman of cherubic shape. Healy immediately peered upward, as if he was inspecting the wooden crown molding. As she passed him, Healy dropped his eyes and watched her awkwardly traverse the hall with her head bent and her right hand covering the side of her face. Healy thought her manner merely reflected the embarrassment for having been seen coming out of Oxley's room, where she had obviously been sent to satisfy his lust.

But by looking up when she first came out, Healy failed to see the angry red scrape marks on her face, caused by Oxley's forcefully pressing her face down on the carpet while he was having his way with her.

Chapter 18

Early the following morning, Oliver Pearcy sat in his office awaiting a visitor with whom he had met several times before. Previously, their meetings had always taken place at a more secretive hour, but the message Pearcy received late the previous evening insisted on a face-to-face communication as early the following day as possible.

While waiting, Pearcy sorted through some notes relating to his legal work in the autumn. One sheet, dating from the end of October, pertained to a complaint he had chosen not to pursue. He had been approached, he assumed, because of his daughter's friendship with Catherine Healy. But he decided to end his involvement before anything was done. He wanted nothing at all to do with the matter.

"Mr. Pearcy?"

Even though he had come to his office expressly for this meeting, Pearcy was nonetheless startled by the visitor's appearance.

"Please sit. Let's get this done as quickly as possible. It wouldn't do to have anyone see you here."

~ # ~

Jamie found troublesome the cab ride to the abandoned house on High Holborn, because his Cate seemed so preoccupied. After they stepped from the cab, he asked what was on her mind.

"It's . . . just that I'm concerned about how Inspector Phillpotts will take the news that we've been in possession of Nedra's belt all this time without informing him." That much was true, she rationalized. But her discomfort was primarily due to her inability to tell Jamie where she had been the previous evening and why she would have to be gone for a time tomorrow evening—or whenever it was that Oxley could next see her. To risk Jamie's disapproval, no matter how briefly, was something she couldn't abide. She still believed telling him about Oxley now would be worse—not for her but for The Acropolis. Were she to inform him and he to protest, she would forgo seeing Oxley, thereby destroying her best chance to effect a quick reopening of the theatre.

Jamie wrapped his arm around her shoulder and kissed her now frozen cheek. "I'll think of something to tell Phillpotts. Don't let it worry you."

"Tell me more about your time in Bristol. Did your father behave?"

"Better than I expected. But then everyone there deferred to his opinion on how the local shooting occurred. Even the head of the Bristol force acknowledged my father's opinion as the one he'd proceed on. My father is always congenial when everyone else sees things his way."

"Did he talk about me?"

"Not exactly—or directly, I should say."

"But . . ."

"No, no. He merely railed against the practice of allowing women to take their own parts on the public stage."

"He would really prefer young men and boys to act them as they do in the schools?"

"He only made the observation to stimulate a reaction from me."

"So Jamie, did you speak up for actresses—in particular the one now standing before you?"

"In a manner of speaking. The gentleman we were conversing with did it for me. And he paid you a very fine compliment as well."

"And what was this gentleman's name?"

"I am ashamed to say I don't know. I never asked. In any event, he seemed to be an acquaintance of Alfred Nichols and has agreed to see me later today. It's obvious this man knows something about Alfred that might have relevance to the crime."

Thomas Millard had finally arrived by hansom cab. Catherine stood with her hands on her arms folded in mock indignation. "So, Dr. Millard, I understand you believe women have no place on the public stage."

"You have the wrong Millard, my dear. That was my son's sentiment, not mine."

Jamie rolled his eyes and groaned, as Catherine laughed freely, feeling more confident that the elder Millard was ready to accept her as his daughter-in-law. But there was still her father. How soon would it be before word of her marriage reached him in Dublin? Regardless of his promise to her, she felt certain he had at least one man assigned to keeping an eye on her and an ear open for whatever might be said in London about her.

Catherine pointed to the door. "Well, gentlemen, shall we go in?"

Although it was mid-morning, the house was lacerated with shadows. With Millard and his father carrying lanterns, they entered and gave a cursory examination of the ground floor. All appeared the same as it did when they were there last.

Thomas placed his hand on his son's arm. "You and I will go upstairs. Catherine, please remain here. It may be too dangerous for you to climb up to the other rooms."

Had the elder Millard not been her-father-in-law, she would have simply thanked him for his concern and then mounted the stairs regardless. As it was, she saw an opportunity to enhance her standing with him while refusing to honor his request.

"If I promise to hold tightly to your arm, can I accompany you up the stairs?"

Thomas was unprepared to feel the softness of her body pressed against his arm. "You may indeed, my dear."

They navigated the staircase, being careful to avoid the area of dried blood from Nichols's head wound. The creaking of the top four steps would have been more disturbing at night of course, simply from the sound alone, but it was still dark enough to make Catherine grab both her husband and father-in-law for support. She feared that the entire staircase would collapse before they reached the next floor.

"Look in the room on the right, my boy, and I'll examine this one." Catherine released her husband and accompanied the elder Millard to the room on the left.

Thomas lifted the lantern and moved it about so that they could both see all of the empty room. "Nothing here, it seems."

Catherine politely asked for the lantern and bent down to the floor. "Can you see these? They are impressions of the furniture that had been once been in this room. A bed was positioned here." She pointed to the four depressions in the wooden floor.

The elder Millard helped her up and she examined the walls. Before she could finish, Jamie called out to them.

They entered the other room and observed a bare wooden table and two battered chairs, devoid of cushions, in the Queen Anne style.

"Did you find anything, Jamie?"

"Take a look at this." Jamie lowered his lantern to the edge of the table.

His father leaned so far forward that his nose ended up only inches from the table's edge. "Hmm. Blood."

"Belonging to Mr. Nichols, do you think?"

"Impossible, my boy."

"Why?"

Upon first viewing the blood, Cate lowered her lantern to the floor and bent over almost ninety degrees. Keeping that position, she moved slowly out of the room to the top of the staircase. "Your father's right, Jamie," she said from outside the room.

"Why do you say so, Cate?"

She stepped back into the room. "Because there aren't any blood drops leading out of this room to the staircase."

"I assume he wasn't shot here, but perhaps he received a gash or a cut and staunched it before moving down the stairs."

"I don't think so, Jamie."

"Why not, Cate?"

"Your father would have noted such a wound when he did his post-mortem examination."

Thomas slapped his son on the back. "That's an intelligent girl you have there, my boy. I saw nothing on the body that would account for that much blood being pooled on the table the way it is here."

Jamie grinned without embarrassment. "Very good, Cate. So, did the blood come from a wound on the murderer, then? Perhaps an altercation of some kind between Nichols and the man? Could Nichols have delivered a blow and then left the room, only to be shot out of anger?" Jamie immediately realized his possible error of deduction. "But that would have meant the killer either left the room ahead of Alfred or pushed his way past him to get to the bottom of the staircase before turning to shoot him."

"The former possibility seems more likely than the latter, my boy, yet still I don't think it happened that way."

Catherine came to Jamie's side and reached for his hand. "But there's a small problem with either of those possibilities being true, if you will indulge me."

Jamie loved his wife even more for her thoughtfulness and manner whenever she was forced to contradict him. Still, he offered the perfunctory "Of course we will indulge you. Go on, Cate."

"Alfred Nichols was hardly a man who would deliver a blow with his fists against another man. Even if he struck out in anger or in self-defense, I cannot imagine his having enough power behind the blow to cause such a gash." Before either man had a chance to consider other causes of the wound, Catherine challenged her own conclusion. "Yet one might argue that Alfred could have used a blunt instrument or a knife of some kind to strike a blow. Still I feel that—"

The elder Millard interrupted. "What's this?" He had begun searching the floor near the bottom of the wall and had discovered what was apparently a mauve handkerchief crumpled against the baseboard of the floor. It was apparently mauve, but the color had been mixed with the copious amount of dried blood on the fabric.

Jamie expressed his frustration. "We keep finding such things. Bloody handkerchiefs lying in the same place both here and in the secret chamber at The Acropolis."

"Do you think this belonged to Mr. Nichols, Dr. Millard?"

"Likely so, my dear. It goes well with what he was wearing when he was shot, and my examination of the body and the clothing revealed no handkerchief."

Subsequent inspection of the room turned up nothing else of value. Jamie remarked, "Regardless of who caused the wound, we can't ignore the possibility that two others were involved in Alfred's death. One might well have been up in this room talking with him, while the other waited on the floor below."

"I am inclined to think so, my son. And it might well have been that these two men had some kind of confrontation in this room, while Nichols was with them. One of those two men struck a blow, which opened up a wound on the other man—exactly where on his body I cannot be sure. The hand and wrist area probably—perhaps even the forehead. In any event, that man—the man who leveled the blow might well have left the room and walked down the stairs to the floor below. And then Nichols and the other man—in whatever order—headed down, and the one below shot Nichols. Damn it, James. It's even possible that given the darkness of the house Nichols might have been shot by mistake."

"It's possible, father—very possible. Cate, what do you . . ." Millard saw that his wife had moved toward the door. "Cate?"

She came back to him and grabbed his wrist. "Jamie, I heard someone come in downstairs."

They listened and in a moment heard the sound of footsteps starting up the staircase. Jamie pulled his wife and father to the far wall and stood defiantly in front of them. Having no weapon, he had little choice but to grab one of the worn Queen Anne chairs and wrench free one the legs. He was only able to crack the joint slightly when he heard the footsteps reach the top of the stairs.

The light from the intruder's lantern spilled into the room. After a slight delay, the man stepped into the doorway. Jamie felt Catherine brush past him.

"Cate!"

She sighed. "You nearly frightened us to death, Inspector."

Phillpotts held up the lantern and saw the three of them on the other side of the room. "Then I suppose I should have sent up my card before I mounted the stairs."

Chapter 19

"I will hand her this note as soon as she returns, Mr. Isaacs."

"Thank you, Miss Pearcy. And please give my regards to your father."

Alice seemed pleasantly surprised. "Oh, you know my father?"

Isaacs said nothing but kept his eyes locked on those of the attractive young woman standing before him.

"Do you, Mr. Isaacs?"

"I know more *of* him than know him, Miss Pearcy. But do say that I send my regards. Adieu."

Alice watched the young man until his carriage pulled away. She was disappointed he didn't look back and smile before he stepped inside the vehicle, because she found him quite handsome.

"What did Mr. Isaacs want, Alice?"

"He asked me to give this note to Catherine."

She had momentarily forgotten the presence of George Wooten—the young man who had been her companion at The Acropolis the night of the murders and who so wanted to please her and make her his wife. A fate no less dreadful than being maimed, she believed. All she had to do was say yes and she could be the bride of a mortuary assistant—that is, if she dared risk being disowned by her father and sent to live all alone on one of the remotest islands off the coast of Scotland.

"Well, what do you think is in the note?"

"I don't know, George. It's not for me to know."

"You're not at all a curious, then?"

Alice had to laugh at such a presumption. Her father once joked that he expected his daughter to end up buried in a cat's cemetery because of her rampant curiosity.

Wooten continued prodding her. "If it were in my hands, I know I'd take a peek at what has to be a letter from the First Lord of the Treasury."

"What do you mean?" Alice's eyes took on their habitual feline shape.

"That was Mr. Isaacs. He's Lord Oxley's secretary, don't you know that?"

Alice only knew that Isaacs was a messenger from someone in the government. She had no idea he was secretary to Oxley. She grimaced. Why hadn't she made more of an effort to get Isaacs to stay or to invite him to return at another time? Surely, he wasn't married. Her mind raced to the desired end of all possibilities. Yes, to be the wife of the secretary to the First Lord of the Treasury. Poor George looked even worse at this moment.

"Open it, Alice. Use steam. Or say you opened it by mistake but that you hadn't read a word before you realized it was for Miss Healy. Come on—do it. If it's an invitation of some kind from Lord Oxley to Miss Healy, might we then assume that he and she have—"

"I know what you are implying, Mr. Wooten, and you need to be aware that I don't like it."

"'Mr. Wooten' now, is it? I suppose I had best take my leave and give you ample opportunity to think about what you'd be giving up if you were foolish enough to reject me. I'll call on you again tomorrow or the next day."

"Or the day after that." Alice was staring at the sealed note.

"Fine, fine. Or the day after that."

After she closed the door behind him, she sat on the sofa with the letter still clutched in her hands. "Steam?"

~ # ~

Upon his return to The Acropolis, Henry Jaynes stood at the back of the house and frowned at the empty seats. He sickened at the thought that they might well be empty for weeks to come. His imagination brought to his ear the melodious and commanding voices of the players captivating an appreciative audience night after night. More and more patrons had begun to come to The Acropolis since the beginning of the new season, primarily to see the two newest additions to the company, Edward Ludmore and Catherine Healy, but then they found the rest of the actors worthy of their allegiance as well—including the gifted James Millard.

Jaynes was at least relieved to know that no one came to hear Charles Donovan, unless it was to take wagers on when the man would miss an entrance or drop a line—common occurrences over the past several months, when his backstage brandy became more his demanding muse. Nor did anyone make a special trip to The Acropolis to see the bit player Alfred Nichols. And surely no one came to get a glimpse of the omnipresent theatre manager Morris Roberts-Smythe. The deaths of these three men, therefore, could have no real effect on the growing numbers who were shifting their loyalties to The Acropolis. And now the theatre was closed, not to be reopened until Scotland Yard and the government deemed it cleansed enough to do so. Jaynes had sincerely believed that in the immediate wake of the killings the theatre would simply stage an evening of tribute for the slain men and then go about its business.

The acting manager stepped further into the house and closed his eyes, trying to think of what else he could do to influence those who held The Acropolis hostage. But again, he couldn't help visualizing the stage during a performance. He had stood where he was now standing, watching the play unfold and listening to the sighs, the laughter, the shouts, and even the sobbing of those in attendance. Curiously, he believed he could now hear the faint voice of Ned Ludmore. But the sound wasn't something he had imagined or recalled. Rather, the actor was sitting in one of the stage boxes, speaking to someone whom Jaynes couldn't identify owing to the position of Ludmore's body.

For a moment, Jaynes batted aside his feelings over Ludmore's desire to quit The Acropolis and strained to see the other person conversing in the box. The voice was feminine and familiar. It belonged to Nedra Alexander.

~ # ~

Apparently out of courtesy and possibly other chivalric promptings, Denham Phillpotts allowed Catherine Healy to leave the abandoned house on High Holborn after she showed him where she had found the black belt and had finally presented it to him. He was particularly interested in the inscription and asked Catherine if she knew what it meant. She feigned ignorance in response to that question and the subsequent one, "Do you have any idea to whom this article of clothing belongs?" She couldn't bring herself to implicate Nedra Alexander—not at this time.

Catherine assumed that someone at the Yard would easily translate the Bulgarian inscription, but she understood that she would be withholding evidence by not mentioning her recent conversation with Nedra. Catherine feared the woman was involved in something she perhaps didn't understand. It might well have had something to do with the shooting at this abandoned house, but perhaps not. Catherine had more to discover before sharing all that she knew.

Phillpotts's skeptical look made clear that he wasn't swayed by Catherine's declaration of ignorance. He generally held the view—as many did—that one cannot trust the word of an actor. Who better to disguise the truth than one who assumes the identities of so many characters? Still, Phillpotts gave no indication that he was going to scold her for keeping the belt so long after it was found, let alone to bring charges against her for doing so. But she expected Phillpotts to ask James and Thomas Millard about the inscription and the owner of the belt as soon as she left the house on High Holborn. How wise of her to keep these bits of information from her husband and father-in-law as well.

Jamie accompanied her down to the cab. "Are you going back to the Pearcy's now?"

"No, my darling. I need to stop at The Acropolis to pick up something that my friend Aydin Kormaz sent there for me."

"Another of the many with whom I have to compete. Alas."

"You have no one to compete with. They all compete with you—and they all fail by comparison."

"You are so very kind to say so. But I fear that someday someone will come along who can offer you more than you can possibly refuse. If not in appearance, then in possessions—or . . ." Jamie paused for the dramatic effect.

His tone was so overtly playful that no one could have taken him seriously, but still Catherine's face dropped. For a brief moment she was certain that he had found out about her previous or future meeting with Lord Oxley. She tried to rally with a broad though awkward smile.

"Cate? Did I say something wrong? I was only joking, you must know that."

"I know. But sometimes *any* thought of being apart from you saddens me terribly."

"Then be of good cheer. That will never happen."

As the hansom cab pulled away, Catherine pondered whether she should cancel the yet unscheduled meeting with Oxley. Soon a thought hit her. While at The Acropolis to retrieve Kormaz's gift, she would see if Henry Jaynes was on the premises and ask him if he had heard any firm news about the theatre's reopening. There was a chance, then, that the next meeting with Oxley would be completely unnecessary.

~ # ~

"The time? It's a minute past noon, Bernhard."

"I don't know what's wrong with me. I didn't awaken until 11:30."

"In this weather, it's often a miracle I wake up at all. Anyway, it's good to see you. You haven't been in here for days."

Sam Peele, the proprietor of the Crooked Staff pub in Chelsea, had taken an instant liking to Schneider the first time the bit player from The Acropolis patronized his establishment, some four months earlier.

Peele poured the German a dark ale. "Say, Bernhard, who was that actor fellow you came in here with last week? That older fellow with a taste for cheap brandy? It struck me because you always come in alone. I've never seen you here in the company of anyone else."

"Name was Donovan." Schneider downed half of his beer and began shuffling the glass between his hands.

"Was that it? Strange sort of gent, he was. Come in like he hated everything about his life. Then after a few drinks, old Mr. Donovan became the most congenial gentleman you'd ever wish to see. That is, until he said something that upset you mightily."

"Really? I don't remember."

Schneider finished the other half of his beer. Peele poured him another. "Yes, after a few brandies that broken-down bloke began spouting off facts about London, and you tried to quiet him down, but he wouldn't cease his jabbering."

"Is that so?"

"Indeed he wouldn't. I remember you stood up and grabbed this Donovan chap by his shirt right after he claimed there was probably ten thousand professional whores working in London alone and added that not all of them was walking the streets. We all heard that, but then he whispered something to you that none of us could hear, and you threatened to kill him if he didn't shut his mouth. You were in a prickly way that afternoon, Bernhard. What was it he said that set you off so?"

"None of your damned business." Schneider slammed his beer glass on the floor and pushed his way out of the Crooked Staff.

Peele looked to those standing about. "Jesus, assist me. What was that all about?"

One of Peele's workers began picking up the broken glass and blotting the spill on the floor. "Sam, don't you know that this Donovan fellow was one of the ones killed at The Acropolis the other night?"

"That old actor who was in here was one of the ones killed? Then the heavens cover my hide, I'm lucky the German didn't kill *me* just now for what I said."

~ # ~

"So you are in after all. How are you, Henry?"

Catherine's warm greeting was the very tonic Jaynes needed. "Catherine, do sit. I've just had a mind for some hot chocolate. Would you care for some?"

"I would adore some, Henry—yes, thank you."

Jaynes prepared her the drink in his Oriental porcelain chocolate pot, frothing it with his special whisk. "Here you are. This should chase away the chill."

"I have no doubt." She took a small sip. "It's so delicious. Nothing tastes more exquisite than hot chocolate on a cold January day."

"So, Catherine, what brings you to this empty place?"

"I had to collect something sent here for me, but I was hoping to see you and have you tell me that our reopening is nigh."

"I'm deeply sorry to disappoint you, dearest Catherine, but nothing has changed. I have spoken with Mr. Hawkins at the London City Council, but to no avail. I'm afraid that we need friends in higher places if we hope to affect any immediate action."

Catherine dropped her head and stared at her hands, which were now folded on her lap. "I see."

"You're not drinking, Catherine. Is the chocolate not to your liking?"

"Oh no, it's exquisite. I'm afraid that I'm just so disheartened by our situation here at The Acropolis." She lifted her hands from her lap and wrapped her fingers around the warm cup.

Jaynes sighed wearily. "You must feel as helpless as I do at this point."

She said nothing but lifted the chocolate to her mouth. Jaynes could see that her eyes were turned away from him.

"Catherine, from your manner I fear that you have come to tell me something rather serious."

"What? No, Henry. Nothing like that."

"It will utterly break my heart if you have decided to move to another house." Jaynes recalled the teasing words of Emma Cons at the Old Vic promising to steal Miss Healy from The Acropolis. "Please don't tell me that someone has approached you and promised to nurture your career more effectively than we could possibly do here."

She knew Jaynes was speaking only hypothetically, but guilt again made her wonder if he had heard of Lord Oxley's interest in her future. "Henry, no one has made me any such offer. I can't even think of leaving The Acropolis. Nor does my . . . fellow actor and gifted colleague James Millard." Once more, she had almost betrayed herself and said "my husband."

"It soothes me to hear you say so, dearest Catherine. But I still can't help fearing that if the theatre stays dark too much longer, you and Mr. Millard will renege on your assurances to me."

"Henry, I am going to . . ." She didn't complete her thought but only because she had firmly resolved to meet with Oxley again. It was the only unselfish thing to do.

"I understand why you couldn't finish what you were about the say, Catherine."

"No, it's not that, Henry, I promise you."

"And the damned thing is that I may not be long in this office even if The Acropolis reopens soon and if you and James remain in the company. The owners haven't made their decision on my fate and aren't likely to until all has been resolved."

"Henry, there is no one else who could take on the responsibilities of managing this theatre as well as you. You've been here a long time. The actors and crew both like and respect you. The owners wouldn't wish to alienate the entire company by bringing someone in from the outside—especially not now, after what has just happened."

Jaynes reached for her hand. She hesitated but placed it in his. "I can't tell you how much your support means to me. I will never forget your kindness today."

Catherine saw that his eyes were moistening. He slowly slipped her hand from his.

"And on top of all this, Inspector Phillpotts has it in his head that I was the one who—"

She slapped her open hand on the desk. "Oh that is ludicrous, Henry. I cannot imagine why he would ever think such a thing. The Inspector is such a difficult man to understand." In truth, Catherine found Phillpotts nothing short of intriguing in his behavioral contradictions and apparent flights of investigative fancy. "I have it in mind to speak to him about the way he is tormenting you, dear Henry."

"No, Catherine, please don't do that. I feel he would only make things worse for me if you complained to him directly. Can I ask you not to intercede in *this* matter?"

She smiled warmly. "But you would have no objection to my speaking to the owners about your being promoted to theatre manager, I suppose?"

"No objection whatsoever."

Catherine was gratified to hear the poor man finally laugh. "Henry, whatever I can do on your behalf, you know that I will."

"Thank you, dearest Catherine. Thank you ever so much."

Michael Healy walked past Oliver Pearcy's house, still debating whether he should see his daughter on this unscheduled stop in London. After he had made up his mind to come and warn her about Oxley's potentially sordid plans for her future, he sent a telegraph message to his widowed sister in Basingstoke, a town less than fifty miles southwest of London. He hadn't been with her in over two years, and she was anxious to come up to London to see Catherine, but she was afraid of the city and only felt comfortable traveling there if her brother accompanied her.

Healy decided. He wouldn't meet with his daughter now. He was still considerably agitated by the situation with Oxley and still unsure what Oxley might have said to Catherine during their dinner together. She would easily read his face and be able to discern that he was worried about her—which then might lead to frustration on her part and tension between them.

From a concealed location, Healy saw the hansom cab stop in front of the Pearcy's. His daughter emerged and went directly into the house, looking as radiant as she always did on a winter's day. He was so happy she was the kind of beautiful young woman who constantly glowed rather than periodically glittered. Yes, he would take the train to Basingstoke without seeing Catherine. Still, he would remain the rest of the day in London to find out exactly what the First Lord of the Treasury was up to.

~ # ~

"Tonight?"

"What did you say, Catherine?"

"Hmm? No, nothing, Alice." Catherine was visibly affected by the note from Oxley with its two apologies. One for the interrupted meal at the Charing Cross Hotel and the second for having to move up their meeting to this evening instead of tomorrow night.

> *The demands of my position in Her Majesty's government force*
> *me to test your patience and good will, Miss Healy. But I assume that*
> *a discussion about your theatre and your career is deemed important*
> *enough for you to forgive any breach of propriety this request might*
> *convey. I will have Mr. Isaacs collect you at 7:45 tonight. Alas, dinner*
> *cannot be in our plans for this evening, since I must return to my duties*
> *as soon as we are finished with our discussion. Therefore, we will be*
> *judicious in the use of our time together. I do hope that arrangement is*
> *satisfactory to you.*

Alice was grateful Catherine hadn't noticed that one third of the envelope's flap was unsealed. Her conscience had awakened in time to prevent any further effort to open the envelope. Alice couldn't believe she had allowed the annoying George Wooten to tempt her so easily.

"Is it from anyone I know, Catherine?"

"No. It's simply a matter of theatre business. Business I'm afraid I have to address tonight."

"Tonight?"

"Yes. I'm to see someone in the government about the reopening of The Acropolis."

"And who in the government might that be, if I may ask?"

"I'm not really sure. I can only hope that it will be someone who has enough influence to push matters along."

Catherine's lifeless response informed Alice that her friend was lying about the person she was going to see. "Will Jamie be going with you?" Alice flashed her cat eyes again.

"No. He has another appointment to keep at roughly the same time." Catherine was relieved that this was indeed true, for her husband was to meet the man on the train at 8:00 p.m. "Alice, I must ask that you say nothing to Jamie about my going out tonight."

"Oh, and why is that?"

Catherine wished to throttle her young friend. "Because I hope to surprise him if I come back with assurances that the theatre will reopen in a day or two. Besides that, I don't want him holding out too much hope that my mission will succeed. You have no idea how infuriating it is to get the government to act on even the simplest matter."

"Should I say anything specific to Jamie if he returns before you do?"

"No, just tell him you don't know exactly where I've gone, but that I told you I would be safe and would explain everything when I get back." In fact, Catherine was wagering she'd return before her husband. After all, Lord Oxley noted specifically that their meeting would be relatively brief. Regardless, she knew that when she returned she would be free to tell Jamie everything—a moment she was both pleasantly anticipating and utterly dreading. She feared her explanation would only incur her husband's disapproval and, worse, an emotional demonstration of it.

Chapter 20

"I should go now, my darling Cate. I wish to be at the address on High Holborn exactly at eight. The gentleman said he had one hour to spare, and I intend to find out all I can about Nichols in that time. If I find that the man hasn't much to tell, I'll return earlier."

"You must promise me you won't return alone to that dreadful house."

"You have my solemn promise."

Catherine smiled and kissed her husband fully on the lips—as she had never done before when they had parted for a short period of time. "And you are sure Inspector Phillpotts isn't planning on charging you and your father with obstructing the investigation?"

"Oh, so you assume you are in no danger of being charged?" Millard smiled and tenderly brushed her cheek with the back of his fingers.

"Never. He likes me too much. Can't you tell?"

"I most certainly *can* tell. Well, now I must head to my appointment with the well-dressed and congenial gentleman from the train."

"I expect to learn his name when I see you later this evening."

"It will be the first thing I'll ask him."

Less than fifteen minutes later, David Isaacs was leading Catherine to Lord Oxley's carriage. Catherine turned to find Alice standing at the front door wearing a look of surprise mixed with one of considerable disapproval. Catherine was uncertain whether her young friend was envious of the transportation or jealous of Catherine's being on the arm of the handsome young man who had escorted her down to the street. Catherine saw Oliver Pearcy pull his daughter back inside the house, but the attorney remained in the doorway watching the carriage pull away. Catherine assumed the identity of the man she was about to see was no longer a secret, because in his position as a prominent London attorney, Pearcy would certainly know whom Mr. Isaacs worked for.

~ # ~

Patrick Copsey stared at the ten pound note given him by a well-dressed gentleman an hour earlier. After Copsey initially expressed an unwillingness to deliver a message to Mr. James Millard at a location off High Holborn, the gentleman doubled the payment, repeating that he needed someone who knew Mr. Millard by sight and that the message contained important information Millard had requested. Copsey carefully examined the script on the outside of the envelope to satisfy himself it bore no resemblance to the odd handwriting on the note sending him off to The Lyceum and to High Holborn on the nights Morris-Smythe, Donovan, and Nichols were murdered. Still, he had vowed to deliver no more messages, given what had happened a few nights earlier.

But ten pounds was too much to turn down. Clare and the baby needed the money. The Acropolis might not reopen for weeks, and Copsey had already promised Clare he would take whatever miscellaneous tasks came his way, provided they paid him fairly. The man offering the money was at least well-dressed and refined in manner. Copsey concluded that the gentleman's scheduled meeting with Millard was legitimate.

But it was only after the gentleman had disappeared that Copsey wondered how the man knew where Copsey was staying and why he chose him to deliver the message. Perhaps he had already gone to Millard's lodging and found him away. Copsey grinned, thinking that Millard was usually elsewhere—most often in the company of the beautiful Catherine Healy. Feeling more relaxed and looking once again at the ten pound note, Copsey chose to ignore all further unanswered questions about the errand.

~ # ~

The weather had undergone considerable change during the late afternoon. The icy cold gave way to warmer conditions and the accompanying menace of fog. Catherine was amazed the driver could find his way through the streets. Perhaps he had become used to the conditions, but this was her first year living in London, and she couldn't imagine how anyone could traverse the city when it was like this.

Although it was worse in November, the intrusion of fog throughout December and now in January had lowered her spirits and heightened her anxiety and feeling of vulnerability. From what Jamie said, the fog could extend a full three miles from the center of the city. It was a creeping yellow pestilence affecting everyone in its path.

As the carriage struggled its way along, Catherine thought of other unpleasant colors at this time of the year. There was the black mist that dropped from the sky and swept horizontally along the streets—all from the coal fires that burned during these months. Nedra Alexander had warned her to avoid a white shawl when she ventured out at this time of year, because the soot would invariably turn it gray. If predictions held true, the more frequent use of motor cars would only make things worse in years to come. In contrast, the clear and cold, snow-fallen days of winter, such as those of the past week, were always so exhilarating. Catherine had often thought of traveling to the Scandinavian countries to experience even more days of such natural winter bliss.

The carriage came to a stop, and Catherine couldn't be sure if the driver had been blinded by the pernicious fog or if they had arrived at their destination. It was only at this moment she realized she had never asked where she was meeting Oxley. Did she simply assume they would return to the Charing Cross Hotel? Isaacs leaned toward her. "We've arrived, Miss Healy." These were the first words he had spoken to her since they departed from the Pearcy home. Isaacs exited the coach and extended his hand to help her out. She looked around but could see very little, given the conditions. The sound of horses' hooves and carriage wheels on the pavement and a distant cry of a street vendor comforted her only momentarily, for she had no idea where in the city she was.

"Be careful of your step, Miss Healy." Isaacs had taken her arm and was leading her up the steps to an unfamiliar residence, with all but one room completely dark.

~ # ~

After inspecting the grounds of the closed Acropolis theatre, Michael Healy met one of his London contacts at a public house on Chancery Lane, which ran north and south between Fleet Street and High Holborn. Healy bought his pub companion two pints, while he pumped the man for information regarding the recent activities of the First Lord of the Treasury. Healy's contact worked in the Prime Minister's office and was able to give a fairly full account of Oxley's social schedule, which included last night's dinner meeting at the Charing Cross Hotel and a planned "brief sojourn" of some kind this evening at his "hideaway house" on High Holborn. Having witnessed both his daughter's return to the Pearcy's and the embarrassed young woman's leaving Oxley's room at the Charing Cross Hotel, Healy was confident the Lord Treasurer's rendezvous for this night was either with that same young lady or with one of similar moral standing.

As the men started on their second pint, Healy heard the proprietor raise his voice to one of the men who had been sitting gloomily inside the pub before Healy had arrived.

"I told you five minutes ago what time it was. And five minutes before that, and five minutes before that. So stop asking me what time it is."

Healy's long experience informed him that some kind of physical confrontation was likely imminent. The pub master's face suggested that he was in his fifties, but it also bore marks of several previous violent altercations—forehead scars and a bent nose being the most obvious. The man demanding the time was at least twenty years younger and a good twenty pounds heavier than the proprietor. Even though he wore his heavy coat, it was evident that he was a powerful man. Healy slid his chair backward, ready to rise and intercede if a punch were thrown or a glass tossed. He knew he had no business getting involved in what wasn't all that uncommon in such establishments, but he couldn't help being what he was, regardless of where he was.

The younger man made his way to the counter behind which the proprietor stood. "I'll ask you once again. What is the exact time?"

Healy rose as the owner leaned forward, bringing his face to within a foot of the customer's. "And I'll tell you for the last time. It is presently four minutes to eight. Now I'm telling you for the first *and* the last time to take your business elsewhere. Go back to the East End, where you evidently come from."

The younger man smiled. "And a very good place to be from. I'll leave—just as soon as I finish my drink. I believe I've already paid you for it." The man downed the whisky, politely handed the empty glass to the proprietor, checked the pockets of his coat, and walked slowly toward the door, apparently testing his balance. Satisfied that he had control of his legs, the man pushed open the door and headed briskly up Chancery Lane.

"Where are you going, Michael?" Healy's companion was surprised by the Irishman's desire to leave so soon. "It's only a couple of minutes to eight."

"Joseph, I have a train to catch in the morning. I appreciate all you've told me. Here, have yourself another. This one's on me." Healy tossed a coin to the proprietor, who poured Joseph another pint.

As soon as Healy stepped outside, he checked the conditions and muttered, "May the devil choke on this infernal fog."

~ # ~

Millard held up the gentleman's card, making sure he had the address right. "It should be the next building on the left."

The cab driver was grateful they hadn't gone past the location in the dense yellow fog. "Shall I wait, sir?"

"I'm tempted to say yes, but it could be a full hour, so you'd better find another passenger. Here." Jamie paid the fare. "But if you're in this area at nine, then by all means drive by this spot."

"Not sure I could even see you, given the fog."

"Just call out 'Mr. Millard' and I'll shout back if I hear you."

"Very good, sir. But I can't be promising I'll return."

"Not a problem, my good man." Millard knew he could always walk west on High Holborn and find another hansom cab back to the Pearcy's.

The structure Jamie now contemplated was apparently an office of some kind, although there wasn't an identifying sign above the door or on the brick exterior. Peering into the window, he saw no one inside. He walked around to the eastern end of the building, which ran along an abbreviated side street. Looking into one of the side windows, he spotted a dim light coming from what was obviously a back room of some kind. Stepping further down the side street, Jamie discovered a narrow access lane at the rear of the building.

Jamie groped his way into the area through an even thicker pocket of fog and at once heard several quick footsteps behind him. "Hello? Hello?" He was about to turn back toward the side street when he felt a muscular forearm lock around his neck. Millard was healthy and strong, but he was helpless in the grip of someone far more powerful. He tried to pull the man's top hand free, but the assailant kept it wrapped tightly around the other wrist. Jamie managed to lift his legs and press them into the narrow brick wall at the back of the building. He bent his knees and shoved himself backward as forcefully as he could. Both he and the man slammed into the wall across the narrow access lane, but the man's death grip remained unbroken.

Millard suddenly lost the sense of the immense pressure around his neck, even as the assailant's forearm still pressed tightly against it. Jamie knew he was losing consciousness. His arms and legs became useless; his eyes dropped shut. He detected the odor of whisky on the man a moment before he lost consciousness. The last thing he heard was the sound of a violent thud the moment his body slipped to the ground.

Michael Healy stood over the assailant, holding a .22 caliber Open Top Pocket model revolver. He already had the pistol in his hand when he made the turn into the access area behind the building and clubbed Millard's assailant with it.

Healy left his friend Joseph at the pub because he sensed that the younger man who confronted the proprietor was up to no good—because those who constantly ask the time often have an appointment with mischief. And Healy was used to following his hunches. After finding the younger man walking north on Chancery Lane, Healy watched him cross the street and pause on the other side. Although the fog impeded his vision, Healy thought the man was looking for an address and making sure of his directions. After the man turned left off High Holborn, Healy closed the distance between them. Soon the younger man disappeared into a bank of denser fog. It was only the sound of a struggle behind the building in the narrow access lane that brought Healy to where James Millard was being assaulted.

"Stay right down where you are, young man." The assailant rubbed the back of his head as he struggled to his feet. Healy placed his finger on the trigger of his pistol.

"You busted open my head, you bastard." The man shoved his left hand inside his coat pocket and withdrew an ugly looking knife. He took a menacing step forward. "I'll cut your miserable throat, you—" The threat was abruptly terminated by a bullet from Healy's pistol. The assailant fell dead across Millard's feet.

Healy checked Millard and found him unconscious but alive. Deciding to remain with the victim until he regained consciousness, Healy wondered if the sound of the pistol's report would soon bring others to the scene. He didn't have to wait long for an answer.

~ # ~

"Miss Healy, please excuse my delay. I trust Mr. Isaacs has tended to your needs. I see he has made you tea. Good, good." Catherine thought the First Lord of the Treasury looked highly embarrassed for his tardiness. "Mr. Isaacs, will you excuse us? Miss Healy and I have but a little time together this evening, and we do need to discuss her career."

Isaacs nodded and left through the front door of what appeared to be a small but attractive residence. Catherine assumed Isaacs would wait down by the carriage. Much to her dismay, she looked but saw and heard no evidence that anyone else was in the house with them. "Lord Oxley, before we discuss my career, I do so wish to talk about—"

"About the reopening of The Acropolis—yes, yes, of course." Oxley poured more tea. Catherine was cautiously grateful and pleased by Oxley's respect for her wishes.

"To move directly to the matter, Lord Oxley, is there anything you can do to convince the government and the city to permit a quick reopening of our theatre? Your assistance would be so very much appreciated—by the actors, by the stage hands, by Mr. Jaynes our acting manager, and most certainly by our patrons."

"Of which I am one."

She greeted his seeming exuberance with a resigned smile. "Yes, you most assuredly are our most important patron."

"Please know that I am at your service, my dear Catherine. I have no greater desire than to assist you and your theatre, especially at this most difficult time in its short history. So tell me, how would you evaluate the way you have been presented to the London public?"

"I'm sorry, Lord Oxley, I don't understand."

"I mean, do you feel as though your performances have received the proper amount of advertising—in the papers, on the playbills, in preview articles?"

"I am most satisfied with the advertising. In fact, I am often embarrassed by it because I feel other members of the company deserve more attention than they receive."

"Mr. Ludmore, for example?"

Catherine weighed her words carefully. "Mr. Ludmore may well agree with you that he hasn't received all the attention he might deserve. But Mr. Morris-Smythe thought very highly of him and had been thinking of more creative ways to publicize Ned's impressive talent."

"But Mr. Morris-Smythe is now dead."

Oxley's reply gave Catherine an opening. "Indeed, and it is a tragedy. But I know Henry Jaynes, should he be named the new manager of The Acropolis, would do very well by Mr. Ludmore and nurture his career to Ned's satisfaction."

"And would Mr. Jaynes nurture yours similarly, dearest Catherine?"

"I'm sure he would. We have a splendid relationship. I cannot imagine his ever allowing his estimation of my contributions to fall into indifference."

"You may be correct, dearest one, but from what I know of the man, he seems too passive and tepid by nature to do the best for his star actress."

Catherine was troubled not only by Oxley's returning the discussion to her specifically but also by his free usage of endearing terms such as "my dearest Catherine" and "dearest one."

"Please Lord Oxley, I feel somewhat uncomfortable talking about myself. Can we speak only of—"

Again he interrupted. "But why would you feel uncomfortable, dearest Catherine? You cannot convince me that you are oblivious to your beauty and theatrical gifts. Had you been so, I greatly doubt you would have left Dublin to come and perform in our city." Oxley laughed. "Of course escaping from Dublin would . . ." He caught himself, thereby preventing the full force of the insult from affecting his lovely guest. "Forgive me. I'm getting off the point."

"Yes, Lord Oxley, you certainly are." Catherine couldn't believe her effrontery. And yet she felt better for having chided him.

"And once more I must rely on your forgiveness." He waited for her response, but she merely nodded ambiguously. "Allow me to ask one more question about you before we talk about The Acropolis."

She had no choice but to accede. "If you wish, Lord Oxley."

"Regardless of who becomes the permanent manager of your theatre—whether it is Mr. Jaynes or someone else—no one can more effectively nurture your career than I. I will see to it that you play only the leading roles you most desire to act. That you are paid more than any other leading actress in the West End. And that you will come to no harm while you are in my care."

"Harm, Lord Oxley?"

He paused. "Yes, harm from a disturbed patron who might become obsessed by your charms or from any deranged woman who might be envious of your fame or resentful of the effect you have on the man to whom she has devoted herself."

Catherine was dismayed by the specificity of his explanation. "Lord Oxley, you are making me *most* uncomfortable. Please don't speak of such things."

"Need I remind you that three members of your company have been murdered? There is no way to know at present if others at The Acropolis might also be targets of whoever committed those crimes. I can see to it that you are protected. No one else can do this for you. But I can and I will."

"Do you mean that you would have me followed and watched wherever I happened to go, Lord Oxley?" Catherine feared what Oxley might say next.

"To have you watched and followed would be unsavory as well as cumbersome. There is a better way."

Catherine heard nothing but the cracking of wood in the attractive fireplace. The rest of her sensations were completely numb.

"Lord Oxley, where are we?"

"What?" He was evidently taken aback by her question. "We are in a small pleasant house in the city, where I often come to get away from my governmental responsibilities."

"And you would wish to keep me here, so that I would be safe from the harm caused by disturbed theatre patrons, jealous women, and diabolical murderers?"

Oxley paused, unsure how to characterize the ambiguous tone that accompanied her question. "To be most truthful—in part, yes. You would stay here and live both safely and luxuriantly. You would want for

156

nothing. Your career would continue as before, but with the guarantees I promised you a moment ago. There would be *no* restriction on your having guests or on your traveling to Ireland to see your father. Of course in that event, I would insist that you be escorted—for reasons of your personal safety."

"You said 'in part' just now, Lord Oxley. May I know what you intend the other part to be?" She looked around the room and examined the portraits on the walls. She refused to look at him.

"Dearest Catherine, I believe I have made no secret of my admiration for you. That you are sitting here at this moment is irrefutable evidence that you have judged my attentions favorably."

"I think you have been mistaken in your assumptions, Lord Oxley."

Oxley's smile dropped. "Have I been mistaken in your desire to have The Acropolis reopen at once?" She moved her gaze to the dancing flames in the fireplace. They seemed to be mocking her predicament.

Oxley stood. "Shall I ask that again, Miss Healy?"

Although she was sitting alone with Oxley in one of his lodgings at some undisclosed location, she couldn't help feeling somewhat relieved by his flash of anger and now apparent refusal to call her "dear Catherine."

"I don't believe that you care a pin's fee about The Acropolis, Lord Oxley." She rose from her seat and stepped away from where they had been sitting. "Now please have your carriage take me back to Mr. Pearcy's home." She was also comforted by having made the request forcefully without any indication of her growing anxiety and fear, as her father had often advised. He had taught her to "Stand in the middle and turn your mind a full clock's circumference so that you don't miss anything." Now she literally turned in a circle and evaluated the entire room, looking for a way to escape or, if that was impossible, for a weapon of some kind to strike a blow should Oxley attempt to grab or harm her. But he was now placed between her and her handbag, in which she always kept a small single-shot Remington Derringer pistol her father provided her before she left Dublin.

"You really wish to leave without discussing the theatre's reopening? In spite of your cynicism, Catherine, I am most willing to see to it that you will be acting again in two days."

"Provided I . . .?"

"Provided you allow me to show you how devoted a patron I can be. Discard that mask of aloofness and propriety, my lovely Catherine. I can make your life all the sweeter in so many ways. I only ask you to make mine sweeter in but one way."

"I will leave even if you don't call the carriage." She gave Oxley a mere second to respond. He merely smiled. "Excuse me, then. I will take my handbag and depart."

Catherine attempted to cross in front of Oxley to retrieve her handbag. But as soon as she stepped past him, she felt his hand gently close around her wrist.

Chapter 21

"Healy? What in the blazes are you doing in London?" Phillpotts raised his lantern in the curdled fog, providing an eerie illumination of the access lane. He noted the pistol in Healy's hand.

"Biding the time on my way to Basingstoke, Inspector. But it seems I have also been saving a man's life . . . while unfortunately taking another in the process." The two men stared at each other as they had done once or twice previously, when each was ascending the ranks.

"And I suppose I don't need to remind you that this isn't Dublin. We do things differently here."

"Then you let innocent men die in London, Inspector?"

Phillpotts ignored the insult. "Just tell me why you happened to be behind this building."

Healy informed Phillpotts of his movements since leaving the public house and of his suspicions regarding the man lying dead on the ground. "You recognize him, Inspector?"

"Looks like one of the many East End toughs who frequently make their way to this section of London for a little amusement and mayhem. And what about this fellow here?" Phillpotts lowered the lantern to get a look at the man's face.

"The victim of the assault. Don't know who he is."

"Good Christ. James Millard."

"Who did you say, Phillpotts? Millard? The actor Millard?" Healy knew the name from his daughter but hadn't met the man when he visited The Acropolis early the previous autumn.

"Yes, the actor Millard. Here, give me a hand." Jamie began to come to as Phillpotts and Healy lifted him into a sitting position. Soon he was able to speak.

"What happened? I only remember . . . an arm around my throat."

Phillpotts looked at Healy for the explanation.

"He had you around the neck, pressing his forearm into the artery here." Healy touched the area on the right side Millard's neck. "Enough pressure here will cause a man to lose consciousness, owing to the interruption of blood flow to the brain." Healy sighed at the realization that the assailant might not have been attempting to strangle his victim—only to incapacitate him.

Jamie rubbed his neck and struggled to his feet. "I assume then that you came to my rescue?" Healy nodded. "I am deeply grateful for your assistance, sir." Millard blinked his eyes several times as he began to regain all of his faculties. "Inspector Phillpotts? What are you doing here?"

"An anonymous note, Millard. Another of those damned anonymous notes told me to come to this address because someone else from The Acropolis was about to be murdered—by someone else from the theatre. How curious that I immediately thought of you."

"As the intended victim of the murder or the murderer himself, Inspector?"

"I'll leave you to wonder."

"Well, as it turned out, I was the intended victim. Now who was supposed to have murdered me?"

"Finch!"

Phillpott's associate stepped around the corner of the narrow lane from the side street. In one hand he held a lantern. In the other he held the wrist of a young man whose hands were locked in cuffs.

Jamie saw the young man's face appearing out of the clotted mist. "Patrick!"

Copsey's face mushroomed with surprise and hope. "Mr. Millard, what are you doing here? Please tell them I didn't come here to kill you or anyone." Healy found the near farcical nature of the scene too amusing to suppress his chuckle.

"Wait. What's that in your hand?" Phillpotts had noticed that Healy had bent down and pulled something from inside the clothing of the dead man.

"A pistol, Inspector. It seems that the man had two weapons on him— a knife and a firearm. Perhaps it's good fortune for me that he reached for his knife when he started to come at me."

For the next ten minutes, Phillpotts and Healy examined the area but found nothing unusual. Finally they left further examination to the coroner and the two investigators just arriving from the Yard. Phillpotts instructed them to take the body to Dr. Thomas Millard for examination. Phillpotts would have no one else do it. "I don't care if the old man has gone early to bed, Finch. Just have the body taken to him. This could be the same man who killed Roberts-Smythe and the actor Donovan."

His memory now unclouded, Millard told Phillpotts and Healy about the gentleman on the train and the invitation to meet him at this address. Phillpotts barely paid attention as he insisted that Copsey remain in handcuffs for the time being.

As they walked on, Healy whispered to Millard. "That lad couldn't stir himself to squash a bug, to say nothing of killing a man. But that stubborn Inspector Pisspotts just can't bring himself to admit that all isn't what he'd hoped it to be."

Millard appreciated the wit expressed by the man who may have saved his life. "Damn it, sir. I just realized that I don't even know your name."

"The name's Healy, Mr. Millard. Michael Healy from Dublin. Since you're an actor at The Acropolis, you must know my daughter Catherine."

~ # ~

"Believe me, Edward, I didn't have any idea you knew about that secret room."

"Oh, I knew about it, Nedra. But I'm shocked to learn you knew about it as well. I wouldn't have thought . . ."

"What? What do you mean?"

Nedra Alexander and Edward Ludmore stood before the door leading to the small room at the back of the old furniture and properties storage area at The Acropolis. Although it was now past 9:00 p.m., Ludmore had once more gained entrance by explaining to the two policemen that they were going in to collect personal items and several copies of bound plays for study.

Ludmore relished the advantage he had over Nedra. "If you want me to keep what I know from the rest of the company—and the police—then remind me who designed this secret area. Why Roberts-Smythe told you about it, I can't guess, but perhaps you and he were—"

"No, no. Stop, stop! I'll tell you, but I want to hear you promise me again that you will never expose me. Not to anyone."

"Just make sure to send me the envelope with what I require."

"And you will send one back to me, as you promised?"

"We have agreed that I would."

Nedra's couldn't suppress her emotions. "But I want to hear you one more time swear to me that you won't speak of what you know—not to anyone."

"Don't snivel, Nedra. It doesn't become you." Ludmore's face and manner reflected his insufferable arrogance. She hated herself for ever finding those traits appealing.

"Just renew your vow to me. I have to be protected."

"Don't presume to impose conditions upon me, Nedra. You forget what I know—and have seen—and possess. Just tell me who constructed all of this."

"You are no gentleman, Edward Ludmore." She attempted to daub the tears running down her face, but Ludmore pulled her hands apart and squeezed her wrists until she began to lose her balance. "Damn you, Nedra. I asked you what his name was."

"You're hurting me. Please stop. All right, all right. "The builder's name is Isaacs. Edmund Isaacs."

~ # ~

"And just where did she go, Alice?" Millard had returned to the Pearcy home.

"I really don't know, Jamie. Would you like something warm to drink?"

"Then how long has she been gone?"

"I think some two hours or so. She should be back any time now—I'm sure."

Millard could see from her face and manner that she wasn't at all sure. Alice had overheard several bold tales of Lord Oxley's kept women and illegitimate children scattered throughout city and throughout the British Isles. But beyond such exaggerated gossip, Alice was certain that the First Lord of the Treasury was a seducer, and it only made sense therefore that he would make an attempt on the lovely actress Catherine

Healy.

"Jamie, she went to see someone in the government about the reopening of The Acropolis."

"At this time of night?"

"It seemed to be the only time they could meet, and Catherine was most anxious to settle the matter as soon as possible."

Millard momentarily relaxed hearing Alice's plausible explanation—until he remembered what had happened to him behind the building on High Holborn.

"Why are you rubbing your neck, Jamie? Have you injured yourself?"

"It's nothing. I'm fine, Alice." He could see that she was looking over every inch of him.

"And how did your clothing get so filthy? You look almost ghastly."

"Let's just say that I was assisting Inspector Phillpotts in an arrest."

"And you were hurt in the attempt? And did the man who did this to you harm anyone else? Did he resist arrest by the Inspector?"

Jamie was taken aback by the rapid firing of her questions. "No. All was quickly taken care of." He thought it best to keep her unaware of the man's fate. "Alice, did anyone come here looking for Cate?" Millard wished first to know if her father had made an earlier appearance at the Pearcy's. And he was still incredulous over having met Healy under such violent circumstances. But Millard was keen to learn if the gentleman on the train had come to the Pearcy's and spoken to Cate or asked Alice about Cate's whereabouts.

"Someone came, but only to pick her up and take her to . . ." Alice's shoulders slumped as she brought the back of her right hand to her mouth in the familiar attitude of one who has let the cat out of the bag.

"What do you mean, Alice?"

"Oh, dear. She should have returned by now, so I must tell you. Mr. Isaacs came to the door and escorted Catherine down to the carriage."

"Mr. Isaacs? Do you mean the architect and builder Isaacs?"

"I don't think so. He works for Lord Oxley—as his secretary."

"That's the architect's son. Are you telling me that Cate was to meet Lord Oxley tonight?"

"I'm sure I'm not supposed to tell you, but yes, she was to meet Lord Oxley. But only about the reopening of The Acropolis."

Jamie would have laughed at Alice's remark had Cate made it home before him on this miserable fog-laden night. "I have no doubt she was to meet him *only* about the reopening of the theatre, Alice." Yet Jamie knew from others that the First Lord of the Treasury had vowed to use his influence to remove Michael Healy from his post as chief Inspector of the Dublin force—on the grounds that Healy once and perhaps still belonged to an Irish independence group bent on violence against the British government. Millard feared his wife had found out about Oxley's possible designs against her father and decided to speak with the First Lord of the Treasury about that as well as the reopening of The Acropolis. And there was also the matter of Oxley's reputation with younger women.

"Do you know where she was to meet Oxley? And how do you know she was to meet with him, again?"

"She wouldn't tell me whom she was to see or where she was to see him, but my father said that Mr. Isaacs worked for Lord Oxley, and so she must have gone to meet him—somewhere. Now I'm frightened for her, Jamie."

~ # ~

Catherine couldn't stop trembling. From the moment Oxley placed his hand around her wrist to prevent her from gathering her handbag, she had resisted giving in to her fears. But now she felt overcome by all that had happened since she arrived at Oxley's private residence. She was presently in a place where her vision was severely limited. She felt almost as if she were blind. Although a warmer night than the ones previous, a chill nevertheless permeated her body, exacerbated by the shivering caused by her emotional distress. How could she ever have believed Oxley would respect her wish to speak only of The Acropolis and its company? Why had she briefly suppressed the judgment her father had so carefully inculcated in her? At the very least she should have told her husband of the planned meetings with the First Lord of the Treasury.

She could hear voices, although she couldn't see any of those who shouted various epithets in the near distance. Yet it was the fresh memory of Oxley's words as she was attempting to leave that spoke the loudest.

"Come, come. Where are you going, my dear?"

"Lord Oxley, I am trying to retrieve my bag. As I have already stated, I wish to leave. I trust you are gentleman enough to let me pass and to call your carriage."

"May we not speak further, dearest Catherine?"

"And I must insist that you refrain from calling me by that designation ever again."

"You don't mean that."

"I do mean that. Please let me pass." She stared down at his hand, still clasped about her wrist.

He uncurled his fingers but kept the palm of his hand pressed against her skin. "I apologize for any insult I have unintentionally paid you tonight."

"I wish to go, Lord Oxley." She softly moved her arm and freed herself from his touch.

"Can we not sit back down so that we may speak of what most concerns you?"

"I believe I have just now spoken of what most concerns me."

Oxley positioned himself to prevent the retrieval of her bag. He didn't reply to Catherine's rejection of his advances, but his manner made clear that he had certainly felt it. He shook his head and sighed. "You have forced me to speak frankly and bluntly. You must have gathered from my two notes and from our meeting last night that I am most enamored of you. That you have encouraged these feelings from me, you cannot doubt."

"Encouraged them? That is utterly a false supposition, and you are surely aware that it is so."

Oxley lifted his hand and waved away her protest. "Your defiance and impertinence aside, I will forget all of this and allow you to leave."

"But I will not forget it, sir. Allowing me to leave is the very least you should do after your rude behavior to me."

"I trust that you will reconsider your decision on my offer after two days' time. I will trust that you will agree to see me again to discuss the fate of The Acropolis, if nothing else. I wish our next meeting could be sooner but I will be forced to delay having again the pleasure of your company, owing to the Queen's business."

"And do you think that *this* is the Queen's business, Lord Oxley? I can assure you here and now that I will *not* meet you two evenings hence—or two months hence—or at any time hence. I am left only to lament for the

rest of my life that I agreed to meet with you last night and tonight—
under the most blatant of false pretences."

"On the contrary, my dearest one. You were well aware of what I
would expect from you for the promise of assisting you in your career."

"I wanted you to assist The Acropolis—and only The Acropolis."

Oxley stepped toward the side table and poured himself a brandy.
Catherine picked up her bag and took several steps to the door before he
continued. "Another man in my position would demand that you comply
with his wishes or risk seeing the end of your stay on the London stage.
How sad it would be to see you limp home to Dublin and ply your trade
there for the rest of your career. Of course, I am not such a man." The wry
smile on his lips as he lifted the brandy glass to his lips convinced her
otherwise. "I will call the carriage now, Miss Healy."

Oxley had taken several steps toward the front door before she was
able to speak. She realized she could have quietly left the lodging and
lamented her misfortune during the carriage ride back to the Pearcy's.
But she recalled one more special lesson her father had taught her so
many years ago, when she was being tormented by several older girls
near her home in Dublin. She would have the last word, and not even a
man of such standing and power as Oxley could stop her from having it.

"You may do your worst, Lord Oxley, but I can assure you that I will
have one final performance in London before I return home to Ireland. It
may not be at The Acropolis, but it will be at another major house in the
West End. And in the middle of that performance, whatever role it may
happen to be, I will step from my character and address the audience in
my own voice. I will inform them of every word you have said, every
threat you have implied, and every cruel action you have taken this
evening. I will not dress you in anonymity—either by the designation "a
powerful man in government" or even "a member of the ministry." I will
state your name most plainly and ask every patron in the theatre if a man
such as you should be representing Her Majesty as First Lord of the
Treasury. I will name you, Lord Oxley. I will most certainly name you."

Shivering in the fog, she remained gratified that she had rejected
Oxley's insistence that she take his carriage back to the Pearcy's. Her only
thought was to leave Oxley's presence immediately, even though she
didn't know where she was. At first she felt safe walking rapidly away
from the residence, but after a few moments she felt her vulnerability to

other potential hazards in the depressing and impenetrable fog.

Hearing horses' hooves in the distance, she ran toward the sound, and to her considerable good fortune she came upon a cab seeking a passenger. Seeing that she was trembling, the driver offered his heavy coat, under which she sought both warmth and escape from the consequences of her actions tonight. By now Oxley was surely feeling the humiliation of her attack on his manhood and gross disrespect of his elevated position. He would have his revenge, she knew. If not directly against her, then against those closest to her. The cabman's heavy coat did little to lessen her trembling.

Chapter 22

After being freed from the handcuffs, Copsey was allowed to return to his lodging, with the proviso that he remain in London to be available for further questioning about whom he saw at the theatre the night of Roberts-Smythe's and Donovan's murders. The young man once more assured Phillpotts that he saw no one backstage who didn't belong there, and other than Ned Ludmore's frequent grousing about the talents and commitment of his fellow actors, Copsey never heard anything of a threatening nature from or between anyone in the company.

Copsey gave the matter further thought as he made his way through the ponderous fog to where he, Clare, and the baby were staying. Who would use him in such criminal schemes and why? Was he simply a convenient and pliable messenger, easily manipulated? Had the perpetrator of the plot intended him to come upon the dead body of James Millard and take blame for killing him?

Michael Healy had explained this and further possibilities to him while Phillpotts fumed about other matters. Either the bloody knife would be resting next to Millard's body so that Copsey would walk upon the scene and perhaps be found with the murder weapon in his hand—or someone would kill Copsey but make it appear as if Millard had done so before he expired. Healy was more inclined to believe Copsey would be dispatched, leaving the murderer to place the knife in Copsey's grip, making it appear as though he had stabbed Millard. The pistol earlier discovered on the assailant's person would be used to shoot Copsey—the weapon then being placed in Millard's hand to finalize the deception.

Reminding himself of Michael Healy's observations made Copsey less sure that someone was truly out to destroy him personally. Were Roberts-Smythe still alive, Copsey might have suspected him of doing so, because two months earlier Copsey had refused an astonishing request made of him by the theatre manager—even though Roberts-Smythe never seemed to hold the refusal against him afterwards. Still, Copsey was convinced he was being used to destroy Jamie Millard.

But now a new thought intruded on his speculations—one seemingly preposterous but troubling nonetheless. Could his involvement have anything to do with Clare Paget, the mother of his child? Over the last several weeks he had begun to think more often of her hazy past. She had told him only that she was brought up by a couple other than her real mother and father. Curiously, she met with indifference all of Copsey's efforts to learn more of her history, although on a few occasions she became upset over his questions, particularly when he spoke of their taking formal marriage vows—something she didn't feel worthy of doing, she told him, since she wasn't eighteen and didn't have a dowry to offer. She pointed to others she knew in London who had chosen cohabitation. The city wasn't as concerned as it used to be about such arrangements, she had conveniently added. Still, Copsey knew it made no sense to connect her to what happened that night at The Acropolis and the events of this night on High Holborn, but he couldn't help wondering.

~ # ~

"My dearest Cate, are you all right? You're shaking so."

Millard pressed her face into his chest, rubbing her shoulders in an attempt to bring warmth to her chilled body.

"It's so very cold outside, Jamie. A most horrible night." She lifted her head and met his lips with her own. They had forgotten that Alice Pearcy was standing only a few feet away.

"Sorry, Alice. You shouldn't have to witness to such a public demonstration of affection." Despite her shaky emotional state, Catherine couldn't resist punctuating her remark with a smile.

"Are you going to add that I'm only seventeen and therefore am not able to understand the longings of grown-up men and women?"

Jamie got out his reply before Catherine could. "No, Alice. It's because that at seventeen you *do* understand them—and accordingly they aren't appropriate for you to witness."

"If you think I don't know what you two are up to whenever you both go up those stairs, then . . ."

It was Catherine's turn. "Thank you, Alice. That will more than do."

It was a bit of a chore convincing Alice to leave the room, for the young woman seemed intent on knowing all the particulars of Catherine's evening. Alice could see that the meeting with Lord Oxley had not gone well. In addition, she wanted to hear more of Jamie's explanation for the soreness on the right side of his neck. But at seventeen she was also mature enough to understand a husband and wife's need to explain everything to each other first. Alice decided to withdraw from the room without offering tea.

At first neither Catherine nor Jamie spoke, each having difficulty determining how much to tell the other. Finally she noticed the dirt on his clothing and on one side of his face. She took his hands and saw the scraped skin at the top of his fingers. She had been so overwrought when she first arrived that she had been oblivious to his appearance.

"Jamie, what happened to you?" She gently rubbed her cheek on his hands.

"It is nothing, my love. Tell me about your evening."

"No, I insist you first tell me what happened. Did you fall?"

Millard nodded and told her of the assault in the access lane off High Holborn. He explained that he had been rendered unconscious and that his life was saved by a man who had followed the assailant to the location, because of the assailant's suspicious behavior at a pub.

Shocked by the account, Catherine nodded her head and said that following the assailant was "something my father would do." She was startled by Jamie's broad grin, but even more so by the revelation that it was indeed her father who likely saved her husband's life.

"And he told you who he was?" For the first time since she had made it back to the Pearcy's she felt relaxed enough to sit.

"He did. And you can imagine my surprise. When he found out I was an actor at The Acropolis, he said—almost innocently—that I must then know you." Both of them wanted to laugh out loud but decided against it. They didn't want to draw Alice back down the stairs.

"Did you . . .?"

"No, I didn't. I was tempted to tell him, but given all that had happened, I thought it best to wait. In any event, did I say that poor Patrick was put in handcuffs for being there?"

"Patrick was there?"

"He too received a note telling him to come to the address. As did

Inspector Phillpotts. All of us to be there roughly at the same time."

"Three notes asking all of you to arrive at the same spot at the same time. Let me think . . ." She walked to her handbag and withdrew the small notebook into which she had entered facts and thoughts regarding the three murders.

Jamie knew she would place the pieces of the information into an analytical pattern. He had already seen her sit at one of the tables and place pieces of paper with relevant details and speculations about the crimes in a circle, drawing imaginary lines with her finger, connecting various pieces of paper. He took the notebook from her hand. "No, no, Cate. Don't think of all that now. You must tell me what happened tonight with you. You looked so distraught when I came to the door. You say you've been shivering because of the cold, but it's relatively warm this evening, owing to the fog. Something else has affected you. Please tell me what happened." Her eyes expanded but she said nothing. "So, Cate. What did Lord Oxley say?"

His question jolted her as if it was electricity. She turned her face away from him. "How did you know I went to see Lord Oxley?"

"Alice told me without telling me. I simply assumed that you went to see him about the reopening of the theatre."

"Yes, that was the only reason I met with him. The only reason."

Jamie was confused by her insistence on that point. "Of course it was your only reason for going, my darling. And I take it that he wasn't sympathetic to your appeal."

"No. He wasn't." She found it impossible to elaborate further. There were too many questions coursing through her mind which she had no time to satisfactorily answer. How much she should tell her husband? Should she at least mention Oxley's interest in assisting her career? What of the two notes he had written her? What of last night's meeting at the Charing Cross Hotel? Should she inform Jamie that tonight she met Oxley at one of his private residences and not at his family address or in his office on Downing Street? And how much should she tell him about Oxley's deplorable behavior and implied threats and about her reaction to them?

But what use would it be to further upset her husband, who tonight had almost been the victim of a homicide? Even if he hadn't been assaulted, wouldn't telling him about Oxley's offer to keep her as his mistress, as well as his encircling her wrist to detain her when she wished to leave, only make Jamie miserable and place him in the position of demanding satisfaction from the First Lord of the Treasury? Yet what satisfaction could he expect to have—and even if he gained it, what would be the cost to him and to the both of them?

"Cate, you're not telling me anything specific."

She could ponder the impossibilities no further. "Jamie, Lord Oxley infuriated me by . . ."

"By what, Cate?" His face tightened into a look of deep concern and growing anxiety.

"By his refusing to see the wisdom of using his influence to quickly reopen The Acropolis. I had such high hopes that he would. He misled me to believe he would take up the matter immediately. That is all, my dearest one."

"Are you certain that is all, Cate?"

"You are such the chivalrous gentleman. How fortunate I am that you care so much for my well-being." She once more kissed him tenderly.

Satisfied with her account and warmed by her kiss, Jamie reached for his coat with reluctance. "You'll have to forgive me, but I must leave for a time. I'm expected at the hospital—the morgue rather—to meet with Phillpotts and my father, who will be examining the body of the man who assaulted me."

"The man my father shot?"

"Yes, thank heavens, the same."

"But, I don't want you going away any more tonight, given the dreadful fog and all that has happened to you. Can it not wait until morning?"

"I'm sorry, but the good inspector insists. And I don't believe I can rest well until I see that my father is all right. I cannot imagine he would be a victim in the larger plot that someone has evidently weaved to torment us all, but I need to see him for my own sake if not for his. I refused to go with Phillpotts earlier because I had to come here and see you first."

"But . . ."

"Cate, I'll be safe. I have one of Phillpotts's men accompanying me. He's outside now, waiting in the hansom. Another will be watching the house here. That reminds me. Has Pearcy gone up to bed?"

Catherine shook her head. "Alice told me he left some time ago for his office and said he would return late—between eleven and midnight."

~ # ~

"Your son is expected soon, Millard. I see no reason to wait any longer. Let us begin."

"You should know, Inspector, that it's helpful to speak with those who were at the scene of a death when conducting a thorough post-mortem examination. Beyond that fact, I will concentrate more fully when I see that my son is indeed all right."

"I have told you he was, didn't I?"

"I prefer to make my own judgment. You don't know him as well as I do."

Phillpotts ignored the joke or insult, whichever one Thomas Millard meant. "But as I say, another at the scene is here to answer at least some of the questions you have. He arrived soon after your son was attacked. And if I didn't say it already, he in all probability saved your son's life by firing the bullet that killed this man."

The elder Millard and Phillpotts were positioned over the prone body of the muscular assailant. Young George Wooten, unhappy to have been roused from his early sleep, stood off to the side next to Michel Healy.

The elder Millard squinted in an attempt to see Healy. "Sir, I cannot express in words how grateful I am to you." He walked to Healy with hand extended. "As my son Jamie likes to say, 'Thanks, thanks, and ever thanks'—or something to that effect."

Healy smiled and shook Millard's hand. "That's Shakespeare, Dr. Millard."

Millard pulled his hand from Healy's. "From the sound of your voice, you're Irish."

"Indeed I am and proudly so. The name's Michael Healy, from Dublin. I'm chief inspector there."

Millard turned to Phillpotts. "Is this a joke of some kind?"

Phillpotts was hardly pleased to assert the seriousness of the identification. "No, Dr. Millard. He's who he says he is."

"Your daughter's Catherine Healy, then."

Healy's face bloomed with delight. "She most assuredly is. And your boy's one of the actors she works with, I understand."

Thomas's grin immediately made Healy suspicious. "Rather, she works *on* him."

Healy took a few seconds before charitably concluding that the elder Millard simply uttered the wrong preposition.

"Excuse my delay. I came as quickly as I could." Jamie entered the morgue.

Thomas grabbed his son by the coat sleeves. "My boy, I can't tell you how relieved I am that you are breathing and in one piece." Unable to articulate all he felt, the elder Millard embraced his son—something he did only during the Christmas season—and never in front of anyone else.

After further prodding by Phillpotts, everyone stepped to the table and took up positions over the deceased man. The elder Millard was again in his element. His son continued to marvel at the vigor and nimbleness of his father's mind was when he engaged in examining the dead.

"All right, then. Help me remove the man's clothing, George. And Jamie, give a hand too, if you don't mind." After the deceased was completely naked, the elder Millard bent forward to look at the fatal wound. "Since we know Mr. Healy's pistol caused this damage, we can dispense with the probing and removal of the bullet—at least for now. From what I can see here, I am going to assume that the bullet traversed the descending aorta, causing rapid blood loss and a speedy death. The man's chest is considerably muscular, as are the arms and legs. Hmm, this is interesting."

"What is it?" Phillpotts hovered over the doctor's left shoulder.

"This wasn't the first bullet wound this man has suffered, Inspector. Look here." Millard pointed to scars on the man's right shoulder and the inside of the right arm. "The scar tissue looks of a similar consistency. These two wounds may well have been inflicted on the same occasion."

"And the significance, Dr. Millard?" Looking at the corpse, young Wooten was shaky but steady enough.

"Good boy, George. Ask questions. That's how you learn. The significance would be that this man was no stranger to violent altercations."

"But the bullet wounds to his left shoulder and arm may simply have been the result of his being a victim of someone else's violence. Isn't that possible, doctor?" Wishing to be contrary, Phillpotts seemed satisfied by his assessment.

"Anything is possible, Inspector, but you don't seem to notice the scars on his hands—on his left hand, particularly—the likely result of both hammering something with his fists and receiving cuts from his own, if not someone else's, knife."

The younger Millard added, "And several of the fingers seem dislocated, as well, father."

"Good for you, Jamie. I might venture to say that this fellow has bashed more than his share of faces, and gripped one or more men by the throat and attempted to strangle them—successfully I rather imagine."

"The same could be said for the feet and toes, doctor." Michael Healy was at the foot of the table, doing what he had done so many times in Dublin. The elder Millard moved down to Healy's position.

Jamie was curious to see how his father would receive the assistance from the Irish Catholic investigator—the father of the daughter-in-law Thomas didn't yet know he had.

"Yes, well done, Mr. Healy. You have a good eye for this kind of thing."

"Too much experience with this kind of thing, I'm afraid."

Jamie shook his head. Once again his father's behavior defied prediction. For all of Thomas's railing against the Irish, the Catholics, and the theatre, he blew so much of his hot air harmlessly over the heads of than he did seriously into the faces of those he professed to dislike.

Thomas continued, "This husky lad has likely kicked into submission or to death a poor soul or two. The left foot was broken at some time. The three smaller toes are almost mashed." The elder Millard looked up the table toward Phillpotts. "Of course, Inspector, it's always possible that this fellow got stepped on by a draught horse or had his feet run over by an old hackney coach."

The old doctor's chuckle did nothing to alleviate Phillpotts's irritation at the slow pace of the examination. Still, the inspector checked himself. "So, doctor, do you think that this man might have been responsible for the death of Roberts-Smythe at The Acropolis?"

Thomas took no time to ponder the matter. "No, I don't. That is, I don't believe he killed the theatre manager. I judged the killer as being right handed, based on the angle of the stab wound to Robert-Smythe's back. This man is left handed."

175

"You are certain of that, Millard?"

"Yes, Inspector, I am. First, I believe the bullet wounds to this man's right arm and shoulder came from one or two shots from an adversary *while* this man's left arm was extended, either with a knife or pistol in his hand."

Phillpotts couldn't let the assumption stand unchallenged. "Ah, but you couldn't know, not having been in that narrow lane off High Holborn."

"But *I* was, Phillpotts." Healy nodded his head. "It was exactly the way he came at me in that access lane. With his left arm extended."

Phillpotts countered that the man might have been in an awkward position, causing him to grab the knife with his left hand, rather than with his right.

Jamie interrupted. "But the scars are mainly on his left hand and on his left foot, Inspector. He would obviously punch either a face or a wall with his strongest hand—and kick a prone body with his strongest foot."

Healy smiled. "It seems you have missed your calling, Mr. Millard. Instead of trodding the boards, you should have followed the same path as your father—or as Inspector Phillpotts here."

"Sometimes, Mr. Healy, I believe I am still on that path." Jamie wished that Cate was standing next to him to hear all of this. He felt she would have applauded his remark.

Phillpotts was almost remarkable in his ability to ask pertinent questions in the face of what he felt were a humiliating series of contradictions from both Millards and his Irish rival. "Is there a chance that the knife was the same one used to kill Roberts-Smythe?"

"Ah, good question, Inspector." Finally, Phillpotts had received some positive acknowledgement. "George, bring me that knife. George! Get the knife, boy."

Wooten had seemingly stepped into a daydream—about Alice Pearcy, no doubt. He ran to the far table and ran back with haste. The men backed up as soon when they saw the blade end being run toward them.

Jamie deftly took the knife out of the boy's hands. "George," he said gently, "never run with a knife in your hand, and always present it handle first. Like this."

"Oh. Thank you. I'll remember that next time, Mr. Millard."

The elder Millard took the blade from his son. "I have notes about the mortal wound to Roberts-Smythe's back. Let me check them." Pulling a sheaf of papers from his small desk, Millard easily found his notes. Jamie had amused Cate with tales of his father's uncanny ability to locate what he needed in unorganized mounds of notes and scrap heaps of paper.

"No, it's not the same knife. Let me state it plainly. The wound in Roberts-Smythe's back was caused by a blade that narrows at a steeper angle than this knife, which narrows more gradually."

Phillpotts hesitated, making sure his next question wouldn't be ridiculed. "Then we can dismiss the possibility that this man had anything to do with the other murders."

Once more Thomas shook his head. "No, we can't do that, Inspector. It's possible this man was the one who dispatched Donovan and moved his body. It's also possible, I suppose, that he shot that Nichols fellow on the stairs of the abandoned house on High Holborn."

Phillpotts was at least grateful that there was no hint of derision in Thomas Millard's reply.

A weary George Wooten asked, "Well, are we finished now, Dr. Millard?"

Once more the elder Millard shook his head. "No, my boy. We haven't gone through his clothing yet."

Phillpotts grabbed the man's coat, Jamie the trousers, Healy the shirt, and young George the shoes and socks.

The men found two ten pound notes, a few coins, a soiled handkerchief, a small flask of cheap whiskey, crumbs from some bread or a muffin, and a broken pencil.

Thomas sighed. "Nothing of significance here, gentlemen."

"Wait."

"What is it, George?"

"Something in this sock, sir. A folded note." Young Wooten had discovered a piece of paper folded several times inside one of the woolen socks the men had rolled off the dead man's feet. Phillpotts took the paper and unfolded it. In the same unusual script he had seen before, the note included the same address on High Holborn that he, James Millard, and Patrick Copsey had been given and a time several minutes before the other men were to be there. The note had no signature, nor any initials.

George turned to the Inspector. "Strange place for the note to be hidden— inside his sock, isn't it?"

"Not at all strange, Mr. Wooten," offered Phillpotts. "The assailant couldn't risk losing the address by having it in one of his pockets, where it might tumble out." The inspector looked at the others for a response, but for once none of them offered a contradictory opinion.

Chapter 23

At ten the next morning, Catherine headed toward The Acropolis for another meeting with Nedra Alexander, who had sent word earlier that she needed to see Catherine at the theatre "before the noon hour." Nedra had underlined the passage, "Please come. It is most important. I feel it cannot wait until a more congenial time."

Jamie accompanied his wife. Given the events of the previous night, neither wished to be apart from the other. The fog hadn't entirely dissipated, but the city had at least come more clearly into view. Traveling in the hansom cab, Catherine and Jamie inhaled the familiar odors of street food, and the sight of the vendors selling such staples as pea soup, baked potatoes, sweetmeats, and meat pies. They both enjoyed other welcoming aromas—Chelsea buns, spice cakes, crumpet, and muffins offered by the vendors. Although for the moment, she felt content, Catherine knew more serious matters awaited her at The Acropolis.

"Jamie, I'm sure Nedra is going to tell me more about that belt." Catherine found it more terrifying than coincidental that her husband was assaulted on the same street on which stood the abandoned house where she found the black velvet belt and where Alfred Nichols was murdered.

"You are no doubt right, Cate. I'll wander about the theatre while you speak with her. But I promise you I won't be far out of your sight."

"We can't go on living in such a state of apprehension, my darling."

"At least for today we can, Cate."

As they stepped into the theatre, they found Nedra sitting in the first row behind the orchestra pit. Staring pensively at one of the upper stage boxes, she was oblivious of their arrival until Catherine whispered "Nedra." Clearly, she was disconcerted by Jamie's appearance.

Millard sought to put her at ease. "Good morning, Nedra. I needed to come to The Acropolis to inventory my costumes and stage props. Call me if you need anything, Cate." He mounted the stage and headed off without waiting for Nedra to reply. Before he disappeared he turned and gave Catherine a look that assured her that he'd be at her side in seconds if she saw anyone in the theatre she didn't recognize.

"I'm afraid I was rude to James by my reaction and silence, Catherine."

"No, not at all, Nedra. He understands that our meeting is to be private."

"Oh, Catherine, I've had so much joy on this stage. I'm so blessed to have the opportunity to perform here. I've never experienced such gratification and sense of purpose. Don't you feel as though out on that stage you are free from everything that has ever plagued you?"

"I'm in complete agreement, Nedra. I have always felt I escape every misery of life as soon as I enter the theatre."

"*No.* Enter onto the stage. *Onto the stage.*" Nedra's cheeks rose in an attitude of anger. Her voice took on the quality of one of the villainous queens she had always been asked to play. But just as quickly her demeanor transformed into that of a vulnerable child. "Oh, Catherine. I don't know what to do."

"What is it, Nedra? Tell me, please."

"I don't know. Perhaps I have invited you here for no reason." She stood as if to go.

Catherine grabbed her forearm to detain her. Nedra winced in pain. Catherine released her arm and moved her fingers to the sleeve of Nedra's dress.

"Did I hurt your arm? I didn't think I squeezed you that tightly. Did I?" Catherine frowned recalling Oxley's behavior the previous night.

"I . . . I hurt it when . . ." Nedra wouldn't complete her thought. She merely shook her head as Catherine gently pulled her back down into the theatre seat.

"Nedra, did you wish to speak about your black velvet belt with the inscription?"

Nedra took a quick look around the theatre. "I know we haven't been intimate friends, Catherine"

Nedra had never felt close to any of the other women in the company. This fact partially led to the assumption that Nedra's preference for men included granting favors of a scandalous kind. Catherine's instincts as well as tangible evidence convinced her that the rumors were not far removed from the truth.

"It's all right, Nedra. You know I like you and have always enjoyed our scenes together on stage. You are a wonderful actress."

Nedra offered a half smile. "I am most grateful that you think me worthy of your praise, Catherine. You are to me the—"

"No, no. Please just tell me more about the velvet belt I showed you at the Savoy Hotel."

"It was a gift."

"From . . . ?"

"The overused phrase would be 'an admirer,' I suppose. And to some degree that would be true." Nedra began lightly patting the place on her arm where Catherine had grabbed her. She was careful not to rub the spot.

"To some degree?"

"Yes." Nedra offered no elaboration.

"Did you ever discover that it was missing before I showed it to you?"

Nedra offered a weak "No."

"I didn't tell you at the Savoy because you wished not to speak about it then, but this belt was found at a location where a murder occurred."

Nedra's evinced neither shock nor even mild surprise at Catherine's revelation. She remained silent, not asking who the victim was. Nor did she offer any explanation that the belt must have been stolen from the theatre or from her London residence.

"Nedra, were you ever at an abandoned house on High Holborn?"

"High Holborn?" She asked as if she had never heard of the street. "I might have. I cannot say for sure."

"Are you aware of what the inscription says on the inside of the belt?"

"I'm sure it's likely complimentary. Catherine, where is the belt now?"

"I have it."

"Do the police know?"

Catherine was annoyed by the matter-of-fact tone of Nedra's questions. "No, they do not. I wished to speak to you about it before I told them."

"Will you be in legal difficulty for having withheld it from them?"

Frustrated by Nedra's questions and the bland manner in which they were asked, Catherine recalled still another lesson taught by her father. Often there comes a time, he said, when a witness evinces a desire to reveal important information but quickly balks at doing so when the questions become too specific. Michael Healy assured his daughter that in such cases, a more aggressive and otherwise unpleasant approach is needed—which includes a promise to walk away and leave the witness to his or her own devices. Catherine knew such a time had come with Nedra Alexander.

"Nedra, it seems I have wasted my time coming here to speak with you. And in believing you wanted my assistance. I assumed you wished to discuss important matters, but I now realize you are not prepared to do that. I must say I'm disappointed you would take advantage of my time in this way."

Nedra's softy apologized. "Then I am most sorry, Catherine."

"If you will excuse me, I will go backstage and find Jamie."

"No, don't. Stay with me." Nedra took a deep breath of resolve.

"All right, Nedra. Confide in me, then."

"I've made mistakes. Many of them. I no longer control my own life. I have given that privilege away."

Catherine caught sight of her husband standing in the stage left wings. She told him with her expression that she was all right. He retreated from sight. "Nedra, who controls your life?"

She directed her gaze the rear of the stage. "I mustn't say."

Catherine knew it would be unwise to prod her with preliminary questions such as "Is it anyone I have met?" This was no parlor game. "Nedra, go on. Tell me why you think you have given your life away."

"I gave it away years ago. I made a terrible mistake when I was a girl of fifteen." She continued to stare at the back of the empty stage.

"What kind of mistake do you mean?"

"You must know. You've heard what everyone has said about me."

"There is always the opportunity to regain control of your life, Nedra."

"You cannot understand."

"Look at me." She finally turned toward Catherine. "Nedra, do you have faith in God's forgiveness?"

"No. Only a strong belief in his just retribution."

Catherine despaired of comforting Nedra in this vein. Religious commonplaces wouldn't do. "Tell me who has hurt you and I will speak up for you and express my indignation on your behalf."

"Denial and shame, Catherine. They are what I know best." Nedra gently brushed her hand across her arm. "Were you aware that Mr. Roberts-Smythe was going to release me after we completed our run of *Hamlet*?"

"What? You cannot mean that."

"Oh, yes. He said he would speak to me officially at run's end but that I would be advised to look for other theatrical opportunities in the meantime."

Catherine stared into Nedra's eyes, half expecting an admission that she had killed Morris Roberts-Smythe. Such an expectation was of course absurd, for how could this woman have dispatched the theatre manager, Charles Donovan, and Alfred Nichols—not to mention plotted the assault on Jamie?

Nedra's eyes closed before Catherine could find anything else to read in them. When they reopened, she stood and squeezed Catherine's hand. Nedra made her way up the aisle and out of the theatre.

"Catherine?"

Catherine was startled by the voice. It didn't belong to her husband. She spun her shoulders and saw the concerned face of Henry Jaynes standing at the foot of the stage. Jamie was situated to Jaynes's left.

"Catherine, is Nedra all right?"

"She is upset, Henry, by . . . by all that has happened here last week."

"I understand. It has been an almost unbearable strain on us all."

"Cate?"

"Yes, Jamie."

"Henry and I have found something you should see. Come."

She quickly made her way to the side door and met them on the stage. "What is it?"

"This way, Cate." The three of them headed toward the stage-left wings.

~ # ~

The gentleman boarded a small vessel at Portsmouth for the trip across the channel to Le Havre. He wasn't fleeing the country because events had gone awry in the narrow access lane off High Holborn. The plan all along had been that after getting James Millard to go to the address on High Holborn, the gentleman would travel to France, where he would remain until the spring. Besides, it wasn't his fault in the least that someone had interfered with the scheme—one much too elaborate, the gentleman thought. And too imperfect as well, for given what Catherine Healy had absorbed about criminal investigation from her father and her active involvement in the matter, which would likely continue unabated, she also should have been swept up in the plot to implicate and dispatch Patrick Copsey and James Millard. But the gentleman's specific instructions were to leave her out of it.

Introducing himself to Jamie Millard on the train and inviting him to discuss Alfred Nichols at the High Holborn address was yet another of the many such manipulations the gentleman had brought off the past few years in London and as far as Edinburgh in the north and Bristol on the west coast. He possessed an irresistible charm—an ingratiating manner that easily won the trust of men and women alike. And he was paid rather well for his services, which never included any physical action on his part. Others were better suited to perform the more sordid tasks.

The gentleman examined the small notebook he kept in the pocket of his inner coat, which consisted of various bits of cryptic information regarding the jobs he had agreed to do and a series of code names and sobriquets of those he had made and was to make contact with. The gentleman made certain that a loss of this notebook would implicate neither him nor those who employed him. As he turned the pages, he glanced at a list of names he had jotted down several nights earlier. The one he chose would be his identity the next few months in France. He quickly determined to use "Jean Lambert." He smiled at how benign the name sounded. "Lambert": the fair lamb. Perhaps when he returned to England in the spring he would simply modify the name to John

Lambert—this time pronouncing the terminal "t."

The gentleman continued to flip through the pages, stopping at the entry noting the amount of "five hundred pounds" next to the name "Dear Old Ash Jenny Rye." The gentleman had half the amount in another pocket of his inner coat; the other half of the ripe sum would be waiting for him at La Havre. He had already received confirmation that the money was there. Fortunately, both halves were delivered before "Dear Old Ash Jenny Rye" got the news that the events at High Holborn didn't go as planned.

~ # ~

"And where did you find this, Henry?" Catherine held in her hand a pale gray handkerchief containing a stain of what was surely dried blood lying directly in the middle of the square fabric. "This was likely folded so that the center was blotted against a cut or wound of some kind." Both she and Jamie recalled the bloody articles in the secret room at The Acropolis and at the abandoned house on High Holborn.

Jamie explained that Jaynes found it lying crumpled on the floor just inside the door of the old costume storage space—at the other end from the secret recess. "Henry says he was looking for anything else that might help with the investigation."

Jaynes nodded. "That's true, Catherine. I raised and lowered my lantern up and down the wall behind the door so that I wouldn't miss anything. I found this item almost immediately and brought it to my office. It was then I heard voices in the house, and when I realized you and Nedra were speaking, I returned here so that I wouldn't intrude on your private conversation. It was only when I heard the sound of footsteps near my office that I came out again. Then I saw James. In any event, James has just told me about the hidden room at the back of the old costume and properties storage area."

Catherine was confused. "Didn't Inspector Phillpotts ask you about that room when he questioned you about the murders, Henry?"

"No, Catherine, he did not."

"That is strange," Jamie added. "I would have thought the inspector would have at least taken you to the room if you claimed no knowledge of it."

"I was never consulted during the renovations—either by being shown the architect's plans or during the actual construction. I was away from London when the work was being done, and when I returned it was completed. You recall my absence, don't you, James?"

"I do. Henry, I haven't told you that there is a very narrow door inside the hidden room that leads down to a rear exit from the theatre."

"I don't understand."

"We'll show you in a moment, but can you think of anything Mr. Roberts-Smythe may have wanted brought into the theatre without anyone's knowing it?"

Jaynes thought for a moment. "I cannot recall anything. What do you think it might have been, James?"

"I have no idea. I was hoping you would."

"Then I have let you down. I apologize. So what shall we do with that handkerchief?" Jaynes pointed to the object still in Catherine's hands.

"Give it Inspector Phillpotts, of course." Catherine saw the fear on Jaynes's face. "Come now, Henry. Do you really believe he views you as a prime suspect?"

"He does, Catherine. There can be no doubt. At least he wishes to treat me as such." Jaynes paused. "And there is reason for it."

Jamie scoffed at Jaynes's assumption. "Come now, Henry. What reason could there possibly be?"

"There is a history between Denham Phillpotts and me. He hates me for what he believes I am responsible for years ago—many years ago."

"Henry, please tell us what happened between you." Catherine gestured for all of them to sit.

Jaynes took his place behind his desk. "Very well, then. The truth is that in my youth I ardently courted the inspector's younger sister."

Jamie refused to look at Catherine, for fear they would both grin disrespectfully. The image of Henry Jaynes as a youthful Lothario was simply comic. His slender frame and unsymmetrical facial features would classify him, even most charitably, as "especially plain" for a man.

"I knew she loved me and would have married me, except . . ."

The serious tone of Jaynes's voice forced Millard to drop his emerging smile. "Go on, Henry."

"Forgive me, both of you. This is most difficult." Jaynes closed his eyes. "She would have married me except for the fact that I broke it off between us."

Catherine was frankly surprised he would have done such a thing, yet she felt badly for assuming Jaynes would have jumped at any chance to marry a woman who would have him. "Henry, why did you break it off?"

"I came to see that she was emotionally unstable. She had flights of fancy without the usual charm that often accompanies them. She suspected me of betraying her trust. That is, that I had informed others what she told me about herself—about her fears and her other suspicions. I tried desperately to assure her of my caring and loyalty, but to no avail. She took all I said in that regard as a lie or an exaggeration. I'm not proud of the fact, but after a time I grew weary of even attempting to assure her of my love. And then I realized I no longer loved her. I deeply regretted losing the feeling of romance and affection, but I knew I was feeling only pity, mixed with resentment over her treatment of me. And so I walked with her in Lincoln's Inn Fields, where she always loved to go, and told her that we must part."

"And Phillpotts couldn't forgive the fact that you rejected his sister?"

"If it were only that, James. No, he couldn't forgive me because that very night his sister took her own life by jumping from Waterloo Bridge."

"Oh no, Henry." Catherine reached across the desk and took both of his hands. "I'm so deeply sorry. Dear man, you've had to live with that tragedy for all these years."

"Yes. And I've also had to live with the thought that at some point, Phillpotts would exact his revenge in a way I couldn't predict. And now I'm afraid he has found his opportunity."

Jamie sighed in exasperation. "Henry, he can't make a case on absolutely no evidence. He only means to frighten you with the prospect of charging you."

"You shouldn't underestimate the good Inspector, James. Even if he has never been shown to be corrupt and even if he otherwise does his job by the book, we are talking here about the death of his sister, whom I am sure he loved deeply. A death from a suicide he believes I caused." Jaynes picked up the handkerchief from the table and extended it toward Catherine. "He will claim that this is mine and that I 'conveniently' found it in some attempt to appear as though I was looking for evidence—even though that is exactly what I was doing. The blood, he will claim, belongs to Roberts-Smythe and came to be on this handkerchief when I wiped my hand after stabbing him—or some such thing."

"That is utterly preposterous, Henry."

"It may be, James, but Phillpotts will claim it nonetheless."

Catherine took the handkerchief from Jaynes. She once more examined the blood stain in the center, but this time she paid careful attention to the edges, which were not touched by the blood. And there it was. "Jamie, look here."

Millard took the handkerchief and saw that on the other side were three minuscule initials running on the very edge of the handkerchief—"MRS." It took him but a second to identify the owner. ""Morris Roberts-Smythe."

Chapter 24

Nedra stood across from the lodging she had been seeking for several days. Having paid someone to discover the address for her, she had walked the entire distance from her own house, unwilling to take a cab for fear of arriving before she had time to decide on her course of action. Would she go directly to the door or remain across the street, waiting patiently for someone to come out before revealing herself? Perhaps she wouldn't make herself known at all, but rather observe what she could from afar. That would at least give her some hope and a small degree of pleasure as well as save her from a devastating rejection.

A man grabbed her arm from behind.

"And what are you doing here, Nedra? A little far from home, isn't it?"

Because it wasn't the voice she expected, she took some comfort in the man's Teutonic accent, as she had the previous May when he replaced an ailing actor in the small role of the Doctor in The Acropolis's production of *Macbeth*. It was the first night of Nedra's unsuccessful and brief run as Lady Macbeth, and she found a supportive colleague in Bernhard Schneider. Following the first night's tepid response during her curtain call, the German made a gallant effort to nurse her wounded spirits with equal measures of sympathy and physical affection, to which she responded willingly. But the term of her affections for Schneider soon expired, to be replaced by a feeling that he had taken advantage of her emotional vulnerability. Before the week was out she ceased speaking to him entirely.

"Bernhard, what are you doing here? I pray you've not been following me."

"Oh, I have. Yet you seemed so distraught that I thought it best to let you compose yourself before speaking to you. It's a lesson I should have learned last spring."

"And what do you want? You surely don't believe we should attempt to breathe life into an unfortunate relationship that months ago died its natural death."

Schneider laughed. "What is this speech you are talking, Nedra?"

"I see your English has not improved much since you joined the company."

His hands curled into fists. He wondered if he would have struck her had it been dark or the fog as thick as it was yesterday. "You think that by merely ignoring me all would be forgotten?"

"As a matter of fact, I had thought that—yes. I have nothing I can give or even say to you. Now, please respect my wishes and leave."

"I will be far away from you soon enough. In fact, that is why I wanted to see you one last time."

"Then I wish you well wherever you may go. Back to Germany, I presume?"

"It's possible." Schneider continued studying her face.

"Why are you looking at me like that, Bernhard?"

"I'm just thinking that these are the most words we have exchanged off stage since last spring."

"Again, please take my sincere good wishes and leave me alone."

"What are you looking at across the street?"

"Nothing."

Schneider laughed. "I would have been gone before today, but that was impossible."

"Why is that?" She wanted to end their conversation, not extend it. But she couldn't suppress her curiosity.

"I believe you know why."

"I have no idea what you're talking about."

"I was on my way out of the country when I was discovered and brought back to London. Inspector Phillpotts has since refused me permission to leave the city."

"And why are you telling me all of this?"

"Very well, since you wish to play the role of the country ingénue, I believe I am a suspect in the murders at The Acropolis because you have given false testimony against me."

"That is completely untrue. I have no reason to believe you were in any way involved in those horrible acts. Now please go. I will say nothing to Inspector Phillpotts that I have even seen you."

"If I am again stopped from leaving and again returned to London, I will tell what I know about your behavior and associations and ruin you. I promise you that."

Nedra put her hands to her mouth and began to sob. Schneider doubted the sincerity of her emotional outburst, but realized that her crying would soon encourage others on the street to come to her defense, and he couldn't afford any kind of scene. Besides, he had made his point.

"*Auf wiedersehen,* Nedra."

Seeing two men coming across the street to assist her, Nedra began walking in the opposite direction from Schneider's path. She had failed to catch sight of those she had expressly come to see in the lodging across the street. She would have to come here again.

~ # ~

"And your father left early for his office?" Catherine had just sat down to her mid-day meal.

Alice Pearcy shrugged. "It appears so. When I awoke he was gone. Nor did I see him when he retuned late last night. He must have something important to do today, for he hardly ever leaves without kissing me, even if I'm asleep."

Catherine smiled. "Perhaps he kissed you *while* you were asleep."

"I always know it when he does. Anyway, where is Jamie? I had hoped he'd be back by now."

"He's gone to see Inspector Phillpotts about some matters relating to the events at The Acropolis."

"Events I'm not fully aware of, I regret to say. I wish you would tell me everything—especially all that happened to you last night."

Catherine frowned. She utterly detested keeping matters secret. It wasn't in her nature to do so. Her father claimed she had gravitated toward the stage because everything was revealed there. She had agreed at the time, but now she knew the theatre could hold shocking and frightful secrets. There was much she still didn't know about what had happened before and after Morris Roberts-Smythe and Charles Donovan were murdered at The Acropolis. She also didn't know when the theatre would reopen. And what mysteries about Nedra Alexander were left to be revealed? And for now she had to keep from Alice and Jamie the secret of her meeting with Oxley. The only secret she could accept with some pleasure was the fact that James Millard was her lawful husband.

Part of her wanted all of the secrets to be revealed in one fell swoop, so that her life could return to normal. But the other part was highly stimulated by the mysteries surrounding recent events and the irresistible impulse to pursue the matter until she contributed to its resolution. Thinking of her father, she was surprised he hadn't come to see her now that he was in town. That he had actually saved her husband's life was almost too much for Catherine to embrace.

"So you choose silence rather than revelation, Catherine?"

"I'm sorry, Alice. What did you ask again?"

"I see no reason why I have to be so direct, but all right. Why won't you tell me everything about your meeting with Lord Oxley? And please don't answer that it's because I'm only seventeen?"

"Then I cannot provide you an answer at all." Catherine playfully pinched her young friend on the top of her hand.

~ # ~

For once, Phillpotts seemed appreciative. "Well, thank you, Mr. Millard, for a more detailed description of this gentleman on the train who gave you the address on High Holborn. Now to this handkerchief. You say Henry Jaynes discovered it backstage at The Acropolis—inside the door leading into the old costume storage area."

"That's right, Inspector."

"And you believed him?"

Jamie didn't wish to discuss Jaynes, given what he had learned about the acting manager's tragic connection to Phillpotts's sister, but if any time was right for defending Jaynes, this was it.

"Inspector, am I to understand that you are considering Jaynes a suspect in these murders?"

"That isn't your business, Millard."

"I feel that it is, and that your questioning his truthfulness to me just now is your way of letting me know that you do suspect him."

"Think what you will. But I can assure you that a number of persons are suspects at present." Phillpotts paused. "Even you, Mr. Millard."

Jamie's face tightened. "That is absurd, Inspector, and you know it. I was almost murdered myself last night. Or have you forgotten that fact?"

"I have been thinking about that very 'fact,' as you put it. It's very possible that the deceased assailant wasn't trying to kill you at all. His arm was locked around the side of you neck, not around the front. As Healy noted last evening, the effect might have been merely to force you to lose consciousness—not to strangle you. And why didn't the assailant shoot you? He had a pistol on him. Or why not stab you? He had a knife as well. That is, if killing you was actually his intent."

Jamie remained bewildered by Phillpott's serious tone. "What do you mean by that, Inspector?"

"The whole thing could have been a set up job. To make things look other than what they really were."

"You believe I committed the murders of Roberts-Smythe, Donovan, and Alfred Nichols and then orchestrated my own assault? For what possible purpose?"

"I am still thinking that through, Millard. But you must admit that such a staged assault, with notes directing both Copsey and me to be there at the same time, could serve to deflect attention away from you. You are an actor, Millard. Many think a damned good one. Such a staging would come naturally to you. And because that blasted Irishman shot the man whose arms were around your neck, we aren't able to question him, are we?"

Millard wanted to laugh, but given his rising anger he found it impossible to do so. All he could muster at the moment was sarcasm. "So Michael Healy was in on it with me? Then at least Henry Jaynes isn't really your prime suspect."

"I never said that there was only one suspect, did I?"

"If you will excuse me, Inspector, I must be going. That is, if you're not planning to arrest me."

Phillpotts smiled broadly. "Come now, Millard. Don't take all this so personally."

"You're just doing your job—eh, Inspector?"

"That's it exactly. Please give my warmest regards to Miss Healy."

~ # ~

193

Ludmore brought to his nose the envelope just delivered to his lodgings—sent to him, as promised, by Nedra Alexander. It had the same fragrance as the first note she had passed to him, only two weeks after he joined the company the previous summer. She had then played on their Christian names—the diminutive of his, "Ned," and of hers, "Nedra"—adding that "Ned and Nedra" seemed destined for "intimacy before Michaelmas"—on September 29th. Yet it took Ludmore longer to indulge his sexual curiosity, for they met for intimate relations a month later—most fittingly, Ludmore believed, on All Hallow's Eve. Much to his surprise, that was the extent of their passionate exchanges, for she wounded his sensibilities by refusing to repeat the encounter, curtly remarking in early November that "It would no longer be possible, now or at any time in the future."

Since that time, Ludmore used the rejection as motivation for his on-stage interaction with her. For instance, many commented on Hamlet's third act confrontation with his mother Gertrude, given Ludmore's aggressiveness in the scene. Several patrons had even complained to Roberts-Smythe that the moment made them rather uncomfortable. And this was the very scene being played when Morris Roberts-Smythe met his fate behind the arras.

Ludmore counted the amount of cash Nedra sent him in the envelope. It was all there, all the funds he believed he needed for a proper move to New York. She assured him that "a man involved with the securities" supplied her with money beyond what she made as a stage actress. Ludmore had no interest in knowing who her benefactor was, for his only desire was to secure the best passage across the Atlantic and lodging appropriate to his position as London's brightest young actor—Catherine Healy be damned. The agreement with the Manhattan theatre was most generous, but Ludmore wanted more than what they offered for his journey to America.

Ludmore paused before addressing the envelope going back to her—the one with the photograph inside. The photograph she so desperately had to have from him. The photograph Ludmore found backstage the night of Morris-Smythe's murder. It was on the floor near where the manager lay dead. At least one of the actors or stage hands had stepped on and perhaps kicked it in the chaos, for the shoe smudge on the photograph was pronounced, although it didn't obscure what the photograph revealed.

Ludmore had glanced at it often since he retrieved it that night. It fascinated him and surprised him, even though logic suggested that it shouldn't have. He wondered if such things as depicted in the photograph were on her mind the one night they had indulged in their passion. It had been on his—often during the past two months—and he felt somewhat shackled by what he imagined when looking at the photograph. But that was in the past, as were his dealings with Morris Roberts-Smythe. Indeed, he had every reason to leave London, no matter how he broke his contract with The Acropolis. He smiled sardonically. Would the theatre ever be reopened in any event?

Ludmore enclosed the photograph, sealed the letter, and made arrangements that it be delivered to Nedra. Her pain would be heightened upon receiving it, he reasoned, even though she had begged him to send it to her and added to her plea the money he demanded, which he now placed into his handsome leather wallet.

~ # ~

"George?"

"Yes, Dr. Millard."

"Send word to my son and to Inspector Phillpotts that the bullets in the weapon found on the fellow Mr. Healy shot are not the same kind as the one earlier extracted from Mr. Nichols's body at the abandoned house on High Holborn."

"It's interesting."

"What is, my boy?"

"Both men you mentioned were killed on High Holborn."

"It's a long street, George. Not that unusual."

"I suppose not."

But Millard knew his apprentice was right. The abandoned lodging where Nichols died and the access alley behind the building where his son was assaulted—both on High Holborn. Rather "interesting" indeed.

"Which first, Dr. Millard?"

"What do you mean?"

"Should I tell your son first or the inspector first?"

"Tell my son first. Wait until you do so before you find Phillpotts."

"And where might your son be at present, sir?"

The elder Millard chuckled. "Oh, I suspect he's in the company of Miss Healy at the Pearcy home."

Wooten's face radiated with delight. "I shall go to the Pearcy home right away, sir."

After George left on his errand, Millard muttered a bemused, "The poor lad hasn't got the faintest whisper of a chance with young Alice, I'm afraid."

~ # ~

Oliver Pearcy checked his watch and knew it was time to leave his office. He had arrived very early and was able to work alone, but the moment his law partner arrived, he began thinking of a good reason to leave at the very time they were to meet with a client to discuss an impending case. Not theatrically minded, Pearcy merely begged the rest of the morning off, owing to the discomfort of a chest cold.

Pearcy took a cab to the address in Belgrave Square. The architect Isaacs was unable to break free until this hour. Therefore, meeting in Pearcy's office wouldn't do, given that complete privacy was required. The location was ideal—a lavishly furnished though empty house having just gone through substantial renovations. The owners of the impressive home were still in Africa and not expected back until the spring.

When Pearcy arrived, there was no servant to show him in. All the household staff had been removed when the new construction began, and those hired to watch the premises were obviously dismissed for the time being.

"Come in, Pearcy."

Pearcy nodded and entered the impressive study. He saw a bottle of brandy and two glasses on the circular table in the middle of the room.

Isaacs noticed Pearcy contemplating the brandy. "Fits the mid-afternoon better than tea, wouldn't you agree?"

"Perhaps so, Isaacs."

Isaacs poured a small amount into each glass. "Please, sit."

Pearcy had only seen young David Isaacs close up on two occasions, but it was enough to conclude that the son carried his father's features splendidly. His father, Edmund Isaacs, was a noted architect and builder,

196

the man who had renovated The Acropolis Theatre and whose most recent work was the renovation of this and another luxurious residence in Belgrave Square.

"Pearcy, I must admit that your letter came as quite a surprise."

"Because it expressed something completely false—or because it carried a truth you never expected to be revealed?"

"You're an attorney, Pearcy. You can't believe I would answer that."

"Quite right, although my hope was that you would."

"May I ask how you came by this information—or should we call it an accusation?" The elder Isaacs held Pearcy's letter in his hand.

"Since you know that I'm an attorney, you must also know that I'm likely to withhold the identity of the source—at least for now. But may I ask if there is any truth to it?"

"I see we are getting nowhere swatting our verbal shuttlecocks back and forth across the net. Let me make myself clear to you. Truth or no, I am anxious that this go no further. I am sure you have the talent and the persuasive skill to see that it doesn't. I of course wish to reward you for your discretion and cooperation. I simply need to know the amount you would hope to receive."

Pearcy looked about the library. "This room is quite impressive, Isaacs. Did you do much to it during your renovation of the house?"

"Ah, now you have shifted games on me. Is it chess we now play? Am I to sit patiently nursing my brandy while you contemplate your next move? Then let me shorten the game by providing you something more tangible to ponder." Isaacs went to a massive desk pushed against the only wall in the room devoid of books. Smiling, Isaacs drew forth a piece of ivory-colored paper. He took a pen and ceremoniously wrote down an amount. Folding the page, he walked behind Pearcy and placed the folded sheet over Pearcy's shoulder onto the circular table. Isaacs retuned to his seat and downed his brandy.

Pearcy unfolded the paper and stared at the amount. He raised his head and looked into the architect's eyes.

Isaacs nodded. "I can read your thoughts, Pearcy. Let me assure you that the source for your information can easily be convinced—by you, I mean—to forget everything relating to this matter. I challenge you to glance again at the amount I have written and tell me if you don't think I'm right about your persuasive powers.

197

Pearcy again noted the amount and folded the paper twice more. He placed it in his coat pocket.

Isaacs smiled triumphantly. "Good. Now before you leave, let me show you what masterful changes I have made to this house."

~ # ~

When Pearcy returned and opened the door to the law office, his clerk informed him his partner had taken their client to supper and that someone was waiting inside to see him. For a moment, Pearcy feared who it might be. He pressed his fingers against his coat pocket and felt the folded paper resting inside. He sighed and stepped inside his private office.

The identity of the visitor stunned him. Was this related to his visit to Belgrave Square, a case of irony, or merely a coincidence? The son of the man he had just visited stood to greet him. And young David Isaacs was holding an envelope in his hand.

Chapter 25

"And I thought you were going to leave London without seeing me." Catherine had her arm securely in her father's as they began their stroll away from the Pearcy home. Regardless of her self-sufficiency, she was always comforted and strengthened by his physical touch.

"I had intended to bring your aunt up from Basingstoke before seeing you, but that little altercation involving Mr. Millard last evening made impossible my not speaking with you first.

"Thank you for saving him, dearest father."

"A good actor, then? Valuable member of the company?"

She laughed at his joke. "Yes, he is."

Healy was wise enough in the ways of the heart to understand his daughter was in some way attached to the actor. He only hoped it wasn't in the way that first came to mind.

They had agreed to walk for half a mile and then return to Pearcy's for afternoon tea. Elated to be with her father, Catherine hoped he wouldn't see Jamie return to the Pearcy home. Although she had gained much confidence over the past several days that Thomas Millard would welcome her as the wife of his son, she hadn't a shred of confidence her father would accept Jamie as a son-in-law or would ever forgive her for marrying him—an Englishman, a Protestant, and an mere actor.

As they continued their walk, Catherine provided a full picture of what had happened six nights earlier at The Acropolis and all that had transpired since. She wanted to express her thoughts in a way that would elicit her father's endorsement of what she was doing. Her initial fear that he would disapprove of her investigating the crimes was soon dispelled by the tightening of his arm around hers.

"I'm so very proud of you, my dearest Catherine." Michael Healy had never kept his true feelings from her—even if they bruised her own from time to time.

"My dearest father, do you know I have called upon so much of what you have taught me and what I had learned by watching and listening to you?"

"Ah. So you paid attention even when I thought you were more interested in your dolls."

She playfully pinched his arm. "Of course I did. I should only hope I would have made as good a detective as many say I have made an actress."

"The unfortunate limits of your sex, my dearest one."

"Oh, I imagine that as the century turns the 'New Woman' will begin to make her mark as a detective, at least before too many years pass. Perhaps when I am older and no longer wanted on the stage, I can follow your footsteps more directly."

"I fear it will never happen."

"Do you know that women detectives do exist, father?"

"Other than you, you mean?"

"Yes, other than I. I was told that a writer friend of Mr. Arthur Conan Doyle, a Mr. Grant Allen, is working on a book featuring a female detective. There are hopes for its publication next year."

"Oh, so in literary fancy they exist, I see. Well, I can accept that in fiction, your sex may indeed be the official solvers of crime."

She smiled at her incorrigible father. "Just for that, I shall get a copy of Mr. Allen's book when it is published, and when you become very old and feeble and in need of my company, I will read it to you."

She had similarly bantered with him since she was a child, often when he posed hypothetical and actual criminal situations to her and asked how she would set about investigating them. If any one man had given legitimacy to the notion of a female detective, it was Michael Healy.

After they turned and headed back to the Pearcy's, Catherine spoke more fully of her suspicions that Nedra Alexander knew something about the murders. "Every instinct tells me that much can be understood if she reveals what she knows."

Healy listened attentively, as he had all her life to whatever she spoke seriously about. "Catherine, from what you've said, she has begun to reveal some details to you, even if she feels she hasn't. You should see her again and then again after that. Show your concern—which I have no doubt you genuinely feel. Make it impossible for her *not* to confide in you.

Push her on matters she's most unwilling to discuss."

"I fear she will then push me away and say no more about them."

"She may act as if she would, but from what you've told me, she likely feels she must confide in someone. She will therefore remain silent to you only for a brief time."

"Then I will be more insistent."

"Yes, do. But Catherine, you must be on your guard."

"What do you mean?"

"Your description of her reputation, although unsubstantiated, and her past and present state lead me to believe she could be dangerous to you."

"She might wish to harm me, you believe?"

"Not until she tells you something startling, I would imagine. After revealing any secrets to you, she could resent you enough for drawing that out of her that she might wish to—"

"To strike at me—or to murder me?"

Before her father could answer they were in sight of the Pearcy's front door. Standing before it was Nedra Alexander. Alice was pointing toward Catherine.

"Let me venture a guess as to the identity of that woman, who seems to be waiting for you, Catherine."

"Yes, father, it is she."

"Remember what I have said. I'll leave you now and return to the Pearcy home later this evening." Healy kissed his daughter on the forehead and moved briskly across the street.

When she reached the door, a nervous Alice pulled at Catherine's arm. "Come in for a moment, please."

Nedra placed her hand on Catherine's shoulder and insisted that she and Catherine speak immediately. Alice assured Nedra that she simply needed to pass on some household news to Catherine. "I promise it will take but a moment, Miss Alexander."

Nedra nodded and the three women entered the house. Alice beckoned Catherine to another room.

"Alice, do you know you are behaving rather rudely?"

"I'm so sorry, Catherine, but I think this is important. Not two minutes after you and father left on your walk, Mr. Isaacs delivered yet another note for you."

Catherine felt her stomach tighten. "Where is it?"

"Here." Alice held it up. It had been in her hand the entire time. "Are you going to read it now?"

"No. I'll look at it after I have spoken to Nedra."

"Do you want me to hold it?"

Catherine managed to maintain her patience with the effervescently curious Alice Pearcy. "No, I'll go up and put it in my room. Tell Miss Alexander I'll be down in a moment."

Catherine entered her room and placed the letter in the small locked box sitting on her vanity table. When she returned downstairs, Nedra wasn't in the house. She was standing by the road with one of the male servants.

Alice looked out the window. "Miss Alexander is calling for a cab. She wants you to ride with her."

~ # ~

Oliver Pearcy read Lord Oxley's short letter for a third time. If the younger Isaacs hadn't been its deliverer, Pearcy would have thought the letter a forgery of some kind. The request of him was completely absurd. The tone of the message was professional. It included no demand of any kind, yet the implication was clear that Oxley assumed Pearcy would comply with his wishes. Pearcy shook his head. Oxley knew Catherine Healy was his houseguest, if not a *de facto* member of the family. And still the First Lord of the Treasury could write him such a message and ask for his assistance in such a matter? Pearcy felt too much was becoming impossible to control. When had everything begun to shake loose from his grasp? He knew well when it was. When he first spoke to Nedra Alexander about her legal complaint.

They communicated twice about the issue—the first time in his office, the second in the area vicinity of All Souls Church, close to Regents Park. On this occasion, they met for a walk in the late afternoon, which too quickly became early evening by the time Nedra Alexander addressed the matter. Pearcy recalled that she had appeared emboldened by the approaching darkness. And as a widower for over nine years, Pearcy felt his own resistance to her charms weakening as the daylight exhausted itself. Accordingly, he postponed a third meeting when she asked that they again meet away from his office—this time somewhere on High Holborn—the exact location he never bothered to ask. Pearcy sensed there would soon come a time when Nedra would simply disappear into the night, never to be seen again.

~ # ~

"Here, let me help you." Catherine adjusted Nedra's lap blanket. "I want you to be as warm as possible." The driver asked where he should take them.

Nedra's visible unease led to a terse "Can we just move along now?" She looked about, as if she were fearful of being seen.

The driver was frustrated by the lack of specific directions. "Please, either of you Misses, where would you like to be taken?"

Nedra again answered unpleasantly. "East—toward Drury Lane."

Catherine also wanted to know the exact destination for their excursion. "You wish to go to The Acropolis, Nedra?"

"No, I've already been there today, as you no doubt recall. Now I wish to go to High Holborn."

Catherine was taken aback. "What do you want to see there?"

"Nothing, Catherine, I simply wish to ride along High Holborn."

Catherine waited for Nedra to add that she wished to speak about something particular relating to High Holborn, but she merely stared blankly out of the cab and remained silent until they reached Drury Lane.

"Driver, turn toward High Holborn and then east again."

Nedra waited until they were on High Holborn before finally looking at Catherine and taking her hand. "This is the most significant road in the entire city. The most significant road in my entire life."

Catherine could tell by her voice that she was expected to ask why that was so. When she did Nedra continued in a soft, vulnerable voice.

"The course of my life has been determined on this road. No other place in London has had any effect on me. Only here."

Again, Nedra seemed elsewhere, as she stared out at the north side of the street, occasionally looking past Catherine to the south. Once more she had retreated into silence.

Casual talk seemed Catherine's only recourse at the moment. "I believe the poet Milton once had a house here." Catherine pointed to the area where High Holborn adjoined Lincoln's Inn Fields.

Nedra's face and voice regained their usual animation. "That makes me think of another writer of the epic." Nedra folded her hands on her lap and ground her thumbs forcefully into the flesh between the thumb and index finger of each hand. She shook her head in exasperation. "I have always wondered why in his *Iliad* Homer fails to mention Agamemnon's sacrifice of his daughter Iphigenia. I feel she is the one figure from the Greeks who most reflects what I have become."

Catherine was intrigued by the sincerity with which Nedra had expressed the assessment. "Why do you say that, Nedra?"

"For many reasons. First, she was sacrificed by the one who should have loved her more than anyone else."

"But isn't it the point that Agamemnon did love his daughter and that her sacrifice was part of the tragedy of the tale?"

"But did he sacrifice her for love?" Nedra's eyes bore into Catherine's. "Or was it because without such a sacrifice the goddess Artemis wouldn't have allowed him to sail to Troy to satisfy his selfish vanity and lust for war?"

Catherine saw that Nedra's hands were still tightly clenched. "Nedra, it is all mythology. There likely never was such a situation as was depicted." When Nedra ignored her, Catherine continued. "Why do you wish to identify with Iphigenia, Nedra?"

Nedra raised her head and looked sharply into Catherine's eyes. Her voice was strong and disapproving. "When did I say that I *wish* to identify with her? I would have given anything not to have seen myself *in* her."

Catherine felt she couldn't afford to leave this subject. "Nedra, I wonder if Iphigenia agreed to die for reasons of country—seeing that the Greek fleet couldn't sail until the Artemis was appeased."

"No. She likely saw her father as corrupt and evil and felt she had nothing further to live for."

As they passed the deserted lodging on High Holborn where Catherine and Jamie discovered Alfred Nichols's body, the black velvet belt, and the bloody handkerchief, Nedra kept her eyes on the building, even after they had driven past it.

Catherine still felt the time wasn't right for specific questions about the murders. At present she would settle for whatever clues Nedra revealed in her account of Iphigenia. "Nedra, is it possible that she forgave her father for what he felt he had to do?"

Nedra took a final look over her shoulder at the deserted lodging. Once more her reply was short and contemptible. "No, it is *not* possible. No forgiveness. None. Not ever." Suddenly, Nedra's anger evaporated. Her eyes filled with tears. Catherine reached into her bag for a handkerchief and offered it to Nedra, who refused to take or even look at it.

"Catherine, do you know what happened after the Greeks left Troy?"

Catherine was startled by the lifeless voice. "They left a horse, as everyone knows."

"Agamemnon returned to his wife Clytemnestra, who was grieving for her daughter Iphigenia, yet still found the time to satisfy her new lover Aegisthus." Unable to sustain her patience, Catherine desired to move on from the sordid classical tale. "Nedra, I think it is time to take you to your lodging or back to the Pearcy's."

"I am not done." Nedra's voice made clear that she was implacable. Catherine would have to hear the rest of it.

"Very well. Go on, Nedra."

"Tell the driver to turn to the right here." They had reached Fetter Lane.

Catherine did as Nedra requested. "All right, please go on."

"Clytemnestra entangled Agamemnon in a cloth net and stabbed him to death while he bathed." She paused. "And surely she plunged the knife into his back." Smiling now, Nedra took her companion's hands. "I know what you are thinking, Catherine, but you forget that I was on stage at the moment Mr. Roberts-Smythe was killed."

Chapter 26

Jamie headed to his own house before joining Catherine at the Pearcy's. He knew his father would send word about the bullet recovered at the abandoned house on High Holborn and those in the pistol owned by the man who assaulted him the previous night. Even if Alfred Nichols was shot by that weapon, such a fact couldn't prove the deceased man had also murdered Morris Roberts-Smythe and Charles Donovan. And what of the gentleman on the train? Undoubtedly he was somewhat involved, but had he actually been at The Acropolis the night of the killings? Was he the author of all the notes sending Patrick Copsey away from the theatre and both Copsey and Inspector Phillpotts to the address on High Holborn? Clearly, more than one man was involved in these crimes, but how many more?

As he stepped from the hansom cab in front of his residence, Jamie's thoughts turned to motive. Yes, a number of men might have wanted Roberts-Smythe dead—those working under him or those dismissed by him the previous summer. Would the same man or men also want to dispatch Donovan? Or had the poor soul simply been in the way that night? And why shoot Alfred Nichols at the abandoned lodging on High Holborn? What had Nichols seen or known to warrant a bullet to the head? Had he confronted the man or men who were responsible? Or had Nichols been part of the plan to murder Roberts-Smythe and merely suffered the fate of so many assassins whose services were no longer necessary? Had there been a disagreement about payment for the crimes? But who would have had the means to pay the murderer or murderers? And was this the real motive—money? Millard wondered further if the man who had attacked him in the access lane was at The Acropolis during the third act of *Hamlet*. Or was last night's assault the first time the man had attempted to do service for whoever it was who planned the murder of Roberts-Smythe?

Jamie once more tried to rub the soreness from his neck. It was certainly possible the assault was unrelated to the three killings, but he didn't believe it. Was envy a motive, then? Everyone knew he had in effect been demoted by Roberts-Smythe to make his old parts available for Ned Ludmore. Other than Phillpotts, no one could honestly suspect Jamie of the murders. It was true he wasn't on stage when Roberts-Smythe fell behind the arras. He was rather offstage attempting to steal a kiss from his wife. At least that memory made him smile as he reached the front door of his residence.

No, the reason he was attacked could only be a reaction to his unofficially investigating the murders of Roberts-Smythe, Donovan, and Nichols. Millard closed the front door behind him, appreciating more fully now that Cate would also be in similar danger. Instead of awaiting word from his father about the bullets, he would retrieve some clothing from his upstairs bedroom and return to the Pearcy's as fast as he could.

After speaking to his man Peters and his housekeeper Mrs. Leavis, Jamie headed up the steps. Peters remembered that the floors at the top of the stairs had just been scrubbed. "Mr. Millard, wait!" In his rush up the stairs, Peters stumbled two steps below Millard and fell against his employer. As the men toppled comically against the inside wall of the staircase, a bullet slammed into Peters. The servant groaned loudly just as Mrs. Leavis reached the bottom of the staircase. Her piercing howl muffled the sound of someone running from the morning room to the rear door of the house. It was evident the assailant had somehow entered from the rear and took a position that gave him a free shot at anyone climbing the stairs.

Millard heard the rapid footsteps but was unable to make a pursuit because Peters was crumpled against his feet writhing in pain and Mrs. Leavis, who was particularly fond of the older man, had bolted up the stairs in panic, throwing herself over Peters, who had been hit in the back of the shoulder. Jamie was confident Peters would be all right, provided he received quick medical attention. Ordering Mrs. Leavis to call for a physician, Millard did his best to staunch the bleeding and keep Peters assured that his wound wasn't mortal.

An hour later, after the physician had taken care of Peters, Jamie looked around the back of the house, but the setting darkness made difficult his finding anything. He questioned several in the area, all of whom said they had witnessed nothing. As he entered the cab for the ride to Pearcy's, it struck him there wasn't a policeman watching over his house. Evidently, Phillpotts or someone in the city force had pulled the detail.

~ # ~

Catherine wanted time alone to ponder Nedra's account of Iphigenia, including every inflection in her voice and sudden change of her mood. Michael Healy would point to Nedra's life as an actress to explain these disturbing manifestations of voice and personality. But his daughter would disagree, for actors usually left their dramatic flourishes and nuances at the theatre. Most often they spoke plainly, even ponderously from time to time when they engaged in general conversation. That is, unless they truly wished to use their vocal gifts to manipulate or mislead. Catherine refused to believe such was so with Nedra, for in her own way Nedra seemed intent on communicating sincerely. But her unarticulated fears forced her to speak indirectly—through the tragic story of Iphigenia.

Two matters took precedent over Catherine's going upstairs and thinking further about the matter. First, she had to get past Alice, who was begging to know what was discussed between the women in the hansom cab. Catherine told her they talked only of the fate of The Acropolis and Nedra's concern for her future as an actress. Alice sighed in exasperation at Catherine's stubborn dishonesty but decided to pursue the issue no further—for the time being—allowing Catherine to make it to her room with no further protest from her young friend.

The second hindrance to Catherine's consideration of Nedra and Iphigenia was the letter from Lord Oxley. She could postpone reading it no longer. Had Oxley sent her a direct or veiled threat of some kind? Or had he already taken some action to end her stage appearances in London? She opened the envelope with considerable anxiety and began reading.

Dear Miss Healy,

I presume another correspondence from me is the last thing you wish to read. I ask only that you allow me the privilege, as undeserving as it may be, of having this letter read to its conclusion.

First, I deeply regret my behavior the last time we were together. I admit that I behaved abominably. I wish you to know that I have felt little but shame since we parted. I understand it is feeble to excuse my actions by confessing a momentary lapse of decorum owing to a heightened sense of infatuation, made all the more inexcusable by the fact that we were alone.

As a small gesture of my regret and my high regard for you, I will by the end of the day tomorrow speak to Scotland Yard and the appropriate city officials and ask that The Acropolis Theatre be reopened in no more than three day's time. In addition, since I understand your desire to see Mr. Henry Jaynes elevated to the position of permanent theatre manager, I will also speak to the owners of the theatre, two of whom are expected back from Italy tomorrow, and strongly encourage them to make the appointment of Mr. Jaynes to the position.

I ask nothing from you but your willingness to consider forgiveness as it relates to my recent actions. I do not wish to intrude on your privacy in any way.

Before I close, let me send you one further offer of assistance. Know that I will act only with your permission, again because I wish to respect your privacy.

With all that has happened recently, I am willing to assign several men to watch the Pearcy home and anywhere else you may wish. The offer extends to accompanying you (at a discreet distance of course) wherever you may go until the man responsible for these horrendous acts is apprehended. The same may be said about anyone else you wish to see protected, either one of the Pearcy family or anyone else you feel in danger. Once more, I will assign no one until I hear from you directly.

Finally, I hope these promises and offers of assistance will in some small way help to mitigate my deplorable behavior when we were last together. I appeal to your kindness and generosity to take my offers in the true spirit in which they are given.

Catherine immediately read the letter a second time, looking for the smallest sign of Oxley's insincerity and for every possible implication wrapped inside each congenial word. Was it possible the man was honestly contrite? She felt proud for having warned him what she would do if he attempted to interfere with her stage career. She just might have intimidated him enough to prompt a respectful letter and possibly a genuine commitment to the immediate fortunes of The Acropolis and to Henry Jaynes. Her father had educated her to the practices of ruffians, who when meeting unexpected resistance, often become apologetic and overly deferential. In any event, she thought of how marvelous it would be if Oxley actually followed through on his promises.

She refused to trust him completely, of course. His inappropriate familiarity, his sordid offer to keep her, and his ungentlemanly implied threat could not so easily be forgotten or forgiven. That would take time, but she wondered if the contempt she had for him was indeed mitigated by this at least seemingly generous letter. And that offer to assign someone to watch over her and over anyone else for whom she feared was almost too unbearably tempting to accept. After what had happened to her husband the night before, could she afford to remain silent on this offer? If Oxley wished to show himself as honorable, then she and the rest of the company would be performing again very soon, perhaps under the official management of Henry Jaynes. She didn't need to communicate with Oxley about that. But should she wait until she was certain about the reopening and Jaynes's appointment before asking for Oxley's men to watch over Jamie?

She decided to make her decision about the matter the following morning, after a night's sleep and further consideration. But there could be no opportunity to consult openly with her husband, since he yet remained unaware of what really happened between her and Oxley at the private residence on High Holborn. Perhaps she could simply mention that the First Lord of the Treasury, a supporter of The Acropolis Theatre, was concerned about the well-being of the actors and therefore offered to protect them. Yes, the police had a man assigned to The Acropolis, and others at her husband's home and at the Pearcy's, but they had not prevented Jamie from his assault the previous night.

"Catherine!" Alice was knocking on the door.

"Yes?" She placed Oxley's letter back inside the locked box.

"Jamie's father is here."

Catherine opened the door. "Is he here to see Jamie?" She hoped he was. At this time, she couldn't bear to have the elder Millard sit her down and tell her she wasn't the right woman for his son.

"If I had to guess, I would say that he's here to see you, Catherine. He's carrying a box of Treacle tarts. He must have found out you love them so. Unless your husband likes them as much as you do."

Catherine shook her head. "Jamie's taste buds have a blind spot. He doesn't like them at all." Alice began laughing. "What are you giggling on about?"

"Blind taste buds? My, what nonsense they teach girls in Ireland."

Catherine headed down the stairs—right after she had playfully tugged Alice's pretty nose.

~ # ~

"Thank you for your time, Mr. Isaacs." Phillpotts watched the fully-bearded architect lower himself into the chair.

"You are welcome to it, Inspector, but this is not the best moment *for* it, I'm afraid. I am working late overseeing several renovations in both Belgrave and Grosvenor Squares."

"I appreciate the demands on your time, Mr. Isaacs, but be assured that I won't keep you long. Besides, I am particularly anxious for my supper. My work causes me to miss too many midday meals, I'm afraid."

"So, what can I do for you, Inspector?"

"I am curious about one aspect of the renovations you did for The Acropolis Theatre."

"I see." Isaacs pushed his torso squarely into the chair and offered nothing further.

"Well, can you tell me something about those renovations?"

"They were done last year, Inspector. By the request of and to the satisfaction, I should add, of Mr. Roberts-Smythe."

Phillpotts wondered if the man was always this succinct or if he was unwilling to speak openly about his work at The Acropolis. "Yes, of course. But having been there myself after his murder, I discovered backstage that curious and cramped room at the rear of the former costume and properties storage area."

"Again, I was instructed by Mr. Roberts-Smythe to construct it that way."

"Yes, yes, I know that. But did you question why Roberts-Smythe wanted that additional room with the inside narrow door leading down to a little used rear exit out of the theatre?"

"Or entrance into it, Inspector."

"Yes—quite so." Phillpotts attempted to translate Isaacs's slightly changed expression. "So now, why didn't you question him about it?"

"I never ask such questions of those who hire me, Inspector."

"But *I* am not hiring you, Isaacs. Rather, I am in my own crude way *requiring* you to answer my question."

Isaacs lowered his eyes and stared at the half-empty bottle of whisky at the top of Phillpotts's desk. "Crude way, indeed."

"Let me be more elegant, then. What is your best guess as to why Roberts-Smythe asked for those unusual adjustments to the interior of The Acropolis? But before you answer, would you like a drink?"

"I have another two hours of work tonight, I'm afraid. Thank you, no."

Phillpotts lifted the bottle. He saw Isaacs contemplate the liquor with disdain. "I'm sure you're used to something more expensive, Isaacs, but I find this concoction ends my day just as well as it starts my morning."

"I'm sure it does, Inspector." Isaacs looked over his shoulder toward the door.

"Was Henry Jaynes privy to the design of the areas I just mentioned?"

"Jaynes, Inspector?"

"Yes. Jaynes."

"I have no idea if Mr. Roberts-Smythe consulted him about it."

"Did Jaynes speak with you during the renovations?"

"Not that I recall. Wait. I believe he was out of town at the time." Isaacs studied Phillpott's face. "You seem disappointed by my answer, Inspector."

"Just another question or two, Isaacs and then you'll be free to return to your work."

"Then by all means, ask them."

"As part of the renovations, you constructed those storage compartments in and near the backstage area of The Acropolis, which they call 'The Honeycombs,' I believe. That's correct, isn't it?"

"It is."

"And in one of those compartments was found the body of the actor Charles Donovan. Were you aware of that, Mr. Isaacs?"

"The murders have been no secret, Inspector."

"Quite true, sir. Now, you have no doubt been acquainted with many members of the company." Phillpotts shuffled the short whisky glass back and forth, moving it closer to Isaacs each time. "And I would assume you knew at least some of those who were in the audience that night. Not to mention whatever you might have heard about the murders from your son David, who works for Lord Oxley. At least I believe he still does."

Isaacs's disinterested manner concealed his confusion over Phillpott's apparent implications. "You are correct, Inspector, but I haven't talked to my son about the events at The Acropolis. We are both very busy men."

"Of course. Now, did you examine your notes and plans relating to the renovations before you came to see me."

"And why the devil would I do that? But even if I did, what difference would it make?" Isaacs stood and immediately moved to the office door.

Phillpotts finished his drink. "None, I suppose, but I'm still troubled by that small room and the exit down to the street at the rear of the theatre. Now if you could just tell me what you believed Roberts-Smythe's reasons for wanting it might be."

As his patience fled, it left a grimace of indignation in its place. "Damn you, Inspector. I have already said or implied that a man's reasons are not my business when it comes to construction and renovation. Payment is my only concern."

"And your reputation?"

"Yes, Inspector, and my reputation. Without it, I wouldn't have met with the success I have."

"Or the associations with highly influential men?"

Visibly frustrated, Isaacs leaned his head back against the door. "I assume Roberts-Smythe wanted that small room for more . . . for private reasons, Inspector. And he was most insistent that it included an inside door and a way to get to and from to the street behind the theatre."

"And he never told you specifically why he wanted these additions? Why not, do you think?"

"For the last time—I didn't ask him, and he never told me."

"And he knew that you wouldn't ask, eh?" Phillpotts stood and moved toward Isaacs, who was still pressed against the office door.

"I'm sure he felt confident I wouldn't't."

"Because of your sterling reputation for discretion?"

Isaacs emitted a labored sigh. "Inspector, I have no doubt that over the years you have come upon some rather wildly decorated or unusually constructed rooms and niches in your investigations."

"Isaacs, are you implying that Roberts-Smythe was using that area as a secret opium den?" Phillpotts immediate laughter assured Isaacs he wasn't serious. Having closed the distance between them, Phillpotts was a mere two feet in front of Isaacs. If his intentions were to menace, he was doing a fairly good job of it.

"Inspector, I long ago decided not to make it my business to ask or to question the uses to which anyone put a large room or even a small niche."

Phillpotts leaned close enough for Isaacs to smell the inexpensive whisky on his breath. "Perhaps it would have been wiser if you had."

"Is that all, Inspector? I really must return to my work."

Phillpotts turned and walked back to his desk. "Thank you for your time, Mr. Isaacs."

Chapter 27

"How did you know I have such a weakness for Treacle tarts, Dr. Millard?"

"I overheard my son comment on your fondness for them, Miss Healy. Fortunately I haven't lost that much of my hearing since I passed the age of sixty. I only act as though I have. That way, I hear what otherwise wouldn't be intended for my ears."

Alice laughed broadly at the joke and deftly reached for one of the tarts.

Catherine cocked her head in an attitude of disapproval. "Alice, I think it only polite you ask before you take one."

Alice smoothly withdrew her hand from the tray on which the tarts had just been placed. "My apologies. Dr. Millard, would it be all right if I took one?"

"My dear, you will have to ask Miss Healy. I have given them to her."

"Catherine, may I?"

"You shouldn't. It might spoil your supper." The young woman looked as though she were about to cry. "I'm only teasing, Alice. Of course you may take one—into the other room."

Alice gratefully snatched one of the Treacle tarts, but only reluctantly left the room to Catherine and Thomas Millard.

Thomas waved to her as she disappeared. "I'm quite surprised by how quickly her heart began breaking when you told her she couldn't have a tart." Catherine laughed. "Alice is going to make a splendid performer on the public stage—that is, if she can ever convince her father to let her appear in a play. She can shift her moods in the wink of an eye—far better than I can."

"So you're saying that sincerity is not a virtue of the good actress?"

Catherine withheld her reply for a moment. She knew she couldn't converse at all with the elder Millard if she feared he would take everything she said as a mark against her. It was time to give her instincts and natural playfulness their rein. "A good actress must be able to convey sincerity at all times, Dr. Millard. But also duplicity when the occasion calls for it."

Thomas looked completely confused. "Do you mean on stage or off?"

"Both." Catherine tapped his hand. "I am only teasing you, you know."

"Is your teasing an example of your sincerity or your duplicity, Miss Healy?" She was completely charmed by his impish smile, as well as his witty reply. Once more she permitted his playfulness to calm her fears that he would disown his son the moment he heard of Jamie's marriage to an Irish Catholic actress.

"I trust your son will soon be here."

"Well, if he's not, my visit hasn't been in vain. I can see why so many attend the plays at The Acropolis this past season."

"That is most kind of you, sir. But surely your son is another reason they come. He is a masterful actor, I hope you know."

"I am? Well, I thought I would never hear you admit it, Cate." She hadn't heard her husband come in the front door.

"Look what your father has brought me."

Jamie's smile at the thoughtfulness of his father was soon replaced by a more serious expression. "I have something to reveal to the both of you. Perhaps you should sit down, Cate." After Jamie removed his winter coat, Catherine noticed the blood stains on his waistcoat and shirt. It was all she could do to sit before her legs gave way. On the several times she accompanied her father to the scene of a crime, he praised her for standing up to the sight of blood without resorting to "swooning like all the other girls." But this was her husband with blood on his clothing, and she was frankly surprised that her immediate reaction was more in keeping with her father's description of her sex.

After Jamie explained what had happened to his man Peters, his shaken father revealed what he had discovered about the bullets found in the abandoned house on High Holborn and in the pistol carried by the man who had assaulted his son the night before. "Now I had best go and see about the bullet taken by the unfortunate Peters." Thomas thought further. "What about Phillpotts? When are you going to tell him about the shooting at your residence?"

"I have already sent one of my neighbors to inform him."

John Vance

"Good. All right, I'll leave you now. Are you properly armed, my boy?"

"Yes. Right here." Jamie went to his heavy coat and took the pistol from the pocket.

Catherine could think of nothing at this moment but Oxley's offer to protect all of them if she so wished it. But how best to communicate that desire to the First Lord of the Treasury?

Her musings were interrupted by a knock on the front door. Alice, who was still in another room savoring the aftertaste of her tart, called out to one of the servants, "The door!" She bounded into the room and saw Jamie holding a pistol with blood stains on his waistcoat and the upper part of his shirt. "Oh, dear!" But before she could learn what had happened, the servant came scurrying into the room and on through to the front door. She immediately returned with Mrs. Leavis.

Jamie was most surprised to see his housekeeper. "Mrs. Leavis, what are you doing here? I told you not to worry—that I'd be safe."

"Well, I'm not about to accept that assurance, Mr. Millard, just because you said so. But the fact is I came here to show you what I discovered on the floor at the entrance of the morning room. She held a section of a torn photograph. "Sometimes, things are right under our noses, sir. You looked all over outside the rear of the house, but not in the morning room. The man must have dropped this or it fell out his pocket when he pulled out his pistol."

"Let me see that." Jamie took the piece of the photograph and showed it to Catherine. "It looks like we have the upper left-hand corner of the picture."

Catherine's eyes expanded. "Look at the face. The rip is right through the left ear downward, but you can clearly see the woman's eyes and hair." The eyes of the woman in the photograph wore a dreamy yet frightened expression. "I know these eyes, Jamie."

As the elder Millard retrieved his coat for his return trip to the hospital, Catherine said goodnight and went upstairs to her room, leaving Alice and the younger Millard to say their farewells to Thomas and to Mrs. Leavis.

Mrs. Leavis began wrapping the comforter around her neck. "Oh, I almost forgot. Mr. Millard, will you again be spending the night at your father's? I must say you should at least allow me to come and have a proper supper prepared for the both of you. Heaven only knows what

217

kind of meals you gentlemen have been taking, given that you have been spending so many nights together."

The expressions on Jamie's and Alice's faces were poles apart. Jamie's mouth had opened and his eyes shut almost convulsively, rivaling the popular impression of a man having just breathed his last. On the other hand, Alice's eyes expanded in anticipation of some delicious catastrophe about to occur. As for the elder Millard, his mouth, eyes, and all the rest of him remained unmodified. His son could only hope his father's complaints about his progressive loss of hearing were no exaggeration.

Mrs. Leavis shook the edge of her comforter at Jamie. "Well, I will ask again. Are you staying with your father tonight, Mr. Millard?"

"Yes he is, and I'm getting rather tired of his nightly visits, Mrs. Leavis. Like one of Mr. Dickens's Christmas ghosts, he haunts my every sleeping hour. He's old enough now to sleep by himself, don't you think?" The old doctor took the edge of the comforter from her hand and wrapped it once more around her neck.

After Mrs. Leavis left grumbling about not being given permission to prepare a meal for the two men, Jamie stared at his father, who acted as though he hadn't bothered to consider the implications of what he'd just heard. Were Jamie able to think coherently, he would have forced himself to confess the marriage so his father wouldn't believe the worst of his son's judgment and especially of Cate's virtue. But all Jamie could push out of his throat was an anemic "Father, I . . ."

Thomas quickly interrupted. "Must go, my boy. Have much to do." He smiled, doffed his winter hat, and joined the policeman who was at the street waiting to accompany him.

~ # ~

Alone in her room, Catherine contemplated further Nedra Alexander's impassioned recounting of the myth of Iphigenia. Catherine softly and slowly bit down on her lower lip, as she invariably did whenever pondering anything seriously. To Nedra at least, Iphigenia was betrayed by her father. Was Nedra's father alive? Catherine didn't recall her ever speaking of him. Although Nedra mentioned no father, she surely had a man who served such a role in her life. There was no escaping the conclusion that Morris Roberts-Smythe might well have been that man.

When Catherine first joined the company, she noted the glances Nedra gave Roberts-Smythe whenever the manager addressed the company. Catherine had even caught Nedra looking at him in that way when the manager simply passed them in the theatre, whether it was in rehearsal or in performance. The look suggested respect and admiration, but something else. A look that transcended what one gives even to a revered colleague or employer. It wasn't in the manner of a lover or a woman in the throes of infatuation, but there was something there that made Nedra seem as though she needed something from Roberts-Smythe and was afraid he would stop providing it. The exact look that rivaled the expression of the woman in the torn photograph—the woman whose eyes and forehead had immediately brought Nedra Alexander to mind.

Was it possible Nedra's life had paralleled in some way the mythological tale of sacrifice, betrayal, lust, and murder? Had she experienced any of these horrors or had she merely seen them happen to another? If so, Catherine could only imagine what that might have done to destroy Nedra's spirits and alter her behavior. And if she had experienced anything resembling these abominations, did they occur years earlier, when she was a girl—or more recently? Or was she experiencing them now?

~ # ~

Before he left his office for home, Oliver Pearcy placed Lord Oxley's letter in his strong box. He couldn't risk having the letter read by anyone, especially those residing at his house. The correspondence bedeviled him. What was Oxley up to? The appeal to Pearcy's patriotism was one thing, but predicting dire consequences for Pearcy's legal career and the future of his entire family infuriated the attorney. It didn't matter to him that the First Lord of the Treasury professed genuine concern and wrote the letter in a tone that couldn't be construed as a threat. But Pearcy knew it was a threat. He had little doubt that Oxley's promise to suppress any rumors about to come to the attention of the newspapers and possibly the police was purely an ultimatum, regardless of the tactful manner in which it was expressed. Oxley had to assume Pearcy would have great difficulty refusing the request made of him.

Therefore I ask only that you find the occasion, while Miss Healy is away from the house, to enter her room and look for any correspondence she may have lying about or carefully concealed that was sent from Ireland particularly. It is with the deepest regret that I ask you to do this service for Her Majesty. Not simply regret over having you do something you will certainly find intrusive and ungentlemanly, but also regret that such a brilliant artist as Miss Healy might well be involved in treasonous activity against the crown. I assure you the evidence we have pointing to her as an agent for one or more of the violent Irish independence organizations is strong enough to compel me to request this service of you.

To Pearcy's mind, Catherine Healy was no such thing. But Oxley's insistence on the matter suggested there might at least be evidence enough to warrant a discreet examination of her correspondence, in case others were attempting to use her for treacherous purposes or solicit from her information to aid their cause. Pearcy felt he could justify doing Oxley's bidding—again since the motive was a matter of protecting his country. But Pearcy also realized he was motivated first and foremost by a fear of being exposed and therefore harming his children and his career. Yet how did Oxley discover what he had been doing besides his legal duties?

~ # ~

Henry Jaynes returned to his office, as he had done at least once a day since the night of the murders. Nothing had come from the owners of The Acropolis regarding their plans for the next several months. They would of course expect Jaynes to honor Roberts-Smythe's scheduled stagings for February, March, and April—once again, if the theatre reopened by the end of the month and the owners kept him on as acting manager during that time. Jaynes felt confident they wouldn't replace him in the immediate aftermath of the murders, especially since he had Catherine Healy and other members of the company, as well as Emma Cons at the Old Vic, speaking on his behalf. But what of the following 1898/1899 season—and those after that? Would he be appointed manager full-time?

Jaynes examined a list of possible plays for the next season. If he became the theatre's permanent manager, he wanted to include more of the modern naturalistic dramas, particularly those of Ibsen, as well as the work of contemporary playwrights—Bernard Shaw for example. There was much else Jaynes wished to change about The Acropolis if he had the opportunity to manage it, but he agreed with Roberts-Smythe that securing the talents of the best available actors was paramount to the theatre's future success. And now Edward Ludmore had decided to take his skills to New York. Jaynes thought of securing an attorney and forcing Ludmore to honor his contract or to make him pay dearly for the privilege of breaking it, but given the current situation, the most prudent course was to let the actor sail to Manhattan, fail miserably with the less refined American audiences, and then plead for reinstatement in London for the 1898/99 season.

Jaynes set down his pen and took his glass of Scotch whisky to Roberts-Smythe's office. He entered and sighed at the untidiness resulting from the recent police investigation. A number of books had been scattered on the desk and two had been dropped on the floor. Jaynes placed his drink on the desk and bent to retrieve the two books for re-shelving. If he was anything, he was a most tidy man.

"Moving in so soon, Jaynes?"

Jaynes was so startled by Phillpotts's intrusion that he lost his balance and fell forward to his knees. "Damn you, Phillpotts." Jaynes struggled to his feet.

"Did you really expect not to see me again, Jaynes?"

"I was only *hoping* not to see you again, Inspector. Let me venture a guess. You've finally come to arrest me for the murders of Roberts-Smythe and Charles Donovan."

"I must admit that it's far more enjoyable having you wonder when exactly I will be doing so rather than actually confronting you with any formal charges."

"You are behaving so damned absurdly. You realize that, don't you? All to avenge something in the past that you have always greatly misrepresented in your mind."

"Is that what my sister's death is to you, Jaynes? A misrepresentation?"

Exasperated, Jaynes attempted to return his office, but Phillpotts blocked his way. "I must say, Jaynes, I think it quite revealing hearing you punctuate your assertions with all those quaint 'damns.'"

"No man could be expected to maintain decorous speech in the face of your persecution, Inspector."

"Not persecution at all, Jaynes. Simple justice, that is all."

"Your sister was deeply disturbed. When will you accept that? She took her own life. I never—"

"It was at your prompting."

"My prompting?"

"You drove her to it. Other than the loss of a sister I dearly loved, my largest regret is that I have never known exactly what you did to her to make her think her life wasn't worth living."

"You're mad, Inspector. You're undeniably mad."

"Save the dramatic stage-speech, Jaynes. I am not an appreciative audience. Yet I will admit that madness is sometimes a goal worthy of one's effort."

"You are simply spouting nonsense, Inspector. I regrettably ended the relationship with your sister—as happens dozens of times a day between young men and women who believed they were in love but then realized the error of their perceptions. I never wished your sister to . . . Wait. Wait. I see now. You are attempting to make me express myself irrationally by accusing and persecuting me. Just waiting for me to say something you can misrepresent in court, isn't that it?"

"I've been making some inquiries about you, Henry." Phillpotts turned deftly and walked out of the office. Jaynes reached for the glass of whisky. His hand quivered as he picked it up. "Why won't you leave me alone? Why won't everyone simply leave me alone?"

~ # ~

Catherine sat on the edge of her bed, ruminating on Nedra's black velvet belt with the inscription Aydin Kormaz had translated for her. Who presented Nedra with that gift—or had she purchased it herself? Had she ever been to the eastern part of the Mediterranean? If so, had she gone with a family member or with a man passionately interested in her? Who then? Only one name came to Catherine's mind at the moment. Morris Roberts-Smythe. The manager had taken several trips to the Mediterranean, Aegean, and Black Seas and often commented on his affection for Egypt, Greece, Bulgaria, Romania, and Turkey. Catherine questioned her own earlier assessment of Nedra and Roberts-Smythe's relationship. Could there have been a more intimate aspect to it? For the first time, she thought of Roberts-Smythe as a man with needs. Had he occasionally acted on them—and with Nedra Alexander? Catherine pressed her fingers against her temples. Had Roberts-Smythe used the small secret room at the end of the old storage are for something carnal?

Resigning herself to another meeting with Nedra the following morning, Catherine took out a piece of stationary to answer Lord Oxley's most recent correspondence. His promise to protect her and anyone else she wished to keep safe was impossible to ignore. How many other assaults on her husband would be attempted in the days ahead? There were also the Pearcys and the elder Millard, whose lives could also be in jeopardy. Should she simply list these names and politely ask Oxley to have someone watch over them until the murderer was apprehended? She wouldn't solicit any protection for herself. That way, the First Lord of the Treasury would understand he was to expect no further communications from her. She decided to write as much in the passive voice as possible to put further distance between them.

Your generous offer to protect those closest to me is very much appreciated. The names of the Pearcy family and those of my fellow actor James Millard and his father Dr. Thomas Millard would be offered by me as those I would most wish to have so protected.

She frowned at the stilted prose, evidently the result of the clumsy passive voice. But she also disliked calling her husband a "fellow actor." She knew Oxley would wonder why she had singled out Jamie from all the others at The Acropolis—that is, if Oxley didn't already know the nature of their relationship. Oxley might simply ignore the request to guard Jamie and his father, out of misplaced envy if for no other reason. Or he might even attempt to harm them out of the same motive.

Catherine put down her pen and tore what she had written into several pieces. She couldn't accept Oxley's offer—any part of it. She knew what he would expect from her if she did.

Chapter 28

"David?"

"Yes, Lord Oxley."

"The murders at The Acropolis occurred a week ago tonight, did they not?"

"I believe so, yes."

The First Lord of the Treasury stood in front of his office window, gazing at the street below. "It's been a long and most unproductive day. What time is it now?"

"Half past three in the afternoon, Lord Oxley."

"David, I want you to return to the home of the attorney Pearcy and ask to speak to Miss Healy. Inform her that I would like a reply to the offer I made in my last letter. Tell her also that she must give you the reply at once, for events dictate immediate action on my part if she wishes to accept. Do you have all that, David?"

"Yes, Lord Oxley. But what shall I say if she asks me what those events are to which you must take immediate action?"

"Provide no answer. Let her wonder. Go now, and don't leave there without speaking directly to her. If she is away, learn where she is and find her. Do *not* come back until you have her answer."

"Yes, Lord Oxley."

Before Isaacs reached the door, Oxley turned from the window. "David, there is one more thing. Go to this address before you go to the Pearcy home." Oxley wrote the address and handed it to Isaacs. "I want you to tell me what you observe and whether you see anyone familiar."

"I understand, Lord Oxley."

Oxley sat at his desk and contemplated the several possibilities that lay before him. Surely he would find success in one of them.

~ # ~

The blow struck Nedra fully against her cheek and mouth. It was delivered by the back of a thick and filthy hand. She remained upright but only barely. Perhaps she had braced herself, knowing the blow was inevitable the moment she said no to his demand.

The late afternoon brought a strong frigid wind along with the rapid approach of darkness. Nedra had come with her housekeeper Betty to the home of another actress at the end of Drury Lane—right before it connected to High Holborn. After dismissing Betty, Nedra delivered a small birthday gift and walked immediately to High Holborn, turning east and ending up at the abandoned lodging where the body of Alfred Nichols was found almost a week before. She felt she had no choice but to meet the man at the location he specified. He said he needed to clear up a few matters with her. And she well knew why he had chosen this place.

"You'll give me what you've given to every other man, or I'll do more with this little fellow than you're used to in your little games." Nedra saw him draw forth a wicked looking knife from the inside of his boot.

"Please, don't threaten me. Not now."

"Not now? What are you saying, woman?"

"You said you needed some answers from me. I'll provide them if you'll just leave me alone. Please, John, don't do this."

Backing toward the staircase where Nichols's was shot, Nedra's heels hit the bottom step, causing her to fall rearward. Her elbows slammed into one of the steps, but she was too overcome with fear to feel the pain. She looked up at the man with whom she had once bantered teasingly backstage at The Acropolis. He was new to the company then and had heard about the amorous propensities of the actress who played women older than her age but whose physical charms still commanded the kind of attention younger women envied, though never admitted to openly.

He was handsome enough, she had thought then, though his rough features and bulky physique suppressed any desire ever to kiss him passionately. She could indulge in flirtation but nothing more, even though she understood he wanted more—wanted what he had just told her she had given freely to others. Freely? If he only knew at what heavy price she had paid for every one of her intimate encounters.

At thirty-three, John Metcalfe was only slightly older than Nedra. Like Bernhard Schneider and Alfred Nichols, he was one of the three characters on stage at the opening of *Hamlet*—the Francisco of the evening. The first to go off stage, Metcalfe was instructed by Roberts-Smythe to leave the theatre early, as were the other men. But Metcalfe had come back into the theatre that night through the little known entrance at the rear of The Acropolis and up the narrow stairway to the door leading into the small, sparse, and secret room at the end of the old storage area.

"I thought you'd appreciate giving me my due right here in this lovely abandoned house, Nedra—right upstairs in that room where you sacrificed a few drops of blood against your will. And by the way, how is your arm? Has the cut mended? Or has there been another added since I saw you last?" Metcalfe grabbed her arm while she lay on the stairs and squeezed where he remembered seeing her bleed. She grimaced, showing him that he had found the spot, although she did not cry out.

Metcalfe began undoing his trousers. "Then again, this staircase is just as good a place as any." His heavy coat was still on his back. He looked over his shoulder. The inside of the abandoned lodging was almost completely dark now. "Not a mouse stirring."

"What?" Nedra watched him unsnapping the leather braces and pulling down his trousers.

"'Not a mouse stirring.' It's one of my few lines as Francisco at the beginning of the play. I take it you never listened to me give my lines, did you?"

Nedra's voice betrayed her growing panic. "I was getting ready to enter the stage in the second scene. I couldn't . . . I couldn't."

"Here's more of the pathetically little I had to say—which so perfectly fits this present occasion and what you're about to give me." His trousers dropped below his knees. "For this relief much thanks. 'Tis bitter cold, / And I am sick at heart." He grabbed the banister with his right hand and began to lower himself over her.

"Dearest John, why are you sick at heart?" Nedra desperately hoped her caring manner might prevent what was about to happen to her.

Metcalf laughed crudely as he began pulling at her clothing. "So now you are concerned for my happiness, is that right, *Miss* Alexander? Well, I'll tell you why I'm sick at heart."

She couldn't understand why she wasn't grabbing at his hands as they pulled roughly at her dress and moved it up her torso. Was it a numbing fear or a dispiriting familiarity with a moment such as this?

"Please, John. Don't."

"I'm sick at heart because I failed to kill James Millard earlier today."

Nedra placed both of her hands on either side of him as he lowered his face over hers to seize a kiss.

"No, John."

"Yet I have been successful at other things I set out to do, and I am well fortified with funds." His mouth assaulted hers, as her hands began batting at the sides of the heavy coat he still wore. "But there is further business to be done before I leave this city for good and live the life of a proper gentleman. And one of those things I am about to do." He pressed himself down upon her. He took satisfaction in feeling her hands cease their slapping against his sides and in sensing one of them gently glide up his clothing.

Metcalfe lifted his head and bore his eyes into Nedra's. "And now let me speak one final line from Francisco's meager batch of words in the opening scene. Since you never listened to what I said, I'll remind you that Marcellus asks who has relieved him, and my character Francisco says, "Bernardo hath my place." And you know that Bernardo was played by our late friend Alfred Nichols. One of the many men you have warmed in your bed and who paid such a dear price for his pleasure. Well, now it is I who has his place."

As Metcalf began to place himself into her body, Nedra screamed as loudly as she could. She wanted to blunt the sound of the pistol she fired into Metcalfe's upper chest. The pistol she had felt and drew forth from his coat pocket while he was attempting to grind his lips against hers.

Metcalfe fell forward, pinning her against the stairs. She managed to move her head toward the wall to avoid as much of the blood from the wound as possible, but given her twisted positioning on the stairs, she was unable to push his body off hers. She had to call for help and hoped that someone was nearby to respond. Yet before she could adjust her body and muster enough breath to call out, she heard the sound of footsteps running into the abandoned lodging.

In a moment, she felt Metcalfe's body lift from hers. Staring at the ceiling and still lying on her back, Nedra heard the body drop to the floor at the foot of the stairs. As she frantically pushed her clothing down to cover herself, she lowered her eyes and saw the man now bending over her. She screamed a second time—this time even more loudly than the first.

~ # ~

"Cate, come here. Look out the window. See? Those three men—there, there, and there." Jamie pointed directly across the street and then to the left and right. "Unless we are about to be robbed, I assume they're watching over us. But I can't believe they are all police. None of them is wearing a uniform."

Catherine drew back from the downstairs window. Who else could they be but Lord Oxley's men? Soon she was flush with indignation. She knew what he had done. He had sent these men to make her feel as though she had agreed to his offer. He had taken her silence as assent. Now he would expect her gratitude and more.

"Cate, what's the matter?"

"Nothing. I . . . I was just worried about my father. I hope he made the train to Basingstoke."

~ # ~

Oliver Pearcy had insisted his daughter continue to entertain young George Wooten, who came calling ten minutes earlier. Wishing the young man to leave, Alice objected to both her father's insistence and her brother Matthew's snickering. She needed no distractions in her quest to learn from Catherine and Jamie all that had happened to them the past two days.

Leaving his daughter and Wooten in the parlor, with one of the servants keeping a watchful though completely unnecessary eye on them, Pearcy escorted his son upstairs for his nightly studies. Pearcy shut the boy's door and took several steps down the hall until he stood before Catherine Healy's room. She and Millard were still downstairs, perhaps trying to rescue Alice from George Wooten's inane conversation.

Pearcy was attuned to the sounds of his house. He would know the moment anyone began mounting the stairs. Even so, he was taking a serious gamble going into the room and searching for any evidence of his boarder's involvement with Irish nationalists. Pearcy cursed silently. All had been going so well, and now he was forced to do the bidding of Oxley. All because of the concessions he made to those impulses that too often governed his decisions and obscured his better judgment.

Pearcy pulled back the delicate curtain on the window in Catherine's room. The view was excellent, and he spotted the three men standing across the street. He immediately recognized two of them. All three were stepping toward a hansom cab that had just pulled up to the far side of the street. A man stepped from it. Pearcy couldn't see his face, but he had no doubt who it was.

~ # ~

"Cate, did you say you were worried about your father getting his train for Basingstoke?"

She had no choice but to continue her fabrication. She couldn't mention her suspicions about the three men outside because she would then have to reveal her meetings with Oxley and his letters to her. She despaired. When would she ever find the courage to tell her husband everything? "Yes, I am concerned, Jamie. If he missed the train, my aunt will be alarmed."

"Sorry to hear it, for your father has indeed missed his train to Basingstoke."

"How can you know that?" She assumed her husband was being jocular and would now deliver a line to make them both laugh.

"Because he's just arrived outside this house in a hansom."

"My father?" Catherine peered out the downstairs window and witnessed Michael Healy speaking to one of the men across the street. He then nodded to the man and stepped back into the cab. Catherine couldn't believe her father was going away without coming to the house.

Catherine turned from the window. She was determined to chase the cab down the street if necessary. Jamie grabbed for her arm. "Wait, the cab is turning around. It's stopping in front of this house."

Catherine was relieved. Being with her father this evening would be most comforting. She touched her hair to be sure each strand was in place and took her position near the front door. "Jamie, come from the window. He might look up and see you staring at him."

"What's this? He's helping a woman out of the cab."

"My aunt? Did she come by herself to London, then? I'm most surprised. She has always refused my invitations for her to do so."

"I don't know your aunt, so I couldn't be sure if she is . . . Oh, good God. It's not your aunt."

"No?" Catherine felt queasy at the next intruding thought. She softly spoke her suspicion. "Can my father actually have a lady friend here in London?"

Jamie stepped back from the window. His tone was somber. "I hope not, Cate. The woman is Nedra Alexander."

~ # ~

After they entered and were brought tea, Michael Healy explained that he took it upon himself to examine further the area where he had shot the still un-indentified man who had assaulted Jamie. Having found nothing else relating to the event, Healy walked to the abandoned lodging where Cate and Jamie had found the body of one of the Acropolis's actors. "After you told me about the murder there, I decided that before I left London I would have a look about. As I approached the vacant building, I heard a pistol shot and then ran inside, with my own weapon drawn. I turned to my left and saw a man lying on Miss Alexander. I pulled the body from her and bent over to see if she was harmed. When she screamed, I backed away and assured her I was only there to help."

Nedra nestled further into the sofa, still trembling. "I was so afraid he was going to hurt me. I didn't know who he was, Catherine. I didn't believe anything he said about wanting to assist me—until he informed me he was your father and that we had met last autumn when he came to visit you at The Acropolis—and that he was the chief inspector of the Dublin police. It was only then that I found the strength to rise from the stairs and go to him. Oh, look at me. I must look utterly hideous."

Catherine and Alice took Nedra upstairs and washed all the traces of blood and filth from her body and gave her fresh clothing to change into. Oliver Pearcy had come down the stairs the moment Michael Healy and Nedra entered the house, followed soon afterward by his son.

Following their return downstairs, Nedra identified her assailant as the actor John Metcalfe and revealed most of what he had said to her. Catherine and Jamie were appalled that they had simply ignored him as a suspect in the murders of Roberts-Smythe, Donovan, and Nichols. Catherine was too ashamed to look at her father. Sensing her embarrassment, Michael Healy reached for her hand.

Nedra refused Alice's offer of food. "But he only admitted directly to an attempt on your life, James. He never came out and said he had murdered anyone else. He just made it clear that Alfred Nichols deserved what happened to him because . . ." She wouldn't finish. She had her eyes on young Alice and didn't wish the girl to know that their surprise guest had given herself to Nichols—as well as to other men. "John said he was going to leave London because he had done some or most of what he had set out to do, but not all—and I'm sure he meant more than just killing you, James."

Millard shook his head. "It seems fairly certain that he murdered Roberts-Smythe and Donovan. Metcalfe was a strong man, powerful enough to drive a blade deeply into Roberts-Smythe and to strangle Charles and then lift and place his body in the storage compartment backstage. And I have little doubt he shot Alfred. We can have my father check the bullet you fired into him with the one taken from Alfred—and with that removed from the shoulder of my man Peters. They will all match, I'm sure. Now we need to consider his motive for all this incomprehensible mayhem."

Michael Healy interrupted. "But what of the gentleman you said you and your father met on the train and the man I killed in the access lane off High Holborn? You will have to consider their connection to Metcalfe as well, James."

Catherine was relieved that her father's addendum to Jamie's assessment was spoken in a tone of professional courtesy, investigator to fellow investigator.

Jamie respectfully nodded. "Of course. We must also consider what you have just noted, Mr. Healy. Only then can we know everything."

Suddenly Nedra stood and grabbed Catherine's wrists and spoke to her as if no one else were in the room. "Catherine, I must speak with you, and I don't want anyone else to hear."

Catherine glanced at her husband and her father, who both gestured that she should again take Nedra upstairs.

"Let us go up to my room, Nedra. No one will disturb us there."

When she and Nedra entered the room, Catherine noticed that the locked box where she kept her correspondence was on the wrong side of the table where she usually kept it. But that wasn't all that unusual, given the housekeeper's inability to return things to their proper place.

~ # ~

"Father, why are you looking up the stairs?" Matthew Pearcy judged his father's behavior as most peculiar.

"I just wanted to be sure Miss Healy and Miss Alexander didn't stumble on their way up, that's all."

"But they have already gone into Miss Healy's room."

"Matthew, I suggest that you return to your reading."

Pearcy recalled that he had picked up the locked box in Catherine's room and attempted to ascertain how much correspondence she might have in it. But when he was forced to come down after Michael Healy arrived with Nedra Alexander, he couldn't be sure he had returned the box to its same place on the vanity table. Regardless, he now had something Lord Oxley might wish to know. The two men Pearcy recognized outside his house were suspected of plotting violent acts against the English government in the name of Irish independence. He knew them because he had taken their case a year earlier—truly believing in their innocence—and negotiated their release from custody provided they leave London immediately and return to Dublin.

Would Oxley be satisfied with the fact that they had violated the terms of their release and returned, without Pearcy having to tell him anything about the nature of Catherine Healy's correspondence, which from what he just read was only social and not political? And if Oxley demanded something about her to satisfy his suspicious nature, then Pearcy could reveal her secret marriage to James Millard. After all, they had concealed it only because of their respective fathers' likely objections to the match, which they both hoped to lessen in time. Would these bits of information placate Oxley enough to suppress what he knew about Pearcy? And as if to mock his precarious situation, Nedra Alexander was sitting in his own house. Since she arrived, she had refused to speak or even to look at him.

Chapter 29

For a full minute, Nedra stood frozen in the center of Catherine's room, saying nothing. Finally, she sat on the edge of the bed.

"Catherine, please come and take my hand." Nedra patted the bed, and Catherine took the place beside her. "It has become too much for me. I must confide in someone, and you are the only one I can trust."

The despair in Nedra's voice and her forlorn gaze convinced Catherine of Nedra's sincerity. "Nedra, you can tell me whatever you want—about anything."

Nedra squeezed Catherine's hand so tightly the sensation bordered on pain. "I fear whatever I say will make you think so much less of me than you must already do."

"It won't. And if it helps you at all, I have always believed your life to have been a difficult one."

Rather than expressing her relief at Catherine's understanding, Nedra's expression and voice altered, as they had when the women were riding along High Holborn. "Not just my past, Catherine. But my present. My very now."

"Just tell me something, Nedra."

Nedra rose from the bed and made her way to the door. Catherine assumed she was leaving the room, having now changed her mind about revealing what she had experienced and perhaps what she knew about the killings. But Nedra merely checked to see if the door was secure.

"Nedra, tell me why you insisted on riding along High Holborn and why you—"

"Why I looked at the abandoned house even after we had passed it?"

"Yes. Why did you do that and why did you say the street had such meaning in your life?"

"I once lived in that now abandoned house, Catherine. Or should I say I was kept there."

233

"Kept?"

"Kept there as a kept woman is kept. But I was no woman. I was only a girl of sixteen." Catherine's body sagged at the revelation. Nedra stepped to the window and peered down at the street. "I remained there until I went off to have the child."

"The child? Oh, dearest God. Who was the child's father?"

"She was a beautiful infant, Catherine. They took her from me so that she wouldn't be raised in scandal, or so he told me. I believe he thought I would never find out where my daughter went."

"Please, Nedra. Who is the 'he' you refer to?"

Nedra turned from the window and caught her reflection in the mirror above Catherine's vanity table. "I assumed the child would be taken to another part of England or even further away. I used to imagine she would go to America and that I would eventually go there and find her. Silly of me, wasn't it?"

"And you never discovered what happened to your daughter?"

"No. I learned from . . . someone else that she lived in London and always had from the time she was taken from me."

Watching Nedra study herself in the mirror, Catherine decided for the moment not to push her for the name of this "someone." "Have you seen your daughter?"

"Seen her? Oh, yes. But she has not seen me. Unless she has come to The Acropolis. But she wouldn't have known that the woman playing Gertrude in *Hamlet* was her mother."

"You have seen her but you haven't approached her?"

"I couldn't. She would ask me why I had abandoned her. That question I have always dreaded. I could never give a satisfactory answer, don't you see? She would never believe me if I simply said I had no choice but to leave her to someone else's care."

Catherine rose from the bed and went to her. "Where is your daughter living now?"

"She is now as young as I was when I gave birth to her. And . . ." Nedra was barely audible.

"Nedra?"

"And she has just had a child herself."

Catherine tried to smile. "She is indeed very young, but this is a wonderful moment for her—and for you, Nedra. May I ask the name of her husband?"

"She's had no church or civil ceremony. And do you know it was I who advised that such an arrangement as she now has with her child's father was acceptable in the eyes of God."

Catherine was confused. "But you said you have never approached her."

"I haven't. I gave that advice to the man she is living with—the father of the child—my grandchild."

"But how do you know him, Nedra?"

"As you know him. As a fellow employee of The Acropolis. The father is Patrick Copsey."

"Patrick?" Catherine gently turned Nedra's face away from the mirror. "Then your daughter's name is Clare. I have met her, Nedra. Jamie has as well. And we have seen the child." Catherine immediately regretted saying so.

Nedra's manner became more agitated. She once again stepped to the window. "You have met her? Her name is Clare? I have never known her name."

"You must go to her and the child. Clare and Patrick will understand. I will arrange a meeting tomorrow, if you wish it."

"No." Nedra was emphatic, her voice bordering on hostility. "I cannot let my daughter know who I am. When she learns about me, she will hate me. I couldn't bear her censure. It's best she knows nothing."

"But Nedra, your daughter doesn't have to know anything about what you may have done in the past—or even done more recently."

"Her father will see to it that she knows."

"Patrick you mean?" Catherine believed Nedra had misunderstood her comment.

"No, I mean Clare's father—the man who kept me in that horrid house on High Holborn."

"Does she know him—her father?"

"No. He has never owned her and he will never do so. He will deny everything as it relates to me. I went to him when I learned my daughter was with child. He denied ever having kept me at that dreadful house. He never knew me, he said—except for having seen me on the stage. Never knew me otherwise—not in any way."

"Then we will be sure that only you and Clare know. I won't tell anyone what you have told me."

"But there is also Patrick." Nedra's voice was almost completely drained of emotion.

"Patrick is a good fellow. He has no malice in him, Nedra."

"Catherine, don't you know that last spring I stole a kiss from him in the wings one evening night before I was to go on stage. It was just an act of harmless flirtation and I had no idea he would become the father of my daughter's child, but you can imagine how sickened he would be upon learning who I really am."

"Oh Nedra, Patrick would not hold that against you. He probably doesn't even remember the occasion."

"But he knows my reputation. You can't tell me that you haven't heard of my brief romances with several of the actors."

"Nedra, there is no need for you to chastise yourself for what you have—"

Once more she refused to allow Catherine to finish her point. "Alfred Nichols was one of those actors, did you know that? Yes Alfred, who was murdered in the house where I was once kept—where I came to be with child. And there were other men who weren't in our profession. And there were others I fear I led on but refused to give in to, such as John Metcalfe. You see, Catherine, I have suffered for rejecting men as well as for receiving them." She folded her arms across her chest. Her hands were trembling.

"Nedra, who are some of the others you have just mentioned?"

"No, no. I cannot tell you—not now, not now."

Catherine doubted Nedra would ever tell her. Had she been threatened by one or more of these men if she didn't keep silent? Once more, Catherine conjured thoughts of Oxley.

Nedra leaned her back against the window panes and took several long breaths either to prevent herself from breaking down or to prepare herself for what she would reveal next. "Catherine, it seems God made me to be used so. But I cannot say that I have been blameless. The attentions of some I sought because I was attracted to them naturally, as a woman is to a man. Others because I wanted something from them. And still others for whom I at first felt compassion but who used me to satisfy what they required only for themselves. And some have done things to others *because* of me."

Catherine remained silent. She knew Nedra was about to reveal something even more disturbing than what she had so far confessed.

"I have been deeply humiliated, Catherine. Made to do things I utterly despised. But I believed I had no choice. You must understand. My survival has depended on my many unwilling concessions. And then there was my daughter's fate. I couldn't risk having her harmed in any way."

Nedra began to roll up the sleeve of her dress. Catherine saw two fresh wounds on her arm, right below the elbow.

"Do you see these, Catherine? They were given to me so that I would better understand how necessary was my silence about everything that has happened to me. In both a secret room at The Acropolis and in an upstairs room at the house on High Holborn, I was cut on my arm with a knife. I willingly extended my arm so that the cuts could be made. That's how debased I have become."

"No, Nedra. It's not that way. You knew you would suffer more if you didn't comply."

"You are kind, but don't you see that my confessing this to you now may end up destroying me and my daughter? But I have to trust that you will help me and see at least that my daughter and granddaughter will always be safe."

"I will, Nedra. No one will hurt you again. Nor will anyone harm Clare and the baby. I promise you."

Nedra pressed the fingernails of both hands into her forehead. Catherine could she was in considerable distress.

"Nedra, is there more you wish to tell me?" Nedra shook her head, but only tentatively. "There is, isn't there?" Catherine grabbed Nedra's wrists and pulled them away from her face. "Look at you arm, Nedra. You didn't deserve these wounds. Do you hear me?"

Catherine's forceful emphasis immediately calmed Nedra. She took one more look at the wounds on her arm and slowly rolled down the sleeve of her dress. "You are correct, Catherine. There is more. Very well, I will tell you everything. No matter what it costs me, I will tell you everything.

~ # ~

Jamie stepped back into the house, after speaking with Michael Healy about those presently watching the Pearcy house. Healy had asked him not to mention these men to Inspector Phillpotts, leaving Jamie to conclude that they had somehow run afoul of the law. He didn't care. Cate's safety was the only matter that concerned him now.

Millard and Healy entered the house and noticed Oliver Pearcy sitting in a corner of the morning room, seemingly lost in thought. Before Jamie could ask Pearcy if he was all right, Catherine entered the room. Jamie could see she was serious and anxious.

"Jamie, we need to go to The Acropolis right now."

"I don't understand."

"Please. You need to go with me. Father, I should like you there as well.

George, go and ask Dr. Millard to come to the theatre. And ask him this as well." Catherine whispered into Wooten's ear.

"May I go too?"

"No, Alice. You need to stay here with your brother. But I want you to have one of the servants find Mr. Jaynes at his home and another to locate Inspector Phillpotts either at his home or in his office at Scotland Yard. The servants are to tell Mr. Jaynes and the Inspector to go immediately to The Acropolis."

Catherine's commanding tone persuaded Alice to refrain from insisting that she be allowed to go with them to the theatre. "All right, Catherine, I'll send the servants right away."

There was a knock on the door. Matthew Pearcy opened it to reveal David Isaacs.

"I should like to see Miss Healy."

Matthew asked him to wait and went to the morning room to tell Catherine.

"Mr. Isaacs? Good. Have him come in, Matthew."

Isaacs came into the room and was startled at the sight of Jamie and Michael Healy standing on either side of Catherine. "Miss Healy, may we speak privately for a moment?"

"Somehow I expected to see you this evening, Mr. Isaacs. I will speak to you at The Acropolis Theatre, where we are headed this very minute."

Isaacs was flustered. Given Lord Oxley's insistence, he knew he had no choice but to accede to Catherine's wishes. With Michael Healy showing him the door, Isaacs left the house and boarded his carriage for the ride to The Acropolis. He hadn't bothered to offer passage to anyone in the house.

"What was that all about, Cate? And you were up with Nedra for quite some time. What did she tell you?"

She whispered, "Jamie, my darling, I will explain everything once we get to The Acropolis."

Catherine informed the others that Nedra Alexander would be staying in her room and instructed Alice to provide her with anything she required. "Father, will your men remain and continue watching the house while we are away?"

"Two of them will, my dearest. The other will follow us to The Acropolis." Although he didn't know exactly what his daughter was up to, Healy's manner showed not only confidence in her judgment but also unmistakable fatherly pride.

After Millard and Healy left the house, Oliver Pearcy was hesitant to go. Catherine extended her hand. "Oliver, you must come as well."

"Is my presence really necessary, Catherine? I have legal work to finish for the morning. I won't disturb Miss Alexander, I assure you."

"Why would you think that I would imagine such a thing, Oliver? In any event, your presence *is* required. Come. Walk me to down to the street." Capitulating, Pearcy donned his coat and hat and took her arm.

Chapter 30

Upon arriving at The Acropolis, Catherine found David Isaacs waiting impatiently in front of the main entrance.

"Miss Healy, I must have a word with you. In private, if you will indulge me."

She shook her head. "No, Mr. Isaacs, I will speak with you inside the theatre."

"Under normal circumstances, Miss Healy, I would act more the gentleman and not insist, but I must speak with you now. I am to return to Downing Street as quickly as possible."

"You must forgive my incompliancy, Mr. Isaacs, but I will not speak to you now about your business. If you wish, you may return to Lord Oxley and tell him you refused to honor my request that you wait, but that is completely up to you. Otherwise, I suggest you come in and wait like a gentleman for me to respond to the question I know you wish to ask of me."

Isaacs appeared chastened. "I could never make demands of you, Miss Healy. Very well, I will do as you wish." With no further delay, they all entered the theatre and waited in the lobby for the arrival of Jaynes, Phillpotts, and the elder Millard.

Henry Jaynes was the first to appear. "I received your message, Catherine. May I ask what this is all about? Please tell me our theatre will be reopening soon."

Jamie shook his head. "I'm sorry, Henry, but we are here on another matter."

Jaynes whispered to him, "Are we all in some danger, then?"

"Perhaps so, Henry. Perhaps so."

Jaynes noticed the attorney standing apart from the others. "Very good to see you again, Pearcy. How are your children?" Jaynes glanced at Michael Healy, whom he recalled meeting in this past autumn, and nodded his greeting. "Well, James, are we meeting to discuss what to do about our predicament?"

Jamie couldn't answer. He trusted his wife to make everything clear as soon as his father and Phillpotts joined them.

Jaynes offered his office for the meeting. "It's not very large, but I believe the six of us can manage to sit in there all right."

Jaynes started to lead them through the house, but Healy stopped him. "I'm afraid we have two others coming, Mr. Jaynes."

"Two others?"

"Yes, Mr. Millard's father and Denham Phillpotts."

"Phillpotts?"

Jamie understood Jaynes's apprehension. He lowered his voice as he assured Jaynes the inspector wouldn't attempt any harassment since the rest of them would be there as witnesses.

"I don't believe you know him as well as I do, James. All right, where shall we meet, then? Here?"

Healy already knew from his daughter where she wished them to congregate. "Mr. Jaynes, we shall be gathering on stage."

"I see." Jamie could tell the acting manager was puzzled. But then so was he.

Jaynes offered to bring chairs to the stage and asked for the other men's assistance. Millard, Healy, and Pearcy went off with him, while Isaacs escorted Catherine through the house to the empty stage. The interior of the theatre was dimly lit, giving it a grand though Gothic feel. The gilt edgings and handsomely decorated boxes were lost amid the shards of shadow that ran through the interior like elaborate and menacing web work.

"Might we speak now that the others are getting the chairs, Miss Healy?"

"No we may not, Mr. Isaacs. But I assure you that it will be soon. Just have patience." Isaacs found her manner disquieting. Normally, there was a lilt in Catherine Healy's voice that pleased all who heard her speak socially. There was no trace of that now.

By the time Catherine and Isaacs walked on the stage, eight chairs had been set in a rough circle. Jamie assumed his wife wanted the chairs configured as they often were when a cast met to read through a play they were to start rehearsing. Catherine nodded appreciatively when she saw how the men had set the chairs, but she had no intention of sitting until the other men arrived.

Thomas Millard was the next to enter the theatre. "I think I would have preferred having this meeting in one of the luxury boxes up there. How the devil do I get up to where you are?" Jamie directed his father to the side door to Thomas's right.

When the elder Millard joined the others, he looked completely satisfied at the arrangement of chairs. He preferred teaching young surgeons and physicians more intimately in small groups gathered similarly than in the larger hospital amphitheatres. Millard knew everyone on the stage except for David Isaacs, who was most agitated with the situation and barely acknowledged the elder Millard when he was introduced. Thomas whispered to his son—though not inaudibly—that Isaacs was giving "evidence of vulgar impertinence." Jamie informed his father, more quietly, that Cate would soon explain why they had all been summoned to The Acropolis.

The elder Millard continued to break the uncomfortable silence. "If it's all the same to you, I'll be the first to take his seat. I assume there are no seating cards glued to the back or to the underneath of these chairs. Mr. Jaynes, do you have something strong and drinkable to warm this ancient carcass of mine?"

"Of course. May I get you the same, gentleman? Tea for you, Catherine?" Jamie, Healy, and Pearcy nodded. Since removing their heavy coats in the lobby, the men felt the chill of the near empty theatre. After Catherine declined the offer of tea and after receiving no indication from Isaacs that he would join them in a hearty beverage, Jaynes headed toward his office.

Following another two minutes of casual talk among the Millards and Michael Healy, a voice shot forward from the darkness at the back of the house. "Once more it seems you have disobeyed my instructions to suppress your active involvement in this affair, Miss Healy and Mr. Millard. And I see your father has remained in London to assist in the investigation. Not enough crime to entertain you in Dublin, Healy?"

Thomas grabbed his son's coat sleeve. "The man is eaten up with envy and insecurity, my boy."

Phillpotts made his way through the house and up to the stage. "Ah, yes. Very charming seating arrangements we have here. We are to sit in a circle. Are we to conjure up the face of the murderer? Or are we to hold hands and call Roberts-Smythe, Donovan, and Nichols back from the dead so that they may name their assassins?" Phillpotts acknowledged the other men with a quick nod. Only one handshake was offered—to David Isaacs. "Miss Healy, I hope you can explain why all these men are here and why I have been asked to join them. If it has anything to do with the latest attempt on Mr. Millard's life, let me assure you that I've just been informed of it."

As Phillpotts spoke, Jamie caught sight of Henry Jaynes at the edge of the stage holding a tray with several glasses of brandy.

Jaynes expressed shock. "An attempt on Mr. Millard's life?"

Jamie took his drink from the tray. "It was unsuccessful, Henry, as you can see. The bullet hit my man Peters in the shoulder, but he's going to be all right." Millard appreciated the horrified look on Jaynes's face. The acting manager must have wondered how many more of the company would be slain. Because he wished to spare Jaynes the knowledge of another actor's death and since Phillpotts hadn't mentioned it, Jamie added nothing about John Metcalfe's assault on Nedra Alexander and Michael Healy's killing him earlier. By sparing them all another bout of chastisement from Phillpotts, Jamie was doing his best to assist his wife in whatever it was she was about to do.

"Would you care for something to drink, Inspector?"

Phillpotts waved off the offer and stepped toward Jaynes. "Good to see you, Jaynes. I assume you have come before these present to plead your case. I see you have retained the services of Mr. Pearcy."

Jamie's sigh registered his irritation. "Inspector, that is entirely uncalled for."

"Perhaps not entirely, Mr. Millard." Phillpotts stared icily at Jaynes, who directed a grateful nod toward Jamie.

Michael Healy approached his daughter. "Should we sit now, Catherine?"

"Yes." Catherine turned and looked directly upstage left, to the spot where Roberts-Smythe's body had fallen exactly a week earlier.

"Come sit next to your father, my boy." The elder Millard tapped the seat nearest to his right. Jamie took his place, as did the others in the circular configuration of chairs. Looking from the foot of the stage, Catherine claimed the seat at twelve o'clock; her father was to her left.

Following in clockwise order were Jaynes, Pearcy, Jamie, Thomas, Phillpotts, and Isaacs, who was immediately to Catherine's right. Catherine and Jamie were directly across the circle from each other. So were Phillpotts and Jaynes. Every one of the men turned their attention to Catherine, waiting for her to begin.

Her emotions surpassed any she had ever felt while waiting in the wings for an initial stage entrance. She had always had the comfort of knowing that the moment she began speaking, her nervousness would vanish, regardless of the role she was about to perform. But there had been nothing in her stage experience to compare with the consequences of what she was about to say before this intimate audience. How would she begin? She came equipped with no lines memorized or any outline prepared. There was only the account Nedra had provided in her anguished confession in Catherine's room. Catherine wondered how she would shape that account in front of these men, who so far had remained reluctantly though respectfully silent. She understood she needed both her husband's and her father's presence to provide her the security to carry on.

She was sitting properly, with her hands folded on her lap, one on top of the other, as if she had just arrived for a Sunday visit. She debated whether to stand and move to the center of the circle of chairs, following the pattern she had used figuratively, and at times literally, when she contemplated the intricacies of a crime. But she realized she hadn't the strength to lift her torso. Could she even lift her hands? Perhaps once she commenced, she would be able to control her body.

Jamie finished his drink and placed the glass on the floor under his chair. The other men followed suit one by one, their staggered though coordinated movement adding further awkwardness to the moment.

"Nedra Alexander." Catherine paused before continuing. "Nedra Alexander has confided in me this evening." She chose not to look at each man to gauge his reaction. She directed her eyes between Jamie and his father and into the house. It was as dark as it always was when she performed on stage—the darkness being the reflection of an actor's conflicting emotions of security and fear.

"As some of you either know or have guessed, Nedra is not married, nor has she ever been. But she has a daughter, who lives in London and who has recently delivered a child. The daughter's name is Clare Paget.

The father of the baby is Patrick Copsey. They are residing together but are unmarried."

Phillpotts sighed. "Miss Healy, am I to believe that you have invited me to this séance to discuss your concern over a scandalous family situation? Any embarrassment this might now bring to The Acropolis Theatre is, I suppose, regrettable, but what relevance does it have to the murders we are trying to solve?"

Catherine turned to him. "Inspector if I am permitted to finish *all* I have to say without interruption, I believe you will be satisfied."

Although still agitated, Phillpotts conceded. "Very well, Miss Healy. I relent, but only out of respect for you."

"Nedra hasn't made her identity known to her daughter, nor has she paid any kind of visit to her or to the infant. How she came to have Clare is an unfortunate and most deplorable tale." She paused once more, closing her eyes for several second before reopening them. "Nedra was a kept woman when she was carrying the child—if one may call a sixteen year-old girl a woman. She was kept at the abandoned house on High Holborn where Alfred Nichols was shot to death. You may recall, Inspector, the black velvet belt I said I discovered there not long ago. Yes, that belt belonged to Nedra. It was a special present purchased for her at a shop on the Isle of Cyprus. But it wasn't a gift from the man who kept her at that house years earlier. Someone else had purchased it for her. This belt, which may well have been used to strangle Charles Donovan, had been forcibly taken from Nedra only recently by yet another man whose attentions she had several times rejected. A man who vowed that he would have her. A man who has only today attempted to violate her. A man Nedra was forced to shoot to protect herself."

"What is this?" Phillpotts had so far only been told that another man lay dead in the abandoned house on High Holborn.

"Inspector, please. You will know everything if you will allow me to reveal it in my own way."

Phillpotts winced in anger but said nothing more.

"That man was John Metcalfe. Another of our actors, Inspector. You probably spoke to him after the deaths of Mr. Roberts-Smythe and Charles Donovan. It was Metcalfe who stabbed Mr. Roberts-Smythe and strangled poor Charles and placed his body in one of the storage recesses. And it was John Metcalfe who shot Alfred Nichols at the abandoned house on High Holborn. And John Metcalfe who today entered Jamie's house and shot at him on the stairway. And why did John Metcalfe kill Alfred and shoot at Jamie? He knew Alfred had actually been with Nedra, as rumor had it, and he couldn't bear the thought that both Alfred and Mr. Schneider had experienced such an intimacy with the woman he desired but wasn't permitted to have. You see, Inspector, Messrs. Nichols, Schneider, and Metcalfe were always in competition with each other—from seeking the affections of a woman to coveting the largest of the small parts available in a production."

Phillpotts was mortified that he had never suspected Metcalfe. He realized now that Metcalfe's disparaging account of Henry Jaynes earned the actor his approval and therefore muffled his investigative instincts.

"But why did he try to kill me, Cate?"

Catherine forgave Jamie for interrupting. "Because he believed Nedra had lain with you as well." Catherine saw the astonishment on her husband's face. "I know there was no truth to his assumption. But a man with such a jealous nature sees much when there is sometimes nothing at all.

Phillpotts put up one finger, much like a schoolboy. "Since Mr. Millard was permitted a question, let me simply ask then why Metcalfe murdered Charles Donovan. He surely didn't believe Donovan was another rival for the attentions of Miss Alexander."

"No Inspector, he did not. Nedra doesn't know for certain, but I would conclude that poor Charles was killed merely because he was supposed to be waiting behind the arras as the character Polonius during the scene—in the very place where Metcalfe was to murder Mr. Roberts-Smythe. Poor Charles couldn't be permitted to impede or to witness the crime, of course." Catherine anticipated the next most obvious question, forwarded by Phillpotts. "So did Metcalfe kill Mr. Roberts-Smythe merely because Mr. Metcalfe was bitter over the types of roles he was contracted to play?"

"I have no doubt that such a fact made Mr. Metcalfe's killing him much easier. But there is more to it than that."

"Then it was Morris Roberts-Smythe who kept Nedra Alexander when she was sixteen and Roberts-Smythe who is the father of her daughter."

Catherine shook her head. "No, Inspector. Mr. Roberts-Smythe was not the father of Clare Paget."

"Really?" Phillpotts stared into Henry Jaynes eyes and began to shape a cruel smile.

Instead of directing her attention to Jaynes, Catherine turned to her right. "It was *your* father, Mr. Isaacs."

"Isaacs?"

"Yes, Inspector. It was Mr. Edmund Isaacs who took a sixteen-year-old girl to that place on High Holborn, fathered her child, and then abandoned her, without ever offering her or their daughter any assistance."

David Isaacs stood up, his face ashen. He offered no denial or protest. It was clear to all of them that he too was stunned by the revelation. Without so much as a gesture of parting, he left the stage the way he had come on. When he reappeared, he walked briskly up the main aisle. Suddenly he stopped. He was stone still for several moments until he finally turned back toward the others. Catherine rose from her chair and walked to the foot of the stage. Isaacs stepped toward her, numbed by the revelation but determined still to take Catherine's answer back to his employer. She looked down at him from the stage. "The answer is no, Mr. Isaacs. I wish none of Lord Oxley's assistance in any matter that relates to me." Catherine remained at the foot of the stage until Isaacs made his way out of the theatre.

Thomas Millard turned to his son, "Then that's it? The case is closed up? But then why was *I* asked to—"

"Wait, father." Although he too was anxious for the next revelation, Jamie knew his wife would explain all in due time and with a comforting look encouraged his father to remain silent.

Michael Healy gently intruded. "Not quite closed up, Dr. Millard. What of that gentleman on the train you and James both met, and who was the man who first assaulted your son in the access lane on High Holborn?"

The elder Millard sighed. "It seems obvious. They were accomplices of Metcalfe's, the both of them."

Catherine had come back up stage and was standing behind her father-in-law. She placed her hand on his shoulder. "Yes, Dr. Millard. All of these men were accomplices, but *each* man was instructed by another man, who was truly responsible for everything."

"Not, the elder Isaacs, then?"

"No, Dr. Millard, not Edmund Isaacs."

Chapter 31

"Shall I remove Mr. Isaacs's chair, Cate?"

"No, Jamie, leave it. It still has some relevance." She returned to her seat.

Jamie was certain she would soon make clear her meaning, but Phillpotts hardly shared Millard's confidence. "An empty chair has relevance? Miss Healy, please relate the rest of what you have learned from Nedra Alexander. Better yet, could you drive on through the details and inform us who was most responsible for the murders and the attacks on Mr. Millard?"

Catherine ignored Phillpott's request and continued as she had intended. "Nedra revealed to me that she was subjected to emotional humiliation, physical pain, and personal degradation. Following her abandonment by Edmund Isaacs, she assumed she had no choice but to place her newborn child in the care of others. Several of London's self-proclaimed guardians of morality advised her to forget about the child and lead a life of penance and hard work. She was even told she would never be worthy of a marriage and that household service would be her lot."

Thomas Millard puffed in exasperation. "May God provide these moral guardians little comfort both in this life and in the next. Ah, dear Catherine, I've gone against your wishes and interrupted you. My apologies." The elder Millard patted all of his pockets, searching for his pipe and tobacco, which he had left in the hansom cab that brought him to the theatre.

After she smiled at Thomas to assure him his apology was unnecessary, Catherine continued. "But Nedra refused to heed that advice and by the time she was eighteen, she came to realize she could make her way by her daring and willingness to please those who had the power to assist her. She became an actress and unfortunately continued her indiscriminant ways with men. The nature of her relationships with them seemed to bring out the worst behavior of these men—members of The Acropolis's company included. Over the years, she has been struck several times in the face and pushed violently to the floor and up against walls. And you now know what John Metcalfe attempted to do to her. Yet there was more. Recently she received two cuts on her arm, each between two and three inches long, made with a small knife—the second directly below the first. These cuts were deliberately and carefully made."

Phillpotts petulantly smacked his hands on his knees. "Miss Healy, our sympathies go out to the woman, but I beg you, can we dispense with all of this detail for the time being? I'm sure the rest of these gentlemen agree that we have been here long enough."

Phillpotts quickly looked to the others for support. Jamie's and Michael Healy's faces suggested their disapproval; Thomas Millard seemed occupied in thought; Henry Jaynes stared at the empty chair; and Oliver Pearcy kept his glance toward the stage floor.

"Very well, Inspector. I am sorry to have taken up so much of your time with these 'details,' as you put it. You will not insult me if you leave now. I will send word to your office of what I will very shortly reveal. I trust that will be satisfactory to you."

Phillpotts was staggered by Catherine's stark invitation for him to leave. It took him several moments to respond. Finally he folded his arms petulantly across his chest. "I will gladly wait until you are ready to reveal all you have learned."

"Thank you, Inspector. I have decided to reveal every detail, because I want you to know all of what has happened to Nedra Alexander. Throughout her difficult life, no one has taken her side. She was a young girl seduced and then abandoned by an older man of accomplishment, who soon found her both an embarrassment and a threat to his reputation. For all her faults—or sins if you wish to call them so—she is still a vulnerable woman with inconsistent feelings and deep-rooted fears, which have made her susceptible to betrayal and abuse."

Catherine couldn't believe she had come this far in her defense of Nedra with her emotions in check and her voice steady. Fearing she might be unable to sustain her strength, she left her seat and began walking slowly around the eight chairs.

"Nedra was made to pose for photographs. Photographs of the kind many men decry but nonetheless desire to examine or possess. She didn't know she would be photographed in such a shameful manner and initially refused. But she was threatened and finally relented."

"Excuse me, Cate. Threatened with physical violence?"

"No, Jamie. With something even worse to her. She was told that if she refused, her daughter—whose name she didn't even know—would be made aware of her identity and would suffer consequences as well. The photographs were taken—a full dozen of them, much to her utter dismay. But some of these photographs were seen by others and stolen. A torn section of one of them was dropped by John Metcalfe at Jamie's house. The rest of it was in his possession when he was killed by Nedra at the house on High Holborn moments before my father arrived."

Michael Healy tapped the pocket of his coat. "I have the torn photograph here, Inspector."

"Inspector Phillpotts, Morris Roberts-Smythe became aware of the photographs and of the man who ordered them taken. Nedra wrote Mr. Roberts-Smythe a letter revealing that information. She was distraught. She felt she had to tell someone and somehow put an end to the abuse she was enduring."

Catherine ceased for a moment and took a deep breath in an attempt to steady her nerves. How she wished she didn't have to say what was coming next.

Her voice slightly quivered. "But it wasn't the first time she had tried to solicit support. Another man she had sought assistance from had failed her by not believing her story, which admittedly she had only told in part." Having said that much, her voice regained its steadiness. "Mr. Roberts-Smythe was therefore her last hope because he was a well-respected man of considerable accomplishment in London and would be believed. Being true to his generally cautious nature, he took it upon himself to secure further proof before seeking a confrontation with the man who had so abused Nedra. Roberts-Smythe made an investigation and discovered the photographs and several concealed pieces of correspondence. When he was certain of what he had in his possession, he approached the man, who was then speaking with Nedra, and demanded to see them both in the morning. That was on the night of his murder, an hour and a half before the performance of *Hamlet* began. Sometime afterward, a note was left on Roberts-Smythe's desk."

"How was that fact known, Catherine?" Michael Healy never permitted speculation to go unchallenged, even by his daughter.

"Because after the murder, Nedra ran to Roberts-Smythe's office, fearful that he had left unconcealed one or more of the scandalous photographs taken of her. She couldn't bear the thought of anyone else seeing them. She found no photographs but did discover the note. She has given it to me, and I have it here."

Catherine withdrew the folded note from the inside of her jacket sleeve. She read it aloud.

Sir, Mr. Donovan is in a bad way tonight. The first-act scene with Polonius and Laertes did not go well. We fear he will not be standing soberly when he is to make his entrance behind the arras in the third act. He has a bottle of his brandy situated back there.

"There is no signature on this note. All of us knew that Mr. Roberts-Smythe rarely watched performances after opening night. He chose instead to be in the lobby conducting business and checking on receipts for the evening. But he would invariably return to his office at the midpoint of a performance. Someone likely placed the note there after the play began. Concerned, Roberts-Smythe made his way to where Charles should have been in the third act to confront him and found him missing. It was at this moment that he was stabbed by John Metcalfe. Patrick Copsey wasn't at his station there, for he had been instructed to leave The Acropolis on a false errand to The Lyceum. You see, gentlemen, the man who was responsible for these crimes never touched those who died. Others did his despicable work for him."

Henry Jaynes stood up and pointed to the empty chair. "That damned scoundrel Ned Ludmore! Now I see why you wanted that chair left vacant, dearest Catherine. You were telling us that the one responsible should have been sitting here among us. I'm sure he's by now out of country on a ship to America. Believe me, I was aghast when he told me he wished to break his contract with The Acropolis, but now I know why. How diabolically clever to have Roberts-Smythe and poor Charles murdered at the moment he was on stage acting Hamlet—and on stage with Nedra Alexander, the woman he so abused. I can't begin to imagine what terror she felt at the moment of discovery in the play, knowing what Ludmore had made her do and what he had just had done to Roberts-Smythe and Charles. The vicious hellish bastard!"

Jaynes almost collapsed from the intensity of his outburst. Breathing heavily, he grabbed the back of his chair and managed to remain standing, perspiration forming on his brow. All during his impassioned speech, his eyes had not moved from the empty chair directly across from him.

Finally, he realized that no one had said anything. Without glancing toward Catherine's chair, Jaynes offered an exhausted apology. "Dearest Catherine, I beg your forgiveness. You wanted to be the one to reveal Ludmore's name, and I have unthinkingly upstaged you. You will pardon me, won't you?" He raised his eyes and saw her standing now directly behind the empty seat.

"No, Henry, you did not upstage me. But I'm afraid I cannot and will not forgive you, for it is you who are responsible for all of these horrific crimes."

"Jaynes?" Denham Phillpotts was flabbergasted.

Catherine nodded sadly. "Yes, Inspector. Henry Jaynes was the man who has so deeply hurt and abused Nedra. It was he who forced her to sit for those awful photographs. And he who threatened to expose her to her daughter and to harm Clare should Nedra reveal anything about his actions and his sordid desires. Henry Jaynes fooled us all by playing a character—one we all wished to assist and protect."

"Cate, this simply can't be." Jamie could only hope his wife had made some dreadful mistake. He looked at Jaynes, who stood immobile—his eyes tightly closed, his lips moving in an attitude of silent prayer.

Catherine went on. "When Roberts-Smythe learned the truth, Henry Jaynes had him murdered by John Metcalfe, who had just previously strangled Charles Donovan, as he was also likely instructed. What we all didn't know was that Mr. Jaynes is a man of means, a man who had lost his legitimate investments in his youth but then set about to regain his fortune through several parliamentary associations, successful financial speculations, and fraudulent investment promises he has cleverly continued to this day—anonymously transferring money from rightful accounts to his own. He has also involved himself over the years in manufactured and counterfeit deeds and forgeries and the ruination of private shareholders, from small tradesmen to members of the government. He has done all of this while passing a relatively quiet existence as assistant theatre manager of The Acropolis."

"Nedra Alexander has told you all of this?" Michael Healy wished to stress to his daughter how serious these charges were.

"Yes, father. She knows too much to have simply made it up."

"But again, *how* would she know?" Michael Healy looked at Jaynes, who remained frozen in his place, still muttering something inaudibly. His hand gripped tightly the chair that held him upright.

"It seems Mr. Jaynes needed to boast about his abominable accomplishments, and he believed Nedra's devotion to him was such that she would admire him for all he had done. In any event, he felt he had enough power over Nedra to keep her from betraying him. Inspector Phillpotts, we owe you an apology for criticizing your belief that Mr. Jaynes was in some way responsible for these crimes."

Phillpotts remained too stupefied to respond. Several times, he had brazenly crossed professional boundaries by asserting that Jaynes was involved, but in truth he thought no such thing. He had only wished to torment Jaynes for what he believed the man had done to hasten his sister's suicide.

Catherine knew it would deeply grieve Phillpotts, but she felt it was only right that he knew even more about his sister's death. "Dr. Millard, I assume George Wooten asked you on my behalf to check your records about Miss Phillpotts's death many years ago."

"Yes, and I did check it. That was why I was delayed in arriving here."

"And what did your records show other than the cause of death?"

The elder Millard looked at Phillpotts, whose eyes were now wedged closed. "On her lower arm were two cuts of two to three inches in length, one on top of the other—obviously made with a knife."

Phillpotts large body began to tremble. Michael Healy stepped forward to prevent him from lurching at Jaynes. "Inspector, it might be best to have two of your men come inside and place Mr. Jaynes in custody. Dr. Millard, would you walk to the lobby with the Inspector?"

Catherine came to Phillpotts. "Please, Inspector, go out and send in your men."

Phillpotts was too overwrought to protest. He realized every second he remained in Jaynes's presence would make him less able to restrain himself from killing the man. The elder Millard took Phillpotts by the elbow and led him across the stage and out through the house into the theatre lobby.

Still startled by the revelation, Jamie waited for Jaynes to proclaim his innocence, but the man made no attempt to do so. Instead he took his hand off the chair and opened his eyes. He stood completely erect and spoke calmly, in a voice that belied both his unimpressive physical appearance and the general manner he had presented to those who knew and worked closely with him.

"You should have let the Inspector remain, Mr. Healy. He has long wished to kill me, and he'll set about it in any event. I will never live to stand before a judge and jury."

Jamie found an emerging disgust quickly erasing his bewilderment. He asked his wife, while staring into Jaynes's almost placid face, "Catherine, why did he maim Miss Phillpotts and Nedra Alexander in that particular way?"

Jaynes held up his hand. "Miss Healy doesn't have the answer, Mr. Millard. Nedra didn't know. You see, back then I wanted Miss Phillpotts to leave me alone. Indeed, I remember actively wishing she was dead. Yes, I was tired of her cloying ways, but more than that I feared her because she was deeply disturbed. In desperation, she claimed to be with child. I believed then and to this day that she was lying in some desperate attempt to keep my attentions. But when she refused to part from me as I demanded, I resorted to violence and took the edge of a knife and made two cuts on her arm. I wanted to awaken her senses—to make her understand I would be dangerous to her if she failed to leave me alone. It was at a time when I discovered that my investments had been lost in the same kind of fraudulent scheme I would later use to my personal advantage. My wounding Miss Phillpotts in that way must have filled her with enough fear and despair that in her disturbed state she jumped to her death. I regret to say that it was best for both of us that she did so."

Jamie couldn't believe the man before him was Henry Jaynes. The pacing of his speech had altered, the tone had slightly deepened. In manner and voice, Jaynes reminded him of an actor shedding all trappings of a character after a performance had ended. "And what of Miss Alexander, then?"

Jaynes's deportment remained chillingly dispassionate. "To be blunt, I suppose I wanted her dead as well. I cut her arm twice—once in the secret room at the end of the old costume and properties area and once in the upstairs room at the abandoned house on High Holborn, at the same time

Metcalfe shot Nichols on the stairs. She told you that too, didn't she, dear Catherine?"

Catherine met his gaze as she answered. "Yes. She said that the two of you were forced to step over Mr. Nichols's body as you descended the chairs."

Jaynes continued. "I came to the conclusion that, like Miss Phillpotts, Nedra was more than vulnerable and pliable. She was emotionally disturbed. If she didn't end her own life, I knew I would have to have it done. You see, for over a year and a half I believed she was the one woman I could take into my confidence. Perhaps I was completely naïve, since I had not formed a passionate alliance with any female since the death of Miss Phillpotts. In any event, whenever Nedra and I lay together, I couldn't resist the compelling urge to confide in her."

Catherine lifted her chin and asked the next question without any hesitation. "And those erotic photographs of Nedra? They were for your prurient amusement only?"

"No, not in the least. I insisted on them merely to have something else with which to ensure her discretion, other than threats of violence. But I soon realized these photographs wouldn't be enough. It was only then that I made the cuts on her arm. Even having done that, I knew she had become a danger to me—if nothing else, because of all she knew about me."

"And for that you wanted her dead?"

"In part, Catherine—yes. But Nedra had also confided in me. She spoke of her unfortunate past, the child she had to abandon, and her need for the attention and protection of men. Never having felt the emotion, I had no feelings of jealousy over her past relationships, but I discovered that her desire for the attention of men wasn't simply relegated to her past. I soon had evidence she was betraying me with members of the company, most notably with Alfred Nichols."

"And Mr. Roberts-Smythe?"

Jaynes laughed at Jamie's question in a manner unfamiliar to them. "No, James. Roberts-Smythe had no interest in women. And his interest in young men was limited to watching, not participating. Catherine, forgive me for being inelegant, but the man was practically impotent."

"And just how would you know that, Jaynes?"

"My connections in this city, Mr. Healy. For instance, Edmund Isaacs, the subject of your daughter's first revelation, informed me that several young men were invited to the secret room to amuse Roberts-Smythe with their dallying. But I was already aware of the room and the use to which it was put, because Ned Ludmore spoke to me about Roberts-Smythe showing him the room and the hidden stairway going down to the back of the theatre. Roberts-Smythe hinted that Ludmore bring a male companion to the room through that passageway, to be joined by Roberts-Smythe." Jaynes smiled. "Apparently, Roberts-Smythe misjudged Ned Ludmore's preferences. I also know that young Copsey was approached by Roberts-Smythe for the same reason."

Jamie took a step closer to Catherine and her father, who were now standing directly across from Jaynes. "And why didn't Ludmore and Copsey say anything publicly or at least to me?"

"That's simple, James. Roberts-Smythe threatened Copsey with the loss of his job and a bad reference should he wish to find another position in the city, and Roberts-Smythe secured Ludmore's silence by an additional payment per performance. Roberts-Smythe feared losing Ludmore to another theatre for several reasons, one obviously being his concern that Ned would then feel free to reveal what he knew about that secret room."

Catherine remained unaffected by Jaynes's account. She had other questions to ask. "And the blood stained handkerchiefs found in that room and upstairs of the house on High Holborn—the blood was from the cuts you inflicted on Nedra's arm. Were the handkerchiefs yours, Mr. Jaynes?"

"No. They belonged to Roberts-Smythe. He kept a dozen or more of them in his desk. They were a long-time sartorial affectation of his. As you imply, I daubed the blood from Nedra's arm with the handkerchiefs and deliberately left them in both places. You may remember that I also claimed to find another handkerchief near the door of the old storage room. As you know, that too belonged to Roberts-Smythe."

"So that he would be blamed for Miss Alexander's death, that is, once you had her killed by Metcalfe."

"In large part, Mr. Healy. But your daughter and Mr. Millard made their discoveries a little too soon, I'm afraid. I mistakenly believed I had thought of everything."

"And why did Roberts-Smythe have to die—since he had no interest in Nedra? You wanted his job, then?"

"No, Mr. Millard. Miss Healy has already alluded to the reason. I had Roberts-Smythe killed only because he had found me out. He had seen the photographs of Nedra and she had spoken to him, accusing me of abusing her. I would have been ruined, if not arrested. Yes, of course I wanted his position, but I would never have killed him for it. I was more than content to show the public only what they saw—the dedicated and greatly underestimated assistant manager of The Acropolis Theatre. Miss Healy has explained accurately why and how Roberts-Smythe was murdered."

"And your reason for twice attempting to kill me? Did you believe I was having a relationship with Nedra?"

"On the contrary, James. I never thought any such thing. I have always been very fond of you. In the access lane behind that office on High Holborn, you were only to be rendered unconscious by the forearm hold the man had on the side of your neck. My intention in ordering that done was to frighten you and Miss Healy from pursuing the matter further. Therefore, Mr. Healy didn't save your life, although his killing the man seemed to me not at all a bad thing. And dear Catherine, please know I never intended you any harm. You were never in any danger— ever. My affections for you remain as they always have been."

She was horrified by the sentiment and by the gentle manner in which it was delivered.

Jaynes went on. "James, John Metcalfe shot at you on his own accord. I was stunned to hear that he had done so. He was told only to silence Nedra Alexander. Your life was to be spared. Those were specifically my instructions."

"Jaynes, you made a serious miscalculation in your scheme by allowing Metcalfe to remain in London."

"He would not have lived out the day, Mr. Healy. Nedra informed me that he had stolen from her bedroom one of her gloves and a velvet belt, which he then left in the secret room and at the house on High Holborn, in order, I suppose, to implicate her in Roberts-Smythe's and Nichols's deaths. The man was an idiot and unworthy of the trust I put in him. Arrangements had been made to have him dispatched after he strangled Nedra. Ironic, isn't it, that both you and Nedra did me favors, Mr. Healy?"

Jamie lightly pressed the palm of his hand against Healy's chest to prevent him from approaching Jaynes. "So who was the man on the train who spoke to me and my father?"

"You need only know that he was handsomely paid. He was a man with a reputation. One who has performed services for several very important men in London and in other European cities. The man you met on the train could be depended on. Quite adept with puzzles, codes, and word games—a connoisseur of the finest brandies and wines." Jaynes's face took on a mercurial expression. "Oh, there were others who assisted me whom I didn't have to pay. For example and as Miss Healy noted, Nedra sought assistance from another, who apparently refused to believe her story about what I had done to her. Or was it because you feared that any involvement in the matter would leave you vulnerable to exposure yourself, Mr. Pearcy?

Chapter 32

"Oliver?" Catherine was totally unprepared for this revelation. Concentrating on every word spoken by Jaynes, she failed to observe that Pearcy hadn't moved from his chair since he first sat down or offered a single reaction to anything Jaynes had admitted. "Oliver, is this true?"

Pearcy finally rose and walked to the foot of the stage, followed by Catherine. "It is. Nedra recently came to me for help, saying she had no one else to go to. She spoke only in generalities, but tried to make me understand that Henry Jaynes was abusing her and that she feared for her life."

"Oliver, why didn't you tell us about this?"

"I had already judged the woman to be overly theatrical, even outside the confines of The Acropolis. But the truth is that I didn't *want* to believe her. I couldn't imagine Henry Jaynes behaving in such an abusive fashion, and I was concerned that my involvement would upset you and cause embarrassment and difficulties for the theatre. I therefore concluded that simply ignoring her request for assistance would be in all of our best interests. But now that I have heard what she has confessed to you and what this man has done to her, I find myself deeply ashamed of my unwillingness to hear her further." Catherine pressed her hand gently on Pearcy's shoulder.

"So very admirable of you, Pearcy. So very admirable." Jaynes was shaking his head in sarcastic sympathy. "Still, there was another reason for your unwillingness to assist her, wasn't there? You didn't want to support her accusations against me because you feared retribution, isn't that right?"

Jamie shook his head in frustration. "What are you talking about, Jaynes?"

"Some four months ago, Mr. Pearcy had occasion to meet Nedra Alexander after a production at The Acropolis. Charmed by her flirtatious ways, he invited her to dine with him, and later that evening, perhaps feeling the loss of his wife or the want of a woman's affections, he made a fumbling attempt to kiss Miss Alexander, and when she refused his advance, he told her something that deeply wounded her."

"That was not my intention, Jaynes, and Nedra knew it." Pearcy was clearly anguished.

Jamie wished to grab Jaynes by the throat. "How could you possibly know what he said, Jaynes?"

"You have not been listening at all—have you, James? I had Nedra followed and watched because she had clumsily broken off an engagement with me that very evening. Pearcy knew from the family who took Nedra's child sixteen years ago that Nedra was completely unaware her daughter was living in London—and yet you informed Nedra nevertheless—didn't you Pearcy? When she left you that night, she went immediately to where her daughter was staying with the intention of seeing her—that is, until she despaired of explaining her disreputable past to the daughter she had abandoned. She told me all of this, you see. So in effect, Pearcy, you filled her heart with the misery that comes from knowledge, when blissful ignorance would have served her better. From that time she began altering her behavior toward me, speaking wildly about confessing her sins and making amends. And as the autumn wore on, I could see that she would soon cause herself and me irreparable harm if she wasn't made to stop. And then more recently she came to you again about my treatment of her—and you sent her away."

Remaining at the foot of the stage, Pearcy turned to Catherine. "All he says is true. And there is more. In my foolish attempt to impress Miss Alexander, I mentioned I had been involved in defending several Irishmen accused of plotting against the crown. I added that I often found myself supporting their general desire for complete independence. The matter came up when Nedra and I were discussing you and your father being from Ireland. Nedra feared that your future on the London stage might be jeopardized by your heritage and rumors about your father's politics. I had just made you the offer to board with us and was trying to win Nedra's favor. Later, I feared that she would reveal my support for the Irish separatists. It appears now that she told Jaynes."

Jaynes nodded matter-of-factly. "She indeed told me, Pearcy, and I immediately told others. They have been keeping an eye on you these past few months. I advised against their confronting you because Catherine was living in your house and her serenity was more important to me than your persecution. So now you should reconsider your occasional visits to check on the welfare of these men and your periodic financial assistance to their families. Once they publicly brand you as a friend of the Irish Nationalists, your name—as well as that of your family—will be ruined, even if you escape incarceration or execution."

Jaynes continued, but in a voice reminiscent of a stern headmaster. "You have always involved yourself in others' affairs, Pearcy—all in the name of charity and compassion—and where has it left you? Perhaps our attorney friend has not told you, Catherine, that sixteen years ago he arranged foster care for Nedra's daughter and tried, in vain, to secure a place for the girl upon the death of Mr. Paget last year. But young Clare decided instead to place her fate in the hands of young Copsey."

Pearcy took a deep breath, as though he had suddenly awakened from a frightful dream. Without responding to Jaynes or even looking at the others, he walked off the stage and out through the house, passing Phillpotts men, who had started down the aisle toward the stage.

Jaynes sighed. "It seems that I won't be named manager of The Acropolis after all."

Jamie had one further question for Jaynes. "Tell me. Why subject yourself to the mundane responsibilities of assistant manager of The Acropolis when you had enough money to live whatever life of leisure you desired?"

"A life of leisure and comfort doesn't allow one to play a role, James. 'All the world's a stage,' as Shakespeare said. 'And all the men and women merely players.' I memorized that passage when I was a boy, and nothing I have read since has filled me with the same sense of excitement and purpose. I always wished to be an actor, and I think I've demonstrated to all of you that I could have been a masterful one. But auditions at the Haymarket and at the Adelphi some thirty years ago were unsuccessful. I didn't have "the look" for the leads and I didn't seem impressive enough to be hired as even a bit player. Each year I studied and perfected my craft, but the criticisms were always the same. After five years of the same rejection, I refused to subject myself further to such indignities. Still, as the years went on I reveled in those moments when I could become someone else in my financial transactions, in my duties here at

The Acropolis, and even in my imagination. I took special delight in altering the general pitch of my voice and even the script of my handwriting."

Catherine and Jamie now understood why they were unable to recognize the hand that composed the notes to Patrick Copsey and Denham Phillpotts.

Jaynes took several quick breaths as he heard Phillpotts's men mounting the stage from the side door. "It was utterly exhilarating playing the part of the hapless victim of Inspector Phillpotts's harassment, as well as a harmless and helpful soul who provided information and tangible evidence to mislead the investigation. You see, I had all a true actor needs. Undeniable talent, unwavering commitment, and deep-rooted passion."

Phillpotts's men came onto the stage. Catherine, Jamie, and Michael Healy stepped back, leaving room for the men to take Jaynes away.

After nodding politely to the men, Henry Jaynes turned toward the house, stepped to the foot of the stage, and stood as majestically erect as he possibly could.

"Come, come, and sit you down. You shall not budge!

You go not till I set you up a glass

Where you may see the inmost part of you."

Jaynes had spoken Hamlet's words, a moment before he stabs through the arras and kills Polonius. Phillpotts men took a step toward him, but Jaynes was not finished.

"Diseases desperate grown

By desperate appliance are relieved."

Millard was to speak this passage as the murderous Claudius later in the play. He would never see these words in the same light again.

"Thus conscience does make cowards of us all,

And thus the native hue of resolution

Is sicklied o'er with the pale cast of thought."

At the completion of these words from Hamlet's famous third-act soliloquy, Jaynes's shoulders dropped to their normal sloped posture. He turned back to the others and once more nodded.

"Gentlemen, my time upon the stage is complete. Take me where you will."

Chapter 33

Edward Ludmore sat in a Liverpool tavern waiting to board a steam ship for New York, a voyage of only six or seven days—a far cry from the forty-six days it took his grandfather to cross by sail half a century earlier. And Ludmore was quite anxious to leave England and all the events at The Acropolis behind. Although never ordered to remain in London, Ludmore feared Denham Phillpotts would eventually detain and charge him for planning the murders. Ludmore would have much to account for in that event—such as his duplicity and ill-treatment of both Henry Jaynes and Nedra Alexander, his knowledge of the secret room and of Roberts-Smythe's carnal inclinations, and the additional payment he received from Roberts-Smythe for his silence about the goings on in the hidden chamber. There was also the business of his detailed accounting of everything relating to Catherine Healy at The Acropolis—her manner, her preferences, her conversation, and even particular aspects of her physical appearance—the last of these being provided by the youngest female member of the company. This information about Catherine Healy was requested by David Isaacs, on behalf of his employer, Lord Oxley.

Finishing his coffee, Ludmore glanced at a letter he composed several days earlier, which implored Oxley's assistance should Ludmore become a suspect in the murders. True, he had left London easily enough, but he couldn't feel entirely safe until he was out to sea.

The tavern door opened to a man in ship's uniform. "All setting sail for New York are now asked to board."

~ # ~

"*Monsieur Lambert, désirez-vous autre chose?*"

The gentleman shook his head. "*Non, merci.*" His breakfast had been more than sufficient; he required nothing else to eat. At present he was writing an order for the wine he would have at this evening's dinner, a *Chateau d'Yquem* 1890, from the Sauternes, Gironde region of France. He thought of the superb 1884 vintage he had recently enjoyed in London. The gentleman looked forward to returning to England in the spring for another assignment.

"Excusez-moi, monsieur." The waiter handed the gentleman a telegram. "Henry Jaynes arrested for Acropolis murders. No others implicated."

He finished his coffee and pulled out the notebook he always kept with him. He turned to the page that related to his recent London activities. "I'm going to miss you, Jaynes. Not only did you pay me very well for my services, but you were one of the best anagrams I've ever concocted." How delighted he had been when he scrambled the letters of Jaynes's first and last names and came up with the melodious "Ash Jenny Rye."

~ # ~

"I cannot express fully my deepest gratitude to you, Lord Oxley."

"You expected me to dismiss you, David?"

"Indeed I did. Your reaction last night to Miss Healy's reply strongly suggested my services would no longer be wanted."

"I tend to become agitated when I'm disappointed. You certainly know that."

"Again, I am most grateful you wish me to continue in my position."

"But I must say it was unfortunate you left The Acropolis before Henry Jaynes confessed his guilt. Quite a shock, to say the least. But I should like to know if he identified any of his more highly placed financial relationships."

"Even if he did, no one could draw any connection to you, Lord Oxley. And even if one was made, who would believe it?"

"Yes, we were quite right to keep our distance from him directly. In any event, I shall miss his monthly contributions. You know, I am completely perplexed as to why he arranged those murders of Roberts-Smythe and the two actors. David, I want the details. I assume Oliver Pearcy was there for the entire confession. Find out from him exactly what Jaynes said and who if anyone he identified as part of financial dealings."

"And if Mr. Pearcy is reluctant?"

"Just remind him that we are aware of his associations with London's Irish separatists. I doubt you will need to say any more than that. He will comply."

"Lord Oxley?"

"What is it, David?"

"What of Miss Healy? Do you wish me to deliver another message from you?"

"Not now. Not for awhile. Let her return to the stage and regain her sense of serenity. Perhaps in the early spring she'll be in a more receptive mood. What was it Tennyson wrote? 'In the spring a young man's fancy lightly turns to thoughts of love.'"

"A young woman's as well, Lord Oxley?"

"Exactly, David. Exactly."

"But when do you suppose The Acropolis will reopen?"

"It will raise its curtain again in a week's time. I communicated with the theatre's owners yesterday morning and strongly encouraged them to reopen as soon as feasible—even if the murders weren't solved. But now that they have been, the owners need only to announce the name of the new theatre manager." Oxley let out a satisfied chuckle. "He's someone I highly recommended to them."

"I'm most curious. Had you intended Jaynes for the position after Mr. Roberts-Smythe's murder, Lord Oxley?"

"Jaynes? Never. He was much better suited to continue his financial activities in the more anonymous post of assistant theatre manager. Now, David, spend the rest of your morning on your work and then in the late afternoon have that talk with Pearcy."

After Isaacs closed the door, Oxley opened his desk drawer and retrieved a woman's silk handkerchief, laced with delicate embroidery. It once belonged to Catherine Healy. It had been purloined from her dressing table at The Acropolis by one of the young actresses and then given to Edward Ludmore, who passed it on to David Isaacs. Oxley brought the handkerchief to his lips. The fragrance was still palpable. In early December, Oxley had seen one of Catherine's characters draw this handkerchief across her cheek to her young suitor in a gesture that said,

"I love you." Oxley was on that December evening determined to possess the handkerchief. Now sitting alone in his office, he renewed his determination to possess the woman.

~ # ~

"Really, Catherine? The theatre to reopen in just seven days?"

"Yes, Alice. The message came this morning from one of the owners, who informed me they have named Mr. Richard Stempson as the new manager of The Acropolis. Last season, Mr. Stempson was assistant manager of The Criterion, which became insolvent this past summer." Catherine chose to postpone thinking about how she would evaluate Stempson, whom she had never met, in light of her horribly erroneous impression of Henry Jaynes.

Catherine also decided the time wasn't right for speaking to her husband about Lord Oxley. Her earlier reasons for postponing her admission still applied, and now she had Oliver Pearcy and his family to worry about, knowing that others, likely Oxley, were made aware of Pearcy's assistance to those in sympathy with Irish nationalism. Were Jamie to make a protest either publically or in a private meeting, Oxley could make matters horribly difficult for all of them.

And then there was the matter of her marriage to Jamie. Michael Healy had left earlier in the morning, on his way to Basingstoke to bring back his sister to visit Catherine. Since the appearance of her aunt would only complicate matters, Catherine thought it also wise to wait for another time. But she would then have to take Jamie to Dublin to confess their marriage. Michael Healy would never accept receiving such startling news by mail—and he had vowed never to use "that damned contraption"—the telephone.

Still, Catherine was considerably gratified by Denham Phillpotts's visit to the Pearcy house, after they had all returned from The Acropolis. Although he remained deeply affected by the full truth of his sister's relationship with Jaynes, Phillpotts questioned Nedra Alexander gently and assured her she was now safe from harm and that her life would soon begin to return to "the warmth and the sun." He promised to cause no problems over Michael Healy's involvement in the two shootings or over Catherine and Jamie's failure to obey his instructions to stay out of the matter.

As for Oliver Pearcy, the previous night he had immediately set about making amends by learning from Jamie where Patrick Copsey and Clare were presently residing. He spoke to them both, revealing what he had learned and emphasizing how much Nedra desired to see her daughter and grandchild. He arranged a late morning meeting between mother and daughter and upon returning home apologized to Nedra for his failure to assist her when she was in need. He informed Nedra of his visit to Clare and the meeting he had scheduled for the next day. Calling a hansom cab to take Nedra home, Pearcy promised to establish a small account for the Copsey's new family and do his best to encourage a marriage between Patrick and Clare.

"Must leave now. Matthew, go down to the street and call me a cab and I'll give you sixpence for your efforts." As young Pearcy gleefully headed out the door, Thomas Millard grabbed his coat. "I have four fresh dead bodies to examine before my next meal. Young Mr. Wooten is likely anxious for my arrival. He's not comfortable among the dead, I'm afraid." He winked at Alice, who rolled her eyes. Thomas continued. "Pearcy, you were very kind to ask me and my son to come here and join you for breakfast. Jamie, I thought you'd be home sleeping off your most trying night. You seem to have arrived here quite early."

As the elder Millard donned his coat, Catherine hurriedly decided that now was the time to confess that she was his daughter-in-law.

"Dr. Millard, may I ask you to take off your coat and sit for just a moment or two more. I have something important I should like to say to you."

Catherine felt Alice's hand gripping her own in girlish anticipation. Catherine had to wrench it free in order to lift it above the table. Jamie sat down as well, a wide grin dominating his features. She wanted to chide him for his visible delight in knowing that she, and not he, would be making the difficult admission.

"Dr. Millard, I plead for your forgiveness even before you hear what I have to say." Catherine caught Oliver Pearcy trying to suppress a chuckle and having a very hard time doing so. "As I say, Dr. Millard, I do hope you will find it in your heart to—"

"May I ask that you stop calling me 'Dr. Millard'?"

Catherine was ruffled by the interruption. "Oh, yes, of course. Well, it will take some getting used to, but I will try. "I hope, . . . Thomas, that you will find it in your heart to . . .'"

"Thomas? Is that appropriate given our vast age difference, young lady?"

"I . . . I apologize. I just assumed . . . Then you wish me to call you 'Mr. Millard,' then?"

"Jamie, I told you these actress types are a little slow to comprehend what isn't written on the page for them to memorize."

Jamie had nothing to offer but a wide-eyed look. "Pardon me, father?"

The elder Millard pounded his fist in the table, sending several cups and dishes leaping several inches from their moorings. "Damn it, Catherine. Don't you think it's about time you called me 'Father' like the boy does? It may be the only thing of value you may ever gain by having married the offspring here. That is, the right and distinct privilege of calling me father."

Catherine's eyes reminded Alice of one who is about to lose consciousness, but soon they filled with joyous tears. "Then you knew, all the time . . . father?"

"No, dear Catherine, not all the time. But in the past few weeks I began to doubt no longer. The way you are in each other's company reminded me either of those who wish dearly to marry or those who are freshly married. Had you been married more than several months, I wouldn't have seen such rapturous looks."

Jamie barked playfully, "Father, that is offensively cynical, you know."

"My boy, cynicism is often the term applied to the truth by those too ignorant or indolent to accept it. I think Mr. Wilde or Mr. Shaw may have said that—or something like it, at any rate."

By this time, Catherine had made her way around the table to Thomas's chair. She bent over and pressed her cheek next to his. "You are the most adorable man I have ever known."

"And you can be the most adorable woman I have ever known—provided you change your occupation, your religion, and your nationality."

Catherine had no other thought but to kiss Thomas Millard's irresistibly incorrigible face.

~ # ~

That night as they lay together in bed, Catherine and Jamie felt confident they would regain the sleep the previous night hadn't permitted them. They were both eager to return to the stage, although they were uncertain how things would fare with the new theatre manager. How different would life at The Acropolis be? And how would they feel walking over the very spots where real deaths had occurred? Catherine only knew that she never wanted to spend another minute on High Holborn if she could help it.

Catherine and Jamie were also relieved to learn from the owner's letter that Mr. Stempson would cancel the remaining scheduled performances of *Hamlet*. They spoke of possible roles they might be assigned and teased each other about who would be more memorable in their parts, delaying their sleep until they felt their emotions had properly settled.

"Jamie?"

"Yes, Cate?"

"I should be flogged for saying this, but in spite of the many horrors we have just endured, I have never felt more engaged in my efforts than I have this past week. I experienced a kind of stimulation no stage role has ever provided me." She grimaced in preparation for her next admission. "I think I should very much like to do it again."

Jamie smiled. "Who knows, my love, perhaps you will. But for now I wonder, before we fall asleep, if you could draw forth some enthusiasm, if not stimulation, for another kind of effort—which common decency forbids me to name."

Jamie placed his fingers lightly on Catherine's face and turned it toward his own. They didn't need to articulate well-rehearsed lines about how they loved and needed each other. Both knew that at this moment all dialogue was superfluous.

—The End—

View other Black Rose Writing titles at www.blackrosewriting.com/books

and use promo code PRINT to receive a 20% discount when purchasing.

BLACK ROSE

writing™

www.ingramcontent.com/pod-product-compliance
Lightning Source LLC
Chambersburg PA
CBHW010443100726
47904CB00008B/2465